SKYSEED

SKYSEED

BILL McGUIRE

The Book Guild Ltd

First published in Great Britain in 2020 by
The Book Guild Ltd
9 Priory Business Park
Wistow Road, Kibworth
Leicestershire, LE8 0RX
Freephone: 0800 999 2982
www.bookguild.co.uk
Email: info@bookguild.co.uk
Twitter: @bookguild

Typeset in 11pt Minion Pro

Printed and bound by CPI Group (UK) Ltd, Croydon, CR0 4YY

ISBN 978 1913208 882

British Library Cataloguing in Publication Data.
A catalogue record for this book is available from the British Library.

For my sons, Fraser and Jake, my niece Katie, my nephew Joe, and all of their generation. May they never reap the whirlwind of our inaction and incompetence.

PROLOGUE

Sergio Rojas tried to shout, but the wet ash clogging his mouth made him retch. Bending over, he used a forefinger to clear out the worst of the muck, spitting out long strings of grey slime. Standing upright, he peered out at the torrent of ash and pumice that had been coming down now for what seemed like days. Moving to the doorway of the shack in which he had taken refuge, he bellowed into the stifling blackness, willing there to be an answering cry. But beyond the mind-numbing clatter of pumice falling on the corrugated iron roof, there was nothing.

He moved back into the shack's interior and winced with pain as he eased his scalded body into a sitting position. Leaning back against the adobe wall, he closed his eyes and tried to make some sense of the nightmare of the last few hours. It had all happened so fast. The detonation announcing the start of their journey into hell had blown in the windows and dumped him and his wife, Bernita, out of bed. Even before they had gathered their thoughts, pumice fragments were battering the roof above, the clamour a counterpoint to the jet-engine roar of an eruption in full spate.

Sergio played over what happened next as a series of disconnected cameos, as if in a film trailer. Still dazed, they grabbed some clothes and yanked them on. Bernita picked up screaming Hector from his cot, wrapping him in a blanket and clutching him close. Sergio kicked and pushed at the outside door, forcing it open against the rapidly accumulating volcanic debris, and made a gap wide enough to squeeze through. Outside the rain of pumice and ash made it impossible to see further than a few metres, and as soon as they lost sight of their home they struggled to find their bearings. Sergio held out a restraining hand, and they paused while he turned full circle. After a few moments, he came to a decision and pointed hopefully into the blackness. Trudging through drifts of hot ash and rock that already reached almost to their knees, they followed a route through a cluster of scrubby bushes that he prayed would take them away from the volcano.

They inched forwards, Sergio in front, arms outstretched in anticipation of unexpected obstacles masked by the volcanic deluge. As they stumbled on, the already stifling air became hotter still, sucking the sweat from their bodies even as it formed. Scraps of hot pumice blistered their arms and legs and set Hector's blanket smouldering. The baby had stopped screaming, but Bernita had no opportunity to check if he was all right.

As if things couldn't get any worse, it started to rain. A torrential downpour of enormous drops coalesced around ash particles blasted high into the atmosphere. In seconds, the ground was transformed into a quagmire of sucking mud from which they could barely lift their legs. He called a halt as they found themselves under the wide canopy of a tree, its branches almost touching the ground under the weight of ash. They made the most of the shelter to clear their clogged mouths and scrape away thick layers of ashy mud from their faces. Hector's blanket was sodden now, and the child was still except for the occasional dry cough that wracked his overheated body. But Bernita was able to do nothing except cover his face as best she could and hope against hope that he survived until they found somewhere safe beyond the volcano's reach.

Sergio had been dimly aware that scientists were concerned about the volcano's increasing rumblings and the possibility of a major blast, but they lived nearly twenty kilometres away, surely much too far, he had thought, for them to be in any danger. Now, as they searched the blackness for any chink of light that might guide them in the direction of safety, he wondered if they would ever find sanctuary from the volcano's seemingly limitless fury.

He hugged his wife and son close before taking Bernita's hand and pushing through the drooping branches and out, once more, into the barrage from above. If anything, the rain – of water and pulverised rock – was even heavier, and they struggled to make any headway through the deepening, glutinous, mud. Without warning, he felt Bernita's tight grasp loosen and her hand slip from his. He turned at the sound of a small cry just in time to see his wife and child slide down a steep slope, along the unseen edge of which they must have been walking for some time. Without hesitation, he followed, hurtling into the darkness on his back, his passage lubricated by a mixture of mud and water.

Then he was in the air and falling. The torrent of muddy water that ended his fall shocked him like an ice bath. It took just a second or two to realise that his body had been fooled. The water wasn't freezing at all, but close to boiling point. Screaming as the agony started to build, he fought to heave himself out of the flood, but his hands could find no purchase on the steep, muck-mired bank. The churning waters carried him downstream, where he came to rest up against a fallen tree, along which he was able to scramble to the bank. He lay in the darkness, skin lobster-red and throbbing, mind numb. The pain was excruciating, but he had to find Bernita and the baby. He struggled to his feet and slipped and slithered along the edge of the boiling cascade as it continued to tumble downhill.

He followed the torrent until the gradient flattened out and it turned into a sluggish and gently steaming creek. For hour after hour he ploughed through the mud, the rain and the continuing deluge of pumice and ash, calling out all the time. Lightning spawned by the eruption periodically splintered the darkness, revealing a blasted, featureless, plain on which nothing lived or moved. His legs eventually failed him and he was crawling on all fours when he – quite literally – collided with the shack, a jagged piece of corrugated iron drawing blood from his temple. Struggling upright, he dragged open the makeshift door against the drifted ash and collapsed on the earth floor inside.

He lay on his back, bone-weary, bereft and overcome with loss. Much of his exposed arms and legs were blistered, but the pain had subsided to a dull ache that pulsed in sympathy with his heartbeat. His mouth was clogged with ash and he was desperately thirsty, but there was no water to be had. After a time, he dragged himself painfully to his feet and stood at the open doorway, peering into a blizzard of ash and pumice. He shouted for Bernita until his throat ached and no voice would come.

Despite the pain and the din outside, Sergio fell into a troubled sleep. When he awoke, the rattle of falling pumice on the roof had diminished, but now there was something else, a barely audible susurration, like the rustling of the grass on the high plains. The sound grew rapidly, becoming first a loud hissing and then a soft roar. At the same time a pale glow illuminated the shack's interior and for a moment he thought it was a car's headlight beams. His spirits lifted briefly, and he moved as quickly as he was able to the doorway, but the hoped-for vehicle was not there, just an eerie, dull-red glow, off in the direction – he assumed – of the volcano.

Turning away, Sergio sought to relieve the pain of his scalds by stretching out on the floor of the shack. Soon, a hot wind sprang up, clawing at the flimsy walls. Within seconds, it became a howling banshee that tore off the roof and carried it away into the darkness, drenching him with dislodged ash and pumice so that he scrambled to his feet to brush the debris from his head and shoulders. The glow was brightening quickly now and in the far corner of the shack it picked out a child's teddy that looked familiar. Hector had one just like it. A surge of hope overcame the pain and despair and Sergio walked over to pick it up. It was the last move he would ever make. Through the roof space, the open doorway and the two, small, glassless windows, came a hurricane blast of boiling gas and incandescent ash and pumice that gathered him up and hurled him against the shack wall.

The shock made him gasp. The first intake of scorching gas tore his vocal chords and windpipe to shreds. The second destroyed his lungs. His mouth gaped wide in a silent scream that would never come. The last sound he heard, overlaid on the crackling and sighing of the gas cloud, was a repetitive popping. It was the sound of his skull sutures unzipping as the water in his brain turned to pressurised steam and blew his head apart.

***

Karl Slater put on a burst of speed as he crested the tussocky slope that climbed steeply out of the village, then paused to suck air at a drystone wall where the ground levelled out. He was out of shape, seriously out of shape. Too many working lunches, not enough workouts. His side was already cramping and he bent over to stifle the pain. Easing himself upright as the discomfort passed, he took in the widescreen view to the west and south, where gritstone crags like tumbledown castles capped green, rolling hills.

It was late September and the air was bitter. Patches of snow and ice lurked in the shadows, the first year they had persisted throughout the summer in the English Peak District. He turned to watch a line of dark cloud coming in fast from the north, gravid with the first of the winter's snow. A little way off, a mountain hare squatted on its haunches, ears alert, watching and waiting for his next move. It already bore its white winter coat, a sure sign that the all too brief summer was at an end.

He shivered beneath his fleece and wondered if next year would bring any summer at all. The climate had deteriorated so quickly he wondered how long it was going to be possible to stay in the village. The winters were already grim, and he knew that much of the high ground of Scotland, the Lake District and the northern Pennines were already shrouded in snow all year round. The official word was that they were over the worst, but all the signs said otherwise. In any case, he would know more when he met up with Jane that evening.

He took a deep breath and launched himself down the slope on the next stage of his run. The hare's eyes widened as he bore down on it. Then it turned and fled in the direction of a nearby copse.

The promised heavy snow arrived during the early afternoon and played havoc with the rail timetable. Sheffield station was steeped in a miasma of diesel fumes, sulphurous smoke and steam, and overflowing with disgruntled passengers. After a number of platform alterations, the announcer settled on number four for the next London train. A tide of desperate travellers swept Karl up and over the bridge and down onto the platform, where he shoehorned himself into one of ten already packed carriages and was lucky enough to commandeer a last remaining seat. Departure time came and went, with no explanation or apology. For a time, he watched the snowflakes melt on the window, then closed his eyes, leant back in his seat, and resigned himself to a frustrating few hours. Finally, twenty minutes late, the train nudged forwards, faltered, then juddered onward again. Couplings clattered, and he heard the familiar 'chuff – chuff – chuff' of an engine getting up steam. Incrementally, the train eased itself out of the station and – with a struggle – began to pick up speed. It was going to be a long, slow journey.

The train crawled into London's St Pancras International terminus more than two hours late. Rather than fight his way through the crush to the tube, Karl decided to brave the blizzard conditions. Turning up his collar, he made for the small hotel in Bloomsbury that he used on the rare occasions, these days, that he was down in the capital. At least the weather had kept the smog at bay, so he didn't need his face mask.

Dumping his bag, he called Jane and arranged to meet an hour later in a small pub around the corner. The place was pretty much empty when he arrived and he ruffled the snow from his unkempt nest of brown curls and matching beard as he waited to order at the bar. Jane was already there, half hidden in the shadows at a table close to the enormous coal fire, hands clasped around a large glass of red wine. He took his pint over and sat down opposite. Jane greeted him with a crooked grin and leant forwards to plant a kiss on his cheek. He smiled in return. It was nice to see her again, but by God she looked tired. Her eyes were ringed with shadows and he was shocked to see that there were one or two streaks of grey in her long, brown hair.

He waded straight in. 'How does it look?'

Jane Haliwell stretched out an arm, palm down, and waggled her hand from side to side. 'Touch and go, I'm afraid.'

'I'd heard things were improving,' said Karl. 'It's a fair few years since the last of the ash settled out.'

'Well,' Jane was cagey, 'it's not that straightforward.'

'So what are we talking now?' queried Karl.

Jane looked down at the dregs of wine in her glass. 'I've just come from the commission – the latest figures aren't good. Carbon dioxide levels are down around the two hundred parts per million mark.'

Karl gasped. 'Jesus Christ!'

Jane continued, 'The concentration of carbon in the atmosphere has more than halved in just seven years.'

Karl shook his head and was quiet for a few moments, digesting the news. 'What about global temperatures?'

'Still dropping, as you'd expect,' said Jane, twiddling the stem of her glass.

'So, what's the official line?'

Jane's mirthless smile said it all. 'For what it's worth, both the WMO and the Met Office are saying the worst is over. It's the government's angle too, but that's understandable. People are shit scared already.'

'And what do you think?'

Jane puffed out her cheeks. 'I think we're screwed.'

Karl lay naked on the bed. Outside, the snow continued to fall, but the room was overheated and stuffy and sleep just wouldn't come. Turning his head, he watched Jane's exposed breasts rise and fall as she slept. They hadn't planned this. It had been solace rather than sex, a commodity much valued in a world going to hell in a handcart. Her prosthetic lay in the corner of the room and the smooth stump that ended her left leg just below the knee peeped out from the bottom of the sheet. He looked away and stared at the ceiling. The sight of Jane's maimed leg never failed to bring with it a sharp pang of guilt. He knew it wasn't his fault, but sometimes it didn't feel that way. *Seven years,* he thought. *Just seven years since this whole thing blew up. What the hell were they thinking?* The stupid bastards had called it 'the fix'. In fact, it wasn't a fix at all. It was a fuck-up, the mother of all fuck-ups.

PART ONE

REVELATION

IT HAD BEEN SWELTERING DOWN ON THE COAST AND it was a blessed relief to have an excuse to get out of the conference hall in Santa Cruz and away from the endless presentations, most of which barely touched upon Karl's field. He had neither seen nor heard from Andy Perkins for years, and it had been a surprise to get a text from him. Karl hadn't even known he was on the island, but it seemed he was doing a tour at the Roque de los Muchachos astronomical observatory perched high up on the rim of one of the island's ancient volcanoes. Andy had spotted Karl's name on a conference poster and invited him to lunch, and to pick his brains – as he put it – about a little problem the astronomers had.

As Karl negotiated another tight hairpin, the morning sun blasted through the hire jeep's windshield and near blinded him. He squinted uncomfortably and tried to ignore the pounding headache. Not for the first time in his life, he had discovered that heat and a hangover didn't mix, and he badly needed to clear his head of the dregs of the previous night's binge. By the time he had negotiated the wildly snaking road to the rim of the giant Taburiente caldera, three double cortados and a combination of the pine-scented air and cooling breeze had worked their wizardry.

With time to spare, he pulled the jeep off the road and sauntered across to the edge of the colossal natural amphitheatre – the legacy of a prodigious volcanic landslide in the distant past. He had climbed more than two kilometres in the last hour or so and the view was stupendous . All around, the sun sparkled on a brilliant blue sea, except behind and below, where Santa Cruz was swathed in a bank of thick cloud. Far off in the east, the great Teide volcano towered over the heat-hazed holiday island of Tenerife. To the west, reflected sunlight flashed from the domes of the giant telescopes that together made up the observatory, clinging precariously to the edge of the kilometre-high cliffs that marked the far side of the caldera. He looked at his watch. Visually sated, he clambered back into the jeep and drove at a leisurely pace along the empty road that tracked the vertiginous drop to the caldera floor far below.

The security guard at the barrier to the telescope complex phoned ahead, and Andy was there to greet him outside the residence where astronomers lived, for months at a time, in self-imposed purdah. Andy had booked a couple of packed lunches, which he carried in a crumpled brown paper bag.

Still the last of the big spenders, thought Karl, a little ungraciously. He was reminded of the petty disputes over money matters that occasionally dogged the time they shared a flat during their university days in Manchester.

Andy had pale blond hair that was already thinning and a pallor to match. Clearly, astronomers didn't get out much, and in any case working on his tan was not the reason he was here. Amongst its fleet of telescopes was Andy's baby, until lately the world's largest, and perhaps most unimaginatively named, Gran Telescopio Canarias. Andy was in the business of locating exoplanets and was already something of a celebrity, within the small cabal of planet spotters, for discovering the closest Earth-like world to our own.

Karl followed as Andy led the way towards the caldera edge. He couldn't help noticing that his friend's spare frame was already surrendering to the hidden perils of a sedentary existence, and the beginnings of a pot belly bobbed up and down as he made heavy weather of negotiating the rocky track. They stopped at a flat outcrop close to the rim where Andy made a show of taking in the breathtaking – but surely now familiar – view of the caldera, to give himself time to catch his breath in the thin air. Once his chest had stopped heaving, he turned and pointed out the various telescopes to Karl. They came in every shape and sizes – thirteen in all – targeting everything from distant galaxies to our own sun. By the time Andy had finished his pitch, Karl's eyes were starting to glaze over, and he was glad to relax on a rock and eat. Mind you, a cold tortilla between a couple of slices of dry roll, he could take or leave.

The conversation meandered pleasantly, from old times to recent activities. Andy regaled Karl with his newest discovery of an Earth-like planet in the habitable zone of a nearby star, which could harbour life. In return, Karl gave a blow-by-blow account of his near-death experience, three months earlier, during the massive eruption of Bolivia's Uturuncu volcano. This brought a frown to Andy's face and revealed the reason for the lunch invitation.

The skies high above La Palma provided some of the best seeing conditions for astronomers anywhere on the planet, explained Andy, but not any more. For months they had been having problems with a murky atmosphere that made it next to impossible to get their work done.

'It's really pissing me off,' Andy said. 'I only have another couple of months left on this tour and I'm sat twiddling my thumbs. Seeing conditions have to be spot on to pick up a tiny planet orbiting a star light years out, and they are nothing like that.'

Karl said he sympathised but wasn't sure how he could help.

'Uturuncu!' Andy almost spat the word. It appeared that the general feeling within the observatory community was that the recent eruption was to blame. Many an expletive-filled diatribe had bounced off the walls of the common room, about volcanoes in general and Uturuncu in particular. 'I know this is your bag,' he continued, 'so I thought I'd get it from the horse's mouth, as it were.'

Karl shrugged. 'What can I say? The eruption has pumped out a huge volume of ash – almost a hundred cubic kilometres, it looks like – but most of it is still circling in the tropics. There's a good chance it will edge polewards in the coming months, but as of now the cloud is still way to the south.'

It wasn't what Andy wanted to hear. In anger, he hurled the piece of rock he had been toying with far into the caldera. 'Shit! Then what the fuck is it?'

Karl couldn't resist. 'Maybe your lenses need a bit of a clean?'

Andy was not amused, and said so. 'I can't sit around here with a finger up my arse. ID'ing exoplanets is a very competitive field and I have a reputation to maintain. I need to keep my hat in the ring.'

Karl thought it sounded more like bean counting than real science, but sensibly decided that this would not be the most diplomatic thing to say. Instead he offered a placatory way forward. 'Look, I've a project on the go at the moment, checking out Uturuncu ash loading of the atmosphere. The aviation industry lost a shed load of money due to airspace closures and engine damage, and they're getting jumpy about taking another hit so have come up with some decent cash. I'm trying to get a handle on how the size and characteristics of the ash particles change with distance from the volcano. The idea is that this can help aircraft builders and operators know more about what sort of ash their engines and airframes might have to cope with following another eruption big enough to spawn an ash cloud that spreads across much of the Earth.'

Andy looked less than impressed. 'And your point is?'

'I've samples from right across the planet. Some from areas impacted by the Uturuncu ash cloud, but also controls from further afield. One was collected by a high-altitude aircraft flying a route across the Canaries. If you like, I can take a look when I get back to the UK. It might not pinpoint the cause, but it could narrow down the possibilities.'

It was a straw worth clutching at, and Andy expressed his enthusiasm and thanks. Now he had simmered down, the two continued to make small talk, and concluded by agreeing tentative arrangements to meet when they were both back in the UK. A stiff breeze was getting up when they shook hands and said their goodbyes, and Karl had a brief wrestling match trying to install the jeep's detachable canvas roof before giving up.

He was about to start the engine when the opening bars of The Stranglers' 'No More Heroes' alerted him to a text message. It was his lab technician – Steve Carob – back in Sheffield, letting him know that the samples of ash from the stratosphere above Australia, South Africa and Argentina had now all arrived, so that the portfolio was complete. Karl allowed himself a celebratory fist pump and set off down the mountain with a smile on his face.

It had taken a great deal of time and effort to blag samples from atmospheric science colleagues around the world, and getting the bureaucracy sorted before the samples could be shipped had been a pain, but it had worked out. All of a sudden the tedium of another four days of dull presentations, only partially rescued by four nights of boozy partying, weighed heavily on his mind. He needed to get back to the lab – he wanted to get back – but his talk was scheduled for the last day of the conference so he would have to tough it out. *Still*, he thought, as a tricky hairpin opened up yet another spectacular vista, *there are far worse places to be cooped up.*

JANE HALIWELL FELT THE NEED TO SLUMP, BUT THE austere high-backed chair allowed nothing but a bolt upright posture. It had been a long and frustrating day. Six hours of pointless hogwash at the Climate Impacts Task Force meeting, down the road in the Cabinet Office. By the end, she had wanted nothing more than to be at home with her son and a wee dram of the golden liquid. But it was not to be. One of the PM's lackeys had seen to that, which was why she instead found herself fidgeting and fretting outside the glorious leader's office waiting for the summons. Jane knew Prime Minister Bannerman – had met him on quite a few occasions – and she liked him, even if his response to the growing climate chaos was feeble. He would say it was pragmatic, but in her book, pragmatism was an admission of defeat, the absence of the backbone to do what was needed, what was right.

She looked at her watch yet again – it was becoming a nervous tick – and swore under her breath. He'd asked for the meeting, so why the hell was she still hanging around after close on an hour? Checking her phone one more time for messages wasted a few more minutes, then she stood and stretched, hands thrust deep into the small of her back. She began to pace back and forth and had managed half a dozen traverses of the large anteroom when the PM's door finally opened and a head appeared. Instantly recognisable, it belonged to Norbert Aitken, Nobby to friends and enemies alike.

The PM's chief of staff hailed from a crumbling estate on the edge of Glasgow and looked the part: shaven head, dark, penetrating eyes and a flattened nose – legacy of a Glasgow 'kiss' bestowed during one of the pub fights that had passed for sport in his younger days. An old-school socialist, Aitken had clung like a limpet to Duncan Bannerman's coat-tails as a conspiracy of charisma, erudition and the ineptitude of the competition wafted his boss to the highest level in the rarefied atmosphere of national politics. So now, from lowly beginnings as a humble constituency agent, Aitken squatted in the most influential unelected position in the land. Most of the younger political journos were in thrall to him and – only partly tongue in cheek – labelled him the real Deputy PM. The more world-weary had seen his kind before and were less impressed. Cynically and lavatorially, they had him tagged as the throne behind the man.

Aitken's default expression was just this side of bleak. From previous experience, Jane could tell that he was working at a smile, but as usual it was largely a wasted effort, the resulting rictus being far more unsettling than a straight face. 'The Prime Minster will see you now, Professor Haliwell.'

Over the years the edges had been knocked off Aitken's Glaswegian patois, and it was now at least recognisable as a version of English. Nonetheless, the combination of nasal Glaswegian whine and ex-smoker's gravelly tones sounded a discordant knell within the hallowed premises of Downing Street. Nobby ushered Jane into the PM's study, then left, closing the door quietly behind him. As always, he would listen in on the intercom in the next room.

'Professor – Jane – thanks for staying on.' Duncan Bannerman gestured to a sofa and took an armchair the other side of a low table on which the paraphernalia of afternoon tea rested. There was no apology for the long wait, but then she hadn't expected one. Politicians had it drilled into them early on never to apologise – about anything.

'Tea?'

Jane said that would be very nice and the PM did the honours, before leaning back in his chair and turning on the charm.

'So, Jane, how goes it in the ivory tower?'

Jane gave a wry smile. 'Well, the university auctioned off the ivory years ago and the tower is a new accommodation block for loaded foreign students.'

Duncan laughed out loud and slapped his knees. 'Don't knock it, Jane, higher education's the only thing that brings in the cash these days. At least it's something we still lead the world in.'

Jane's expression was non-committal.

'And how's my nephew doing?'

'Campbell's coming along fine,' she said. 'We'll make an academic of him yet.' She said it to take the rise, and she could tell by Duncan's pursed lips that it had worked. It was common knowledge that, with no children of his own, and none planned, Duncan was pinning his hopes on his sister's son to follow in his footsteps. She'd heard from an insider that he even dreamt of building a dynasty. A new natural law; Scotland and England both, forever ruled by Scots. She almost laughed out loud at the thought of such risible ambition from a man who seemed so rooted. The PM changed the subject and put on his serious face. 'Jane. I know you need to get away, but I wanted to have a quick chat.' He paused, choosing his words. 'I appreciate how you feel about the country's efforts – my efforts – to meet emissions reductions targets, and I know you think we – I'm – making a hash of things.'

Jane made to speak, but Duncan held up a hand. 'And you are right to do so. I don't like it either, but you have to understand my position. The economy is tanking, unemployment is at record levels. After the last election, my majority's wafer thin—'

Jane could hold back no longer. 'Before the election, you were a supporter of the leave it in the ground campaign, made a big thing of it. I guess it was just a vote winner. Nothing more.' Duncan's face, rosy at the best of times, took on a deeper hue. Other than this, he managed to keep his displeasure at the accusation in check. 'That's disingenuous, Jane. Keeping the remaining North Sea oil and gas where it is was always something I felt strongly about – still do – but my hands now are tied. You must see that. Parliament would never let me get away with turning my back as long as there are hydrocarbons still to be squeezed out. It's money in the bank.'

Jane's face was stony, but she said nothing. Duncan made a weak attempt at levity to try and defuse the situation. 'It could be worse. Some of my Welsh colleagues are pushing for reopening the coal mines.' He was only half joking.

Jane was unmoved. She felt she knew Duncan well enough to leave her words unminced. 'Prime Minister, we can't afford not to keep the remaining oil and gas where it is. For fuck's sake, look around you. You can see where things are going. What was the final bill for last year's east coast floods? Seventy billion, eighty? And the Coventry tornado. Two hundred dead. Whole streets wiped off the face of the planet. Face it, the shit's hit the fan, and we're already up to our necks in it.' Duncan raised both arms, as if to ward off the tirade, head bent in apparent submission, but he said nothing. After a few moments, he reached for his cup of tea and took a couple of sips.

It took Jane a while to realise that the PM wasn't going to rise to the bait, and she shook her head in exasperation. Sometimes – most of the time, these days – she wondered why she bothered.

'So, why am I here?' Duncan put his cup down and looked her in the eye. She hadn't noticed before, but he seemed all-in. His once-thick red hair appeared to be greying and thinning at the same time, and his blue eyes were dull and ringed with shadow. Not for the first time, she wondered why anyone would ever want to be Prime Minister? It wasn't a job; it was a sentence. Duncan seemed nonplussed. 'Do you know, Jane, I'm not quite sure.' He paused to massage his forehead. 'I guess I just needed to talk things over, bounce ideas off someone.' He paused again, shifting his position in the chair, fiddling with his blood-red tie, playing for time.

'The oil and gas are sacrosanct, Jane, as I said, but there has to be something else we can do… surely? I know our emissions reductions have stalled and I am getting it in the neck at home and abroad over this. For God's sake, Jane, I need a lifeline.'

Jane looked at the PM for a long moment, then shook her head. 'Prime Minister, you know what needs to be done. Nothing's changed. Our priority has to be slashing emissions, not GDP growth. Nothing else will do. Killing off the proposed Heathrow runway would be a start. Kickstarting the stalled renewables and transport decarbonation drives, a crash programme in energy efficiency. It's the same old stuff. I'm afraid there's just no silver bullet.'

She made a face then. 'Between you and me, even if we do all this and leave the hydrocarbons in the ground, it's doubtful we'll make much of difference at this late stage. Not while the US and other big polluters are still hanging back.' Duncan nodded and chewed for a few moments at his bottom lip. 'Speaking of silver bullets, Jane, I keep having my ear bent about this geoengineering lark, the idea of hacking the planet to sort out climate breakdown once and for all. What—'

Jane bridled, sitting upright on the sofa, eyes wide. 'Prime Minister, don't go there. It's a real can of worms.' Duncan continued, 'That's as may be, but can it work?'

Jane shook her head vigorously. 'It's untried, untested and there are just too many things that can go wrong. Surely we've fucked with the planet enough already?'

'But I'm hearing more and more voices raised in favour. Some pretty big hitters in the science community too.'

'Not climate scientists.' Jane was adamant. 'Engineers, physicists, people who like to fiddle, to experiment, and to hell with the consequences. Well, we're bang in the middle of one planetary experiment and the ramifications are plain for all to see. More buggering around is the last thing we need.' Duncan shrugged. 'If we can't – or won't – make the required changes to the way we live, perhaps it's the only thing left?'

Jane snorted in derision. 'So what are we talking here? Making artificial clouds to reflect the sun's rays? Billions of tonnes of sulphur pumped into the atmosphere to cool things down, giant mirrors in space? Jesus!' Duncan shook his head. 'Give me a break, Jane, I know nothing of the specifics. I'm just thinking out loud.' Then he grinned, and for a moment looked his old self. 'I take it, though, that you're not a fan?'

'Prime Minister, we have no idea what the knock-on effects of any technofix would be. The climate system is incredibly complex and we still don't know how everything fits together. More interfering could have unpredictable and potentially devastating consequences. To put it bluntly, there is a fair chance that all it would do is leave us in an even bigger hole.' Duncan looked thoughtful for a time, then stood abruptly and held out a hand. 'Well, thanks for coming in, Jane, I really appreciate it.'

Taken by surprise, she took the proffered hand but remained seated.

'Don't get up. I'm needed elsewhere, so please, take your time.' The PM headed for the door, pausing only to steal a glance in the enormous baroque mirror above the fireplace and smooth his red locks.

The door clicked shut, leaving Jane bemused and a little peeved at the sudden and unsatisfactory conclusion to the audience.

'Well,' she murmured, 'what the hell was that all about?'

JUNE 2028
SURREY
ENGLAND

'Good to meet you, Professor Haliwell.' It was the first time Jane had met Dan Mitchell and she had to admit he was impressive. His handshake was firm and his smile wide. He towered a good foot above her, which wasn't saying much, given that most people did, and his body looked hard and well looked after. Very different from the academic meteorologists she knew, whose physiques had been largely forged through a combination of beer and curry.

It was just a week since the dean had called her into his office and said that the MOD were keen to have one of their RAF meteorologists join her team on secondment. Apparently they were very interested in her work on atmospheric dust loading, which they felt might help them better understand the potential impact of dust in the stratosphere on the new generation of super-fast jets.

Her first reaction had been irritation. She had enough on her plate without having some military arse foisted upon her. But when she thought it over, she decided that she could

16

always do with an extra pair of hands around the lab, especially if someone else was paying. She had communicated with Captain Mitchell by email and on the phone, and he seemed like a pleasant enough guy, an impression reinforced when he turned up at the lab on the following Monday.

She was pleased to see that he was in mufti – albeit smart mufti – rather than wearing a uniform, and his black hair was lightly gelled and sported a quiff. The style was short, but not the squaddie's buzzcut that, for some reason, she had been expecting. Sizing him up as they chatted over coffee, she placed him in his mid-thirties – maybe a little older.

As they talked, Jane tried not to be too obvious as she sought to ferret out a bit more about Dan's background, but he seemed open and happy to talk about his life and career. He was divorced, so they had that in common, and there was no significant other at the moment. The RAF had sponsored his meteorology degree at Reading – a while ago now, he admitted – but he was keen to brush up. Since then, he had done a few stints as base meteorologist in the UK and overseas, before working on secondment at Rolls Royce, who were building the engines for a new hypersonic transport. All in all, she was impressed. He seemed the real deal and he might actually prove to be more a help than the anticipated hindrance.

K ARL JUMPED OFF THE BUS AND STRUGGLED TO GET his umbrella up in the gusty wind. It was bucketing down, as it had been ever since he got back. He had thought there couldn't possibly be any more to come, but the news sources were all talking of a 'river in the sky' that could last another week. Apparently there was a narrow corridor of concentrated moisture in the atmosphere above northern England that showed no sign of dispersing.

Head down, umbrella thrust forwards like a shield against the elements, he trudged up the long hill that led to the department and his small lab. Turning, he used his back to open the main door, while shaking his umbrella outside. He wanted to check for parcels, but there was no-one in reception, so he picked up his post from the rack and headed down the stairs into the basement.

The dingy corridor, all peeling paint and exposed utility pipes, was almost as damp as outside, but the smell of freshly brewed coffee raised his spirits as he pushed open the door to his office. Dumping his backpack on a chair, he popped open his laptop and fired it up, before heading off to pin down the source of the aroma. He found it two doors down in Steve's den. His technician was laidback – quite literally. Stretched out in his desk chair so that his black dreadlocks almost touched the floor, trainer-shod feet resting on an old packing crate. His head was nodding in time to music on his bright blue wireless headphones, which he yanked off as soon as he saw Karl.

'Marley?' queried Karl.

Steve rolled his eyes. 'Pu-lease. Sibelius.'

Karl laughed out loud. Steve had been with him for more than a year now, but the posh, privately educated, accent still came as a surprise, especially if he had been away for a time.

Steve may have looked like some streetwise kid from the estate down the road, but the reality was quite different. In fact, classical music and the theatre formed a much bigger part of Steve's life than reggae and ganja. His father was a Jamaican government minister, sufficiently well off to buy his son the best. Winchester-educated, Steve took a first in natural sciences at Cambridge before opting to work under Karl while studying part-time for his PhD. He was quite simply the most brilliant student Karl had ever come across.

They high-fived and Karl slumped into a battered old armchair that had no business hogging half the floor space of the tiny, cluttered room. From an assorted collection of a dozen or so used mugs, Steve selected a couple that were only mildly disgusting, gave them a quick rinse and filled them with coffee. Karl took his straight, but Steve added milk and a couple of sugars before sitting down on the crate opposite. They raised their mugs to each other.

'Good trip?' said Steve, after taking a couple of sips.

Karl made a so-so face. 'The talk went fine, but I could've done without the rest of it. Stratosphere chemistry, mostly.

God, it was dire. But at least the food and the partying were good. Who'd have thought atmospheric scientists knew how to have a good time? How've things been here?'

It was Steve's turn to grimace. 'Wet. I don't think the sun's been out since you left, and it was snowing in Buxton at the weekend. Snow in late June, for God's sake! So much for global heating!' Before Karl could even open his mouth, Steve raised his arms in supplication, fully aware of his boss's bellicose views on climate breakdown deniers. 'OK, OK. Just joking!'

Steve peered more closely at Karl. 'Man, you got a tan. How'd you manage that closeted away in a conference hall?'

'Well, you see—' Karl started.

'You've been skiving, haven't you? Sandy beach, rum and Coke in one hand, maybe a nice young lady in the other? I know you too well. How many talks did you actually sit in on?'

Karl couldn't help smiling. 'One or two, one or two.' He slapped both hands on his knees and stood up. 'Anyway, enough about me – the samples!'

Steve eyed him for a few seconds before deciding to rein back. He would get the dirt later.

'Yup. All here. They arrived on campus just after you left, but there was a bit of a mix-up in the post room, so it took another couple of days for them to get to us.'

Karl rolled his eyes and swore under his breath.

'But!' Steve held up a conciliatory finger. 'I've been working on them round the clock and I've put together a representative batch for the SEM. They're ready to go and you're booked in for two this afternoon.'

'You're a star!' Karl rubbed his hands together in delight and anticipation. He drained his coffee and headed for the door. 'I have meetings this morning, but I'll see you in the SEM suite after lunch.' Patting Steve playfully on the back, he left in high spirits.

The Scanning Electron Microscope was ancient and, by modern standards, huge. Along with all its associated kit, it filled an entire room. But it still worked and provided much better images than a lot of its newer competitors. Steve had prepared and loaded the first batch of samples, and Karl had been going through them now for an hour or so. Pulling back from the binocular eyepiece, he massaged his eyes, leant back in his chair and stared at the ceiling.

The quality of the imaging was excellent, and the ash grains looked fresh and unaffected by the powerful high-altitude winds that had carried them thousands of kilometres from the eruption site. But there was something else. A sign of the times, the image was peppered with micro-plastic fragments, but both these and the spiky ash grains were far outnumbered by a host of microspheres of various sizes. Karl was stumped. He had never seen anything like it and had no idea what the enigmatic particles might be.

He printed off a selection of images – micrographs, as they were known in the trade. The detail was astonishing. An SEM can magnify up to half a million times – 250 times more than the best standard microscope – although he didn't need anything like this to get superb close ups of the ash grains. The SEM's large depth of field also meant that they looked three-dimensional in the micrographs, creating weird and wonderful images that wouldn't look out of place gracing the walls of a contemporary art gallery. He sifted through the pictures for a few minutes, then picked up his phone.

'Steve. Could you pop along when you have a minute? I need to pick your massive brain.'

Steve was there in seconds. Karl stood and beckoned to his technician to sit and look through the eyepiece. 'What do you see?'

Steve was quiet for a few minutes as he examined the sample in view, now and again adjusting the magnification and contrast. After a while he looked up. 'Nothing surprising as far as the ash grains are concerned, so I guess you mean the other stuff.'

Karl nodded. 'What do you think?'

Steve shrugged. 'Never seen anything like them. Are they volcanic?'

'Your guess is as good as mine,' said Karl, passing over the micrographs.

Steve shuffled through the pictures, Karl looking over his shoulder. 'Are they in all the samples?' Karl nodded. When he had finished, Steve shook his head, still none the wiser.

'Let's get a coffee,' said Karl, picking up the micrographs and stuffing them in the pocket of a battered denim jacket.

They made a dash through the continuing downpour to the café in the next building. The place was only half full and they found a table easily. Karl left Steve perusing the photos while he ordered the drinks. When he returned, Steve was pulling at an earlobe – something of a habit when his brain was whirring – and comparing two of the pictures.

Karl raised both eyebrows in anticipation of the forthcoming nugget of wisdom.

'The particles are incredibly regular, aren't they – pretty much perfect spheres.' He paused for a moment. 'I know this is ridiculous, but you don't think they could be artificial, do you?'

Karl was taking a sip of coffee and almost choked at the suggestion. It took a good minute before his coughing fit subsided and his eyes stopped watering. Even then, all he could manage was a strangulated, 'artificial?!'

'Well, they just seem to be too perfect to be natural, that's all,' Steve said defensively.

Karl cleared his tubes of the last dregs of inhaled coffee and picked up one of the images. He had to admit, Steve did have a point. He knew volcanoes and he knew pretty much everything there was to know about what came out of volcanoes, and he had never seen anything like this. And it wasn't just the unnaturally perfect sphericity of the objects that was odd, it was the sheer number, far outweighing the ash grains and the micro-plastic.

The silence was broken by Steve clearing his throat for attention. 'I know you're going to think this is bonkers, but you know what they remind me of?'

'Surprise me,' said Karl.

Steve hesitated before speaking again, in two minds about whether it was a good idea. He was not an especially arrogant young man, but like all research students starting out on an academic career, he was acutely aware of what others might think of him. Not making a fool of himself was something of a priority, and what he was about to suggest could make him a laughing stock if it got out. He paused a little longer and licked his lips nervously. *Oh, what the hell!*

'I happened to catch a bit of a biotech programme the other night, while waiting for the England game to start. It was about these new nanobots they're trialling to reduce blood cholesterol.'

Karl looked a little bemused, wondering to himself where this was going.

Steve continued, 'The bots were injected into the bloodstream, where they extracted bad cholesterol through a chemical reaction between the cholesterol and chemicals in an outer shell. The idea seemed to be that the bots stayed in the bloodstream permanently, monitoring cholesterol levels and – you know – soaking up the excess as… needed…' Steve's voice trailed off as Karl's face took on an increasingly exasperated expression.

'That's all very interesting, Steve, but I'm afraid I really don't get the connection.'

'The thing is,' continued Steve, 'the image they showed of the bots in the blood looked very like this. The same simple spherical structure, and because they had absorbed different amounts of cholesterol, there was a big size range – just as we're seeing here.'

Karl was becoming increasingly frustrated. 'So what are you saying exactly, that these bots have somehow got into the atmosphere?'

Steve shook his head vigorously and held up both hands in denial. 'Not at all, but, you know, if these things are artificial, maybe they're something similar...' His voice trailed off again and he became sullen. 'Anyway, I thought it was worth a mention.' He looked down at his hands, face hidden beneath a curtain of dreadlocks, and wished he hadn't said anything at all.

Karl lightened up. The one thing he didn't want to do was stymie Steve's imagination and lateral thinking. They were the two things that set him apart from all the other research students he had come across. He leant across the low table between them and punched Steve amiably on the shoulder. 'No worries, Steve. You're right. We have to consider every possibility. What was it Sherlock Holmes was always saying? When you have ruled out the impossible, whatever's left – however unlikely – must be the truth. Something along those lines, anyway. But let's not get carried away, there is almost certainly a natural explanation. Just one we're not familiar with – yet.'

Steve's face brightened. 'Hey, what about some sort of nucleation phenomenon? Like those little balls that form when raindrops fall through an ash cloud? Umm – accretionary lapilli?'

Karl nodded. 'Yeah. Condensing water droplets act as nuclei that the ash particles stick to. That's one of the first things I considered.'

He picked up one of the images. 'Accretionary lapilli are spherical, all right, but these things...' he gestured at the picture, 'these are actually smaller – some much smaller – than the ash particles themselves, so it just doesn't fit.'

Karl sighed, tossed the micrograph onto the table and leant back in his chair. 'There are two possibilities – either they are volcanic or they aren't. I've seen my fair share of volcanic ejecta and my gut feeling is that these aren't. I could be wrong, but I don't think so. Take a look at this.' He handed Steve an image he had been keeping back. 'What do you see?'

Steve took the picture and gave it a quick once-over. 'No ash.'

'Right,' said Karl. 'Plenty of spheres, some micro-plastic, but no spiky ash grains.'

'Where's it from?' queried Steve.

'It's the Canary Islands flyover sample I asked you to work on this morning. The Uturunca ash hasn't reached this far north, so a volcanic source for the spheres is out.'

Steve made a face in response.

'In which case,' continued Karl, 'we need to speak to someone who knows about all the other stuff hanging out up there.' Karl pointed skywards, to the ceiling upon which the rain drummed steadily. 'And I think I know the very person.'

The two made a dash back to the lab. If anything, the rain was getting heavier, and the damp chill and the gloom made it feel more like a winter evening than a late afternoon in early July. Steve made his apologies and headed off, saying he had a Finzi concert to get to at the City Hall. Karl headed for his study and parked himself in front of the laptop. He hunted through his address book, until he found the contact he was looking for, and thought for a bit about the best way to approach things. He hadn't been in touch with Jane for quite a while, so there were the inevitable introductory pleasantries. Then he got down to the gist of the matter and pinged off the message.

FRANK POZNAN TILTED HIS HEAD BACK AS FAR AS IT would go, without toppling him over backwards, and stared open-mouthed at the astonishing show overhead. He had been at the university in Fairbanks, now, for more than twenty years, and had seen the aurorae on countless occasions, but never anything like this. The curtains of iridescent green, blue and yellow seemed almost solid as they flickered and flashed across the sky. The air fizzed and crackled, and Frank's scalp crawled as static charges sifted through what remained of his hair, detaching his comb-over so that it waved like a quivering candle flame above his head. The spectacle was even more astonishing, given that the mid-summer sun was barely below the horizon, and the sky far from completely dark.

It was a little before two in the morning and the air was unusually balmy. He had driven the pick-up over from Fairbanks straight after his last class and pitched his small tent in his favourite spot on the Chena River. Dense forest crowded close to the water on either side, leaving a small grassy glade reached by a difficult to find path. It was where he came when he needed to fish and when he had something on his mind.

He could see things were dying down a little, the flickering drapes slowly washing out and the fizzles and hisses fading away. Returning to his tent, he poured himself coffee from a flask, zipped himself in, and then crawled into his sleeping bag. Pulling out a sheaf of black-and-white images, he drew himself closer to his camping lantern and shuffled through them for a few minutes. Then he turned out the light and lay back on his inflatable pillow. He knew he needed to sleep if he was going to provide any sort of match for the grayling in the morning, but his brain was whirring and his mind's eye crowded out by the countless tiny spheres that packed the dust samples retrieved from the surface of the Bering Glacier.

He hadn't had the time to get any analysis done, so he had no idea what they were made of, but the regularity of form had convinced him from the very first that they must be artificial. As to source and purpose, he hadn't a clue. Still, maybe Dick, one of the research guys over at DARPA, could shed some light. He'd heard on the grapevine that the Defense Department had recently put a couple of new satellites up to look at atmospheric conditions ahead of the first tests of the new hypersonic transport plane. He also knew that Dick had a foot in the door, so maybe he had some low-down on this stuff.

Frank's exhaustion eventually won out and he slept for a good eight hours. He was woken by the sun blazing through the thin material of the tent and the rapidly increasing warmth. Irritated at losing prime fishing time, he was out of bed like a shot, donning his fishing jacket with its countless pockets packed with flies, lures and all manner of other angler stuff, and pulling on the rubber waders. He gulped the leftover coffee. It was cold, but he didn't want to waste any time making more on the small stove.

Barely ten minutes after waking, he stood up to his waist in the freezing waters, the chill slowly working its way through the rubber. Selecting his favourite fly, he made the first cast of the day, letting it drift downstream with the current before retrieving it and casting again. It was a while since he'd fished with a fly, but he was soon back in the swing of things.

After a dozen or so casts with no luck, he paused to don dark glasses. The sun had climbed above the trees now and the reflection off the water was blinding. The bugs were up too and in the rush he had forgotten to apply his repellent. They were only going to get worse and he swore under his breath as he realised he would need to head back to his tent and get his protection on. But he had his rhythm now, so he decided to give it another ten minutes. If he could just get one fish in the bag he would feel a lot happier. He cast again and again, pausing only to slap at his exposed forearms as the bugs continued to nip.

A far sharper stinging on the back of his neck brought forth an involuntary cry. 'What the f…?'

He reached up a hand to investigate the source of the pain and was shocked to encounter what felt like a tiny dart. As he turned to look behind, his vision began to blur and his legs gave way. He was unconscious before he hit the icy water, and dead from drowning a few minutes later.

JANE ARRIVED AT THE LAB BEFORE EIGHT. THE endless rain of the last couple of weeks had stopped sometime in the night and she'd been wakened a little after five by summer sunshine blazing through a gap in the curtains. Her teenage son Alistair was staying at a friend's for a few days, and Jane was determined to make the most of it. She was up and out of the door within half an hour. A quick run, a potter in the veg patch and a piece of toast, and then on the road before the morning traffic built up. She was surprised to find that Dan had beaten her in but guessed that he too had been energised by the eventual arrival of summer. The door to the tiny room that was all she could find for him in her space-challenged lab was open and she called out a greeting as she passed. Dan was on the phone but raised a hand in response.

When she got to her study, she opened all the windows, which had been fastened shut against the wet and cold, and breathed in the warm air scented with climbing honeysuckle and early roses planted in the beds beneath. It was far too nice a day to be indoors, but she had a pile of work. Maybe she would leave early and spend a relaxing evening in the garden with a nice, chilled Chablis.

After making a mug of instant coffee, she settled at her laptop and started on the emails, first tackling the dross, as was her habit, before getting into the important stuff. She couldn't help grinning as she saw an email from Karl Slater, which she opened immediately. 'Long time no see...' she read.

Long time no see, indeed, she thought, her mind replaying the last time they had met. A particularly boozy conference in Durham, she recalled. She had been the keynote speaker and Karl one of the conveners. They had taken her out on the piss afterwards, lots of beer and very little food. She was shit-faced by the time she got back to her room and Karl had been the epitome of a gentleman as he helped her – almost fully clothed – into bed. She remembered the following morning too. Probably the worst hangover in a long line of very bad hangovers. Her grin grew even wider at the thought. It would be nice to see Karl again.

She read through the rest of the email, smile morphing gradually into a frown of concentration, and opened the attachment when she had finished. Expanding the image Karl had sent to full screen, she pored over it, frown deepening.

'What the hell is this?' she muttered.

Hitting the reply button, she pinged off a message. Short and to the point. 'Karl, nice to hear. No idea what this is. Send samples over and I will take a look with the probe. Best. Jx.' More work on her plate, just when she didn't need it, but she had always liked a good mystery.

The samples turned up by courier a couple of days later, and she handed them straight over to Dan. For a while now, she had been showing him how to prepare samples for the microprobe. It was a time-consuming business and one that her research students were constantly messing up, so why not make the most of Captain Mitchell while he was around? The nuclear microprobe bombarded a target sample with a tight beam of positively charged particles that allowed the composition of different parts of the sample to be determined with extreme accuracy and precision. To get good results, the samples had to be vacuum-impregnated, mounted in discs of epoxy resin, polished to a flat, flawless surface, and cleaned of any contaminating detritus. A final, rather exotic – but technically vital – flourish, involved coating the samples with an extremely thin layer of gold. Altogether enough to keep Dan employed until the probe was available in a couple of weeks' time. Meanwhile, she had plenty to keep herself occupied.

Jane would never forget the day she took her first good look at Karl's samples. The rain of a few weeks earlier was a distant memory, and the sun had shone from dawn 'til dusk ever since. The temperature had topped thirty-five degrees for several days and it looked as if it was going to be a humdinger of a summer. She had a few household chores to catch up on in the morning, so didn't get to the lab until lunchtime. She grabbed a sandwich in the cafeteria and ate it quickly in her study, while she was working her way through the sample documentation that Dan had sorted out for her. He had prepared twenty discs in all, the first half dozen of which were loaded up. She was ready to roll.

Four hours later, Jane felt drained. She sat in the microprobe's hot seat and stared into space. Then she logged out, powered down, picked up the images and data readouts, and headed along the corridor and out through the door at the end. After the semi-darkness of the probe room, the late afternoon sun was blinding, so she made her way over to a wooden bench in the cool shade of a spreading cherry tree. She sat, clutching the batch of papers to her chest, other hand cradling her head as she gazed up at the mosaic made by the green canopy and a cloudless blue sky.

Dan must have seen her pass his open door, because after a minute or so, he plonked himself down next to her. As a concession to the heat, he had for once swapped his chinos and striped Oxford for belted shorts and a Ralph Lauren polo. Jane stopped scrutinising the sky and gave him a tired smile.

Dan signalled with an upraised chin at the papers. 'Interesting stuff?'

Jane's smile faded. 'Weird stuff. Very weird stuff.' She wasn't quite sure why, but she didn't want to open up to Dan. Not yet, anyway. She needed time to think.

Dan was still watching her, eyebrows raised in expectation. 'Care to share?'

She shook her head and stood suddenly. 'Talk later. I said I'd pick Ali up from his friend's house. See you.' She gave a small wave and headed down the path to her car, still clutching the papers close.

The next morning, she dropped Ali off early and unlocked the door to the empty lab. She had packed Dan off to a workshop on analytical techniques, and all three of her research students were away at a conference in Cambridge. She made the most of the peace and quiet to pore over the images of Karl's samples and the related analytical data, which she had lodged in their own folder on her desktop. She spent a while juggling with the data and zeroing in on individual particles in the images.

Weird was the term she had used to Dan. They were certainly that and then some. Each particle contained a complex core made up of various exotic metals and other compounds. The size of the core was consistent for all the particles, but it was encased in a layer of pure carbon that varied in thickness from particle to particle. The carbon layer was pretty much featureless, but the core had a fine structure reminiscent of nanocircuits she had seen, the purpose of which had her stumped. There were clusters of near-circular structures too, that looked like cellular features and certainly had a chemistry similar to animal flesh. And others that looked like the neurons found in brain tissue. Probably the strangest thing was that some of the larger spheres were girdled by smaller ones that looked almost as if they were about to bud off. Whatever this indicated, it certainly wasn't a natural reproductive process. These particles were artificial constructs – no question. Part organic, maybe, but nothing devised by nature. Who made them, what they were for, and why they were in samples taken from the stratosphere, she had no idea – yet.

She made herself a mug of tea and went out to the bench under the cherry tree to drink it. The sun was hidden behind a curtain of thick stratus, but it was still warm and the increasing humidity spoke of a storm on the way. After a few minutes she drained her tea and, on a whim, headed down to the preparation lab. Armed with a few plastic sample containers, she returned to the cherry tree and, using a spatula, carefully lifted some of the fine surface soil from the surrounding flowerbeds. She placed this in one of the containers, sealed the top and wrote on the side with a marker pen. Stuffing the container in her pocket, she crossed to the university sports field, which abutted the lab, and made a beeline for the long-jump pit, where she filled another container with sand. Then, returning to the lab, she went into the small kitchen next to the common room, stood on a chair and scraped up some of the copious dust on top of one of the cupboards.

Back in her study, she called Geoff Patterson, who ran the probe, to check when next there was a slot free. Luckily, someone had cried off, and there was an entire morning available at the end of the week. It would take her that long to get the samples ready, in any case.

Putting the phone down, she picked up the samples and made for the prep lab. It was quite a while since she had done any sample preparation. That, after all, was what research students and technicians were for. She wasn't quite sure why she was doing this, nor what she expected to find, but she went to work with a will. She had forgotten how satisfying it was to get her hands dirty.

THE FOG WAS REALLY GOING FOR IT THIS MORNING.
Sunny could barely make out the road edge as she nudged her old Beetle through the gloom, and she had to keep weaving back and forth to check her position. She had a progress meeting with her supervisor scheduled for eight thirty and at this rate she was going to be late. Mentally, she kicked herself. She should have known by now how bad the Monterey fogs could get at this time of year. She put her foot down a little harder but quickly lifted it again. The visibility was just too poor. She would much rather be late than be the late Ms Flowerdew.

In any case, Dave was pretty easy-going and he seemed to be pleased with her work. The fog would be gone by ten, as it invariably was, and the forecast was for wall-to-wall sun all day. As a lass who was Manchester born and bred, what more could she ask for? She grinned at the thought of the day ahead. After the meeting she had a boat booked and would be out sampling all afternoon. Then there was the beach party that evening. It was all a far cry from Stockport.

The only cloud on an otherwise unblemished horizon was the sample contamination. In the last few, the phytoplankton had been almost outnumbered by thousands of tiny spheres. She didn't want to seem stupid, so she hadn't mentioned them to her supervisor. First, she wanted to have a bash at shedding some light on the mystery objects herself. As a start, she had pinged off an email to her old tutor back in the UK. There wasn't much floating about in the ocean that could faze him. She hadn't heard anything back but wasn't entirely surprised. She remembered hearing somewhere that he'd been hijacked at short notice to advise on some government project or other. No-one had seen hide nor hair of him for the last six months.

The sign for the bridge over the Amtrak line loomed out of the mist and it looked to be getting a little brighter ahead. Then she saw that it was just a car's headlights. The unmarked black pick-up was parked on her side of the road and as she drew closer she saw there was a policeman standing in front, waving her off the road into what looked like a building site. Sunny guessed there must have been an accident. Not surprising, really. Tourists always drove too fast in the fog. She pulled the car over onto a patch of gravel and waited while the policeman came over. Her throat went dry when he gestured for her to open the door, but his smile reassured her. She got out and opened her mouth to ask what was going on.

The blow from behind was brutal, caving in the back of her skull, blood and grey matter spurting through her bleached locks and down the back of her sun-browned neck. Her legs folded instantly and she collapsed, lifeless, onto the fog-moistened ground. In the distance the sound of a train's horn shattered the eerie silence of the fog. The policeman, and another man in a dark suit, lifted Sunny's body and carried it down the embankment to the single track, where they draped it across the rails. The fog was more dense here and the driver would never see it in time. The two men looked at one another and grinned. That was the problem with students these days. They just couldn't take the pressure. The train's horn sounded again. This time much closer and underpinned by the rumble of wheels grinding on steel.

IMMEDIATELY AFTER THE PROBE SESSION ON THE Friday, Jane picked up the output and marched straight down the corridor and out of the building. Dan's door was open as usual and he waved cheerily as she bustled past. When she didn't respond, he crossed over to the doorway, frowning at her rapidly retreating back. As the fire doors at the end of the corridor crashed shut behind her, he went back to his cramped desk and fired off a brief email.

Jane got straight into her car, threw the papers on the passenger seat and sat biting her lip. She needed somewhere to think. Starting up, she headed for the campus exit. Instead of turning right for home, she swung left, following a winding road through green fields and woodland to a small lakeside park she used to visit when Ali was small. Leaving the car in the pay and display, she stuffed the printouts in her shoulder bag and started walking. The sight of the playground brought memories of Ali there as a toddler, all smiles and chocolate-mouthed, but she banished them and hurried past.

She followed a path along the edge of the lake until she reached her favourite bench. It was set back from the water and half-hidden amongst a stand of self-seeded sycamores that swayed in a gusty wind that was building. A mixed gaggle of mallards and Canada geese approached, hoping to elicit titbits, but she ignored them.

She sat down gratefully and put her head in her hands. To tell the truth, she was still in shock. All the samples she had taken from inside and around the lab contained the enigmatic spheres in huge numbers. She had only had a brief time to think about the implications, but she was already pretty sure what was going on. She remembered reading somewhere, a while back now, about the notion that climate breakdown could be 'cured' by using armies of nanobots to gobble up the vast quantity of carbon pumped into the atmosphere as a result of human excesses. She had laughed it off at the time as a load of neocon guff; a fantasy technofix to keep capitalism in the fast lane, while knocking that pesky global heating on the head. Smoothing the road to consumerism without consequences. The whole idea, she had convinced herself, was preposterous; the ravings of a right-wing commentariat that would never come to pass. But that had been then.

Now, it seemed, someone, some group, some regime, was actually doing it: unilaterally sucking carbon – the principal driver of global heating and climate breakdown – out of the atmosphere. It was the only answer and it explained everything.

The tiny bots were fixing atmospheric carbon, in the same way that the roots of some plants fixed nitrogen from the soil, somehow separating it from oxygen and binding it to their bodies. They were self-replicating too – that's what the budding was all about – so a relatively small initial number could increase exponentially, presumably through scavenging and using the trace elements that natural processes and pollution had spread far and wide throughout the atmosphere. Size population analysis revealed a cut-off at the top end, suggesting that when the bots were sufficiently sated, they were just heavy enough to drift slowly back to Earth, taking their carbon with them. No-one could see it, but it was literally raining carbon. Subversive geoengineering at its most insidious.

Sitting upright again, she reached in her bag for a bottle of mineral water and took a long swig. Taking out the probe data and images, she sifted through them, as if to reassure herself that she hadn't imagined it all. She put the papers down again and blew out her cheeks, expelling the air in a noisy outburst as she wondered what to do next. A feeling was growing that this could be dangerous knowledge, so even as she chided herself for her paranoia, she couldn't help looking around while furtively stuffing the papers back in her bag.

Something like this needed massive backing and a huge organisation. Whoever was responsible clearly didn't want it shouted from the rooftops and that meant that they would likely make life very uncomfortable indeed – or worse – for any potential whistle-blower. Despite the summer warmth, Jane shivered. The more she thought about it, the more she decided she would feel happier and safer once she had shared the knowledge with someone else. Dan was the most convenient, but she wasn't sure. He was bright, helpful and as nice as pie, but what did she really know about him? No, the obvious person was Karl. They were his samples, after all, and she knew he was as honest and guileless as they came. What you saw was what you got. Pleased at coming to a decision, she walked back to the car and retraced the drive back to the university.

Dan was still working, and he looked concerned as he stuck his head round the door and asked if she were OK. Jane thought she made a fair fist at a believable excuse for rushing off earlier – a forgotten dental appointment – and Dan didn't seem suspicious. *For fuck's sake, why would he?* she thought. *Get a grip.*

She pushed open her office door and closed and locked it behind her. Retrieving the probe printouts from her bag, she stuck them on her desk and picked up the phone. She was halfway through dialling Karl's number when she had second thoughts. Even as she scolded herself for the cloak and dagger behaviour, she instead typed up a quick note, printed it and stuffed it in a plain envelope, along with the microprobe data and images. She had everything in a folder on her laptop, so could print out more hard copies whenever she needed them.

The note summarised her thoughts and suggested a meeting place and time early the following week. She looked up Karl's address, scrawled it on the front of the envelope and checked her watch. She was late. Ali was taking his driving test that afternoon and she said she would pick him up. Fingers crossed, he would be driving her around from now on. Nonetheless, something made her eschew the convenience of the departmental mail tray in favour of the corner shop post office on the way to the test centre. She made sure she used recorded delivery, so someone would have to sign for the package.

NOT FOR THE FIRST TIME, SENIOR AIRCRAFTSMAN Taffy Griffiths ruminated on the bunch of Yanks who had been dumped upon them. He hadn't managed to talk to one – in fact, they didn't mix at all with the Brits – but he had heard they were trialling some new rain-making technique. *More rain*, he grumbled to himself, *is the last thing they needed, just at the moment.* He stood in the open doorway of the dreary accommodation block – the Ascension Island 'Hilton', some wag had named it – and shivered, even though the air was warm. The rain was falling so hard that it was bouncing back waist high from the concrete apron beyond. He had never seen rain falling upwards before.

Hardly surprisingly, there was nothing in the air. Landing at RAF Station Ascension was tricky at the best of times, and in this weather and with no instrument landing system in place, it was just the other side of impossible. There might have been nothing in the air, but there was plenty on the ground. A dozen USAF KC-10 tankers were lined up on the far side of the enormous expanse of concrete around which most of the base buildings were clustered, another couple at the end of the taxiway leading to the two-mile long runway.

Grounded for the day, the Yank crews were confined to the compact, tented village that had sprung up six months earlier close to the hardstanding where the tankers were stationed. Taffy cast an envious eye in their direction. The Yanks weren't so much housed in tents, as in what looked like giant, inter-connected yurts that knocked the cheerless RAF accommodation into a cocked hat. Rumour had it they were the height of luxury, with every conceivable mod-con on hand – even a jacuzzi and cinema. But as only the CO had made it inside the surrounding high security fence and none of the crews were let out except to fly, they would probably never know the reality.

The rain seemed to be easing a little now, but Taffy doubted it was anything other than a respite. He had been on base since late the previous year and was beginning to feel that he'd also been on the losing end of a bum deal. He had signed up for a move to an island that was supposed to have a hot, desert climate, but reckoned that in all that time he could count on his hands and feet the number of days the weather had matched expectations.

The first couple of weeks on the island had been a pleasure. The weather was hot and sunny, it was nice and quiet – with just a couple of dozen guys and a few pieces of totty – very little air traffic, and the work was a doddle. Then things started to go downhill. First the weather turned, then one morning all the base personnel were corralled in the big meeting room and given some bull about this cloud-seeding business. They were told that the US were sending in a fleet of KC-10 tankers specially adapted to dump rain-making chemicals into the atmosphere. The story was that it was part of a new programme to try and promote rainfall in drought-hit areas, especially the south-west US, which had apparently been as dry as a bone for more than a decade. There were mutterings and a few raised eyebrows at the time, not least because it had been raining pretty much solidly during the previous week, and they were all desperate for the sun to make an appearance. Assurances that the trials would be undertaken far out over the sea and would have no impact on the island's weather were met with understandable suspicion.

Once the planes and their crews shipped in a few days later, resentment against the newcomers built quickly. The security fences, gun-toting guards and enforced purdah of the crews only served to convince the Brits that whatever the Yanks were doing, it had bugger all to do with rain-making. But with no-one available upon whom to vent their grievances, animosity eventually turned to grudging acceptance and thoughts shifted away from the base within a base to the mundane but necessary business of keeping RAF Ascension bumbling along.

Contrary to Taffy's expectations, the rain stopped, and a watery sun struggled to make itself known through the fragmenting stratus. His shift didn't start for another two hours, so he took the opportunity to stretch his legs. By the time he had crossed the apron, the sun was fully out, the concrete was steaming and the climbing temperatures were bringing out beads of sweat on Taffy's beetle brow. Wiping them away, he crossed the taxiway, and headed for the runway. With no flights expected, the landing lights were all off to save power. His short and somewhat squat frame made hard work of the light scrub, and he was relieved to reach the tarmac. He turned right and walked in the direction of the far end of the runway, which was lost in a mist of evaporating rainfall and a burgeoning heat haze. Only a few years earlier the runway had been partly closed, but now, following repairs to its crumbling surface, it was fully operational again, its status as one of the longest runways in the world restored. As the base vets never tired of pointing out, it was for this reason that it had been selected by NASA, way back, as one of the emergency landing sites for the Space Shuttle.

As the heat and humidity continued to build, the end of the runway felt increasingly like a step too far, and much less tempting than a cold beer in the mess. Taking the shortest route to conditioned air, he recrossed the scrub to the apron, sauntering close to the razor wire compound that enclosed the KC-10s. Half a dozen blue-bereted guards, hard-faced, eyes hidden behind dark glasses, tracked him with their assault rifles as he passed. None responded to his cheery wave.

Beyond the aircraft compound was a large pre-fab that contained the storage tanks for the cloud-seeding chemicals – some silver-based compound that they had been assured was harmless. Taffy followed the high security fence, which marched close to the side of the building, and was approaching its front when there was a loud crash followed by a scream. The front of the prefab was open to the elements, and as the interior came into view, he could see that a forklift had careered into one of the trestle-supported tanks, bringing it down onto the vehicle and trapping its driver by his legs. The man was howling in agony, his cries bringing others running. The tank had split open, and whatever was inside was gushing out over the man's body, before flooding out of the front of the building and down the slight gradient towards Taffy.

The first fingers of liquid streamed under the fence and he shifted his feet out of the way. *It doesn't look very silvery,* he thought. In fact, it was dark, almost black, with the sort of rainbow patina seen on the surface of oily water. He bent down, scooped up a little in his hand and took a closer look, oblivious to the shouted warnings from one of the guards. Instead of resting inertly in the cup of his hand, the liquid seethed and fizzed as if alive. Taffy yelped and shook his hand to get rid of it, but it spread out over his palm in a thin, skin-hugging film. Then the tingling began, very quickly mutating into a pain so excruciating that Taffy failed again to notice the increasingly insistent warnings from the guard. In the end, the bullet that took him four-square in the temple seemed like a mercy.

JULY 2028
SURREY
ENGLAND

I T WAS BARELY SIX, BUT THE BRIGHT YELLOW GLOW
that made a halo around the curtains heralded another hot
day and made further sleep impossible. Jane had tossed and
turned all night and felt dog-tired – physically and mentally.
The knowledge of the bots and what they might already be
doing to the atmosphere was eating away at her. If she could
only share the burden, but there was simply no-one else she
was willing to open up to. Karl should get the package this
morning and they would meet in a couple of days. For now,
she had no choice but to soldier on.

She must have fallen asleep then, despite the glare, as the
next thing she knew the alarm was beeping and she could hear
Ali taking a shower in the bathroom at the end of the landing.
She showered too, in the en-suite, dressed quickly and had
breakfast on the table when Ali came down. She watched him,
enthralled, as he simultaneously munched his cereal and sent
a text. No doubt telling all and sundry that he had passed his
test first time.

All of a sudden he was a man, or very nearly, a real charmer. His open, friendly face and wide, powerful shoulders already had the girls' hearts fluttering. She shook her head in disbelief. Where did the years go? In a couple of months, the holidays would be over and he would be off to Edinburgh to study medicine. Her breath caught in her throat and she had to hold back the tears as she imagined how empty the place would be. There had been just the two of them for so long she was not sure she could bear it.

She took her breakfast things over to the sink, ruffling Ali's hair as she passed. 'Ten minutes. OK?'

He looked up, gave her a smile and raised a thumb in confirmation. When she came back into the kitchen, packed and ready to go, he was waiting by the back door with the car keys in his hands and a look of happy anticipation on his face. He had insisted on driving her to the lab before he headed off to one of the nearby reservoirs for a day pottering about in a sailing dinghy with a few mates.

He held up the keys and jangled them. He was backlit by the sun, so she couldn't see his features, but she knew he would have a grin on his face. 'See you in the car, Mum.'

As she opened the door on another glorious day, she saw Ali in the driver's seat of the ropy, old Renault, leaning forwards to put the key in the ignition. She had her back turned, locking the door, when the bomb went off. The blast picked her up and hurled her against the wall of the house, shattering her lower left leg. The car was a raging fireball, a dark shape at the heart of the flames twisting and turning. She would never forget the screams. Decades later, she would still hear them day and night, the backbeat to the rest of her life.

PRESIDENT ABELINE GORT STOOD ALONE IN THE semi-darkness and looked out across the manicured grounds of the Texas State Capitol through one of its nine hundred windows. Viewed from behind, her tiny frame, silhouetted against the yellow glow of the burning barricades, could be confused with that of a small child. Seen from the front, even in the gloom, it was not a mistake anyone would make. President Gort's face was surprisingly smooth for a woman approaching her sixtieth year. Nonetheless, it was a face that bore, for all to see, the scars of the battles that had taken her from leader of one of the country's minor evangelical churches to the most powerful office in the world. Her cheeks were unwrinkled, but deep furrows ran down from either side of her mouth to the jawline, so that – like a ventriloquist's dummy – her chin seemed to work independently of the rest of her face. Another pair of deep corrugations sliced down either side of the bridge of her nose, separating deep-set, steely-grey eyes that observed the world and everything therein with a cold detachment. Gort had one of those mouths that turned up at the corners. A mouth that always seemed as if it was about to smile, but hardly ever did.

She took a few paces forwards until her face almost touched the window glass. She could just make out the third and highest of the security fences. The first two had been battered down when the demonstrators broke through earlier in the evening. Now a thin shield wall of jittery police and national guardsmen, pinned against a mesh barrier, was all that stood between fifty thousand protestors and the leaders of the free – and not so free – world.

Almost imperceptibly, the President shook her head from side to side, her white pageboy bob trembling in response. She stretched an arm out behind her and clicked her fingers twice. Out of the gloom came a tall, emaciated figure, in a suit at least one size too small.

'Madam President?' A reedy enquiry.

'This has gone far enough. Tell them to fire warning shots.'

The man nodded and retreated into the shadows, talking quietly to a heavy with a head mic.

The gunfire, when it came, could be heard throughout the building. Some of the more timorous dignitaries, waiting in the main reception area to be shipped out by helicopter, actually ducked or looked around for cover amongst the overstuffed armchairs and leather sofas, then looked sheepish as it became clear they were not under attack.

The effect on the protestors was immediate. As one, they stopped pummelling the shield wall, turned and ran, crouching low, arms held over heads in supplication. The police and guardsmen followed, still firing over the heads of the retreating crowd. The President liked what she saw, and her small mouth opened in what might have been a smile but looked more like a grimace, exposing two rows of tiny white teeth that wouldn't have looked out of place on a toddler. She clicked her fingers again, drawing her aide once more from the darkness.

'Jacob. Tell them to keep advancing. I want that scum back beyond the outer barrier before our guests leave. We can't have them' – she nodded in the direction of the reception area – 'thinking we're a soft touch.'

Jacob again retreated to mumble to the head-mic man.

Gort returned her attention to the scene outside. She exuded her trademark calm, but inside she was seething. The security services had been right. It was one hell of a balls-up. They had pleaded with her not to host the G20 meeting in one of the country's most environmentally aware cities. But she was Austin born and bred, and her family had lived there for more than a century and a half, ever since her Huguenot ancestors had moved south from New York. Nothing was going to keep her from showing off her beloved city to the latest crop of world leaders. Now, she had to admit, it had been a very bad call. It hadn't helped, either, that just a week earlier she had turned her back on the latest climate emergency agreement.

It wasn't as if the visiting heads of state had got to see much of the place in any case. Helicoptered in to the ring-fenced and fortified Texas State Capitol, where the meeting was taking place, they glimpsed nothing beyond the vast crowd of protestors and the ten thousand police and national guardsmen ranged against them.

The atmosphere beyond the barriers had been febrile from the start and became more frenzied by the hour. The death of a young woman at the hands of a trigger-happy police officer had raised the temperature even further and served to draw more and more protestors from across the country.

The meeting furnished a focal point for citizen rage like no other in recent times, and the myriad banners reflected this. Smash the banks, screw globalisation, jobs not profits, healthcare for all, no more foreign wars, make America welcoming again, they announced. But, above all, the President's stand on the climate emergency provided the match that had ignited the touchpaper of nationwide dissent.

Since her election late the previous year, Gort had trashed global heating science and shown contempt for the increasingly desperate international initiatives to get on top of greenhouse gas emissions. This had come to a head the previous week, when she had walked out of the Paris II climate conference, which sought to slash global carbon emissions in the face of dangerously escalating extreme weather worldwide. The image of Gort, diminutive, prim and attired entirely in white, flaunting a middle-finger salute as she marched out of the meeting, instantly became an icon worshipped by the alt-right. Already it had spread far and wide to adorn the baseball caps of redneck zealots and the gun stocks of NRA aficionados.

Commentators across the United States and the world had been close to unanimous in bawling out Gort for both the substance and style of her conduct. But there was confusion too. What had the President meant when she said at the brief press conference afterwards that no-one needed to worry about global heating any longer, that she 'had it covered'? Was it hubris or was she just plain nuts? The consensus seemed to be the latter.

Still gazing into the darkness, Gort smiled – grimaced. They would find out soon enough.

Too distant now for the President to follow what was happening, the mix of police and guardsmen continued to force the crowd back. Every now and then they offered encouragement by firing single rounds over the heads of the crouching, scurrying protestors. Even so, it took several minutes to cajole the mob back as far as the crushed and flattened remains of the outer security fence.

The demonstrators sped up as they reached it and space opened up ahead of them, and the security forces followed suit. As they high-stepped over the warped and twisted mesh of the fence panels, a young guardsman caught his boot on a loose wire and stumbled. He bent down to try and release his foot but tumbled forwards. Finger on the trigger of his assault rifle, his right hand hit the ground, loosing a short burst. The trajectory was low, raking the legs of the rearmost demonstrators and cutting them down like a stand of corn. Instead of fleeing, the crowd turned, enraged, and threw themselves at the pursuing security forces. Fingers already on triggers, it was easy for them to lower their sights, bring them to bear on the advancing protestors and let go . More than fifty died in the resulting carnage. But Gort saw none of this. Later the police and national guard would defend their action by claiming they feared for their lives.

Gort slowly became aware that Jacob Adams, her chief of staff, was loitering at her elbow.

'Yes?' she queried without turning.

'The communiqué, Madam President. It's done.'

'Does it suit us?'

'Well, it pretty much offends no-one and commits us to nothing.'

The corners of Gort's mouth turned upwards a little more. 'I think we can go with that.'

Adams proffered a single sheet of paper. 'Would you like to see it?'

'No. Feed it to the media and then get those guys up and out of here.' The President nodded once more in the direction of the reception area where the dignitaries had been waiting for more than four hours as aides argued over the communiqué's precise wording. 'Are the choppers in place?'

'Standing by and ready to go,' announced Adams.

'Good. Get moving, then. Oh, and get that faggot Bannerman in here. We need to head off too.'

Adams gave a small nod – almost a bow – and, signalling for the heavy to follow, left the room.

The meeting could be summed up, without any hyperbole whatsoever, as an unmitigated disaster. The Russians and Saudis had walked out on day one, and the Mexicans and Turks the following evening. In the reception area, heads of state and their aides chafed at the bit. The unending chants from the protestors formed a constant backdrop to conversation, and the waves of hate sweeping the building were almost palpable. Nerves showed on the faces of the dignitaries, and eyes shifted constantly to the windows, beyond which a pitched battle was playing out beneath the cold, white light of the city's unique moonlight towers.

Desperate to ship out of what they mostly agreed was a complete shithole, and away from the company of President Gort, who they unanimously agreed was a complete shit, they clustered together in small groups, where finger-wagging, griping and expletives seemed to be the order of the day. Only UK Prime Minister Duncan Bannerman sat aloof, head down, pretending to fiddle with his phone. Occasionally, he peered furtively across at one group or another, and at one point half stood as if intending to walk over and join in, but instead sat down again and continued fidgeting.

During the good times, Prime Minister Bannerman had been a charming master of small talk, but with the UK out of Europe, bumped off its permanent seat on the UN Security Council and shunned by former friends, his confidence was at rock bottom. Best, he felt, to lie low and hope for better times around the corner.

Like the others, Bannerman was desperate to get away. He missed Jeremy, and the cats, and wanted nothing more than to snuggle up with all three in his Downing Street bed, but for him proceedings weren't yet over. Most of his team were heading back to Blighty, but President Gort had insisted he spend the weekend at her country retreat in the hills close to Bandera. Real cowboy country, she had called it. Two whole days with the obnoxious bigot. He wasn't certain he could hack it, but he knew he had no choice. It really was an invitation he couldn't refuse. This Skyseed business had seen to that.

He wished, for perhaps the thousandth time, that he had never heard of the thing, but it had seemed the only way to stop the UK sinking even deeper into the mire. He jumped as his phone beeped an alert, read the text and put his hand to his mouth. 'For fuck's sake!'

It had been on the cards for a while, but it was still a shock. For the first time in history, the dollar was worth more than the pound. The British media would tear him limb from limb.

Oblivious to the stares, he put his head in his hands and muttered a string of expletives. Then he rubbed his face, put his head back and looked up at the ornate ceiling. More than anything else in the world, what he wanted now was a leadership challenge, a challenge he would cheerfully lose. The obscurity of the backbenches called to him like a siren. Even better, he could revive his career in the press. Some other mug could take a turn at saving the sinking ship that was the British economy. It had been in deep recession ever since the coronavirus pandemic and, as far as he was concerned, it was a basket case.

Head still tilted back, Duncan became aware of a pair of faces looming over him. One, the lumpy, shaved head of chief of staff, Nobby Aitken; the other, the long face of Gort's equivalent, Jacob Adams.

'Time to go boss.' Nobby jerked a thumb at the double doors at the far end of the long room. They stood open, a black-suited, mic'd-up heavy standing either side. Adams said nothing but smiled encouragingly. Bannerman dragged himself slowly to his feet and headed in the direction of the exit, followed by the two aides. He felt utterly drained, but his legs kept moving as if of their own accord. It was like he was walking through treacle, but he kept going, down a long, dimly lit corridor, and out into the night.

THE BIG PLANE CRABBED SIDEWAYS AS THE PILOT
fought the powerful crosswind. Just when it looked to
be too late, she pulled the nose of the fully loaded Swiss Air
A320 around, before dropping it like a stone onto Manchester
airport's single runway. No fun for the passengers, but the only
safe way to land in the conditions. The hard landing evoked
a few screams and dislodged a number of oxygen masks. It
also woke Karl Slater, who had been spark out for the whole
of the two-and-a-quarter-hour flight from Zurich. The trip
had lasted almost half an hour longer than usual due to the
strong north-westerly headwind. Something that Karl did not
begrudge at all. Any extra time for his body to recuperate was
absolutely fine with him. He'd heard of absinthe, of course, but
never tasted it. Never again, either.

Being Manchester, Karl wasn't especially surprised to find
that it was drizzling when he left the terminal building. He
picked up his car, hoped to God that he wasn't still over the
limit and headed east. He was soon climbing high above the

city, into mist and driving rain. There was little traffic and nothing to see but bleak moorland, scattered with sheep, vanishing into the murk. Not much more than an hour after leaving Manchester, he was descending into Sheffield. By the time he reached his lab at the university, the rain had stopped and there was even the odd glimpse of blue through the scudding stratus.

Steve's door was open and Karl knocked on the frame. His technician was hunched over his laptop with his big headphones on as usual and didn't notice. Karl knocked louder and Steve turned, his face splitting in its trademark grin. He removed the headphones, stood and came over. They high-fived.

'How was the land of cuckoo clocks and Toblerone?'

Karl dumped his pull-along and backpack in a corner and slumped into the battered armchair. He scrunched his eyes shut and pinched the bridge of his nose. 'Chocolate boxy as ever.'

He was clearly still the worse for wear, which made Steve's smile grow even wider. 'No doubt a modicum of alcohol was consumed?'

Karl gave a weak grin. 'The fieldwork was fine. Everyone was too knackered to drink much and there wasn't much booze around, anyway. But I had the viva at ETH yesterday.'

Lodged partway up a hill overlooking Zurich, ETH – or, to give it it's full title, the Eidgenössische Technische Hochschule – was one of Europe's leading scientific and technical universities, and probably the only one reachable by cable car.

'How did it go?' enquired Steve.

'Fine,' said Karl. 'Great piece of work, in fact. The kid'll go far. The problem was the partying afterwards.'

Steve put back his head and laughed. 'You're getting old, man.'

'Perhaps you're right.' He was quiet for a moment, while Steve enjoyed his discomfort.

'Ever drunk absinthe?'

Steve shook his head. 'Not as far as I know.'

'Don't. It'll blow your kidneys out through your arse.'

Steve guffawed and slapped Karl on the back. Then his smile evaporated, and he sat down on his desk chair and turned it to face Karl. 'I'm guessing you haven't heard, then.'

Karl looked up, his expression wary. 'Heard what? Are the research grants out? I wasn't expecting them for another week.'

Steve looked down at his hands. 'No. Not yet.' A pause. 'There's been a nasty incident. Jane Haliwell. You said you sent her the samples a few weeks ago.'

Karl waited.

'There's been a bomb attack.'

For a moment, Karl was speechless. Then: 'What the fuck… a bomb? Are you serious?'

Steve nodded. 'I would have emailed you, but somehow it didn't seem the right way.'

'Wait. Is she OK?' said Karl.

'In hospital. The news reports mention life-changing injuries. And she's in a coma.'

Karl shook his head in disbelief. A bomb? He hadn't looked at his phone for a week – crap coverage in the mountains – and the fuss must have died down by the time he checked the news feeds the previous afternoon.

Steve continued, 'There's more. Her son was killed.'

'Oh, for Christ's sake!' Karl had never met the lad, but knew he was everything to Jane.

They sat in silence for a minute or so as Karl digested the news.

'When was this?'

'About a week ago,' said Steve. 'The day after you left.'

'What are the police saying?'

Steve shrugged. 'According to the news, they're not ruling anything out, though they seem to be pretty convinced it was a case of mistaken identity.'

Karl shook his head again. 'Jesus!'

He picked up a stack of post from his pigeonhole and headed for home. There was a meeting with a research student scheduled for later that afternoon, but Karl had cried off. He wasn't up to it, either physically or, after Steve's news, mentally.

By the time he got home – a semi high on the western edge of the city – the sky was entirely blue and the sun burned hot through the still damp air. He brewed a mug of tea and took it and the post out to a table in the long back garden. The weeds had used the opportunity of his recent trip to take over, and some urgent remedial action was needed if he was to rescue his runners and spuds. Beyond the end of the garden, the sun was dipping towards the eastern moors and its rays, passing through the rain-washed atmosphere, were blinding.

He shuffled through the mail, pretty much guessing what each item was from the postmark or by way of expectation. There was one large, brown envelope with a Reading postmark that caught his attention. He turned it over to look at the sender's details and his breath caught in his throat. It was from Jane. He looked at the postmark again. It was dated the day before the bomb blast. For maybe thirty seconds, he just stared at the envelope, too spooked to open it. Then, taking a deep breath, he tore apart one end and pulled out a sheaf of papers, to which was clipped a note.

He read the note quickly and grunted. It had to be a joke – surely? But he knew it wasn't. He turned the envelope over to check the sender's name again. But Jane's easily recognisable scrawl was still there. He re-read the note, more carefully this time, then slowly went through the data sheets and images.

By the time he had finished, the sun had dropped behind the moors, and the air had taken on a damp chill.

'Jesus Christ!' he muttered as the implications started to hit home. What the fuck had he got himself mixed up in? Who the hell would do this? It was insane. Jane's interpretation was spot on. There couldn't be any doubt about that. Someone was pissing around with the climate. Not someone – this was far too big. Some government, then, some multinational; who? Suddenly, it hit him.

Shit! The bomb! It hadn't been mistaken identity at all. The hairs on the back of his neck prickled at the thought, and he felt suddenly weak.

He sat for a few minutes more, mind churning, until a passing shower drove him inside. He contemplated food, but his stomach revolted at the thought. He needed sleep more than anything, and plodded upstairs, papers clutched in one hand. He cleaned his teeth and stood looking in the mirror. His eyes were still bloodshot, a legacy of the previous night's wormwood overload. No doubt another few million brain cells had bitten the dust as a result. He reckoned he had managed about two hours' sleep in his Zurich hotel and maybe another couple on the plane. He was dog tired and even standing up was struggling to keep his eyes open. At the same time, his mind was seething as it continued to make sense of Jane's bombshell.

Well, there's nothing I can do about it now, he thought. He would sleep on it. Perhaps a way forward might reveal itself in the morning.

By the time he woke it was almost mid-day. Briefly, he revelled in the joy of not feeling hungover; a treasured moment that was swiftly crowded out by recollection of the previous night's whammy. He groaned at the thought and lay stupefied for a couple of minutes, before mentally bracing himself and leaping out of bed. A shower, a very strong coffee and a couple of bacon butties smothered with brown sauce did the job, leaving him feeling human for the first time in more than twenty-four hours.

He laid Jane's papers out across the kitchen table and went through them with a fine-toothed comb. There were no holes in the data, and the images and analyses were utterly convincing. So – what should he do about it? Nothing was the obvious answer. Let someone else kick up a fuss. This wasn't the sort of thing that could be kept under wraps for long and others were bound to find out – if they hadn't already. Then again, he couldn't quite quell the prodding thought at the back of his mind that this was a life-changing moment. *Yeah*, he reflected, *just like Jane's life-changing moment.* He wasn't quite ready to risk life or limb for his principles. All in all, he quite liked things as they were. But if he did manage to avoid being blown to kingdom come, this could really get his name out there.

Coming to a decision, he fired up his laptop, opened his email and scrolled down through the address book. He stopped at M.

Ralph Martinez – Captain Martinez – was a USAF meteorologist. They had bumped into one another at a number of international conferences and workshops over the last few years and had just clicked. Karl hadn't before encountered a met guy who could hold his own with a volcanologist in the bar, and that had certainly helped. Ralph's views were not at all what Karl had expected of an officer in the US military, and they had spent many an hour putting the world to rights.

He wasn't at all sure that Ralph was the right person to talk to, but he could think of no-one else. A combination of logic and intuition told him that there was a fair chance that something this big had military involvement somewhere along the line. Ralph was the only one he knew who might be able to shed some light or at least suggest a way forward. God forbid that he was actually involved. In which case, Karl was a crap judge of character, and probably – into the bargain – living on borrowed time.

What the hell, he mused. *In for a penny...*

He started typing. Didn't say much, just that something urgent had come up that required they meet. Last he had heard, Ralph was working out of the USAF base at Mildenhall in Suffolk, so Karl suggested it might be easiest if they met up in London. Maybe the next day, if Ralph were free.

Karl was in the utility room loading the machine with a pile of festering field clothing, when he heard his incoming mail chime. When he checked, he was surprised to find that it was from Ralph. He hadn't expected an instant reply. As it turned out, Ralph was just about to head down to the capital and would be staying overnight. He would be done by mid-morning the next day and could squeeze in a meeting then, before making his way back to base. Karl jumped at the chance and suggested a café that he frequented at St Pancras station, while awaiting trains back up north. Ralph replied immediately in the affirmative.

Satisfied, Karl snapped shut the laptop, shouldered his backpack and headed out the door. After his alpine frolics, he needed to start chipping away at the backlog in the lab.

The day was warm and sunny, and Karl's spirits were lifted by the realisation that he would soon be able to share his burden. He was about to press the remote to unlock the car, when he froze. In his mind, he saw the car lifted off the ground in a massive blast, his burning body tossed like a broken doll high into the air. He grinned to himself. He'd always had an active imagination, but this was stupid. Nonetheless, he couldn't help himself. Setting his bag aside, he lay on the pavement and checked under the car. Nothing out of place as far as he could see. Then he walked around the other side, lay in the road and peered under again. Nothing. He stood and brushed himself down.

As he looked up, he caught the eye of Frank Outram, his diminutive elderly neighbour. Frank was leaning on a garden rake and grinning from ear to ear. 'Lookin' fer bomb then, lad? 'Appen it were one o' them exes o' thine.'

Karl gave a weak smile and muttered something about an odd rattle. Squeezing the remote, he opened the door, started up and headed down the hill and into town. Frank watched him go, shook his head and continued to rake the cuttings off his lawn.

MARINE ONE, THE BIG SIKORSKY THAT FERRIED the President on journeys too short or too remote to require the services of the Air Force One jumbo, clattered through the darkness. They were flying low to avoid a powerful electric storm and periodic lightning flashes lit up rivulets of rainwater that jittered horizontally across the window glass. President Gort was 'in conference' at the front, so Bannerman and his chief of staff were relegated to the inward-facing bench seats at the rear. Gort had made her distaste for Bannerman pretty clear on the handful of occasions they had met, so it was hardly a surprise that she wanted to keep him at arm's length whenever possible. Duncan grinned wryly as he recollected his greeting on her visit to the UK. She had barely connected with his outstretched hand, and it had been hard to miss the way she immediately wiped it on the back of her skirt. He suspected that had been intentional. Well, he'd put up with far worse.

Nobby was snoring loudly opposite, but jumped violently as the intercom announced they would be landing in a few minutes. Forward momentum slowed perceptibly and the craft descended at speed before bouncing once and coming to rest on a large expanse of floodlit lawn. The door was opened from the outside and Gort, Adams and a security agent were ushered out and into a couple of enclosed golf carts that whisked them through the downpour and out of sight. The Brits were beginning to wonder if they had been forgotten when a young head topped by the white cap of the US marines popped through the open doorway and a gloved hand beckoned them forwards. Carefully negotiating the slippery metal steps, they were each provided at the bottom with an umbrella and requested to follow another marine in full ceremonial rig and drenched to the skin. Duncan dined alone in his suite. The President, once again, was tied up, but she would see him in an hour or so in the situation room. Finishing up his perfectly cooked steak, he dabbed his lips with a napkin, leant back in the ornately carved mahogany chair and looked around the room. It was impossible not to be impressed by its size and grandeur, although the mix of Wild West and European Gothic was not really his cup of tea. He wandered over to one of the big arched windows and peered through the rain-streaked glass. He could see nothing beyond an occasional lightning flash. A turning door handle announced the entry of his chief of staff, looking sated and worrying with a wooden pick at a piece of beef lodged between his front teeth. He flicked the pick nonchalantly into the log fire that hissed gently within an enormous iron grate.

'Well. Here we are,' he growled, by way of nothing in particular.

'Guess so. But I wish to hell we weren't.' Duncan slumped onto one of the large leather sofas.

Nobby perched on the edge of an occasional table nearby. Duncan shook his head. 'I don't think I can carry on with this. I really don't.'

Nobby made a face. 'What choice do we have? The country's going down the pan. If we can't get this trade deal in place, we're stuffed. And I don't just mean the economy.' Duncan slammed his palms on his knees and stood up. 'But the risks! What if it goes wrong? Haven't we fucked with the planet enough? And what if it actually works? When word gets out – what then? A lot of people are not going to be happy at the cloak and dagger approach. Not happy at all.'

Nobby just shrugged. Taking risks was why he had entered politics in the first place. Duncan wandered over to the window again and looked out. It was still pouring. 'Why do they even want us on board? They don't need us.'

'Well,' said Nobby, 'you know the Yanks. They might be the most powerful country on the planet, but they almost never go it alone. Look at Iraq and Afghanistan, and the rest. It's almost as if they need someone else alongside to provide reassurance or – more likely – to shift the blame on to when things go wrong, as they nearly always do.' Duncan snorted. 'Yeah, they always need a lapdog, but why is it always the fucking UK?'

Nobby grinned. 'Oh, you know, special relationship and all that.' Duncan was on the point of telling Nobby exactly where he could stick the special relationship, when there was a knock on the door.

In response to Duncan's invitation, a young marine entered and stood to attention just inside the room. It might have been the one who led them through the rain earlier, but it was difficult to say. They all looked the same to him, characterless military clones – scrubbed and manicured. The marine bawled a summons for them to join the President in the situation room, and they followed without a word.

The place was in semi-darkness. A long table with chairs dominated the centre, and there were more seats around the outside to accommodate lackeys and flunkeys. The far wall was faced with a dozen or so flat screens. All were blank, except one showing rolling news on Fox. It looked to Duncan like Austin and they seemed to be loading body bags into military ambulances. President Gort sat at one end of the table, flanked by senior military and security officers. The Fix, as they liked to think of it, or Skyseed – to give it its working codename – was beyond top secret and less than a hundred people in the US and UK knew its true purpose. A good number of them were in the room. Duncan was invited to sit but wasn't introduced. Nobby found a seat up against the wall and nodded to his neighbour, who looked at him blankly and said nothing.

Gort smiled – grimaced at Duncan. 'I hope the accommodation is to your liking, Prime Minister?' Duncan agreed that it was excellent and thanked the President for her hospitality.

'I'm afraid you won't be seeing much of me over the next couple of days,' said Gort. 'There's been a little difficulty back in Austin that I need to take care of. But I hope you can relax and make the most of a few days out of the public eye. I guess you could use it.'

She nodded in the direction of Nobby. 'You too, Mr Aitken.'

Nobby gave a slight bow and murmured his thanks.

Unavoidable pleasantries over, Gort returned to default mode. Her cold stare scanned those sitting around the table, making eye contact with everyone in turn. Few could hold her gaze, and Duncan was not one of them. He looked down at his hands and waited for the President to speak.

'You all know why we're here.' It was a statement, not a question. Muttered affirmations and nods proliferated.

Gort steepled her fingers on the table in front and looked down at them, choosing her words with care.

Looking up: 'We always knew that this was too big to keep under wraps for any length of time. Sooner or later, shit was bound to start hitting the fan. And now it has.'

Gort paused and looked down again. 'The question is, how long do we try and keep the lid on things? The collateral is accumulating, and it can't be long before someone puts two and two together.' Duncan raised a tentative hand, almost as if he were in the classroom. 'Umm. Excuse me, Madam President – collateral?'

Gort looked at the UK Prime Minister with a mix of incredulity and pity. 'You know what collateral is, Mr Bannerman?' It was a rhetorical question. 'People get hurt. Innocent people. With something this big, it's unavoidable.' Duncan looked nonplussed. 'But who—'

Gort cut him short with a raised finger and called over an aide. 'Is Dworak with us now?' The aide nodded. 'Get him on.'

The aide fiddled with a remote and another of the screens lit up. The picture revealed a hairless head as round as a billiard ball sporting a long pale scar running vertically from above the left eye towards the crown. The man to whom the head belonged stopped picking his nose as he noticed he was live and looked sheepish. 'Madam President,' he muttered, with a nod.

Gort turned to Bannerman. 'Mr Dworak occasionally does some work for us. Work that's too sensitive even for the security services – or that we don't wish them to know about. The blackest of black ops. You understand?' Duncan nodded.

'Mr Dworak. Would you fill us in, please.'

The ex-CIA enforcer was never one to use one word when three were available, and his report was – to say the least – comprehensive. The gist of it was that of the hundred or so researchers they had been keeping tabs on, just a handful had picked up on the bots – so far. Blackmail had bought the silence of two, but three others had paid a greater price. Two in the US, and another taken care of by a Brit 'operative'. Then there was the unfortunate accident on the Ascension Island base.

Much to everyone's relief, Gort took the opportunity during one of Dworak's rare pauses for breath to end the proceedings. 'Thank you, Mr Dworak. Much appreciated. Thank you.' Duncan didn't hold back. 'You've killed a British national? What the fuck do you think you're doing? I didn't sign up to this to see UK citizens murdered!'

Gort turned on him, eyes blazing. 'No! You didn't. You signed up to get a trade deal for your shitty little country.'

But Duncan wouldn't back down. 'Who was it? Tell me.'

Gort called over another aide, who handed her a sheet of paper that she scanned briefly. Her eyebrows lifted and she seemed momentarily caught out. She cleared her throat.

'Umm, I believe you know her. One of your climate task force crowd.' Duncan felt his stomach clench in anticipation of what was coming. There was only one woman on the Climate Impacts Task Force.

Gort continued, confirming his fears, 'Jane Haliwell. She was getting too close—'Duncan could keep it in no longer. 'You stupid fuck! Jane was one of my leading advisors. She taught my nephew.'

Gort held up a hand, ignoring the expletive. 'Dworak's guy screwed up. Got her boy instead. The mother's alive, but in an induced coma. She won't cause us any more problems.'

'Jesus!' Duncan shook his head, eyes closed. 'I've had enough of this.'

Gort chided him. 'So. What do you want? Out? Be my guest, but you're in up to your neck. If you leave now, I will personally make sure you get shafted – well and good. And you can say adios to any trade deal. The UK will sink without a trace. Face it. Some people are expendable.'Duncan's shoulders slumped. He knew when he was beaten. 'Couldn't you... I don't know... have used coercion of some sort?' His voice was subdued. 'You said others had been blackmailed.'

The aide whispered in Gort's ear and she nodded. Turning to Duncan, she shook her head. 'Too big a fish, and she was getting far too close. We couldn't take the risk.'

The aide muttered something further and Gort pursed her lips. 'I have to tell you that one of those terminated in the US was also a Brit.' Duncan said nothing, but stared at the President for a long moment, eyes filled with pure hate. Then he put his head in his hands. He had, of course, known of the explosion that killed Jane's boy; it was picked up in his daily briefing a few weeks back. But there had been no names and as the police had been confident that it wasn't terrorism, he had thought no more about it.

Gort looked past him and raised her eyebrows at Nobby Aitken, who gave a slight nod of the head.

She looked around the room. 'OK? Right. Let's move on.'

Dworak was investigating the contents of a nostril again. The President wrinkled her nose in disgust and signalled to an aide for the screen to be turned off.

'So. It seems we still have a lid on things, but at some cost... Yes, admiral?'

A naval officer, whose seniority was established by the colour burst of medal ribbons on his chest, said, 'Madam President, you mentioned Ascension. What's the situation there?'

Gort nodded in Duncan's direction. 'I think Mr Bannerman can bring us up to speed.' Duncan started at his name. His attention had wandered. Too busy pondering his situation – beleaguered at home, bullied abroad. And now this awful business with Jane and her son and the other British national, whoever they were. He made an attempt to pull himself together, turning to the naval officer.

'We've put the base under lockdown. No-one in or out. No communication with the outside world except through military channels. The base commander's been fed a cock-and-bull story about a serious security breach. I doubt for a minute he bought it, but he's playing along – for the moment. The story for public consumption is an anthrax outbreak, the feral sheep, you know.'

The officer nodded, satisfied. 'Very imaginative, Mr Bannerman.'

Gort continued, 'As I was saying. We're still on top of things, but word will get out – sooner rather than later. The question is, do we wait until the cat is well and truly out of the bag, or do we pre-empt? General?'

'I say we go public now?' said an ancient-looking, white-haired man in civvies. 'The seeding is well underway. No-one can stop it now. Let's tell it like it is. Better than letting the media ferret it out. And make no mistake, they will.'

Gort nodded, then sat back and let Jacob Adams answer for her. Adams leant back in his chair and stretched his long legs out in front. His lean, moon-shaped face was dominated by a beak-like nose and framed by a thin, curly beard that followed the jawline. It was hardly surprising that behind his back his subordinates called him 'Abe'. He knew, of course. Rather liked it, in fact.

'You see. It's like the recipe for good comedy.' He paused for effect. 'Timing.'

Gort looked irritated. 'Get on with it, Jacob.'

Her chief of staff sat up straight and continued, 'If the world finds out what we're doing before the outcome is clear, then the good Lord knows what the reaction will be. You saw the hate in Austin. We could be strung up – or worse. But…'

He leant forwards, wide eyes scanning those around the table, reedy voice straining with the passion of a zealot. 'If we can keep the lid on until it looks like we've been successful, then we can expect a very different response. Of course there will be a huge outcry at our somewhat – how can I put it –

unorthodox methods, but the majority would likely shrug their shoulders at a job well done.'

He grinned at the prospect. 'The environmentalists won't have a leg to stand on. They've been ranting on for decades about climate catastrophe. They can hardly complain if it turns out we've solved the problem for them. Even if it was done unilaterally and in secret.'

Adam's eyes seemed to widen even further and a small blob of froth appeared at one corner of his mouth.

'It's a win-win. Trust me. We fuck over the greens, halt global heating in its tracks and clear the way for unfettered growth. Open season for the free market. A pretty fair day's work, if you ask me.'

'And what if it doesn't work?' Duncan looked far from convinced by the chief of staff's almost religious devotion to the project.

Adams opened his mouth to reply but Gort intervened, 'It'll work. It is God's will. He would never allow global heating to destroy our civilisation. That's why he has given us the tools to do the job.'

The President closed her eyes and looked skyward. 'And God said, let us make man in our image, after our likeness: and let him have dominion over the fish of the sea, and over the fowl of the air, and over the cattle—'Duncan cut in, his soft Highland burr the antithesis of the President's grating Texan drawl, '—and over all the Earth, and over every creeping thing that creeps upon the Earth.'

Gort opened her eyes and looked, for a moment, bewildered. 'Mr Bannerman. You surprise me. I didn't take you for a religious man.' Duncan gave a wry smile. 'My father was a church minister. It's not something that sits lightly on a child.'

'Indeed. Then maybe we have something in common after all, Mr Bannerman.'Duncan's pale blue eyes met Gort's cold grey gaze. Along with his voice, they were his biggest asset when turning on the charm. It was how he had reached the top – God help him. But he knew this was neither the time nor the place. 'I doubt that, Madam President. I doubt that very much.'

This time, Duncan held Gort's stare until she felt compelled to turn away. 'Get Petrie up.'

Another screen burst into life to reveal a suited, bespectacled man, sitting some distance from the camera. He was beaming from ear to ear. 'Madam President.' The man bowed his head deeply, as if to a monarch.

'Dr Petrie. Thank you for joining us. What have you got?'

Petrie pushed his square, black-framed glasses further up his pudgy face. He was sweating profusely and had to do this twice before they stayed put. 'Madam President. I am very happy to be able to tell you,' he announced formally, 'that carbon dioxide levels in the atmosphere are falling.' There was a pause while he patted his forehead with a red handkerchief, apologising that the lab air-con was down.

Gort ignored this. 'How quickly?'

Petrie adopted his default lecturing mode. 'Well, we started from a baseline of 515 parts per million carbon equivalent, of which carbon dioxide made up 435 ppm—'

Gort interrupted. 'Forget the technical stuff. I don't have the time. Are we on track?'

Petrie looked a little disconcerted. 'Yes, indeed, Madam President. If anything, levels are dropping faster than predicted.'

Gort leant forwards in the direction of the screen, immediately wary. 'Is that going to be a problem?'

Petrie looked smug. 'Not at all, Madam President. We expected small deviations from our forecast, but I have complete confidence in the model.'

Gort sat back. 'Good, good. Thank you, Dr Petrie. Please keep us informed through the agreed channels.'

Petrie bowed again and Gort's aide switched the screen off, the informal signal for muted conversation and a few handshakes. Duncan looked around at Nobby and raised his eyebrows. Maybe everything was going to be OK after all.

Gort raised a finger and silence reigned almost immediately. 'Gentlemen.' She waited for Duncan to turn back. 'Gentlemen. Good news, I grant you, but it's far too early to be celebrating. Far too early.' While her words called for restraint, the twinkle in her normally expressionless eyes shone a light on the triumph she felt inside.

'I think we will leave it there. Before you go, let us bow our heads.' All did so, some more reverentially than others.

'Lord, thank you for setting us on the road to taking back dominion over our climate. Give us the strength and the will to make Skyseed a success, to do Your work on Earth and to forge a world ordered and ruled by God-fearing people in Your name.'

Muttered 'amens' were followed by the scraping of chairs and the rapid evacuation of the room, leaving only Gort and her chief of staff. They looked at each other but said nothing. They didn't need to. Their expressions spoke for them. They were jubilant.

KARL HALF WALKED, HALF TROTTED ALONG THE platform. A flat-out sprint just wasn't dignified. The train had been late and his carriage was the furthest from the barrier. He knew Ralph didn't have that much time, and he hoped to God he had waited. There was some network problem, so he hadn't been able to text. He needn't have worried. Even before he got to the exit barrier, he could see the USAF Captain's lanky frame stretched out in one of the chairs outside the café-bar he'd suggested. He was dressed casually, and Karl smiled as he saw people turn to look at him as they passed. Ralph was the spitting image of a young Barack Obama, something he had been known to make the most of on more than one occasion.

Ralph had his eyes closed and his earphones in, so he didn't hear Karl's greeting. No-one would have guessed he was an officer in the US military. He was wearing jeans and an *X-Files* T-shirt that warned 'Trust No-one'. Karl wondered if it was worn in his honour. He reached out and tapped the captain on the shoulder.

Ralph's deep brown eyes flew open and his earnest face was transformed by a wide smile. He jumped up, at the same time pulling out his earphones.

'Hey, Karl. How ya doin', man?' Ralph's deep Boston drawl instantly revived memories of many a late-night drunken discourse.

They high-fived and Ralph gave Karl a couple of back slaps that just about knocked him over. The American might have been lean, but he was mighty strong. They both sat down.

'Drink?' said Ralph. 'My coffee's stone cold.'

'Yeah. Sorry about that. The train broke down at Chesterfield and we had to swap over. To be honest, I could do with a beer.'

'Great idea. Me too.' Ralph went into the bar and came back with a couple of bottles of Captain Squib IPA.

'Boston's finest,' he announced, 'although I'm surprised to see it over here.' He gave Karl a sideways look. 'I guess we have globalisation to thank.'

Karl gave a mock scowl. 'Don't get me started.'

They both took swigs straight out of the bottle.

'Jesus,' said Karl, turning the bottle and looking at the label on the back. 'Seven per cent! Bit strong for this time of day.'

Ralph took another gulp, smaller this time. 'Not at all. It's a brew to savour, not get pissed up on. Two max, I promise. Now, what's all this about?'

Karl reached for his backpack and pulled out Jane's papers, note still attached. He dumped them on the small table they were sitting at. 'I think it's probably best if you take a few minutes to have a look at these.'

Ralph took the papers and glanced down at them, his head snapping up when he saw Jane's name. 'Jane Haliwell?! I know her. She was badly injured a couple of weeks ago. A car bomb. Son was killed. Mistaken identity, the police reckon.'

Karl nodded and picked up his beer. 'Just take a look. Let me know what you think. I don't want to be a distraction, so I'm going to leave you for a while. I'll be back in half an hour or so.'

Ralph looked bemused and opened his mouth to say something.

Karl put a finger to his lips and then pointed it at the sheaf of papers. 'Just read. We'll talk in a bit.'

When Karl returned, the papers were resting on the table. Ralph was in pretty much the same position as when Karl had first arrived, stretched out in his chair, eyes closed, earphones in. His bottle of beer was empty.

He opened his eyes as Karl sat down opposite and looked at him for a few moments. Then he stood. 'Let's walk. Oh, and you better have these back.'

Karl put the papers in his bag and they started walking slowly in the direction of the big clock at the far end of the station.

They strolled in silence for a while, then Ralph stopped and they both leant on the metal handrail of the glass safety barrier and looked down at the throng below. They were on the mezzanine, which, as usual, was pretty quiet. Beneath, the main concourse was heaving with shoppers, tourists, commuters and Eurostar passengers.

Ralph's gaze was fixed on the crowd. 'This is big. The biggest.'

Karl turned to look at him and then back down at the crowd. 'You reckon it's kosher, then?'

'No question.'

'You don't seem very surprised,' said Karl.

'I'm not. I'm only surprised it's taken this long.'

'Come again?'

'Pressure to hack a way out of global heating has been growing for decades. Mainly crazy schemes, but some clearly doable, given the will – and the money. Nanotech's always been in the mix – in theory, at least.'

'Who's doing the pushing?' Karl queried.

'All sorts,' said Ralph. He smiled as he watched half a dozen Italian nuns arguing amongst themselves. 'Mainly the alt-right, neocons, evangelicals – you know, the usual suspects. Global heating offends their worldview. Anything that can make it go away always gets their vote.'

'Right,' said Karl, 'capitalism at all costs.'

'That sort of thing,' agreed Ralph.

'So. What do we do? What can we do? Is this a WikiLeaks job?'

Ralph shook his head. 'There isn't enough. If we blow the whistle now, they'll stop and cover their tracks. We'll never know who was responsible. And they'll be in a position to have another crack – maybe try some other scheme – once the fuss has died down. We have to find out who's behind this.'

Ralph continued to look at the bustle below. 'If it's the Chinese or the Russians, then I doubt we'll get any further. If it's our guys, then there might be a way forward.'

Karl waited for more.

'Whoever's responsible, this is black ops. Above top secret. Without a doubt. But they can't keep something this big under wraps for long. Stuff is going to leak out. More and more people, like you and Jane, are going to start asking awkward questions. To buy themselves more time, they need a cover story. Something they can use to obfuscate and confuse, to set a false trail. If we're talking the US here, or the UK, then there's a chance I might be able to spot the cover, at least.'

'How big a chance?' said Karl.

Ralph dragged his eyes away from a girl in a low-cut top, standing immediately below, and looked at Karl. 'Who knows! Not a very big one, I suspect, but it's worth a go.' He looked back, but the girl had gone, replaced by a small tattooed man wearing braces and a green pork-pie hat.

Karl wondered out loud, 'Have you considered the possibility that if we pursue this we could end up like Jane, or worse, like her son?'

Ralph shrugged. 'Of course. But that could happen, anyway, if they – whoever they are – find out who sent Jane those samples…'

Karl stood bolt upright at the suggestion.

Ralph turned and leant back against the safety rail, looking up at the spectacular metal arch that roofed the station. He just couldn't resist it. 'Someone could be watching us right now.'

Karl searched Ralph's face. 'You're joking, right?' He scanned the few people close by on the mezzanine.

'No, sir. I'm deadly serious.' But he couldn't keep a straight face. He slapped Karl on the arm. 'Leave it with me. I'll see what I can ferret out and I'll be discreet. Be sure of that. Now, let's go and have that second beer. I've just got time.'

THE TRIP BACK UP NORTH WAS UNEVENTFUL AND Karl slept most of the way, courtesy of Boston's most potent. By the time he got to the lab, Steve was shrugging on his coat and preparing to leave.

'Off anywhere nice?' said Karl.

'No such luck,' replied Steve. 'If you want me to make those changes to the draft of the Vesuvius paper, it's going to be a quiet night in. I might have time for a pint or two first, though?'

Karl was tempted, but the Captain Squib would do for now. Anyway, he needed to do some serious thinking.

'I'll give it a miss tonight, Steve. There's a heap of stuff I need to get on top of.'

'OK. No worries.' Steve made to go, then turned back. 'Oh, I almost forgot. Chap dropped off an envelope for you. I left it on your desk. Didn't leave a name. Said you'd know what it was about.'

Karl nodded his thanks. *More work, no doubt,* he thought to himself.

After Steve had gone, Karl walked down the corridor to his study and sat at his desk. There was a bit of mail, which Steve had picked up for him from the pigeonholes, and a large padded envelope, which he guessed was the package his student had mentioned. There was no name on the front and no sender's details on the reverse. He tore open one end carefully and pulled out a batch of large black-and-white prints. For a few seconds, he wasn't certain what they showed. Then light dawned. 'Holy shit!'

All of a sudden, he felt slightly sick. It must have been a couple of years back. A party at a student house. He had just heard about a big grant and was celebrating. Consequently he was completely pissed. His memory of the events was blurred, but not blurred enough to stop him cringing every time he thought about it.

There were half a dozen pictures taken from different angles. They were not particularly good, but all the essentials were visible. Karl sat on a chair, naked from the waist up; third year undergrad on his lap, caressing his tonsils with her tongue, one hand down his trousers. He flicked through them one more time. Where the hell did they find them? Presumably someone had uploaded them to the web, in which case getting hold of them wouldn't have been that hard. *Fucking Facebook!* He scanned them one more time before tearing them into very small pieces and stuffing them into his backpack. He would burn them when he got home. Upending the envelope failed to bring forth an explanatory note, but he was in no doubt what the pictures meant. Ralph had made light of it, but he had been right. They – whoever 'they' were – knew he had sent the samples to Jane. The unwritten message was simple. Shut the fuck up or we go public. If the press got hold of this, the university would hang him out to dry. They had a zero-tolerance attitude, these days, towards fraternising with undergrads. And this was fraternisation with knobs on – almost literally. His academic career would be dead and buried.

As if in a dream, he stood, picked up his backpack and headed for the door. As he reached it, his phone rang, although it took a while for The Stranglers to register in his distracted state. He stuffed his hand in his jacket pocket and took it out.

'Hello?'

A gravelly smoker's voice answered immediately, no preamble, London accent, jaunty: 'Did you like the pics, Dr Slater? Nice, aren't they. Really shows off your good side. She's a looker too. Horny little minx, I'll bet.'

'Who the fuck is this?' Karl was livid. 'What do you want?'

There was a sigh on the other end. 'Don't mess me about, mate. You know what we want.'

Karl could think of nothing to say.

The voice continued, 'Simple trade-off. You back off and we don't send the pics to the press.'

Karl was raging inside but tried not to let it show in his voice. 'And if I don't?'

'Ah, now. That would be silly. Very silly indeed. We don't want any more nasty accidents, do we?

Karl snorted at the threat. 'And how will you know?'

The voice at the other end was icy now. 'Oh, don't you worry, we'll know.'

Karl opened his mouth to respond, but the caller had gone.

He stared at his phone and shouted out in rage. Then, calmer, he returned to his desk, sat down – head in hands – and considered the options. They hadn't mentioned Ralph and he guessed they didn't know he'd already passed on the knowledge. That was key. All he had to do was make sure they couldn't get to Ralph through him. Luckily, they had made arrangements to meet again in a couple of weeks, so he didn't need to make contact beforehand. In the meantime, provided he kept to his routine, everything should be fine. He thought it, but he didn't believe it. A mind's eye image of his car being torn apart by a bomb just wouldn't go away. Karl visibly shuddered before pulling himself together and heading home.

AUGUSTUS PETRIE DROVE SLOWLY. HE WOULD BE perfectly happy if he never reached the lab at all today. The grey drizzle and the gloom of the deserted, forest-lined highway along which he trundled matched his mood perfectly. Dread didn't even begin to describe the feeling that coursed through his body.

For two weeks now, they'd known they had a problem, but he'd held off from telling the President. No longer. She had demanded a conference call later in the morning and he had no choice but to come clean.

He still couldn't quite believe the appalling luck that had messed up their carefully laid plans so badly. Their calculations had been meticulous. Bot replication rates were not difficult to pin down based on the steady-state level of available raw material in the atmosphere, and they'd had excellent constraints on that. What they hadn't factored in was the biggest volcanic eruption in more than two hundred years. The stratosphere was flooded with volcanic dust packed with exotic elements and trace metals; it provided all the raw material the self-replicating bots could ever need. Their population had exploded out of control.

Petrie slammed both hands on the steering wheel in frustration. The turning to the lab was coming up and – for a split second – he considered driving straight on. Keeping going, dumping the car in Denver and vanishing into the crowd. It was so tempting.

As he reached the turning, his foot hovered over the accelerator. 'Ah, fuck it!' he muttered, lifting his foot and wrenching the steering wheel to the right. He eased the pick-up onto the narrow driveway that doubled back on itself and followed a winding route through the woods to the lab.

The President was calling at 10:00 local time, and Petrie had asked for a conflab first thing. The three techies were already in the meeting room when he arrived, the atmosphere subdued, but his number two, Dave Beeley, was still chasing some new data. Petrie eased his portly frame into the only chair with arms, at the end of the table, undid his top button and loosened his tie. He opened his briefcase, pulled out some papers and affected to study them while they waited for Beeley. He had given a general nod of greeting but didn't feel like speaking, and no-one said much until the coffee arrived and they had dosed up. His deputy appeared soon after, and Petrie called the meeting to order as soon as Beeley had grabbed himself a drink.

'What have you got, Dave?' said Petrie with a sigh of resignation. He wasn't expecting good news.

'The new data just came in. Samples were taken the day before yesterday.' He paused. 'It's not good, I'm afraid.'

Petrie waved Beeley's apology away. 'Just get on with it.'

'Right, well, bot concentrations are up two per cent in the last week.'

Shock registered on the faces of those around the table, accompanied by a variety of murmured expletives. Petrie grimaced but said nothing. He wasn't entirely surprised.

'Go on.'

'Carbon equivalent ppm is down to 503. The rate of carbon dioxide decline is now around 0.4ppm a week, but this is clearly going to accelerate massively.'

Petrie did a quick mental calculation. A little more than 20ppm a year, and that was just the start. *Jesus*, he thought, *a couple of decades of this and the planet will be a fucking ice ball.*

Petrie knew the answer but asked the question anyway. 'What are the prospects?'

Beeley spread his arms wide. 'Take your pick. Anywhere from hopeless to fucking hopeless.'

Petrie looked down at his papers, nodding at the expected response.

Beeley continued, 'Problem is, we don't have a decent handle on the available raw material the eruption has pumped into the stratosphere. It's too irregularly distributed.'

Petrie took off his glasses and kneaded his eyes with a thumb and forefinger. 'So, what's your gut feeling?'

Beeley shrugged his shoulders. 'We have no idea when the replication rate is going to start to tail off. It could be years.'

Petrie put his head in his hands. 'What in God's name have we done?'

Finally he took his hands away and looked around the room. The bags under his eyes had grown even bigger in recent weeks, his thinning grey hair was mussed and he looked exhausted.

No-one said a word. The question was clearly rhetorical and, in any case, what could they say?

Petrie closed the meeting then and there, and the room emptied quickly, leaving him alone with his thoughts.

There was no way he could spin the news to sound anything other than cataclysmic. He had planned to pick his words carefully, to let the President down gently, but what was the point? He was fucked, the President was fucked, they were all fucked. Physically and mentally hamstrung, he sat staring into space until five minutes before the scheduled call. Then he hauled himself out of his chair, opened the door and trudged down the corridor to the comms room. Dead man walking.

IT WAS LATE ON A WARM SEPTEMBER EVENING WHEN Ralph left the meeting at the huge Brize Norton RAF base in Oxfordshire and headed east. By the time he reached Reading services on the M4 motorway, it was close to ten o'clock and just about dark. There were only two people in the café: a beefy man with a shaved head and tattooed arms, talking loudly into his phone, and Karl, wedged into a corner at the far end. He had a notebook out in front of him, and he was tapping his front teeth with a pen. He looked as if he had the weight of the world on his shoulders.

Ralph walked over and stood in front of him. 'Penny for 'em?'

Karl jumped, then he smiled tentatively. 'Hey, Ralph. How's it hanging?'

They shook hands. Ralph went to the counter to get a coffee and a refill for Karl, and sat down opposite. Karl shifted in his seat and his eyes flicked to the tattooed man and back.

'Something up?' wondered Ralph.

In quiet tones, Karl gave a brief account of the blackmail attempt. He was reticent at first about what was in the pictures, but Ralph dragged it out of him. Despite the seriousness of the situation, Ralph found it hard to keep a straight face, but at least managed to suppress a witty comment. It didn't really come as a surprise. If someone was serious about finding out who sent the samples to Jane, it really wouldn't have been that hard.

'What about the trip down? Were you followed?'

Karl shrugged. 'Not as far as I could tell. But then what do I know? Subterfuge really isn't my thing.' Then he explained the measures he had taken. Karl had done his best to throw any watchers off the scent. He had been down to give a talk the day before at a workshop at Reading University just down the road but hadn't turned up. Instead, he had left his house by the back door and headed up onto the moors. He had walked all day and stayed overnight at a village pub. If someone had been tailing him, he would easily have spotted them in the wide-open spaces of the Peak District. The following morning, he had braved horizontal rain for a few hours before catching a bus to Derby and a train from there to Reading, where he had pottered around for a while before grabbing a bite to eat. A cab had got him to the service station not long before Ralph.

Ralph was impressed. 'Well, not bad for a novice – Agent Slater.'

Karl chuckled and relaxed a little. 'How about you? Any luck?'

Ralph looked smug. 'Maybe, maybe.' It had been two weeks since their meeting at St Pancras station, and he had been busy.

'I don't want to get your hopes up, but there is something,' he said.

Karl leant forwards. 'OK. Let me have it.'

'Well,' began Ralph, scratching his chin, 'there's something called Skyseed.'

Wary of being tracked, Ralph had given his smartphone and his home and work computers a wide berth. Instead, he had bought half a dozen cheap, second-hand laptops. He surmised that whoever was behind the climate hack would be monitoring key search terms and suspicious activity that might flag their scheme was at risk of being rumbled. To counteract this, he only hunted for clues while on the move and used a search engine that didn't track the user or store IP addresses. After each session, he discarded the laptop, taking out the drive and tossing it in a convenient lake or river and dumping the shell.

He tried every term that he thought might bring up something but unearthed nothing that looked suspicious. He was searching on the last laptop, on a rail journey to Manchester, and just about ready to give up, when he struck gold – or what he hoped was gold.

'Tell me more,' said Karl.

'Well,' said Ralph, 'it purports to be a project testing the feasibility of cloud seeding, with a view to promoting rainfall across the south-western US. You know there has been a severe drought there for more than a decade now?'

Karl nodded.

'The website contains no further detail and clicking on "read more" just loops the searcher back to the top of the page. The email address is generic and doesn't work.'

Karl didn't appear convinced. 'Just sounds like a crap website to me. There are plenty of them around.'

'You may be right,' said Ralph, 'but it is also typical of a zombie site.'

'Which is?'

'Pretty much what you'd expect from the name. A site that sits there, apparently dead, but which contains fully developed hidden content that can be made visible in a moment. Brought to life, if you like.'

Karl nodded his head slowly and looked more impressed. 'You did say they would have something like this in place.'

'They were bound to,' said Ralph.'It's a classic smokescreen. If the shit hits the fan, if word of the plot gets out, they will activate the site, plug in a convincing backstory, and claim it's been there all the time.'

'Sweet,' said Karl.'If it's true.'

'There's more,' said Ralph. 'The website is hosted by a company called Drought Solutions.' He paused. 'The postal address for the company is Washington's Pennsylvania Avenue.'

Karl raised his eyebrows.'Not the White House?'

Ralph grinned.'No. But close. The company gives Atlantic House as its base. It's a couple of miles down the road.'

Karl shrugged.'So. What's the significance?'

'Atlantic House,' said Ralph, 'is also the headquarters of Palatine Industries. It's a huge conglomerate with fingers in all sorts of pies, oil and gas, arms, aerospace, shipping. God only knows what else. It's owned entirely by the Malachi brothers – Enoch and Amos. Ring any bells?'

Karl made a face.'The worst sort of capitalist bastards.'

Ralph grinned. 'That's one way of putting it. They're certainly staunch libertarians and promoters of an unfettered market. Through their various foundations and thinktanks they've also done everything they can to dump on global heating and climate breakdown science. And they've opposed emissions reduction measures right down the line.'

Karl grunted.'No surprises there.'

'True,' said Ralph, 'but the brothers have modified their position recently. They still insist that climate breakdown driven by global heating isn't happening, but at the same time they're now pushing for an engineering solution.'

Karl made to speak, but Ralph held up a hand. 'Yeah, I know, there's no logic to it, but when has logic ever been part of a denier's armoury?'

'Anyway. We have a possible zombie site linked to a couple of billionaire deniers with an interest in geoengineering.' Ralph emphasised each point with his forefinger on the sticky surface of the table. 'It could be nothing, but I think it's worth following up.'

'And how the hell do you propose to do that?' Karl was more than sceptical.

'We narrow down the options. This is a huge op, so there can't be that many. Put yourself in their position – whoever they are. Where would you go to do this, seed the atmosphere with these bots?'

'Not difficult,' said Karl. 'The tropics. Best way to get the stuff distributed quickly and widely. The wind systems can carry it into both hemispheres.'

'Right,' said Ralph. 'And how are they getting it up there?'

Karl shrugged. 'Has to be aircraft, surely. I can't see surface cannon getting it high enough. I suppose rockets are a possibility, but we're talking relatively low altitudes here so – again – they don't really fit the bill.'

'My thinking entirely,' said Ralph. 'Plus, I don't see how this can be done without access – official or not – to serious military facilities. So, what do we have?'

Karl opened his mouth to offer his thoughts, but Ralph was in full flow. 'I'll tell you what. A big – probably isolated – USAF base, somewhere in the tropics.' Ralph sat back in his chair and slapped the tabletop. 'Has to be!'

'Do you have anywhere in mind?' said Karl.

Ralph leant forwards again, excitement building in his brown eyes. 'Well, the obvious contender is Guam in the Pacific. US territory, nicely off the beaten track, and a massive military base that covers one third of the island. The perfect place to hide something like this.'

'Seems reasonable.' Karl stuck out his bottom lip. But to get the bots up and doing the business as quickly as possible would surely need more than one base of operations. He was thoughtful for a moment.' Are there similar bases in the Indian Ocean and Atlantic?'

Ralph scratched his head. 'Let me see. In the Atlantic, there's the big base at Thule in Greenland. Much too far north. Other than that, I think we – USAF, that is – have a presence on the Portuguese base on Terceira. Not a very big one, though, and, of course, the Azores are not quite in the tropics.'

'Is there anything further south?' queried Karl.

'Not American, no. There is a RAF base on Ascension Island in the South Atlantic, but—'

Karl interrupted. 'Hang on. Ascension was in the news a while back.' He picked up his smartphone and opened a saved article. 'Yup. Here we are. I bookmarked it because I might be heading down there to do a bit of fieldwork on the volcanics.'

He read out the opening few lines: 'The British Overseas Territory of Ascension Island in the South Atlantic has been placed under lockdown due to an outbreak of anthrax in the feral sheep population... blah, blah, blah... no-one is being allowed to leave the island until further notice, while all incoming flights have been cancelled.'

Karl looked up from his phone. 'You don't think...?'

Ralph shrugged. 'Who knows? It would certainly make an ideal base of operations. But US access to Ascension would have to mean some sort of UK involvement – semi-official, at the very least – which would take the thing to a whole new level.'

Karl ruminated for a few moments, then went on. 'What about the Indian Ocean?'

'No USAF bases,' said Ralph, 'but there is the huge US Navy base on Diego Garcia. You know the one. You Brits kicked out the locals way back and then handed it over to us. Nice.'

'Yes, well. Whoever said we British had scruples? We have considerable experience of grinding the faces of the weak in the dirt.'

'Anyway,' Karl went on. 'Is it a possibility?'

'Oh, without a doubt. The whole place in one enormous military complex. The only people on the island are either US forces or contractors. There are some USAF units there too, and it has a pair of long runways.'

'And,' Ralph's big grin opened up as it dawned on him, 'I know the met guy there, known him for years, in fact. We were at college together. Do you know what? I think it might be fun if I popped out there and had a look around – discreet, like.'

Karl just looked at him. 'You're fucking nuts.'

Ralph made to reply but then held back as the tattooed man sauntered past, still bellowing into his phone. They both waited until he'd left the café, then, before Karl could offer further admonishment, Ralph made a drinking motion.

Karl sighed. 'OK. Americano – just milk – skimmed if they have it.'

Ralph brought the fresh drinks and sat down. 'Look. It's not that big a risk.'

'Yeah, right,' said Karl.

'I've a perfectly valid reason to be there. The new hypersonic transports are going to be using Diego Garcia, and my day job is evaluating atmospheric conditions that could impact their safety and effectiveness, including particulates. It would be perfectly reasonable for me to request permission to visit to check out the local circumstances.'

Karl shook his head. 'Ralph, these people are killers. It's just too dangerous.'

Ralph looked around at the empty café, then leant forwards and fixed his eyes on Karl's, his voice a hoarse whisper, loaded with emotion. 'I know. And they'll kill again if we don't do something – maybe next time it will be one of us. We can't let this go. Not now.'

Karl slowly shook his head again but said nothing.

'Remember why we're doing this, Karl. If we want to blow this thing apart, we need evidence – hard evidence no-one can argue with. If there's any possibility that I might find it on Diego Garcia, then I have to go.'

Karl's shoulders slumped in resignation. 'So. What will you do?'

Ralph held Karl's eyes a little longer, then slapped him a couple of times on the arm. 'That's the spirit.'

'I shouldn't even need to go to the top. I'm certain my immediate boss will give me clearance, and my buddy will deal with things the other end. Hardly anyone will know I'm there. I'll sniff around a bit and be in and out before you know it. If I come back empty-handed, we'll just have to think again.'

Before Karl could answer, Ralph drained his coffee and stood. 'It's getting late. Let's move it, man. Work to do, work to do.'

It was three days on from the meeting with Ralph, and Karl was in a state. They had agreed that, in the circumstances, there could be no contact between them until the whole thing was over – one way or the other. So Karl had no idea if Ralph was still in the country or ferreting around Diego Garcia, if he was alive or dead. He took some, but not much, comfort, from the fact that if Ralph had been unmasked, they would probably have come for him next. Tying up loose ends, as it was known in the trade.

He had barely slept for the last couple of nights, and serious work was near impossible. In a last desperate attempt at distraction he had signed up to a small colloquium on volcanic ash and aviation, being held in Manchester. This was why, at some ungodly hour, he found himself hunched in the rain on a commuter-crammed platform at Sheffield station. The train was near on twenty minutes late and he was already starting to have second thoughts, but he really needed something to keep his mind elsewhere. The meeting was his field and close by, and should be perfect to occupy his thoughts, at least for a couple of days.

A murmur went around the throng as the train finally trundled into view. Just four carriages long, it was far too small for the awaiting crowds, and Karl resigned himself to an hour standing up amongst a press of damp bodies. As the train drew closer, people edged forwards, looking to get on early and grab a seat. Karl was barely a few inches back from the platform edge and hemmed in behind and to either side, something he had always found a little unnerving.

When the train was just a few metres away, brakes squealing as it slowed, he felt a hand on the small of his back. Before he had time to react, it gave a violent shove, propelling him towards the platform's edge. He lost his balance and his arms windmilled as he tried to stop himself falling beneath the grinding wheels of the train. He shouted out, screwing his eyes shut and tensing his whole body as he awaited the arrival of excruciating agony and subsequent oblivion. Then, as he teetered on the very edge of the platform, the same hand took hold of one of his backpack straps and pulled. The train shot past inches from his face, horn blaring. For a few seconds Karl just stood there, eyes bulging, hyperventilating, unable to move.

As the train pulled to a stop, those around him seemed not to have noticed the incident – or chose not to. They surged around him as if he was an island in a raging torrent and jostled one another as they squeezed into the already rammed carriage.

A beeping sound heralded the closure of the doors and the train rumbled off in the direction of Manchester. Karl still hadn't moved, but now he slowly turned and looked around. There was no-one left on the platform other than a young mother with a pushchair and a couple of grizzly toddlers, and a podgy balding man with a small moustache sitting on a bench nearby, reading a paper. He had got his breathing under control, but his legs didn't seem to want to work. Eventually, he managed to coax them in the direction of the ticket barriers and the concourse. All thoughts of the Manchester meeting gone, he boarded a bus in a daze and headed for the lab. When he arrived, he got a coffee from a machine and sat at his desk. Steve was away and no-one else was about, so he was left alone to make sense of what had just happened.

After a few minutes, his abstraction was broken by the familiar Stranglers riff. He looked at his mobile for a few seconds, then picked it up.

'Who's been a naughty boy, then?' It was the same gravelly voice.

Karl said nothing.

'Shook you up a bit, did it?'

Karl nodded, then cleared his throat and managed a strangled, 'Yes.'

'It was meant to, mate. You try pulling a stunt like that again and it'll be the last thing you ever do. Savvy?'

Karl managed to squeeze out another whispered, 'Yes.'

'You stay in full sight, OK. No more slipping under the radar, no sneaking out of back doors. We want you where we can see you.'

Karl muttered something in the affirmative before realising that the caller had gone. He put the phone down and took a few deep breaths. The call hadn't been a surprise. He had been expecting it. The shock of the close encounter with the grim reaper hadn't worn off, but beneath the numbness there was hope too. Clearly 'they' had been pissed off because they had lost him. It was a final warning. But they hadn't picked up on the meeting in the service station. If they had, someone would by now have been scraping his remains off the track at Sheffield station. The way was clear for Ralph. Karl hoped to God that he made the most of it.

He woke from his first decent sleep in days. In spirit he was still with Ralph – wherever that was – but his near-death experience seemed to have steeled him in some way. He'd hardly describe his mood as optimistic, but the sun was shining and he was still alive. A few months ago he would have taken both for granted, but no longer . He breakfasted well and decided to walk to the university.

Now he was certain he was being watched, he found it impossible not to be a bit twitchy. He was constantly turning his head to look behind, peering into people's faces as they passed, looking into cars when they pulled up at lights. It must have added a good fifteen minutes to his journey, but he couldn't help it. When he eventually arrived, Steve was in and hard at work in the prep lab on some new samples. He switched off the polisher as Karl passed the open doorway and beckoned with one hand.

'Phone message. From Jane Haliwell.'

Karl was astonished. 'She was still under a week ago.'

'They brought her out of the induced coma a few days back. She says she's well on the mend. Must be if they've given her phone back.'

Karl couldn't stop beaming. 'That's fantastic news, brilliant!'

Steve rummaged in his pocket and brought out a scrap of paper, which he handed over. 'Her mobile number, in case you don't have it.'

Karl took it and headed for his study, calling over his shoulder to Steve. 'Up for a pint tonight? To celebrate?' Steve's enthusiastic reply followed him up the corridor. Inside, he dumped his bag and made straight for the desk phone. He picked up the receiver, then stopped. 'Shit!' he muttered, and put it down again, frowning. 'What the fuck was he going to say?' Condolences and commiserations, of course, but she was bound to want to know about the samples, what he had done about them, whether anything had happened during the six weeks or so she had been dead to the world. Ralph had said best not to use any form of electronic communication, just in case, and Karl knew his mobile was compromised, but his desk phone? Were they likely to be listening on that? Like most people these days, he used a smartphone for virtually everything. Landlines were a relic from the past that could quite easily slip under the radar. He chewed at a thumbnail for a minute or so, then came to a decision. Fuck it! He'd take the risk. He couldn't very well ignore her call. Not after everything she'd been through.

In the end, it was a bit of an anticlimax. Jane didn't answer, so he left a brief message on her voicemail. Just how pleased he was that she was on the mend and that he would phone later to fill her in. Not much, but enough.

DUNCAN BANNERMAN MADE A MOUE WHEN HIS destination came into view. He'd rather liked the old US embassy in Grosvenor Square. True, the huge eagle above the entrance had been pure kitsch, and the overall ethos was 1960s brutal, but it had a sort of bombastic aspect that matched the times. This new one was cheerless, an ornamented glass cube just south of the river, squatting in its own grounds and surrounded by a moat. A state-of-the-art motte and bailey hemmed in by a cluster of similarly charmless early twenty-first-century high-rise clones.

The prime ministerial Jaguar and its four police motorcycle outriders were waved through security and pulled up at the main entrance, where Bannerman was met by a military attaché. Unusually, this was not an official visit, so he would not be bothering Ambassador Pelman on this occasion. In fact, the whole thing was out of step with protocol. The President's chief of staff, Jacob Adams, had called Number 10 late the previous evening and said that Gort needed to speak to him – urgently. He wouldn't, or couldn't, say why, but he was insistent that they should use a secure line at the embassy, rather than Downing Street comms. It had to be Skyseed. And he doubted it was going to be good news.

Bannerman's fears were confirmed when Gort's face materialised on the giant monitor that occupied almost an entire wall of the secure comms room. He was the only one present. Harry, his protection, remained outside, with a marine sergeant for company. The President looked crushed. Gone was the imperious ruler of barely a month earlier, in her place a tired, undistinguished woman in late middle age. The lines drawn either side of her chin were more strongly etched than ever, the eyes dull.

'Mr Bannerman. Good day. I'm sorry for the subterfuge, but I know you understand the need.' She sounded downbeat, almost apologetic, which made him feel even more uneasy. It must be worse than he thought. Duncan nodded a greeting – 'Madam President' – and waited.

Gort didn't seem sure about what to say next. She looked down at her hands, resting on the desk in front of her, and Duncan could see they were trembling.

She looked up. 'Mr Bannerman. I am afraid I have some bad news. The Good Lord – in his wisdom – has not permitted our little project to accomplish what we wished.'

'Madam President, I'm really sorry to hear that.' Duncan made an effort to sound disappointed, but inside he was overjoyed. His greatest anxiety had always been that the conspiracy would be uncovered. Now, perhaps, they could forget this planet-hacking crap and get back to the real world. Maybe there was even a chance that he could broker a decent trade deal with the US without the unsavoury taint of blackmail hanging over it. But the President was speaking again.

'I beg your pardon…?'

Gort banged her tiny fists on the desk. 'God damn it, man! Listen to me.' Like many on the bigoted right, she thought nothing of bowing to God one minute and blaspheming the next. Duncan just stared as the President's small mouth worked away, struggling with the news she had to impart.

'We are fucked! Do you understand? Fucked?'

A cloak of dread enveloped Duncan. 'You said it hadn't worked?'

'No! I said it hadn't accomplished what we wished. It has worked – is working. It's working only too well.'

The President was calmer now, and silent as she let Duncan digest the implications.

It was only moments before the look of puzzlement on his face turned to one of comprehension. 'Jesus. No!' he whispered. 'What happened?'

Gort slumped back in her chair, massaging her temples. 'The eruption. The big one in Bolivia, back in March. I can't remember its name. It loaded the stratosphere with huge quantities of volcanic ash – as much raw material as the bots could ever need – and more. They're replicating out of control.'

'How bad?'

'We can't be certain yet, but pretty bad. Maybe ice age bad. I'm told atmospheric carbon levels are dropping like a stone.' Duncan put his head back and addressed the ceiling, where a large cobweb momentarily caught his attention. 'For fuck's sake!' He looked at Gort again. 'How soon?'

She shook her head. 'Can't say for sure. Fifty years, they tell me. Could be less.'

'Is there nothing we can do?' said Duncan.

Gort shook her head. 'Pandora's box is well and truly open.' Duncan said nothing. What was there to say? He was stunned. Then it struck him. 'This isn't going to go unnoticed.'

The President nodded silently.

'So, what do you plan to do?'

She shrugged. 'I'm taking advice. The seeding planes are grounded, but still on-site until we have worked out an exit strategy.' Duncan snorted. 'You don't think it might have been a good idea to have one all ready to go?'

Gort shrugged again. 'We were confident, perhaps too confident.' Duncan swore under his breath. 'Perhaps?!'

The President leant forwards. 'Mr Bannerman, this isn't helping. We need to agree an angle, to bluff it out. We're looking at options.' Duncan looked unconvinced. 'Such as?'

'Reduced solar activity, Volcanic cooling, cosmic rays – maybe even the Chinese.'

'No-one's going to fall for any of that garbage. The science is just too well understood. I don't see the Chinese being too pleased either.'

'Who gives a shit? We just need to distract attention while we shut down and bury the whole thing deep – very deep.'

'So. What do you want from me?' said Duncan – worried anew at the thought.

'Nothing. Just sit tight and back up our story – whatever it turns out to be.'

'And the trade deal?'

Gort couldn't help smiling. A real smile. 'Do you really think that's going to matter now?'

'No. I suppose not,' he said flatly. He covered his face with his hands for a few moments as the immensity of the situation finally hit home. Survival was all that concerned him now. When he took his hands away, the screen was dark.

After the late-night meeting with Karl at the motorway services, Ralph had driven straight back to Mildenhall. It was cross-country, so not the easiest of journeys, and it had been the early hours of the morning before he reached home. The fun had started the next day.

The name RAF Mildenhall was deceptive. Officially, the place was a Royal Air Force base – and during the Second World War it had been – but since 1959 it had been a little bit of America on English soil. No stiff upper lips or waxed moustaches any longer, more baseball caps, gum and burgers. The base had been slated for closure, but a change of mind – and a change of President – had secured its future, at least for a while.

Ralph had arranged to meet his immediate superior after lunch. He had nothing much on that morning, so he took the opportunity to do a bit of thinking. He really had no idea what he would find on Diego Garcia. He suspected probably nothing, which would mean back to square one. Then again, there was a logic to the scenario that he and Karl had teased out. He really felt they might be on to something with this Skyseed business. It just didn't feel right. Furthermore, he reckoned he would have heard on the grapevine about any big new project to revisit cloud seeding. Karl was right too; if you wanted to get stuff into the Earth's atmosphere and maximise its spread, then somewhere in the tropics was the place to do it, and what better place than an island military base in the middle of nowhere? There just had to be forces support, almost certainly USAF, but the big unknown was whether or not there was general military involvement. If there was, he was probably stuffed, but he doubted it. Something like this had to be run on a need-to-know basis, with the number of people clued in kept to the bare minimum. That's what he was going with, anyway – wishful thinking or not.

He had checked the base activity schedule first thing and saw he would be thumb-twiddling for a week before he could wheedle a seat on a C-130 heading out to Qatar – the Al Udeid base close to Doha. Provided his boss was OK, he intended to be on it. He could get from there out to Diego Garcia and be on the island a day or two later. In the end, coaxing Major Rice into give his blessing proved to be a doddle. Rice was tied up with supporting base operations, and keeping tabs on a single research meteorologist was barely on his radar. During their encounter, which lasted all of two minutes, the major made it perfectly clear that – provided Ralph sorted out the appropriate paperwork – he wasn't fussed if he flew to the moon and back.

The week went slowly. Ralph tried to focus on his day job, but the wasted time made him increasingly irritable and a pain in the arse to work with. On the day in question, the flight was due to leave late afternoon.

He returned to his quarters after lunch in good spirits and began to gather his things together. It was warm outside and he was heading somewhere even hotter. Nonetheless, he made sure he hunted out his thick, fleece-lined winter jacket. The hold of a C-130 was always perishing. When he had finished, there were still a few hours left before the flight, so he decided a run was in order.

It was a gorgeous early autumn day, not too hot, candyfloss clouds floating gently on a warm breeze. The base squatted amid the low, flat landscape of Suffolk, where the sky was lord. It reminded Ralph of the wide-open spaces and big skies of Kansas, where he had spent many glorious summers at his grandparents' small farm, although on a much smaller scale. That, and there were no tornadoes.

It was good to get some exercise in. There had been too many meetings in recent weeks. Too much jawing and not enough sweating. He followed a set route that took him out of the base and into the surrounding countryside, along winding footpaths through the fields and small woods that dotted the area. At the end of five miles or so, the base perimeter came into view, and he increased his pace, as he always did. Not to impress any onlookers, but because it made him feel that much better when he finally stopped.

Forty-five minutes later, showered, packed and champing at the bit to get off, he closed and locked the door of his quarters and made a beeline for the big Hercules transport plane loading up on one of the concrete aprons half a mile away.

'**M**AJOR SCHROEDER? THIS IS JACOB ADAMS.'

'Sir. What can I do for you, sir?'

Adams just knew Schroeder was saluting the phone. *Fucking martinet*, he said to himself.

'Major. It's a little delicate. Is this line secure?'

'As Fort Knox, sir.'

Adams paused, wondering just how much he should give away. Schroeder was in on the operation so knew the truth about Skyseed. The question was, how much to tell him about why they were pulling the plug? Need-to-know seemed like the best policy or, as Adams thought of it, as little as he could get away with.

'Good. Well, I've got some news. It seems that we've done enough now.' The line may well have been secure, but Adams wasn't taking any risks. He continued to talk in terms nebulous enough to mean nothing to a casual listener. 'So time to pack up and send the boys home.'

'Excuse me, sir?'

'We're all done, Major. You can stand the crews down.'

'But, sir. I understood this was a nine-month deal. Why—'
Adams interrupted. 'Plans change, Major, simple as that.
Plans change.'

There was a muttered expletive on the other end of the
line. 'Sir. We have eighteen aircraft and crews here, flying
round the clock. What am I supposed to do with them?'

Adams made a noise that was the verbal equivalent of
a shrug. A sort of cross between a snort and a sigh. 'Just tell
them the good news. They're going home.'

'But—' Schroeder tried to interrupt. Fact was, a lot of the
guys were enjoying themselves. Easy flying, sun, sea, good food
and a long break from the wife. They were going to be pretty
pissed when they got the news.

'Major. You are aware of the critical importance of this
mission. All you need to know now is that it is over, finished,
terminated, concluded. Is that clear enough for you?' Adams'
voice was as cold as ice.

Schroeder guessed he was going to get nothing more by
way of explanation so turned his attention to the logistics. 'So
when are they shipping out, sir?'

Adams voice relaxed at the turn in the conversation.
'Nothing sorted yet, but we're looking to start things moving
in a few days. In the meantime, the planes and crews stay
grounded. Understand?'

'Sir! And the, umm… cargo?'

'The planes can return with full loads. The rest we'll arrange
to be picked up by ship as soon as we can. In the meantime,
usual protocols apply. Twenty-four-hour guard. Lethal force if
required. Is that all clear?'

'Sir, yes, sir!'

Adams put down the phone, blew out his cheeks and
sat in contemplation for a few moments. Then he picked up
the phone again and dialled an internal number. 'Madam
President. It's done.'

GOD! HE HATED FLYING. WELL, FLYING LIKE THIS, anyway. Strapped into a web seat, facing inwards, ears plugged firmly against the constant racket of the engines, freezing despite the four layers he had on. Then again, the C-130 Hercules was a military transport designed for war, not for comfort. Ralph guessed he was getting old, or soft, or both. Considering the earliest variant had flown way back in 1954, it was a plane he ought to have had great admiration for. Maybe he would – when he was warmer.

It was less than twenty-four hours since they had left the Suffolk countryside behind, but it seemed far longer. They had stopped off at the US Naval Air Station at Sigonella on Sicily's east coast, to load some crates and pick up a couple of other guys headed to Diego Garcia. The view of Mount Etna on the run-in had been stunning. It was into the third week of its latest eruption and fountains of red lava spouted from one of the summit craters, feeding slow-moving flows on the north flank. The spectacle had very nearly made up for the appalling turbulence that rattled every bone in Ralph's body as they had hurtled low over the vineyards and lemon groves of the Catania Plain towards a bumpy touchdown on the coastal strip.

They had landed at sunset and were off again after a couple of hours, heading into the inky blackness of the eastern Mediterranean, the lights of ships glinting far below, the glow of a full moon painting a broad band of silver across the sea. Four hours later, they were on the ground again, this time at the huge multinational Al Udeid air base, close to the Qatari capital, Doha. The middle of the night it might have been, but the thermometer on the outside of the reception building had still registered a blistering thirty-five degrees Celsius.

There had been eight hours to kill before a second Hercules left for Diego Garcia, which Ralph made the most of to refuel. A couple of burgers hit the spot, washed down with a few bottles of Bud. Six hours of sleep on a bunk in the transient quarters and he had felt like a new man. It wasn't to last. First of all, the onward C-130 picked up a technical problem, which left the passengers – a round dozen this time – fulminating in the increasingly baking hold. Then they got as far as speeding down the runway before a warning light had the pilot slamming on the brakes. Back to the apron for more checks before it turned out it was just an indicator fault. They got off the ground four hours late, and Ralph had immediately drifted into a restless slumber.

Now he was awake and bloody freezing. One of the others brought him a coffee, which helped a little, but he wished to God that they were on the ground. Then a burst of crackling on the intercom flagged an announcement from the pilot. Ralph removed his earplugs but still struggled to hear what was being said above the racket of a C-130 in full throat. As he slowly got the gist of what the pilot was saying, his eyes rolled and he mouthed obscenities. There was a huge cyclone crossing their flight path and they would need to make a detour. It would add another hour to the flight.

Ralph knew next to nothing about Diego Garcia, so had checked it out on the web before leaving Mildenhall and printed off some info. He remembered this as they made their approach and dug it out for a quick leaf through. He knew the local population had been hard done by but was appalled by the reality. Of the many blots on the copy book of modern British history, Diego Garcia had to be one of the biggest. It should have been a tropical paradise, and still was in many ways, but no longer for those born and raised there. In fact, the treatment of the population by the British and US governments was nothing short of criminal. The Brits had been ordered nearly ten years earlier by the International Court of Justice to hand the island back but had refused point blank; one of the reasons they had been forced to forfeit their permanent seat on the UN Security Council.

The small atoll was the only inhabited land in the Chagos Archipelago, a cluster of sixty or so tiny islands scattered across the central Indian Ocean to the south of the Maldives. Originally French, it became British during the Napoleonic wars. For a very long time thereafter it remained the quietest of backwaters, its people – around a thousand in all – keeping themselves alive and content tending their coconut plantations. But disaster lay in wait for the Chagossians.

In the late 1960s, the British opened the doors to the United States, who had decided they needed an 'unsinkable aircraft carrier' from which they could build and maintain influence across the region. Diego Garcia fitted the bill perfectly. The US wanted the island but were not so keen on taking its population as part of the deal. They demanded the removal of everyone on Diego Garcia and paid the Brits to do the dirty work. Ever the lapdog, the British were only too pleased to help. The islanders, on the other hand, were desperate to avoid forced removal from their home. But the British had ways, ways that the Nazis would have been proud of. First they rounded up and killed the islanders' pet dogs in front of them, then they prevented anyone who had left the island for medical treatment or some other reason from returning home. They limited available food and medical supplies, and finally herded everyone into overcrowded cargo ships that took them to Mauritius and the Seychelles, where they were abandoned to rot without help or compensation. But, hey, the US got its unsinkable carrier and the Brits got fourteen million dollars knocked off the purchase price of the Polaris missile system, so what was not to like? As for the Chagossians, nearly three quarters of a century on, they were still fighting to be allowed to return.

Ralph looked up from reading. 'Jesus fucking Christ!' he blurted out, causing a few raised eyebrows amongst his fellow passengers. Inside he was livid. Ralph had always had a powerful moral compass. His parents had wired into him the difference between good and evil, right and wrong, but he suspected there was a genetic component too. He just hated injustice. It was visceral. He could almost feel it physically, and it made him mad – real mad. He simmered for a while in sympathy with the fate of the Chagossians, before slowly accepting that there was nothing he could do now. Maybe later.

He read on, exploding with incredulous laughter when he discovered that the US naval base on the island had originally been named 'Camp Justice'. Well, it was either that or cry. The eyebrows lifted again – even higher this time. Ralph grinned, shook his head, and stuffed the printout back in his bag. No more! In response to the pilot's garbled instructions, he fastened his seatbelt, sat back and waited for the wheels to hit dirt.

The Hercules flew low across the atoll before the pilot banked steeply and lined the plane up with one of the two runways. The view was tremendous. The reflected sun sparkled like a jewel in the dead centre of the lagoon enclosed by the palm-covered atoll. The place was a little gem: bright green, set amongst the brilliant blue waters of the Indian Ocean. But it was a gem that was flawed, spoilt by those who cared little for the life that bloomed on the island, but for whom death held a glorious attraction. Now the islanders' homes were gone, bulldozed. The stands of coconut palms were mixed up with fuel storage tanks, staff accommodation blocks and all the paraphernalia of the US military abroad.

Stepping from the foetid interior of the Hercules into the tropical air was a blessed relief. It was hot, but nothing like Qatar. There was little humidity and a stiff sea breeze took the edge off the heat. To all intents and purposes, it was a perfect day. Ralph knew it wasn't going to last. They had dodged the Arabian Sea monster that had barred their way in the night, but now a second cyclone – Nisha – was working its way slowly westwards somewhere to the south. The island was a little north of the Indian Ocean's main cyclone belt, and it looked like it would be spared Nisha's worst. But that still meant eye-watering winds and a truly biblical deluge. Nisha was unusually early, the official cyclone 'season' not due to start until November, but no-one had told Mother Nature. The storm was expected to make herself known the following afternoon. Until then, Ralph determined, he would make the most of the glorious weather.

Along with his flight companions, he sauntered across the concrete apron and over to the terminal building, checked in and completed the inevitable paperwork.

He got the desk sergeant to give Jojo a call, to let him know he'd arrived, and then went outside to sit on a convenient bench and soak up the sun. The sound of the wind in a small stand of coconut palms nearby was soporific and within a few minutes he was dozing.

The screeching of a couple of red-footed boobies having a mid-air tussle overhead intruded on his slumber, accompanied by the noisy arrival of an open-top jeep, which skidded to a halt barely a foot away and nearly made him jump out of his skin.

He was building up steam to give the driver the benefit of his extensive range of invective, when he saw who it was. Frown transformed to wide smile as he stood to greet the diminutive black man, who was vaulting with some grace over the nearside half-door.

'Ralph, ma man. How ya doin'?' They embraced briefly, then shook hands.

Jojo Mackenzie could quite easily have been Ralph's brother. A little older, perhaps, and at least a head shorter, but the same lean physique, the same cropped hair. The facial features weren't too dissimilar either, barring the poorly set broken nose, which gave Jojo's face a slightly lopsided look that the ladies seemed to find irresistible.

Jojo studied Ralph. 'You look tired. How was the flight?'

Ralph grimaced. 'I'm just glad to get out of that tin can and breathe some fresh air.'

'Well, there's plenty of that here,' said Jojo, picking up Ralph's backpack and tossing it into the back of the jeep. 'Nothing fragile in there?' he asked, too late.

Ralph just laughed. Still the same old Jojo. At college he had never been one for formality or protocol. One reason why they got on so well.

Then he noticed the twin silver bars decorating the shoulders of Jojo's uniform. 'So, captain now. You've gone up in the world.'

Jojo caressed the bars on his left shoulder. 'Brand spanking new!' They only came through yesterday.

Ralph couldn't resist it. 'And now you're back where you started.' Jojo had been busted down to First Lieutenant a couple of years back after a dalliance with a two-star general's good lady.

Jojo gave a wicked grin. 'It was worth it, man. She was hot. And I mean real hot!'

Ralph just shook his head in exasperation, then slapped Jojo on the back a couple of times. 'Come on, Casanova. Let's move it.'

Jojo opened the passenger-side door and gestured ostentatiously for Ralph to take a seat. Then he touched his baseball cap in mock respect. 'And where would sir like to go?'

Ralph leant back in the seat and closed his eyes. 'Bed, James. Bed.'

WHAT A DAY. A WARM SUN HAD VANISHED MID-morning beneath a dense layer of black stratus, and the temperature had tanked. Then a gale had sprung up from nowhere and the rain came hammering down. Karl had only nipped across the way to get himself and Steve a sandwich but had been drenched for his pains. He unlocked the door to his study, dumped the shredded remains of his umbrella in the bin and peeled off his soaked jacket. The Met Office had warned of wind and rain, but this was ridiculous. The weather had been swinging wildly for a couple of weeks, and it was impossible not to wonder if it had anything to do with the bots.

His jeans were sodden too, so he locked the door – don't want to shock any unsuspecting lady students – and changed into a pair of shorts he kept handy for his increasingly rare games of squash.

Dress sorted, he sat at his desk to towel his hair dry and contemplated his in-tray. The pile of admin, coursework and reading material had almost reached eye level and was in severe danger of collapse. He had a departmental staff meeting after lunch and a class to teach later. He had managed to persuade Steve to take the practical element, but that still left a couple of tutorials late afternoon. There was a heap of deadlines to meet too – a grant application, early-bird conference registration and paper proofs to go through – all by the end of the following day. Trouble was, his thoughts were half a world away in the middle of the Indian Ocean. Surely he must be there by now? Thinking about what he might have to do if he never heard from Ralph again made him feel a little queasy.

Still, he needed to get on. He had a career to think of – at least for now. But before that, he would try Jane again. The weather might have taken a turn for the worse, but the good news of her recovery still brightened his day. He picked up the desk phone and dialled her number. Still no answer, and he didn't see the point of leaving another message. From his inbox he picked up the proofs of a paper that needed checking over. There was an hour or so before the staff meeting, so he might as well make the most of it. But first – coffee.

Karl closed the door on the departing back of his last student, a middle-aged woman who couldn't resist flirting. Normally, he gave as good as he got, but his heart wasn't in it just at the moment. He knocked back the cold dregs of perhaps his eighth coffee of the day, and checked his mobile, which he always turned off during tutorials. No messages.

When Steve popped his head around the door a couple of minutes later, Karl was sitting at his desk, ruminating and drumming with the fingers of one hand on the peeling laminate top.

Steve made a drinking motion with one hand.

'Give me a second to pack up,' Karl said.

The head vanished, leaving the door ajar. Karl relieved his in-tray of a pile of papers and stuffed them into his backpack. He would get some work done later, he assured himself unconvincingly. His clothes had been dry for a while, so he swapped shorts for jeans and pulled on his denim jacket. It was still pouring down and his umbrella was a lost cause, so he resigned himself to the second soaking of the day.

In the end, Steve had an umbrella big enough for two, so they entered the public bar of The Crown lightly dampened rather than completely drenched. Without a word, Steve headed straight for their usual table in the corner. Karl took the hint. Must be his round, then. It was early doors and the place was just starting to fill. The bar was lined with thirsty punters, but Karl signalled over their heads to the landlord. Two fingers – two pints of the usual. He had to squeeze through to claim his drinks and pay. Then he headed back to Steve.

Karl raised his glass. 'To Jane and a speedy recovery.'

Steve murmured his agreement and they both supped long and deeply, then sat for a minute or so in contented silence. Steve took a second draft, smaller this time, and put down his glass.

'Before I forget,' he said. 'What happened about those SEM samples? You know, the ones packed with the weird spheres?'

Karl took another sip of beer to give himself time to think. He was desperate to let Steve in on what was going on, but it was just too dangerous. He tried to be as laidback as possible. 'Oh, yes. I meant to tell you. Contamination.'

Steve raised his eyebrows. 'Really? What with?'

Karl took another sip. 'Not sure, to be honest.'

Steve looked a bit miffed. 'Look, I prepared those disks. There's no way they were contaminated.'

Karl raised a calming hand. 'Steve, I'm not blaming you. I sent the samples over to Charlie Saunders at Leeds. He reckoned the mounting medium was contaminated – a bad batch – so you're off the hook.

Steve still didn't look convinced, but then smiled. 'Oh, well – mystery solved. So no joint paper on a new phenomenon, then?'

Karl breathed easier and gestured at Steve's empty glass. 'Not this time.'

For another hour and a half they shared rounds, and talked about this and that. Then, feeling pleasantly light-headed, they agreed that their stomachs would appreciate something more substantial. Fish and chips beckoned. Steve shrugged on his coat while Karl headed for the toilet. The place was packed and steamy now, and he had to ease his way through a squeeze of damp bodies to the door at the far end of the bar.

Forcing his way robustly through the throng from the other direction was a short, tubby man with thinning hair and a toothbrush moustache, wearing a grey fleece. Instantly forgettable. As they crossed paths, the man looked Karl in the eye. 'Dr Slater?'

Karl frowned. 'Yes…?'

The man raised an arm and pushed against Karl's chest. Momentarily, there was a sharp, stabbing pain, then – almost instantly – a sudden feeling of wooziness.

The man passed on and was out of the pub door in seconds. Karl tried to continue to the toilet, but his legs started to give way. He tried to speak but could make no sound. Slowly, a black curtain descended in front of his eyes and he knew nothing more.

Ralph slept through the rest of the day and the following night. When he surfaced, the yellow light of a tropical dawn was seeping around the edges of the thick drapes. He felt completely refreshed and absolutely famished. After a quick shower, he put on his uniform – thankfully, shorts and a short-sleeved shirt in light blue were deemed acceptable in the tropics – left his room and went outside. The sun was up, but it was struggling to climb above a towering bank of dark purple cloud that stretched, as far as the eye could see, along the length of the eastern horizon. The advance guard of Cyclone Nisha.

He consulted the base map that Jojo had given him and matched it to what he could see. He was in a part of the island known as Downtown, which sat at the northernmost tip of the western part of the atoll, beyond which it was breached by a stretch of the Indian Ocean . This seemed to be the place for rest and recreation, and there were clubs, a pool, gyms and even a bowling alley. Right now what he needed – according to Jojo – was the consolidated dining facility. Better known, in these parts, as the galley.

The place was bustling with military personnel and contractors coming off night duty, but not over busy, and he managed to grab a window table. The eggs and bacon on his plate vanished in seconds, and he had to hold himself back from going up for more. His waistline wouldn't thank him.

He wasn't due to meet Jojo until eleven, so he had a few hours to kill. It would have been a good time to mooch around, but he was far to the north of the air base. All he could do was wait until Jojo turned up with the jeep. With nothing else to do, he decided he might as well make the most of the sun while it lasted. The bank of approaching cloud was an ominous black now and sending out fingers of grey towards the island. The wind was getting up too, clawing at the stars and stripes that fluttered over his accommodation block and providing an entertaining challenge for the squadrons of acrobatic boobies, terns and frigate birds putting on a show overhead.

He strolled back to his room, picked up a slim, plastic document wallet and headed for the nearest sand. It wasn't far. He followed a path surfaced with crushed coral through a stand of coconut palms, and there it was, a blindingly white beach and, beyond, the ocean, stretching all the way to Africa. Mostly, the atoll was only a mile or two wide at any point, so he could equally well have headed in the opposite direction and still hit the sea in a few minutes. He sat down on the fine, white coral sand in the shade of one of the palms, slightly wary of falling coconuts. There were quite a few fresh ones scattered about and he recalled, with a smile, the time a rather obnoxious colleague had been knocked unconscious by one at a conference in Mexico. It couldn't have happened to a nicer guy, he'd thought at the time. He could remember giving the thumbs up to the sky – nice one, God!

He couldn't see any that looked as if they were about to fall – not that he knew what to look for, in any case – so he gave his attention to a couple of satellite images he had accessed and printed before leaving the UK. What they revealed was the reason why Ralph's visit to Diego Garcia was no longer driven by just an educated hunch.

The two images were taken eight months apart and were essentially identical. But in the more recent of the photos, two additions stood out like turds in a bathtub. First, a couple of warehouse-size sheds had sprouted close to the runways. Second, he had counted fifteen KC-10 aircraft parked on the apron; another at the end of one of the runways, apparently poised for take-off. It was perfectly possible that more could be in the air.

The KC-10 was a military version of the DC-10 airliner, modified as a tanker to support in-flight refuelling of attack aircraft. It wouldn't have been a surprise to see a few of the tankers at Diego Garcia, but sixteen – maybe more – no way. Not unless there was some huge military push on, and he was as confident as he could be that there wasn't.

When he thought about it, it was ingenious, the obvious way of getting the bots up there with minimum fuss and suspicion, and in full view. Really, it couldn't have been easier. Substitute the kerosene in the KC-10s' huge refuelling tanks with the carbon-eating bots and spray them into the atmosphere. The high-level winds would do the rest, spreading them across the planet within weeks. He would bet his last dollar that they were doing the same from Guam, and maybe even Ascension if they – whoever they were – had somehow managed to get the Brits on board.

Well, let's see if he couldn't get a closer look when Jojo turned up with the jeep. He still hadn't decided whether or not to fill Jojo in about the real reason for his visit. They went way back, had shared a room together for a couple of years at college. Hell, one time they had even shared a girlfriend. Ralph winced visibly at the thought. But then again, people changed. He stroked his chin, then came do a decision – or rather, didn't. He would play it by ear.

He looked at his watch. Still an hour before he said he'd meet Jojo. Plenty of time for a snooze. He put the images back in the folder and lay back on the warm sand. He was dozing off when a shadow fell across his face. His first thought was that Nisha's outlying cloud bands had reached the island, but on opening his eyes he saw that the shadow belonged to a large man standing at his feet.

Ralph squinted up at him. He must have been a good six and a half feet tall, and almost half as wide. Muscular, but running to fat. It was barely ten in the morning, but one huge hand enveloped a can of Coors beer, with which he toasted Ralph. 'Mighty fine day.' He had a strong southern drawl that Ralph tried to place. *Alabama, he guessed, or maybe Georgia.*

The man had small, black eyes, a flat-top of jet-black hair showing the first flecks of grey and dark patches of sweat decorating the armpits of his shirt. His belt was fighting a battle with his gut, and clearly losing.

Ralph half sat up, supporting himself on his elbows. Warily, he agreed that it was.

'Haven't seen you around before, uhm…' He looked at Ralph's insignia. '…Captain. New posting?'

'Flying visit, sir,' said Ralph, verbally acknowledging the gold oak leaves that denoted a major. He struggled upright and saluted with one hand, while brushing sand off his rear with the other.

The major gestured at him with the beer. 'No need for formality, Captain. I can see you're chillin.'

Ralph thanked him politely, at the same time trying not to show his distaste for the man. He knew the type only too well.

The major stuck out his free hand. 'Leroy Schroeder.'

Ralph took it and soon wished he hadn't, as it enveloped his like a clammy glove and squeezed almost all feeling out of it. It was a clumsy attempt to put Ralph in his place, but he was having none of it. He had bigger things than point scoring on his mind.

Ralph felt the need to get far away from the major's presence, but the man wanted to talk. 'So, what line you in?'

'I'm a met guy,' said Ralph, without embellishing further.

Schroeder raised black bushy eyebrows. 'Hey, another egghead? We got one of those already. You know Captain Mackenzie?'

Ralph nodded. 'Jojo? Yup. It's him I'm here to see.'

Schroeder slitted his eyes and looked at him oddly. 'Well, now, and why would that be, Captain?'

'Just techie stuff.' Ralph shrugged. 'You know, the new hypersonic transport, vulnerability to atmospheric conditions and the like.'

The major continued to eyeball Ralph, nodding slowly to himself. 'Is that right?' he drawled. 'Is that right?'

Then he seemed to mentally reboot and became business-like. 'Well, boy, it's way over my head, that sort of stuff.'

Ralph bridled visibly at the pejorative term, but, remembering he was trying not to draw undue attention to himself, kept his mouth shut.

Schroeder crushed the now-empty beer can into a small ball of tin and hurled it into the surf. 'Must dash. Duty calls – as they say.' He started to walk away, then turned back. 'Hey, maybe I'll see you in the Officer's Club this evening. It's Tuesday, so there'll be a band.' A desultory wave and he turned again and headed along the beach.

Ralph watched his retreating back with barely contained fury. 'Arsehole!'

He was too angry after the encounter to sleep, so he picked up his folder and headed back to his room. Three quarters of an hour later, the insistent blast of a jeep horn announced Jojo's arrival. Ralph opened the door to see his friend, arm raised, ready to knock.

'Sleep?'

'Like a log,' said Ralph. 'You know me and sleep. Anywhere, anytime.'

'I do indeed,' confirmed Jojo. 'So what now?'

'The grand tour would be nice,' Ralph suggested.

'Fine with me. I'm off duty today, so I'm all yours. But you still haven't told me why you're here. I'm guessing you haven't travelled halfway round the planet just to chew over old times or take a sightseeing tour?'

Ralph gestured to the jeep. 'Could we talk as we go?'

Jojo looked at him strangely. 'Oho. The mystery man. OK. Let's move.'

They climbed aboard and Jojo slammed his foot down, wheels spinning in the crushed coral that surfaced most of the island's minor roads. Ralph had been reminded, the previous day, of Jojo's cavalier driving style, which at college had once left the two of them hanging by their seatbelts in an overturned corvette that Jojo had managed to park in a tree. Surreptitiously, he checked his seatbelt, and braced himself against the dashboard with his arms.

Jojo looked across at him. 'It's good to see you, Ralph. Been too long.'

Ralph agreed. 'Must be ten years now, at least.'

'So what you been doing? I heard you were in on the hypersonic transport project. Sounds like fun.'

'Not as glamorous as you might think. Really just looking at particulate loads in the stratosphere. You know, impacts on windshields, airframe, engines and the like. It's amazing just what dust particles can do when they hit something travelling at Mach six. We've been working with the Rolls Royce guys at Derby, so Mildenhall's been home for the last eighteen months.'

Jojo nodded. 'I passed through once. Had to spend a couple of days there waiting for an onward flight. Damn all to do.'

Jojo took a hump at speed and the jeep was airborne for a few moments before hitting the ground with a bone-shaking crash and hurtling onwards.

Ralph grimaced. 'Well, the nightlife in north-west Suffolk certainly could be better. But if a quiet walk in the English countryside is your thing...' He looked sideways at Jojo, who was making a face, and smiled. 'I guess not.'

'Anyway,' said Ralph, 'I thought you'd got all that out of your system. I heard a while back you were married, a kid too.'

Jojo's hands tightened on the wheel and he suddenly looked dispirited. Ralph hadn't noticed until now, but under the breezy exterior and ready grin, Jojo looked pretty much all in. 'Yeah, well, it didn't work out. Eva and I don't talk any more – unless we have to. Davie's a great kid, but I hardly get to see him.' Jojo seemed close to tears now.

Ralph guessed this wasn't all of it. 'Are you sure you're OK? Is there something else? Something going on here?'

Jojo's expression was bleak. 'Nothing you can help with, Ralph. Let's just forget it. I'll be fine.'

Ralph clutched at a straw. 'It's nothing to do with that creep Schroeder, is it?'

Jojo visibly jumped, as though shocked, and the jeep swerved before he got back on track. 'How the fuck do you know Schroeder?'

'He found me on the beach this morning. Seemed very interested when I let out that I'd come to see you. Gave me the third degree.'

Jojo snorted. 'No. It's not Schroeder. The man's a shit, but harmless enough.' He flicked an indicator, and they turned onto a tarmac road that took them south out of Downtown. The road followed the inner shore of the atoll, slicing through plantations of coconut palms through which – to the left – the enticing, flat, calm waters of the lagoon and its encircling white sand beaches could be glimpsed. The island narrowed considerably here so that the open waters of the Indian Ocean could also be seen to the right, getting choppier by the minute as Nisha rumbled closer. Dark cloud covered perhaps one third of the sky now, and it wouldn't be long before the sun vanished behind a veil of scudding grey.

After a couple of minutes, the uncomfortable silence was broken by Jojo. 'Speaking of the third degree, you still haven't told me why you're here – and I mean the real reason.'

He looked across at Ralph. 'Don't give me any bullshit about wanting to talk about local atmospheric conditions. We could have done that over the phone or by email.'

Ralph had been mulling over his options in the back of his mind, and he knew that he really only had one. He needed help, so he would have to bring Jojo on board and take the risk, which he reckoned was a pretty small one.

'Can we stop somewhere?'

Jojo pulled the jeep over to the side of the road, where it came close to a small beach, and they scrambled out. He led Ralph through a narrow strip of palms and onto the sand and sat down cross-legged. Ralph followed suit.

'OK. So what's this all about?' Jojo was brusque.

Not like him at all, thought Ralph. 'Jojo. It's difficult to know where to start. What I have to say might sound crazy but, believe me, it's not.'

'Just get on with it, for fuck's sake,' Jojo said, exasperated.

Ralph raised his arms in a calming gesture. 'OK. OK. But first, can I ask you a question?'

'Go ahead,' said Jojo.

'Has there been any unusual activity on the island over the past few months? Anything that might have struck you as odd or out of place?'

Jojo had picked up a handful of sand and was dribbling it slowly from his closed fist, making a conical pile. He didn't look up. 'Well, there's the rain-making project, if that's what you mean?'

Ralph expressed surprise. 'Rain-making – out here? I would have thought that was the last thing Diego Garcia needed.' He looked up pointedly at the black cloud surging in from the east.

Jojo continued to evade Ralph's gaze, concentrating instead on the trickling sand. 'They're just testing the method. I think they're using some new chemical compound as the seeding agent. If it works, they want to try it in the south-west. You know, the drought states. I've heard it's so bad now that if it doesn't rain good and hard soon, they're going to have to start shipping people out of Vegas.'

Inside, Ralph was jubilant, but he couldn't show it. 'But why trial it out here? Why not in Nevada or eastern California?'

Jojo had finished dribbling sand and picked up another handful. He shrugged. 'I guess they need some clouds to start with, and Diego Garcia isn't short of those, this time of year.'

'But how can they unravel the effect of the seeding from rainfall events that would have happened anyway?'

Jojo didn't have an answer and just shrugged again. He either wasn't interested or was feigning disinterest. Ralph wasn't sure which. Whatever it was, he decided to take the plunge. 'I'll tell you why,' he said to the top of Jojo's head. 'Because what they've told you is complete bull. The rain-making story is a cover for something completely different. Something illegal and potentially catastrophic.'

Jojo's head snapped up at that and, for a moment, Ralph thought he saw fear in his eyes. Then he looked back down and continued to dribble sand. He sniggered. 'Sure you haven't been watching too much of *The X-Files?*'

Ralph was getting irked by Jojo's attitude, which was completely out of character. 'Jojo. I'm deadly serious. Look at me – please.'

Jojo looked up and this time held Ralph's gaze. His eyes seemed to be saying, *Please, I don't want to know.* But Ralph told him anyway.

When he had finished, they sat in silence for a long time. Jojo's reaction hadn't been at all what Ralph expected. Instead of being sceptical, even disparaging, Jojo seemed accepting of the whole thing. Eventually he spoke. 'So, what do you want of me?' The tenor of his voice was subdued, as if he was resigned to having to do something that he really didn't want to do.'

Ralph took out the two satellite images and laid them side by side on the sand. They had to hold them down to stop the gusting wind carrying them off into the lagoon. 'I know they're spraying the stuff from the KC-10s, and I'm guessing it's stored in these two new sheds. I need to get in there and get a sample. Can you help?'

Jojo shook his head. 'I don't know. It won't be easy. The planes and the sheds are cordoned off, and there are armed guards.'

Ralph frowned. 'Didn't the level of security strike anyone as odd for a rain-making scheme?'

'Not really,' said Jojo. 'Everyone's paranoid these days. You get used to it.'

Ralph frowned in concentration. 'How many guards?'

'A couple for the planes and just the one for the sheds,' said Jojo. 'I guess they don't expect any trouble on a military base in the middle of nowhere, so they're more for show than anything. But you still need to get past them.'

Ralph looked at the images again. The sheds were a fair size. 'It's a big area for a single guard. It can't be that difficult. I'd really appreciate a closer look.'

'Sure.' Jojo sounded far from keen, but in the circumstances, Ralph couldn't really blame him.

They headed back to the jeep and continued south. The sky was seven tenths cloud now and the sun was barely visible through the scud. If anything, though, it felt hotter. The humidity was building as Nisha approached and it would likely get a lot worse before the expected deluge. Jojo drove judiciously now, obviously distracted and clearly wishing he was doing something else. Ralph looked at him askance. This wasn't the Jojo of old, that was certain.

After a while, the coconut palms on the right gave way to row after row of rectangular, low-rise structures – accommodation blocks, by the look of them. These were replaced in turn by what appeared to be admin buildings of various types and then the big, cylindrical tanks of a fuel storage facility. The land on both sides of the road was heavily built up now, and there was a fair bit of traffic.

The main port area came up on the left, and Ralph could see the superstructure of an aircraft carrier towering high over its jetty. He was surprised that the water in the atoll's interior was deep enough, and said so.

'Reckon it's something like a hundred feet,' said Jojo. 'Easily deep enough for the Gerald Ford. It's getting on a bit now, due for replacement soon, I hear.'

Ralph nodded distractedly, the ins and outs of naval procurement holding less than zero interest.

They continued on into the air operations area. Out on the apron next to the terminal building was an assortment of aircraft, including the C-130 that Ralph had come in on and a pair of the new B-3 bombers. The KC-10s were parked a way off on a much larger apron towards the far end of the twin runways.

At Jojo's suggestion, they stopped off at the mess to grab a couple of coffees, which they took out to the jeep. Jojo said his office was close by and excused himself to check out the latest on Nisha. Ralph voted to stay in the jeep. As he drank, he looked up with a discerning weather eye. Cloud covered the entire sky now and was thickening rapidly so that the position of the sun was completely lost. He reckoned the wind was already gusting to force seven, which seemed high considering the storm was supposed to pass by some way off.

Ralph sipped his coffee and watched Jojo leave one of the buildings that hemmed in the apron. After a few paces, he started to jog, and Ralph could see his face was grim as he drew closer.

'Problem?'

Jojo vaulted into the driver's seat and started up the engine, talking at the same time. 'Nisha. She's changed track. The eye's still going to miss us, but we're going to be in range of the eyewall winds. We could see cat two or three windspeeds.'

'Shit!' It wasn't good news. Ralph had intended to put his plan into action that night, after a quick once-over, but this could really screw things up.

Jojo looked across. 'Worst storm to hit the island in more than half a century, it looks like. I'll tell you what, I'm no engineer, but I reckon those new sheds of yours are going to take one hell of a hammering.'

Ralph was silent, weighing up his options in light of the news.

They headed sedately along a small road that paralleled the runways, stopping briefly to watch a pair of F-35 stealth fighters take off. As they climbed east into the storm, the crackling rumble of their afterburners rattled the windshield and set Ralph's back teeth on edge. He wasn't surprised when the planes banked steeply and headed off to the north-west and out of Nisha's reach.

The road skirted the edge of a small bay, where, in the growing gloom, the white sand had taken on a greyish hue, and the now-choppy waters of the lagoon showed white caps.

A few minutes later, Jojo pointed forwards. 'That's them.'

Ralph recognised the new sheds straight ahead. They had been put up on a piece of scrubby ground, close to the runway and the northern end of the main apron known, according to Jojo, as South Ramp. The road crossed the rear of the sheds some way off, before curving around and behind a collection of other buildings that lined the apron.

Jojo pulled the jeep over and raised his eyebrows. What now? Ralph could see the tailplanes of KC-10s through the gaps between the buildings. Suddenly he felt a bit queasy. He was a weatherman, for God's sake. All this James Bond stuff, it just wasn't him. *Well,* he chastised himself, *you should have thought of that earlier. Too late now.*

He took a deep breath, reminded himself why he was doing this and jumped out. Jojo did the same and they followed a path that took them between two low-rise buildings. The wind funnelling through the gap was so strong that they struggled to make headway, and when they reached the edge of the apron, they felt the first drops of warm rain.

The tankers were lined up on the far side, an open expanse of concrete in front. There was no way they could be approached without being seen. The planes were cordoned off by a makeshift metal fence of mesh panels wired together. Patrolling back and forth behind it were two guards wearing green combat fatigues and the blue berets of the USAF security forces.

Ralph's lips moved as he counted the aircraft. 'Eighteen. Is that the lot?'

Jojo shrugged. 'I guess so. I doubt any are still out in these conditions, whatever the hell they're doing up there. Come to think of it, I haven't seen any flying in the last couple of days. Heard a rumour they'd been grounded.'

Grounded or not, it made no difference to Ralph. The planes weren't the target in any case. He turned his attention to the storage facility, which was off to the right. That's where he needed to be. He wasn't entirely surprised to see that the sheds were nothing more than pre-fabricated, open-fronted hangers that looked like they'd been put up in a hurry. They reflected the silvery sheen of unpainted metal and displayed no insignia or signage. Jojo was right. They certainly weren't built to handle hurricane-strength winds.

A fence of the same metal mesh panels formed a barrier to deter the wayward or inquisitive but would do little to scupper a determined attempt at entry. Ralph reckoned that the combination of a pair of bolt cutters and an imaginative diversion should be sufficient.

As Jojo had said, there was a single guard inside the fence. With the rain getting heavier by the minute, he had retreated to the shelter of the closest shed. Perched on a pile of wooden pallets just inside, his assault rifle on the ground next to him, he was trying to read a magazine and fighting a losing battle with the wind. He didn't seem to be expecting any intruders, which was all to the good.

Ralph couldn't see inside from this angle. He was pretty confident of what he would find, but it would be good to confirm. He suggested to Jojo that they should walk out a little way onto the apron, so he could check things out.

In order not to arouse suspicion, they headed southwards, away from the planes and the sheds for a couple of hundred yards. They didn't look back, but Ralph could almost feel the watchful eyes of the guard on them. He called a halt and they stood for a minute or two spouting small talk and randomly pointing in various directions, as though their walk had a purpose. Then they turned and retraced their steps. Ralph tried to keep up the deception that they were engrossed in meaningful conversation and uninterested in their surroundings, while at the same time stealing glances in the direction of the shed interiors. Jojo could have been more help and his one-word answers meant that Ralph had to work all the harder.

But he got what he wanted. Revealed within were rows of bright red, cylindrical tanks, each held above ground by metal trestles. There were no markings on the tanks and nothing at all to suggest – either to the guards or the plane crews – that they contained anything other than a cloud-seeding chemical.

Ralph had seen enough. The rain was torrential now and they were soaked to the skin. They hurried to the jeep and worked together against the wind to pull up the canvas roof and tie it down. The jeep's interior was already drenched and the sides were still open to the elements, but it was better than nothing. Jojo swung the vehicle around and they headed north. The circulation around a hurricane in the southern hemisphere was clockwise, so the wind was coming up at them from the south. It was like being pushed onward by a giant hand.

Neither spoke until they were well on their way and passing the Gerald Ford again. Ralph kept glancing at Jojo, but he didn't seem to notice, his attention focused elsewhere.

Finally, Ralph voiced a question that had been in the back of his mind for some time. 'Do you happen to know who's running the show this end?'

Jojo's mouth turned down and he seemed reluctant to answer. 'Schroeder!'

Ralph was shocked. 'Schroeder? You're kidding me!'

Jojo shook his head. 'All true. Schroeder's in support services, you know, supplies, recreation, catering – stuff like that. I heard whoever's in charge of the project asked for him by name to run things this end.'

Ralph thought further. 'I guess it's not that different. All he has to do is ensure the stuff gets in the planes and the crews do the rest. Thing is, does he know what's really going on or is he just another schmuck going through the motions?'

Jojo wasn't forthcoming.

Ralph felt uneasy. Schroeder was an ignorant, racist, creep, sure, but was there more to him? In other words, was he a threat? *Ah, fuck it,* he thought. He had enough on his plate without adding to it.

When they got back to Ralph's Downtown lodgings, he insisted Jojo come in and dry off, or at least steam for a time. Jojo was reluctant at first, but the lure of a cold beer was persuasive.

Ralph also wanted to make sure that Jojo knew what was to happen that night. Provided the conditions weren't so bad that it was shut, they would meet at eight at the Officer's Club. It wasn't an alibi, as such, but just in case any shit was flying around the next day, it wouldn't hurt for Ralph to be seen having a few beers in public view and then announcing an early night.

Jojo would leave discreetly, after a reasonable interval, and they would reprise today's jaunt. If the predicted hurricane-force winds and biblical deluge didn't do the job, Jojo would provide some sort of distraction. Meanwhile, using the bolt cutters Jojo had promised he could supply, Ralph would cut through the chains holding two of the fence panels together and nip through. He would grab a sample, slip back out and be on a plane the next day, all done and dusted. That was the theory, at least.

SEPTEMBER 2028
SKYSEED STORAGE FACILITY
DIEGO GARCIA, INDIAN OCEAN

B Y SEVEN THIRTY THAT EVENING, RALPH WAS beginning to wonder if he would be forced to scrap his plans. The wind was howling like a banshee around his accommodation block and the rain made a near-continuous hammering on his window. Outside, through the murk, he could see the palms bent almost double.

Fifteen minutes later, he stepped out into a maelstrom of wind, rain and saltwater spume. Within seconds his uniform was saturated and water poured down his face, making it difficult to see. But at least it wasn't cold. The clubhouse was close by, and with a following gale, his feet barely touched the ground as he negotiated his way around the torn-off branches of palm trees and dodged waste bins that rolled around like tumbleweed. He was prepared for the place to be closed and shuttered, but he had failed sufficiently to take into account the siren lure of alcohol. The windows had been boarded up on the outside, but the place was open. With no natural light, it was gloomy inside and swelteringly hot. Ralph guessed that the air-con was down. The low stage at one end of the large room was empty, the band having wisely decided to save themselves for a night when they didn't have to compete with the screaming of hurricane-force winds.

He was surprised to see at least a dozen customers. Most stood, talking quietly in twos and threes. He recognised the sort: resolute drinkers who propped up the bar every night and refused to be put off by a bit of wind. He gave a general nod of greeting, receiving several in return, and tapped on the bar to attract the attention of the steward, who was in conversation at the far end. Jojo wasn't to be seen, so he ordered a couple of beers and took them to a corner table, a safe distance from the big picture windows that shuddered unsettlingly despite the boards.

It was difficult to relax. Every now and then there was the tinkle of breaking glass outside, or a crash as some detached piece of debris collided with an immovable object. The wind seemed to be picking up even more, and its shrieking sounded eerily like human screams. Ralph took a long swig of beer from the bottle and looked around the room. No-one else seemed to be the least fazed. The subdued murmur of polite conversation, holding its own against the backing track of nature's onslaught, reminded him of that British wartime exhortation that had experienced a commercial revival a while back: 'Keep calm and carry on.' In view of what he was going to have to do in the next few hours, it was a piece of advice he felt he would do well to take on board.

Twice since he had sat down, the heavy outside door had burst open, inviting inside a morsel of the pandemonium that reigned beyond the walls. Now the steward locked the door shut, so that anyone wishing to enter had to knock – very loudly.

Almost immediately, the door handle was jiggled up and down, then again, this time more violently. After a pause, a pounding on the door had the steward turning on his heel, releasing the lock and opening the door a fraction, and then a little wider. Jojo's head, dripping water, appeared, followed by the rest of his body, clothed in sodden blue. The steward made to close the door but was brushed aside as it burst wide open to reveal a man mountain moving at pace – Schroeder.

Jojo had stopped just inside the door to squeeze the excess water from his trouser bottoms, and Schroeder almost sent him flying, trundling to a halt just in time.

'Whooee! That's some storm out there. Reminds me of home.' It was almost as if another force of nature had arrived on the scene. Schroeder seemed incapable of talking quietly, and the atmosphere of quiet calm in the face of Nisha's wrath was shattered.

Schroeder gave the steward a friendly slap on the shoulder as he was locking the door once more. 'Hey, Manuel. Get us a Coors, will ya? No, make that two. I've got a thirst on tonight.'

The steward gave a tight smile and returned behind the bar, massaging his shoulder.

Schroeder's beady eyes scanned the room while he brushed water from his flat top. There was nowhere for Ralph to hide. 'Yo, Mackenzie. There's your egghead friend.' He pointed in Ralph's direction and then raised a hand in greeting. Jojo turned to look, saw Ralph had already got him a beer, and came over.

'Sorry about Schroeder,' he muttered. 'He's a difficult man to avoid.'

'So it seems,' said Ralph, who had been wondering at the near-simultaneous arrival of the two.

Jojo took a grateful swig of beer but continued standing as he tried to squeeze more water from his saturated trousers. Everyone in the bar was steaming gently in the heat, and the place was rapidly turning into a sauna. After a minute or so, he gave up and took a seat.

'Did you get the cutters?' Ralph said quietly.

'In the jeep. You're still planning to go through with this? It's fucking godawful out there, and it's going to get worse. I've just checked out the satellite images. The eye is just southeast of us right now, moving due west. The winds are going to swing round to the north in the next hour or so and strengthen as the eye reaches its closest point.'

'I don't have any choice. I'm out of here tomorrow – couldn't swing anything longer. I have to have that sample.'

Jojo was as earnest as Ralph had ever seen him. 'Ralph. I'm begging you. Leave it. Don't interfere. Things'll work out, I'm sure.' He was desperate, pleading.

Ralph's voice was stony. 'I have to do this, Jojo, and I will do it, with or without you.'

Jojo looked down at the table for a good half minute, then sighed in resignation. 'OK. I'll come. For old time's sake. But I'm not happy about it. Not happy at all.'

'That's all I ask, Jojo,' said Ralph. 'Let me get you another beer.'

As Ralph approached the bar, Schroeder left the group he was haranguing and moved to intercept him.

'Hey, Martinez. Let me buy you a drink. You too, Mackenzie.'

Ralph's first thought was to demure, but he quickly decided it would be easier to accept. His second thought queried how Schroeder knew his name. He could have sworn he hadn't told him during their first encounter. *Ah, well, word got around.*

Jojo reluctantly wandered over to join them, and Schroeder handed out the beers. 'Come over and meet the boys.' Introductions made, and without pausing for breath, Schroeder continued with his tirade. 'I was just telling the guys about these fuckin' Chagossians, or whatever they call themselves. They're still trying to get us kicked off the island. Nearly seventy years now and they don't seem to know they're beaten. Jesus – why can't they just take it on the chin?'

Apparently, the islanders – or, to be more accurate, their descendants – were launching another court case to try and get their land back.

Ralph couldn't keep quiet. 'Well, maybe they just want to come home.'

Schroeder upended the first of his beers and drained it, wiping a wayward dribble from his chin with his sleeve. 'Home? This ain't home for them any more. Most of them have never set foot in the place. We're here now and we're not fuckin' budgin.'

Out of the corner of his eye, Ralph could see Jojo looking at him and slowly shaking his head. *Don't wind him up.* The 'guys' said nothing but nodded. Ralph wasn't certain they agreed with Schroeder and suspected they were merely following the line of least resistance. It was obvious that getting into an argument with the man was hard work and frequently, he guessed, didn't end well.

Nonetheless, Ralph just couldn't let it stand. 'How would you feel if someone came and gassed your dogs, restricted your access to food and medicine, and then kicked you out of your home? Pretty mad, I'd guess.'

Schroeder seemed surprised and shocked that someone was standing up to him. His expression hardened and his eyes narrowed. 'What are you, Martinez? Some sort of fuckin' commie?'

Ralph remained calm. 'Just someone who likes to see justice done.'

'Justice!' bellowed the major. 'What's justice got to do with it? We needed this island more than they did. Simple as that. And we paid for it.'

Ralph could feel himself getting uptight. 'Yeah. The British got a special deal on Polaris. The islanders got zilch.'

Schroeder moved a step closer, looking down on him, lip curled in an intimidating sneer. 'Well, boy, why don't you just take it up with the Brits, then? Shouldn't be difficult. You livin' there an' all.'

Ralph had to hold himself back. He had plenty to do that night and a rumble with an outranking officer twice his size wasn't on the list. And he was supposed to be keeping a low profile. So much for that.

He raised both hands in supplication. 'OK. Maybe you're right. All I'm saying is, we need to see it from their point of view too.'

Schroeder seemed placated, even deflated. Ralph got the feeling he was disappointed at the climbdown. 'Yeah, well. OK. But we're here and we're staying.'

As if to acknowledge the end of the argument, they downed their beers in tandem. For a few moments no-one spoke, the howling of the wind beyond the boarded-up windows filling the space. Ralph made the most of the interregnum. 'Right. That's me done. I've a flight out tomorrow and I need an early night. Not that I'm expecting much sleep with this going on.'

Schroeder seemed disappointed. 'Hey. No hard feelings, Martinez. I don't hold a grudge. Have another beer. The night's young.'

Ralph said thanks, but no thanks, and the major seemed accepting. He shook hands all round, told Jojo he would keep in touch and headed for the door.

The steward beat him to it and pulled back the bolts. As they were released, the door was ripped out of his grasp, slamming back against the outside of the building. Jojo had been right, the wind had switched direction. Now it was coming from the north, its strength buoyed by the proximity of the eye. It was going to be one hell of a night.

As agreed, the jeep was parked a few blocks away, in the relative shelter of a stand of palms – which didn't really mean much in the conditions. It was pitch dark and the horizontal rain pounding against Ralph's face actually hurt. It also made it impossible for him to open his eyes for any length of time. He felt, more than saw, the outline of the vehicle, and scrambled into the passenger seat. The canvas roof had been torn off and it pirouetted in the wind, attached by a single fastening. There was no way it could be reattached in the conditions, so Ralph undid the clip and it vanished into the maelstrom. The windshield provided some protection from the driving rain, and he crouched down behind it and waited for Jojo to appear.

After fifteen minutes or so, he thought he could make out a light. It wavered here and there in the darkness but continued to head his way. Eventually, it resolved itself into the glow of a disembodied torch, Jojo's dark outline only visible when he was almost in touching distance. Jojo climbed into the driver's seat, switched on and turned on the lights. He looked across at Ralph, dripping face a picture of misery. 'Sure you want to do this?'

Ralph was adamant. 'No choice, Jojo. Let's go.'

The journey south was like a nightmare. They saw no other vehicles, which was hardly a surprise. A mixture of driving rain and spume reduced visibility to almost zero and limited their speed to twenty miles an hour at best. On half a dozen occasions they had to stop and drag debris out of their path. In several places, the storm surge had swamped the road and they had to negotiate flood water that topped the wheel arches and poured under the doors. The only saving grace was the switch in wind direction, which at least meant they weren't driving into it.

They followed the same route as earlier in the day, circling around the back of the sheds and parking off the road and well out of sight. Jojo grabbed the bolt cutters from the back of the jeep and handed them over. Ralph hefted them, satisfying himself they could do the job, and patted his pockets to make sure the two small metal flasks he had brought out from the

UK were still there, along with the miniature, but powerful, torch that Jojo had provided.

They fought against the wind, barely able to move forwards, until they reached shelter in a passage between two of the low rises bordering the apron. They made their way to the end, holding back while a stream of mangled metal sheeting hurtled past. The wind dropped a little and Ralph leant forwards to check out the sheds. He pulled his head back just in time, as an airborne fuel drum crashed into the corner of the building, gouging out chunks of concrete close to where his head had been. He turned to Jojo, looking rattled, and swallowed hard. 'Jesus!'

It took another minute of watching assorted debris fly past before Ralph felt confident enough to try again. This time, he stepped cautiously out onto the apron, bracing himself against the onslaught of the wind. A pair of tall floodlights swayed violently back and forth, but were still working, bathing the scene in a quavering yellow glow.

Given the conditions, Ralph probably shouldn't have been shocked, but he was. The planes were tied down, and although a few had shifted, they all looked pretty much in good order. But the flimsy sheds were being torn apart. The roof had completely gone from the furthest, although the rows of cylindrical tanks on their trestles seemed to have held up so far. The closest was in better shape, a few of the corrugated metal roof panels had vanished and another was flapping in the wind, attached by a single corner, but most were still in place. The security fence was broken and battered, many of the panels lying on the ground. Of the guard, there was no sign. Suddenly, the flapping metal sheet freed itself and careered in their direction. Ducking back into the passage, they watched as it tumbled past.

Jojo put a hand on Ralph's shoulder. 'We can't go out there with this stuff flying around. We'll get our fucking heads ripped off.'

'Jojo – I'm going.' He handed the bolt cutters over. 'Looks like I won't need these, at least.' He wiped stinging rivulets of rain and salt spray from his eyes and peered out again. The wind was marginally subdued, and there was no immediate debris threat. It was as good a time as any. 'Stay here. Keep an eye out for the guard. If he appears, I'm sure you'll think of something.'

Jojo made to speak, but the sound of an imploding window behind made him flinch and turn. When he looked back, Ralph was gone. Jojo eased his head around the corner of the building and watched Ralph scurry in an awkward crouch across the apron. It was a hundred yards or so to the sheds, and he had to stop and take evasive action three or four times as chunks of detritus continued to career across the concrete. Jojo was only aware that he had been holding his breath when Ralph reached the shelter of the nearest shed without mishap, and he let it out in a rush of relief.

Inside the shed the storm's roar was muted, although the wind wailed through the gaps in the roof and threatened to loosen a couple more metal panels that flapped and struggled to free themselves. It was a huge relief to be out of the pounding rain, and Ralph took the opportunity to wipe excess water off his face. The power in the sheds was out, so there was no internal lighting, and the glow of the floodlights outside did little to penetrate the darkness. He switched on the torch and swept the interior. The closest row of storage tanks was maybe twenty metres away, and he headed in its direction. As he reached the nearest tank, he heard a sharp crack and stopped dead. But there were no further sounds and he guessed it was a bolt shearing as the wind tore at another of the roof panels.

He shone the torch on the tank. It was about the same size as those filled with gasoline on the backs of road tankers, around a five-thousand-gallon capacity, he guessed. He reached in his pocket for one of the flasks. Then: 'Shit, shit, shit!'

He put his head back and looked up at nothing in particular, mouthing further obscenities. He hadn't really given much thought to the specifics of getting a sample, and now the lack of forethought had come back to haunt him. As far as he could see, the only outlet was designed to be connected to a large bore fuel hose. There was no facility for hand sampling, and now he thought about it, why would there be? He hammered the side of the tank with his fists in frustration and despair. 'Fuck it!'

For a while he stood with his head leaning against the side of the tank, racking his brains for a solution. He thought he heard a sound behind him, but before he could turn...

'Raise yer hands and step away from the tank.' The voice was young and wavering. 'Now turn round slowly and drop the torch.'

Ralph couldn't decide whether to submit or make a break for it. He reckoned he might be able to dive under the trestles and get behind the tank, before whoever it was could fire, but what then? If he wanted to live – for at least a little longer – then there was only one option. Another opportunity might present itself.

His shoulders dropped, as if in defeat, his arms went up and he let the torch fall to the ground. He turned slowly to face the USAF security forces guard. He was fresh-faced and looked little more than a boy. His finger was on the trigger of his assault rifle and he was very nervous. He swallowed as Ralph stared at him impassively, and his prominent Adam's apple bobbed up and down. Ralph could quite easily see him shoot first, ask questions later, so determined he would play it straight.

'No trouble now. Ya hear?' Ralph couldn't place the accent but was in no doubt it was either Hicksville or somewhere close by.

The blue-bereted guard gestured with his rifle and Ralph walked slowly towards the open end of the shed.

Jojo watched Ralph stagger as he emerged from the shelter of the shed and took the full force of the wind and rain. The guard followed a safe distance behind, assault rifle pointing at the small of Ralph's back, slight frame struggling against the blow. The dancing floodlights bathed the two figures in a shuddering, sickly yellow glow, but Jojo couldn't make out Ralph's expression. His posture was a lesson in submission, but Jojo knew Ralph better than that. He mouthed his thoughts.

'For fuck's sake, Ralph, don't do anything stupid!'

The hand on his arm was anticipated but still made him jump. Schroeder peered over Jojo's shoulder, lantern-jaw dripping rainwater, beery breath enveloping Jojo's head. 'Atta boy, Cletus. Bring the commie shit to Daddy.' He grinned in the direction of the young guard.

Jojo said nothing.

They continued to watch as the guard ushered Ralph in their direction. Schroeder made to move into the open to take control when an ear-splitting screech stopped him in his tracks. A huge chunk of the nearest shed's roof tore away and spiralled upwards like a Catherine wheel, pieces flaking off and scattering in all directions. Schroeder and Jojo watched, spellbound, as a ragged sheet of corrugated metal flew towards the figures.

Cletus had turned his head at the noise, but Ralph still faced them, wary of making any undue moves. The sheet made a beeline for the transfixed guard, spinning like a frisbee. One razor-sharp edge sliced across his throat, opening up a gash from which a gout of blood spurted, glistening in the yellow light. Ralph turned at last and looked down at the unfortunate guard, now lying prone, hands clutched to his neck, legs flailing weakly. Casually, he picked up the gun and walked slowly and calmly back into the shed.

Jojo turned and looked up at Schroeder, whose eyes were wide – disbelieving. The major's mouth started working, but no words emerged. Eventually: 'Jesus H Christ! Jesus fucking Christ! Fuck it, fuck...' The obscenities continued for a time, after which he seemed deflated and at a loss. Then he reached a hand inside his saturated bomber jacket and pulled out a handgun. 'Give me fifteen. If I'm not out with Martinez by then, follow on.'

Jojo turned, suddenly animated. 'You said you wouldn't harm him. You gave your word.'

Schroeder patted the air with both palms in a placating motion, then gestured with his gun. 'Hey, boy, just chill. It's insurance, that's all. Insurance.' The major headed down the passage away from the apron and vanished.

Even above the roar of the wind, Ralph heard the tearing noise of metal behind him and had to fight the desire to turn. It was clear the guard was shit-scared, and the last thing he needed now was a bullet in the back. There was no further urging onwards, so he stood motionless, hands on head, awaiting instructions. The rain seemed to have eased a little, but the gusts were so powerful now that he could barely stand. Twenty seconds passed and he began to frown. What the fuck was going on? The urge to turn around was overwhelming and eventually he could no longer hold back. Slowly, very slowly, he began to rotate his head, keeping the rest of his body facing the front. Then the corner of his eye caught the guard's body, and he spun around, incredulous. He crossed the short distance that separated them and looked down. The boy was still alive but wouldn't be for much longer. Beneath his hands, now held loosely at his throat, blood pumped slowly from a gaping wound that ran almost from ear to ear. The guard's eyes were closed and his head lay in a wide pool of blood diluted and spread by the falling rain. There was nothing Ralph could do

149

for him. Heavy-hearted at the guard's death, he, nonetheless, couldn't believe his luck. Picking up the abandoned assault rifle, he engaged the safety catch and walked slowly back towards the shed.

Most of the roof had gone now, so there was little shelter inside. The wind howled around the tank trestles and the rain was already forming coalescing pools on the concrete floor. Ralph retrieved his torch and went from tank to tank, fifty in total, but all had the same connection. There were no tools lying around, nothing he could use to try and break through a tank's exterior to get at what was inside. He crouched beneath one of the tanks to get out of the rain and swore quietly in exasperation. To come so far for nothing. It didn't bear thinking about. He sat motionless for maybe five minutes, hands grasping the assault rifle, held vertically before him, stock resting on the ground. Then a smile started to spread and he shook his head. The solution had literally been staring him in the face.

He crept from under the tank, walked a dozen or so steps, and turned. He took the metal flasks from his pocket and put them on the ground at his feet. Then he lifted the rifle and released the safety catch. He was banking that, apart from Jojo, there was no-one around to hear the noise, especially above the commotion of the storm and – in any case – he had no choice. Taking aim, he fired a short, focused burst.

A small, irregular hole blossomed close to the top of the tank. He waited for a few seconds, but nothing appeared. He fired another burst, opening a second hole immediately below – still nothing. The third burst opened another ragged hole a little further down, but still nothing. After the fourth gave the same result, he was beginning to wonder if the tank was empty; then he saw movement in the latest hole.

Slowly, the torchlight revealed dark fluid beginning to fill the breach, unlike anything Ralph had seen before. It fizzed and seethed as if alive, clinging to the side of the tank as it clawed its way downwards in fits and starts around its circumference. Once it had made it halfway, there was nowhere else to go except uphill, so it began to drip slowly through a gap in one of the trestles and onto the concrete. The fluid was pulsing out slowly, so he reckoned he had just caught the surface of the stuff in the tank – as he had been trying to do. A breach lower down could have released a flood. A flask-full or two would be just fine.

The stuff was making a slowly expanding puddle on the ground beneath the tank. Ralph guessed that it was some sort of suspension; the bots contained in a medium or broth. Like mixing seeds with sand before broadcasting, this would make them go further, reducing clumping and spreading them across a greater volume of atmosphere. The fluid appeared dark – almost black – but the surface had the same rainbow sheen as an oil slick. It still shivered imperceptibly, the pool growing by sending out amoeboid fingers that were then gradually assimilated by the expanding mass. He felt a little queasy. He remembered reading, as a kid, about how rogue nanobots might transform the planet and everything on it into grey goo. It had scared the hell out of him at the time, and the idea still gave him the creeps.

He put down the gun and balanced the torch on one of the metal trestles, so that it shone on the dripping fluid. Then he picked up one of the flasks, unscrewed the top and put it back down. He wasn't sure how dangerous the stuff was, but he was damned sure he wasn't going to get any on his skin. He could see nothing lying around that might offer protection, so he shrugged off his sodden shirt and wrapped it around one hand. The air was still warm, but the gale striking his wet skin made him shiver.

He picked up the flask and held it awkwardly in the protected hand. He watched carefully where the drops were falling, and when he was sure, carefully positioned the flask beneath. The first drop went in, but was too close to the rim for comfort, so he shifted the flask's position slightly. The next drop fell centrally, and he held the flask absolutely still as it started to fill.

After a few dozen drops he began to worry about how much the flask would hold. Even with his hand covered, he was still nervous – paranoid, even – that the flask might overflow. He waited for another half dozen drips, then withdrew the flask and screwed on the top with his free hand. Putting it on the floor, he removed the top from the second and placed it in position. The first drop caught the edge and splashed some tiny droplets of the fluid on his shirt. Panicking, he pulled back his arm, unwrapped the shirt and tossed it onto the floor. He retrieved the torch, bent over and shone it on the garment. Half a dozen small holes had appeared in the fabric of one sleeve, each growing visibly in size. *It's hardly surprising,* he thought, *it's mostly carbon, after all.* He kept watching until the holes stopped growing – each now a couple of centimetres across – speculating that the bots were now sated.

Tearing off the affected sleeve with some difficulty – best to be careful – he wrapped the remainder of the shirt around his hand. He wedged the torch between a couple of the trestle's metal beams, placed the flask in position once more and began to collect the drops. There were no more splashes, and after a minute or so, he withdrew the flask to screw on the lid. He was beginning to wonder, for the first time, if he might pull this off after all.

Seconds later, he was kicking himself.

'Well, well, well. Lookee here. If it ain't our visiting egghead. Thought you'd called it a night, Martinez?'

Ralph thumped his head on the side of the tank in frustration and despair. Schroeder! He really should have guessed. Well, shit, he was too close now.

'Temper, temper!' The major chuckled at the outburst. 'No sudden moves now, boy. Just turn around real slow.'

Ralph assumed Schroeder wasn't just bluffing and actually had a gun. He shuffled around slowly to face the major, both arms raised, one holding the uncapped flask.

'That's the way. Now,' Schroeder gestured at the flask, 'put that on the ground, and no funny business.'

Ralph bent forwards as if to comply, then hurled the flask in Schroeder's direction. The major's eyes opened wide in alarm and he threw himself sideways as the contents of the flask flew out in a wide arc. In his desperation to avoid the hot broth, Schroeder slipped on the puddled concrete and crashed to the ground like a felled Redwood, his pistol flying free and clattering into the darkness.

Ralph was onto him in seconds, looking to get in a telling blow before he could recover. But Schroeder was quick for a man his size and deflected Ralph's haymaker with a forearm that felt as if it was made out of granite. Ralph was astride the major now and fighting a losing battle to stop him rising. He tried to pin down Schroeder's arms, but it was like trying to subdue Superman. The major freed one arm, made a fist and jabbed it into Ralph's face. There wasn't much force behind it, but Ralph felt his nose crumple. As his senses reeled, Schroeder rolled over, pinning Ralph to the ground with the weight of his body. His hands scrabbled for Ralph's throat and eventually closed around it like a bear's jaws.

'Ya shouldna done that, boy. Ya really shouldna.'

Schroeder's strength was overwhelming, his grip like a steel vice. Ralph's fingers scrabbled at the major's massive hands, but it was futile. He tried to breathe in but sucked at a vacuum. Darkness began to appear at the edges of his vision and he knew he must black out soon. In desperation, his hands hunted back and forth on the wet concrete, searching for something – anything – that he could use to break Schroeder's death grip.

Because that's what it was. The major's face was inches from his now, eyes bulging, foul breath in his nostrils. Nothing short of Ralph's extinction would stop him now.

His right hand touched something, but he couldn't quite reach it. He stretched out his arm as far as it would go and worked it closer with his fingers until he could grasp it, a thin sliver of metal debris. A veil of darkness was falling across his vision now, and oblivion could be no more than seconds away. With his last ounce of strength, Ralph brought his arm up and around and plunged the metal splinter into the back of Schroeder's thick neck.

The effect was immediate. Blood spurted and the major howled in pain. He released his grip, his hands involuntarily reaching back towards the wound. With everything he had, Ralph brought his knee up into Schroeder's groin, feeling the satisfying squish of soft tissue. This time the big man screamed and rolled to one side.

Ralph staggered upright at once, chest heaving, vision gradually clearing. He shook his head and looked around. Schroeder's pistol was nowhere to be seen, but his own assault rifle was where he had left it below the tank, next to the filled flask. He walked unsteadily towards it and bent down to pick it up. As he did so, he felt a hand grip his ankle and his leg was pulled backwards from under him, sending him sprawling. What the fuck did it take to keep this man down? Schroeder was nearly on top of Ralph's prone form now, pulling himself up on his trouser belt. Ralph reached out, pulled the gun towards him, half turned and jammed the stock hard into the major's face – once, twice – until he cried out in pain and let go.

Ralph made his escape for the second time in a minute, moved away to a safe distance and trained the gun on Schroeder. Neither said a word. Then the major started to climb to his feet. The black hair was plastered to his scalp and his shirt was sodden with a mix of rainwater and blood.

One eye was completely closed, and he stood in a constipated crouch that showed that Ralph's knee had hit the spot.

'No further.' Ralph released the safety catch.

The major raised his hands, as if in acknowledgement of defeat. He was panting, chest heaving, clearly out of shape despite his enormous strength. It was a while before he could get any words out.

'Face it, Martinez. Ya can't win. You'll never get off the island. Not unless ya kill me, and I don't reckon you've got the balls to do that.'

'Try me!' Ralph's demeanour was bullish, but inside he knew Schroeder was right. What the fuck was he going to do now?

The major just shook his head, then rubbed his jaw and wiggled it from side to side, as if testing for damage. For a time they stood in the drenching rain, watching one another. A crash behind him caused Ralph to half turn, and Schroeder's body language suggested he might make the most of it. Ralph turned back and fired off a short burst over the major's head. 'Stay back, Schroeder. I will kill you if I have to. Count on it.'

The major looked a little less sure of himself. He raised his eyebrows at the outburst. 'Maybe ya will, at that, maybe ya will.'

Ralph made to answer.

Then: 'Hold it there, Ralph.'

'Jojo?' Ralph had difficulty making out the figure in the semi-darkness, but he couldn't mistake the voice.

'I'm sorry, Ralph.' Slowly, warily, Jojo moved closer, the dim torchlight unveiling a face that was dripping rainwater and a picture of misery. In his outstretched hand was a pistol. It was pointing at Ralph's chest.

Ralph was incredulous. 'Jojo. What the fuck is this?'

Jojo's voice was close to breaking with emotion. 'I didn't want to do this, Ralph, but I had no choice. They needed local met advice for the seeding and I drew the short straw. They made me an offer I literally couldn't refuse.'

Betrayed, Ralph snorted in derision. 'Right! What was it? Money? Drugs? Women? That was always your weak spot.' Then a light dawned. 'No! Promotion. Jesus Christ, you bought into all this just to be Captain Mackenzie again. You fucking arsehole!'

'No!' Jojo screamed in anguish. 'They threatened my kid, Ralph. They said they'd kill Davie.'

Ralph was speechless.

Schroeder's drawl filled the space. 'Ya fuckin' runt, Mackenzie. What kept ya?'

Jojo ignored him. His attention was on Ralph, his face pleading for understanding.

'Ya hear me, boy? The fuckin' bastard near crippled me. Where ya been?'

Reluctantly, Jojo turned to face the major, gun still trained on Ralph. 'Schroeder. Shut the fuck up.'

'I'm sorry Jojo. Really sorry.' Ralph had found his voice. 'But this thing is bigger than one person, bigger than all of us.' It sounded trite and he knew it.

'You don't have kids, do you, Ralph?'

'You know I don't, Jojo.'

'Well, if you did, you'd know how I feel. I can't lose him. I just can't.' The words were coming out between sobs now and tears mixed with the dribbles of rain coursing down Jojo's face.'

For a time they stood in silence, just the rain hissing on the concrete and the wind howling through the tattered remnants of the roof. The three-body problem in human form, with no obvious solution.

But Schroeder couldn't stop prodding. 'Mackenzie, for fuck's sake, stop shitting yourself and shoot the bastard. Ya know what'll happen otherwise.'

Jojo turned towards Schroeder who, momentarily, had two guns pointed at him. But Ralph wasn't inclined to take advantage.

'Schroeder. One more fucking word. Just one.' The major knew a man on the edge when he saw one and his mouth clamped shut.

Ralph was getting desperate. 'Jojo, please, we can still sort this and save your kid. Make the right move and no-one will be the wiser. Give me thirty-six hours and I'll have blown this whole thing apart. You won't be implicated. They won't touch Davie. What would be the point?'

Jojo's hand wavered, but his voice said he'd made up his mind. 'Ralph, I'm really sorry, but I just can't take the chance.'

For a moment, the keening of the wind and the clatter of flying debris subsided. Ralph heard the quiet click of the safety catch release over the sibilant murmur of the falling rain.

He looked at Jojo, his expression a mixture of acceptance and regret. He had no intention of shooting Schroeder and Jojo knew it. Ralph had never killed a man and didn't intend to start now.

Jojo raised his arm to eye level, his finger tightening on the trigger.

'That's ma boy. Blow the fucker's head off.'

The storm was past its peak now and the shot rang out loud and clear, echoing around the shed's interior. Schroeder's eyes bulged and he clutched at a spreading patch of blood on the left side of his chest. 'Mackenzie, you fuckin'...' His legs gave way before he could finish and he crumpled to the concrete in slo-mo like a high-rise toppled by a demolition squad.

Ralph had closed his eyes at the prospect of imminent death, but they flicked open of their own accord at the shot and Schroeder's exclamation.

Jojo had let the pistol fall to the ground and was hunkered down, face in his hands, weeping.

Ralph walked over, put a consoling hand on his shoulder and squeezed. There were no words. He picked up the gun and headed over to Schroeder, sprawled a way off in the shadows. He didn't need to look too closely. Dead.

He walked back to Jojo and stood next to him, paralysed by events and unsure of what to do next. The worst of the storm was over, the wind nothing more than a force eight and the rain a steady drizzle. It would be dawn in a few hours and the place would be humming. They needed to be done and dusted by then.

'Jojo.' Ralph shook his friend gently by the shoulder. 'Jojo. We have to go. We need to get rid of Schroeder and get the hell out of here.'

Jojo was emotionally drained and half in a daze. He stood slowly and looked at Ralph, face a mask of despair and resignation, voice so quiet Ralph could barely hear him. 'What do you want me to do?'

'Give me a hand with Schroeder.'

Jojo didn't move.

'Jojo. Please. We need to do this – for Davie.' There was no trace of hope in Jojo's eyes, but he helped drag the major's body over to the tank that Ralph had sampled and left it beneath the hose connector outlet.

Ralph rescued the flask he had hurled at Schroeder and quickly, but carefully, filled it from the drops that still fell from the breach. Then he picked up the torch and, hand around Jojo's shoulder, they moved to a safe distance. Turning, he took aim and fired a sustained burst at the tank's outlet valve, ripping it apart and unleashing a deluge of black, seething, fluid that cascaded over Schroeder's body and flooded across the concrete towards them, forcing them to retreat in a hurry. The fluid seemed to cling to the corpse, bubbling and fizzing as the hungry bots got to work. The human body is something like eighteen per cent carbon, one hell of a lot in someone Schroeder's size. They watched mesmerised for a couple of minutes as the man mountain that had once been Major Leroy Schroeder slowly collapsed in on itself beneath its mantle of frothing black. Then Ralph turned and ushered Jojo in the direction of the jeep.

R ALPH'S FLIGHT BACK TO QATAR LEFT JUST AFTER
sunrise and was uneventful. Nisha had pretty much blown
herself out, and one of the runways had already been cleared
of debris. It was the same C-130 that had brought him out
– barely forty-eight hours earlier. This time he was the only
passenger. His body felt pummelled and bruised, and his nose
hurt like hell, but his exhaustion won out. Despite the pain and
the noise he was dead to the world for the entire flight, waking
only when the wheels thudded onto tarmac at Al Udaid.

There was a good twelve hours to kill before a flight left
for the UK, and he used some of the dead time for a visit to
the sick bay. The doctor who saw him was clearly less than
impressed by his formulaic explanation – an argument with
a door – but said nothing. An x-ray of his nose showed that
the bone was cracked, but not badly enough to need setting.
At the doc's instruction a nurse applied some strapping that
would help the fracture heal. There would be bruising and
it would hurt for a few more days yet, but nothing that an

off-the-shelf painkiller couldn't handle. The mess was next on Ralph's to-do list, and after that more sleep in one of the bunkhouses set aside for those passing through.

He was woken by the noisy arrival of a dozen or so grunts on their way to join the forever war in Afghanistan. Feeling refreshed, he tuned out their crude banter and reprised the previous night's events. It was like watching a film and he could barely credit it had really happened. But the two metal flasks nestling in the webbing of his backpack argued otherwise. He had shipped out just a few hours after the night's exploits and the place was already a hornet's nest. It would take days, perhaps weeks, to clear up after the hurricane and repair the damage. In addition, he predicted there would be a deal of head-scratching as base security attempted to tackle the enigma of a dead guard with his throat gaping, a shot-up storage tank, a partially digested corpse, and a lake of something black and nasty that was clearly nothing to do with cloud seeding. Christ only knew what they would make of it.

The whole thing, he reckoned, would be marked down as some sort of score settling gone wrong and quietly buried. If the Skyseeders – as he had begun to think of them – had anything like the influence he suspected, he had no doubt they would stamp down hard. At any rate, he was certain it wouldn't be hitting the news feeds anytime soon. Someone might eventually put two and two together and wonder about the coincidence of the riddle in the storage shed and his flying visit, but by then it would be way too late – or so he hoped.

At least Jojo was in the clear. There was nothing to connect him with the nocturnal mayhem, and with Schroeder gone, the Skyseeders had no reason to doubt Jojo's loyalty. Davie would be fine. And in a day or two, there would no longer be any purpose in threatening him. Right now he needed to give some serious thought to what he was going to do next.

GEORGE CHIDDINGFORD WAS A KIWI, BORN AND raised amongst the temperate rainforest and lush climate of the Coromandel Peninsula, across the bay from Auckland. But he had lived in the UK so long that he had to really work at his accent. This he did as a matter of pride in his heritage and because – as a journalist – there were occasions when not being a Brit conferred a distinct edge.

He didn't cut a particularly striking figure, and the immediate impression he conveyed was one of greyness. For close on half a century, his work ensemble had pulled together a baggy grey sports jacket over shapeless slacks in a matching shade, accessorised by a beige shirt and colourless tie. He was the definitive man in the crowd, instantly forgettable, even when he wasn't in a crowd. Again, not a bad thing for a gentleman of the press.

His very ordinariness lulled people into a false sense of security, and they couldn't seem to stop themselves opening up to him. This was why, approaching the end of his seventh decade, he was still working. If he was honest, the smell of printer's ink – or whatever the hell they used these days – did nothing for him any more. He wanted to be back home, lazing on ninety-mile beach or hauling salmon out of the Waitaki River. It wasn't as if he hadn't tried to escape. He had retired twice, but they kept finding ways of enticing him back. A month earlier he had handed in his resignation for the third and – he was adamant (again) – final time. Friday was supposed to be his last day. But that was before a tall, black American airman had buttonholed him outside the King's Cross headquarters of his paper and dangled in front of him a very tasty morsel that no hack worth the name could have resisted. Which was why he found himself occupying a corner table in the snug of The Hairy Goat at a little after mid-day.

The pub had just opened so there were no other punters. Even if there had been, they would have thought nothing of a saggy, balding man in late middle age, nursing a pint of stout and studying the racing pages.

After about twenty minutes, the door to the main bar opened and the American's head appeared, followed by a hand clutching a pint of bitter. The other held three bags of crisps, in assorted flavours, which he dumped on the table.

'Lunch!' he said with a grin.

George reckoned he was a pretty good judge of character – how could he not be after so long in the business? – and he liked this man. They had only talked for a couple of minutes during the brief encounter that Ralph had engineered first thing that morning, but that was enough. He was straight-talking, uncomplicated and seemed to be on to something very big indeed. George had been hooked within thirty seconds.

Ralph sat down opposite, took a sip of beer and rubbed at the strapping across the bridge of his nose. George had once broken his in a rugby game back home and remembered that it itched like hell when it was healing.

'So. How do you want to do this?' queried Ralph.

George pulled out a small recorder that he placed on the table between them, gave a smile of reassurance and said in his best Kiwi, 'Why don't you start at the beginning, mate?'

George ordered another pint and returned to his seat. Ralph had just gone, leaving behind more than two hours of recorded material, a package of images and data, and a world-weary journo shocked for the first time in decades. He had done more than his fair share of investigative journalism over the years, some impressive scoops too, but nothing like this. This was hold-the-front-page stuff and then some. Hell, this had Pulitzer written all over it. Or would have if he were a Yank. What was worse was that Ralph insisted on simultaneous publication in the US, so he would need to bring Ned Lorenzo at *The New York Times* on board. He would be the lucky bastard that picked up the Pulitzer. He – George – would have to make do with Reporter of the Year at the Brit Press Awards. He winced inwardly. It just didn't have the same ring.

He took another sip of his drink. He needed a while to compose himself and plan the next move. Her indoors – as he increasingly thought of hard-nosed, hard-partying new editor, Miranda Blenkinsop – would be in the driving seat, of course. But he was in no doubt that there was too much material for one edition. He guessed she would clear the decks for two or three days. That would give time for the story to build nicely and for them to get the dirt from the university boffins who now had samples of the bot broth. He looked at his watch, took a last swig of his pint, stuffed the package and the folded-up *Racing Times* in his jacket pocket, and headed for the door, all thought of an impending and sleepy retirement down under long gone.

FOR CENTURIES, BREAKING NEWS HAD MEANT – TO the incumbent of Number 10 Downing Street – the arrival of the morning papers, neatly pressed and warmed by a smoothing iron. For Duncan Bannerman, it meant a new pattern of glowing pixels on the screen of his smartphone. Ever since Gort's hammer blow, he had slept poorly, and tonight was no exception. As he lay awake in the early hours, he could have done with the warm security of Jeremy's body beside him, but his husband was away, working on location in Thailand for a new film about the Vietnam War.

Normally, he had his phone turned off at night. He would never sleep at all otherwise. If the shit ever hit the fan, Nobby or someone else would wake him in any case. But that night, at three in the morning, he had succumbed to an unexplainable desire to turn on his phone, and he now stared open-mouthed at the screen.

He was on the BBC News site, but he had scrolled through the lot and every one led with the same story. The UK's

Guardian newspaper, *The New York Times* and countless other news outlets across the world had simultaneously published what were described as 'explosive' revelations of a clandestine US-UK link-up to 'hack the planet' by artificially slashing atmospheric carbon levels. The evidence was damning and corroborated by university scientists who had somehow got hold of samples of the bots. Skyseed was named and there was even speculation about the bomb attack on Jane Haliwell.

There was a quiet knock on the door, which opened before Duncan could answer. He could just make out Nobby Aitken's bulbous head in the semi-darkness and the screen glow of a smartphone in his hand. He held up his own to show he already knew. Nobby stood in uncomfortable silence for a moment, uncertain what to do next. Coming to a decision, he reached for the light switch and made to come into the room.

'No, Nobby. Just leave it.' Duncan raised a hand, indicating he should come no further.

'There's no urgency. We're dead and buried, in any case. It'll wait 'til morning.'

Nobby bowed his head in acknowledgement, withdrew quietly and closed the door behind him. Duncan lay back on the pillow and stared at the ceiling. He still hadn't moved when his alarm went off at six.

I T HAD BEEN TOUCH AND GO FOR A WHILE. KARL COULD remember nothing at all, but he had managed to piece together some sort of picture from Steve's account. They had been about to leave the pub to get some food, and he had been somewhat the worse for wear but otherwise fine. According to Steve, he'd headed for the toilet and collapsed on the way there. It had been anaphylactic shock, of course, a severe allergic reaction that had been an ever-present threat since he was a child.

Twice before it had happened, once at four years old when a bee had stung him in the garden and much later during his PhD fieldwork in the Caribbean. The first time, he had been lucky to pull through. The second, he had carried an EpiPen, which counteracted the worst effects. Ever since, he had been on antihistamines, but they couldn't handle the intensity of the latest attack. It hadn't helped that, on the night in question, his EpiPen was at home in his other jacket.

The only reason he was still alive was through an astonishing piece of good luck. A couple of paramedics had just finished their shift and were working hard to banish the day's more distressing memories with a few pints. In less than a minute, his throat had swollen so much that breathing was impossible. One of the paramedics had used a narrow-bladed knife from the pub's kitchen to cut into Karl's windpipe to open a new airway and save his life.

That was a week ago. They had kept him in an induced coma for seventy-two hours, and four days after he had come round he felt fine and was champing at the bit to be out of bed and back home. After the bombshell dropped by his consultant, the urge to get as far away from the hospital as possible became desperate. He hadn't understood how it was possible for anaphylactic shock to strike in an English pub on a wet September evening, and now he knew. When he came to, he had noticed a circular bruise on the left side of his chest, at the centre of which was a tiny puncture wound. He hadn't given it much thought, assuming it was the result of some injection or other he had been given on admission. But according to the consultant it was nothing to do with the hospital. Someone in the pub, it appeared, had intentionally injected him with whatever caused the reaction; concentrated bee venom, the doctor reckoned.

Ralph hadn't been scaremongering after all. The bastards had tried to kill him. What he thought of as his Achilles' heel they could have found out easily enough. Maybe next time they would try something more conventional. And he was in no doubt that they would try again.

The hospital had called in the police, but there was really nothing he could tell them – nothing they would take seriously, at any rate. His only hope lay in Ralph doing the business. He'd still heard nothing and was beginning to fear the worst.

It was mid-morning and Karl could hear the rattle of the refreshment trolley approaching in the corridor outside the small side ward. The doctors demanded complete rest, so his laptop and phone were out of bounds. With no other distractions, minor treats like the morning coffee became focal points in otherwise interminably dreary days.

He sat up and plumped his pillows in anticipation. The trolley trundled through the open doorway, followed by Doris, her coverall matching the cheerful shade of her blue rinse.

"Ey up, mi duck. Y'alright?'

Karl couldn't help but smile. However he felt, it was always a pick-me-up to experience Doris' relentlessly optimistic Derbyshire patois a couple of times every day.

'Coffee is it, luv?'

Karl nodded. Doris filled a cup from a large flask, added a drop of milk, perched a digestive on the saucer and handed it over. As usual, she watched until he took his first sip. It took an effort not to grimace. He hadn't the heart to tell her it was probably the worst coffee he had ever tasted. Happy at the sight of another apparently satisfied customer, Doris gave him a big smile, reversed her trolley expertly and headed out the door.

Karl swigged the rest of his coffee, more for something to do than enjoyment, and considered his immediate future. The nurse had said that morning that he could go home, but only after the consultant had signed him off. He was tied up in surgery with some complex procedure, so Karl would have to wait. But he was getting frantic. Now they were on to him, he knew he was a sitting duck, and the longer he lingered in hospital, the greater the chance that he would never leave. He threw back his blankets and settled himself in the bedside chair, fingers of both hands drumming on the wooden arms. After a few moments, he wandered over to the window.

He was on the eighth floor and the room looked west. There should have been a magnificent view of the hills, but steady rain and thick mist ensured there was no sign. After a couple of minutes' staring into the murk, he turned and headed into the corridor. The coffee had gone right through him and he needed to take a leak. Even though everyone wore one, he felt self-conscious in his hospital gown and was pleased that the toilet was empty. Having done the business, he washed his hands, looking in the mirror as he did so. He didn't look half bad, considering he'd been at death's door just a few days earlier. The rest must have done him good.

As he rounded a corner into his own corridor, he heard the distinctive tones of his consultant, an unfeasibly tall and thin Norwegian of few words. He was bent over, talking down to a man who was tall in his own right but hardly seemed so by comparison.

Karl stopped dead, flabbergasted. 'Ralph!' he shouted out and broke into a trot, shouting again.

Both men turned, the doctor looking miffed at the outburst, but Ralph was beaming. Karl grabbed a bemused Ralph in a man hug, slapping him on the back. 'Jesus, Ralph. I thought I'd seen the last of you.' With his consultant looking on, he felt he couldn't come straight out with the question he wanted an answer to, so he took a tangential approach. 'You look as if you've been in the wars.'

Ralph unconsciously reached up to touch the strapping on his nose. 'You could say that, but you should see the other guy.'

The doctor wrinkled his nose in distaste and marched off without a word.

Karl looked at Ralph, desperate to know what had happened, but at the same time terrified that what he might hear would utterly crush his hopes. Ralph knew this, of course, and said nothing. Instead he just handed Karl a small holdall containing his clothes and belongings. 'We need to go.'

Karl took the bag but didn't move. 'Tell me.'

'Well,' said Ralph, milking the moment for all it was worth. 'It's a long story—'

'Jesus, Ralph.' Karl could stand it no longer. 'What's the deal?'

Ralph couldn't maintain the front . 'We did it, man. We fucking did it.' He gave Karl a slap on the shoulder that almost sent him flying. 'Get dressed. I'll bring you up to speed on the way.'

'Where to?' said Karl, too exhilarated to come up with anything else.

'London. Press conference. Jane will be there too. Come on. Let's move it.'

Minutes later, they walked out of the hospital's main entrance, where two waiting heavies joined them and tagged along a few steps behind. Karl looked suddenly nervous, which made Ralph chortle. 'Don't worry. They're with the good guys.'

Ralph stopped by a black Range Rover with tinted windows and waited for one of the heavies to open the rear door. He gestured for Karl to go ahead, then went around the other side and got in beside him. The two heavies occupied the front seats.

The car set off at speed, heading in the direction of the motorway. The driver keyed in a number on the hands-free and spoke briefly. 'Cargo on board.'

Karl looked across at Ralph with raised eyebrows. 'I guess that's us, then?'

Ralph laughed. 'Well, you, anyway. I'm guessing you haven't seen the news today?' he continued, thrusting in Karl's direction a paper he had been carrying under his arm. 'Read that.'

Karl unfolded the paper and stared, speechless, at the front page. Pride of place was given to a picture of a smiling Ralph in full charm mode, pin-smart in USAF captain's threads, next to it a couple of smaller head shots of Jane and Karl. The page-wide headline – 'Planet Earth Hacked' – said it all. The sub-text was 'President Gort and PM Bannerman implicated in illicit geoengineering plot'.

He looked across at Ralph, noticing that, in addition to the strapping on the nose, one cheek was badly grazed. The grin was still in place, but there was something in the way he held himself – harder, more self-contained – that Karl hadn't noticed before. *Must have been tough,* he thought.

Ralph nodded at the paper, and Karl looked down and began to read.

A LITTLE OVER FOUR HOURS LATER, THE RANGE
Rover pulled off Piccadilly and into the paved courtyard
of Burlington House. Most famously home to the Royal
Academy, the splendidly Palladian building also hosted the
apartments of a number of royally accredited learned societies,
including the Geological Society of London.

Normally filled with tourists, the courtyard was instead
heaving with the world's media. OB vans and cars took up
most of the space, their aerials and satellite dishes thrusting
skywards, seeking connection with audiences across the
planet. The car pulled over to the right, edging into a crowd
of disgruntled reporters and photographers jostling for words
and pictures. A couple more heavies held back the horde, while
a third opened the car door and hustled Ralph and Karl into
the building. It was only a little less crowded inside, and the
small party had to run the gauntlet of another media scrum as
they were led by a flunky down some stairs and into a quiet,
book-lined room in the basement.

At the far end sat a small woman, diminished even more by the huge armchair that held her. Leaning against a table to one side was a pair of crutches. Her left leg was missing below the knee. It took a few seconds for Karl to recognise Jane. She looked ten years older than he remembered, face pale and drawn, long red coat draping a frame that seemed to be wasting away. She was smiling, but it was a smile that didn't reach her eyes. She made to stand, but Karl rushed towards her, arms outstretched, half in greeting, half to stop her rising further.

'Jane!'

She flinched visibly with pain and sat back down just as Karl reached her. 'Fucking leg!' she muttered. Karl bent and folded her in his arms. She gripped him tightly around the neck, trying to squeeze the life out of him, and nestled her face in his chest. He could hear nothing, but he could tell from the way her body shuddered that she was weeping. They were tears of loss, but also of relief at the realisation that, even after all she'd been through, good things could still happen.

Ralph stood next to the pair, shifting uncomfortably and unsure of what to do. After a short time, Jane showed her face and sat upright. There were still tears but a big smile too. Releasing Karl from her grip, she held out her arms to Ralph, who bent forwards and gave himself up to an equally enthusiastic hug.

She looked down at herself. 'Sorry, I'm a bit of a sight. I really hadn't planned to be here, and if my consultant had got his way, I would still be tucked up in bed. I know Ralph didn't think it was a good idea either.' She gave him a significant look.

Ralph looked sheepish and a little hurt. 'I was just thinking of you.'

'I know, Ralph. I'm just joshing,' she said. 'But I thought, why the fuck should the boys have all the fun? In any case, I've seen enough of the inside of a hospital to last me a lifetime. Any respite is fine with me.'

'How long is your pass?' asked Karl.

Jane made a face. 'Just thirty-six hours. I have another op booked in for tomorrow night. Nothing big, tidying up, really. But it's still going to be a while before they let me loose for good. And then there'll be time in rehab to follow.'

Ralph had briefly visited Jane since his return from Diego Garcia, but Karl was acutely aware that he hadn't spoken to her since long before the explosion. He put his hand on hers. 'Jane. I can't tell you how sorry I am. You know, the bomb and...' He wasn't sure how to say it.'

Jane looked at him, her once-bright eyes dull and empty, a part of her missing and gone forever. She took his hand in hers and squeezed it. There really wasn't anything to say.

Jane clapped her hands together. 'Anyway, enough about me. Let's hear it all, Ralph – every sordid detail.'

Ralph sat on the edge of the long, polished oak table that dominated the room, while Karl perched on the arm of Jane's chair.

Ralph had brought Jane up to speed when he visited her in hospital the day before and had given Karl the gist on the way down. But he had been sketchy on the shenanigans over in the Indian Ocean. He scratched at the strapping on his nose, an ever-present itch that reminded him that what seemed like a hellish fantasy had actually happened. He was keen to recount the events, had no choice, but the experience had been – if he were honest – distressing and terrifying, so he started tentatively. It became easier as he got into his stride, and he talked for perhaps half an hour, ending on his meeting with George Chiddingford.

When he had finished there was silence. Then Jane beckoned him over and gave him a kiss and a hug. Karl closed his mouth, which had slowly dropped open as Ralph's narrative reached its climax. 'Fucking hell!'

Ralph acknowledged the sentiment with a grimace and one hand went again, of its own accord, to the strapping on his nose. 'It was touch and go. I was lucky, unbelievably lucky. 'I'm proud of what I accomplished, but not of what happened out there...'

Karl leant forwards and stretched out his hand, and Ralph reciprocated. They shook long and vigorously.

'You should be proud. You did what you had to do. Simple as that.'

'What about Jojo – his son?' said Jane.

'Haven't heard from him, but I reckon it'll be fine. He wasn't implicated and this whole thing has been blown wide open now. What would be the point of hurting his kid?'

'Still,' said Karl, 'a brave man to take the risk he did. It would have been easier to kill you and have done with it.'

Ralph shook his head. 'Jojo's better than that. I always knew. Shouldn't have doubted him, really.' He seemed down, subdued.

No-one spoke as they considered how close to failure Ralph had come.

Karl broke the silence, waving the newspaper that Ralph had given him in the car. 'This – the level of detail – in just a couple of days. It's incredible.'

Back on easier ground, Ralph visibly relaxed. 'I know. I can't believe it myself. I went to *The Guardian* because I know this is their sort of thing. I insisted to George that I wanted simultaneous publication in the UK and US, but I never imagined anything like this.'

Jane intervened. 'But how did they dig this deep so quickly?'

'They've done this sort of thing before, many times, and George is an old hand. Once the International Consortium of Investigative Journalists got their claws into it, things just got crazy. In the end the story went out on more than a hundred news outlets at the same time.'

Karl rifled through the pages. 'But the depth of detail here is staggering.'

'Well, the academics really came up trumps, dropped everything once I got the samples to them. There's really no arguing with their conclusions.'

'But there's so much on the seeding operation too,' said Jane.

'Turns out,' said Ralph, 'that the smokescreen was actually pretty thin.'

Karl chuckled at that. 'Must have been if we cracked it.' Ralph and Jane joined in.

'It helped too, that the minute it looked like things might go pear-shaped, some of the bad guys started coming out of the woodwork. This Petrie, who put the idea to Gort and handled the science, especially. Seems like he would say or do anything to save his own skin.'

'Gort!' spat Jane. 'A real nasty piece of work. No surprise there at all. But Bannerman? I was staggered when I heard. I knew him quite well, taught his nephew. Remember when he was elected? It was like he was the new Messiah. I knew things weren't working out for him, but I couldn't believe he would get involved with something like this.'

Ralph shrugged. 'From what I've heard, he got the Jojo treatment. He was made an offer he found impossible to refuse.'

Jane frowned. 'Well, it does explain a very odd encounter I had with him after a meeting of the Climate Impacts Task Force back in the spring.'

Ralph and Karl both raised eyebrows.

'He asked me to stay for a chat afterwards. Just the two of us. He apologised for abandoning the leave it in the ground movement and for not doing more to get emissions down, seemed to be clutching at straws. He raised geoengineering as a potential alternative and I told him what he could do with the whole idea. Skyseed would already have been up and running, so I can only think he was hoping – without giving anything away – for some tacit justification of his actions.'

Karl blew out his cheeks. 'Wow. If only he'd listened to you, but I guess by then it must have been too late.'

'The real surprise,' said Ralph, 'is how few people were in on it. Maybe a hundred or so in the US and only a dozen here in the UK. The rest of the government knew fuck all.'

'So, where do we go from here?' wondered Karl.

'Well,' said Ralph, 'Bannerman is already in custody. They're calling it house arrest – supposedly for his own protection. Gort's still toughing it out, but I can't see either of them surviving. And there's more to come out,' he continued. 'I'm certain of that. The security services are all over it, here and in the US. Once their hackers have finished with the Skyseed files, we'll see the plan laid bare in all its flawed lunacy. And then comes the payback. People are talking impeachment on both sides of the pond, and that's the least Gort and Bannerman deserve.'

Jane was furious, shaking. 'They should jail the fuckers and throw away the key. Even that would be too good for them.'

'It may come to that yet,' said Ralph.

Again there was silence. Jane took a deep breath, visibly trying to pull herself together. Ralph looked down at his hands, mind elsewhere, all of a sudden looking drained.

Karl was beginning to feel a bit peeved at the downbeat atmosphere. Surely they should be celebrating? 'Look on the bright side, dudes. Skyseed is dead in the water, the bad guys are bang to rights and everyone lives happily ever after.'

Jane looked at Ralph, who avoided her stare. No-one said a word.

Karl looked from one to the other. 'What?'

Ralph shifted uncomfortably in his chair. 'Not quite, I'm afraid. Jane – do you want to explain?'

Her body language said, Not really, but she knew she had no choice.

She took a deep breath. 'Hard to believe, I know, but there's actually a fair bit of support for Skyseed.' She watched Karl's eyes open wide in astonishment. 'Not explicit, of course, but mutterings behind the scenes.'

Karl couldn't keep quiet. 'You're fucking joking!'

'Not at all,' Jane continued. 'The idea of hacking our way out of the climate breakdown crisis has been growing for quite a while. The reasoning in some quarters is, OK, so the clandestine way it was done was wrong, but the idea was a good one, so why not keep going?'

Ralph couldn't hold back. 'But they don't know what we know.'

Jane looked across at him in exasperation. *For God's sake. If you want me to explain, let me get on with it,* her expression said.

What she actually said was, 'Ralph's right. Petrie sang like a canary, as they apparently used to say in old gangster movies. And it wasn't a very nice song.'

'Tell me.' Karl thought he knew what was coming.

'Skyseed worked. Trouble is, it worked too well.'

'Shit!' said Karl. She didn't need to explain further. 'How bad?'

'We have no idea. Petrie and his team calculated the bot population they would need to get atmospheric carbon levels down to a safe 350ppm. They took into account the average dust loading to work out how much raw material would be available to the bots, and how quickly and for how long they could replicate.'

'Good luck with that,' said Karl. Jane nodded in agreement. 'They were playing with ballpark figures and would probably have been way out anyway. But something else happened.'

A light came on in Karl's head. 'Dear God! Uturuncu!'

Ralph felt he had been quiet too long and again risked Jane's ire. 'The atmosphere was swamped with the ash, as much raw material as the bots could handle – and some.'

'So,' continued Jane, 'the bots are replicating out of control and carbon levels are plummeting. Petrie knew this weeks ago. It's why the planes were grounded when Ralph arrived on Diego Garcia.'

Karl was utterly defeated; from elation to deflation in less than an hour. 'So, what are the figures?'

'At the moment,' said Jane, 'carbon levels are falling by a little more than half of 1ppm a week, but bot concentrations in samples are increasing rapidly and there's still one hell of a lot of ash up there. In the next couple of years we could see double that.'

Karl was incredulous. 'That's getting on for 50ppm a year.'

Jane and Ralph nodded in unison.

'Jesus Christ.'

'As you know, most of the ash that hasn't been used by the bots will have settled out after a couple of years, but by then it might be too late.'

Ralph intervened for a third time. 'Do you know how Petrie said they referred to the project amongst themselves?'

This is new, thought Jane. 'It wasn't Skyseed, then?'

'Officially, yes. But most of the time they referred to it as "the fix".'

Karl was unimpressed. '*Fuck-up*, more like, '*to end all fuck-ups*'. He shook his head in disbelief. It seemed all they had accomplished had been for nothing. But then, surely something could be done? He voiced the question.

'Well. Hardly surprisingly,' said Jane, 'there's not much appetite for another bash at a technofix, so the only way forward is to chuck as much carbon into the atmosphere as possible as quickly as we can – recarbonation.'

Karl flagged up the obvious flaw. 'Won't the bots soak it all up?'

'As the Uturuncu ash settles out, it's expected that the reduction in raw material will slow replication rates so that bot numbers will start to fall. The hope is that carbon levels can be pushed up quicker than the bots can pull it out of the atmosphere. But it's a suck-it-and-see approach, really. No-one's done the maths yet.'

'Are there any concrete plans to get this recarbonation push going?' said Karl.

'The government invited me onto the COBRA committee addressing the issue,' said Jane. 'I was wired in remotely to the first meeting this morning, so I'm in the loop. I have to admit I was surprised to see politicians actually listening for a change – really listening. Bannerman's out of the picture, of course, but it didn't take too much to convince the rest of the higher-ups that nothing less than a war footing would have any chance of success. The plan is that heads of state will get together in Paris sometime next month to sign an emergency agreement fixing national targets for dumping carbon into the atmosphere.'

Ralph put his head back and guffawed. 'You have to laugh, don't you? God, the irony of it! All that time and effort cajoling and threatening countries to slash carbon emissions, now they probably can't pollute enough.'

'What sort of measures are we talking here?' Karl wanted to know.

'Anything goes, really,' said Jane, 'as long as it pumps out carbon. It'll be a return to the good old days, smoking chimneys, steam engines, smog you can cut with a knife, the lot.'

'Victorian England without the frock coats,' mused Karl.' He had always loved steam, and the thought of its return to the railways provided a crumb of comfort amongst the gloom.

Jane went on, 'Coal is the dirtiest of the hydrocarbons, so a priority has to be burning coal, and as much of it as we can dig out. Uneconomic mines will need to be reopened, and open-cast extraction prioritised so that it can be excavated as quickly as possible. It's going to make one hell of a mess of the environment. Mothballed coal-burning power plants will have to be brought back online and new ones commissioned – lots of them. It's the death knell for renewables – electric cars too. I've heard that cars will be required to meet new high pollution levels.'

Karl shook his head. 'Jesus, the coal and oil company bosses must be pinching themselves. A few weeks back people wanted them locked up.'

For a time they were silent, deep in their own thoughts. *We have to face it*, Karl brooded. *Despite everything that's happened, we've failed to fix the fix.* They hadn't nipped Skyseed in the bud. Instead it had blossomed, casting far and wide an insidious shadow with the potential to bring civilisation to its knees.

He stood and looked out at the crowds passing by. A little girl stopped and bent down to look into the basement window, which was partly below street level, before her mum pulled her away. Karl felt rage building at the injustice of it all, eating away at his insides, looking for a way out. She and billions like her – blameless people, living ordinary lives – knew next to nothing of the climate bombshell that looked like tearing their reality apart. In ignorance and optimism, they made plans for a future that could now be consigned to the past, for a world that they and their children might never see.

Karl turned as the door opened to reveal an innocuous-looking man attired in rumpled grey, accompanied by a pair of heavies in dark suits. Ralph stood to greet the newcomer. 'Jane, Karl. May I present George Chiddingford.' They nodded in concert at the newcomer. 'He's the man you have to thank for all this.'

George held up a hand, as if to say it was nothing. Then: 'We're ready, if you are?'

Karl made to help Jane up out of the chair and pass her crutches. But she had already become quite adept at getting around on her own and shrugged him off with some irritation. She swung her way over to the door and followed one of the heavies through. Karl and Ralph went next, George and the second heavy bringing up the rear.

As they climbed the stairs to the conference room, Karl nodded in the direction of the man mountain leading the way and whispered to Ralph, 'Who are all these gorillas? Special Branch? MI5?'

Ralph laughed and shook his head. 'Far from it. Ex-rugby players. George used to be sports editor in his early days. He called in a favour from an old All Blacks friend who set up a security company in the UK when he retired. Wouldn't want to get on the wrong side of one of these guys, would you?'

Karl was still checking out the one in front and wondering how it was possible to get a neck that was wider than your head. 'Indeed not,' he affirmed.

The party had to run the gauntlet of a sea of journos just to reach the door of the small lecture theatre that was doubling up for the afternoon as a news conference venue. Inside it was packed solid, with no room even to stand. At the back, a forest of television cameras crowded out everything else, cables meandering to a jungle of mics at the front. Jane knew the current society President and had called in a favour or two to get George the room at short notice, but he had clearly underestimated the expected number of journalists by an order of magnitude or even more. Karl suspected that health and safety regs had gone out of the window for the day and hated to think what would happen if there were a fire.

The party made slow passage to a row of tables that had been squeezed onto the small dais at the front. Jane, Ralph and Karl shoehorned themselves into the three chairs, while George – who was chairing the event – made for the lectern.

Rather him than me, thought Ralph. The two heavies stood at the back of the dais, bookending the scene. Standing with arms folded and faces grim, Jane felt they set just the right tone for what was to come. She looked out on a sea of faces, quiet now in expectation. The news was out, had been for several hours, but words and data could only convey so much. Now, all the world and its dog wanted more, the human angle, the lowdown, the dirt. She became aware, suddenly, that the proceedings were up and running, and that the first question had been directed at her. Momentarily, she felt panicked, couldn't speak. She was abruptly aware that the eyes of everyone in the room, and beyond, were upon her and felt sick inside. She wished she was far, far away, but at the same time, she was desperate to tell her part of the Skyseed story. She imagined Ali sitting in the front row, giving her an encouraging smile, as he always had on the rare occasions he sat in on her talks. It helped. She took a deep breath and began to speak.

It was Jane's first week home after months in hospital. She sat at the kitchen table and looked out of the French doors at the whirling leaves in the small courtyard garden. It was late autumn and an easterly gale was working hard at stripping bare the walnut tree in the far corner.

A mug of instant coffee stood untouched at her elbow and her hand clutched a sheaf of unread papers. She would be back in the lab soon and had a huge backlog that required attention. She needed to focus, but her thoughts could never reach beyond an image of a burning car on a sunny summer morning. The blast that sent her crashing into the wall of the house had knocked her senseless, but she had briefly regained consciousness before sinking once more into a darkness from which she didn't emerge for more than a month. What she saw in those few moments of awareness would never leave her. Although the bomb hadn't killed her, she felt that it had – to all intents and purposes – ended her life. No-one could see their child die like that and continue as before.

She tried to pull herself together, gulping a couple of mouthfuls of cold coffee and laying out some data printouts in front of her on the table. *Maybe*, she thought, *heading into the lab would help me concentrate.* Not to forget – never to forget – but to nudge the horrific experience a little further towards the back of her mind. The doctors had said she needed to give it another week before heading back, but what the hell! Another day alone at home and she swore she would go mad.

That afternoon, she discovered – not entirely to her surprise – that being back in the lab wasn't much better. She sat at her laptop, physically there but mentally absent, the events leading up to the explosion churning over and over in her mind. She couldn't help but wonder if there was anything she could have done differently. And – justified or not – there was the guilt. If only she'd cried off the opportunity to take a look at Karl's samples. If only they had been out of the country on that holiday she had booked – and then had to cancel. If only she had refused to have Dan Mitchell foisted on her team. Because, of course, it was Dan. When she came out of her coma, the police had told her that he had vanished the night before the blast. Their investigations had drawn a blank, the RAF denying any knowledge of a captain of that name.

And it became apparent, too, that she hadn't been the only one to be targeted. Others deemed to have been a threat to Skyseed had paid the ultimate price. More than anything, she wished that she had too, if it meant that Ali would still be alive.

To try and cheer herself up, she picked up fish and chips on the way home and ate them in the kitchen from the paper. It had turned bitterly cold and the forecast said there was snow on the way. She turned on the small television on the worktop for the news. There was really only one story – the Paris recarbonation agreement, which would take effect immediately. The battle to save the planet was up and running.

Not, this time, from overheating, but from turning rapidly into a frozen wasteland. Perhaps it was her mood, or maybe an educated hunch, but she couldn't help feeling that the whole thing was futile. She had almost said as much at the last COBRA meeting, which she had joined remotely from her rehab unit, but had managed to bite her lip.

Suddenly she was exhausted. More so, even, than during the months she had spent bed-bound in the hospital. It was barely seven thirty, but she turned off the television and hauled herself up the stairs, her stump hurting like hell under the prosthetic. She paused outside the door to Ali's room. She hadn't entered since that summer morning, hadn't dared. But now she steeled herself and turned the handle. The curtains were still drawn, so she switched on the light then went in. Ali's signature tang struck her like a sledgehammer, overwhelming her with a tsunami of memories. She breathed in deeply and closed her eyes, myriad pictures of the good times jostling in her mind for attention.

After a while she opened them and looked around. She understood that the police had given the place a once-over after the blast, but otherwise she guessed it was exactly as Ali had left it on the final morning of his life. The bed was unmade, the duvet trailing half onto the polished wooden floorboards. On the battered roll-top desk that she had bought for him when he started big school was his driving test certificate, along with a half-eaten packet of mints and a couple of used coffee mugs. A pair of jeans and a shirt lay in a crumpled heap on the chair, three odd dirty socks scattered beneath. The walls were plastered with photos, drawings and certificates, some going back to primary school. On the windowsill was Blue Ted, the soft toy gifted by a close friend to Ali on the day he was born. One eye was gone now and an arm hung by a thread, but she knew that, even in Ali's late teens, he had remained a cherished keepsake.

Her breath caught in her throat at the sight and her eyes filled. The pain was indescribable, unbearable. She gulped air and tried to calm herself. Since regaining consciousness, she had managed to keep her anguish in check. A tear or two had leaked out at the funeral, and when she met up with Karl and Ralph, but that was about it. She had been determined not to let go. If she did, she had felt that it would be tantamount to accepting that Ali was gone – forever – and she hadn't been ready for that, until now.

She lay down on the bed, curled herself into a ball and pulled the duvet over her head. Ali's lingering fragrance enveloped her and drew out her grief in heaving sobs that continued until, utterly drained, she let welcome oblivion take her.

MARCH 2029
WASHINGTON DC
UNITED STATES

GORT HADN'T SLEPT AT ALL. HER CONVICTION IN the Senate had happened late the previous evening. Now she lay alone in her White House bedroom, a disgraced private citizen no longer protected from the law by her position.

Events had moved so fast since Skyseed was exposed, every day bringing some new bombshell. Her administration had done everything in its gift to obfuscate and bewilder, used every piece of legislative machinery it could to place obstacles in the way of those trying to get at the truth. But it had all come to nothing. Too many of those involved in the plot had jumped at the first opportunity, turning state evidence in return for immunity. Gort was left high and dry, along with those too loyal or too slow-witted to desert the sinking ship.

Despite a savage rearguard action by the most extreme element of the Republican right, President Gort was impeached by the House of Representatives four months after the conspiracy was laid bare. By the time she faced trial before the Senate, she was haemorrhaging support, and it took just three weeks for them to vote on her future. By an overwhelming majority, the Senate determined – for the first time in its history – to send the country's head of state packing.

After battling impeachment and conviction for so long, it felt like the end, but she knew that this was just the start of her problems. Now she faced an even bigger fight, for her freedom and, quite possibly, her life. She could see the first grey light of dawn diffusing around the edges of the thick drapes that covered the tall windows of the Presidential bedroom. *Almost certainly*, she thought, *the early light of my last day in the White House.*

Pulling back the bedclothes, she crossed over to the ensuite and retrieved her bathrobe from behind the door. As she knotted the belt around her waist, she heard footsteps approaching, several people walking in unison and with purpose. It was what she had been expecting, dreading. She composed herself and with her hands, smoothed out the folds in her white robe. Chin raised in defiance, expression suitably disdainful, ex-President Gort turned to face the double doors.

PART TWO

RETRIBUTION

MOLLY PATTERSON'S LIFE HAD BEEN ONE CONTINUAL rebellion, a fight against an establishment that she saw as irrational and evil, even if few others did. Greenham Common, the Battle of Orgreave, Stop the War, the People's Climate March, Occupy London, Extinction Rebellion and more. The list was long. Molly was nearly sixty, had avoided relationships, forsaken kids, never owned a house. Forty years of squats, tents and sofas, and where had it got her? The world was still a pile of crap and the parasite elites had tightened their grip even more, squeezing the life out of the people and the planet. She felt as if everything she had done had been for nothing. Forget chaos theory. Her existence had even less impact than the flutter of a butterfly's wing. If she had never existed, she was certain the world would trundle on without changing one jot and with no-one the wiser. Well, enough was enough. This time it would be different. This time everyone would sit up and take notice.

It was just before nine on an icy morning in late spring. The night had been clear and bitterly cold, but snow clouds had flooded in from the east at dawn, and now the sky was white with whirling flakes. She shivered as she peered through the grubby window of her freezing room on the garret floor of the tenement block. The tallest rooftops, she saw, and beyond them the ancient volcanic crags of Arthur's Seat, already had a covering of white.

The hiss of a boiling kettle drew her attention and, crossing to the ramshackle kitchen, she lifted it from the single gas ring. Filling a mug, she dunked a tea bag for a few seconds – there was no milk – and took it through into the bedsit. Everything was laid out on the rickety table, which – with a single chair and a bed – made up the only furniture in the damp-patched room. Slurping her tea, and grimacing at the absence of sugar, she checked things over one last time. Hooded fleece, jam sandwiches wrapped in foil, bottle of tap water, a couple of blagged fags, tram fare's worth of loose change, Webley Mark VI handgun – loaded.

She picked up the Second World War service revolver gingerly. It used to be her father's and she'd handled it countless times before, as a young kid playing cowboys and Indians, and later, Starsky and Hutch with her brother. Now, though – at the other end of her life story – it felt different, felt what it was. Plaything no longer, a lethal weapon.

Her father had always kept it in perfect nick, and when she had unearthed it from amongst her mother's few keepsakes, after her death a year earlier, it was still in working order. All it had needed was a bit of a clean and a dash of oil. There was no ammunition, but that hadn't proved to be a problem. She had been astonished at how easy it was to buy the .455 bullets online, no questions asked. She had gone for just three, based upon the premise that she would probably not be granted the time to fire any more. This wasn't an escapade she expected to survive.

She finished up her tea and returned to the kitchen, rinsing the cup and leaving it to drain. The small act made her smile. Habits were so hard to break, even at death's door. Heading back to the bedsit, she put on the red fleece and zipped the Webley into an inside compartment. It was a tight squeeze, but she felt happier with it there than in an open outside pocket. She packed everything else into a battered, olive brown backpack. For three decades it had been her constant companion. More than that, her lifeboat, her ark. For long periods, it had held her every possession.

She shouldered the pack, her gaze sweeping the room one last time. It left her feeling bleak. This was it. All she had to show for nigh on sixty years. If she hadn't been certain earlier, she was now. Time for the big finale.

She locked the door – habit again – and made her way down the eight flights to the ground floor. She pressed the button to let herself out of the front door and headed down another short flight of stone steps to the road. She stopped to put her hood up and shivered in the chill air. The snow was thicker than ever and the gusting east wind sliced right through the thin fleece.

A grim day for the Grim Reaper, she thought with a wry smile. Turning right, she lowered her head against the strengthening blizzard and set off for the tram stop.

Duncan felt odd being out and about. Once the Skyseed plot had been exposed, his fall from grace had been breakneck. Incarcerated – for his own protection they insisted – impeached by parliament, sacked as an MP, temporarily imprisoned on the basis of an international arrest warrant and interrogated for seventy-two hours.

His lawyers had eventually managed to get him bailed on the premise of deteriorating mental health, which – he had to admit – wasn't entirely fabricated. Anyway, it wasn't as if he could have absconded. Not with one of the most infamous faces on the planet. Once out, he had closeted himself away – along with Jeremy and the cats – in a small country house in Devon, made available by a loyal friend. One of the very few. And, almost seven years on, he was still there.

He had ranted about the injustice of it in an article in the press a week or so earlier. His first foray into the media since he was forced out. If he had thought public sentiment might have lightened up in the intervening period, he was soon dissuaded otherwise. The article had brought across-the-board condemnation, the general feeling seeming to be that he was lucky not to have been hung, drawn and quartered on the spot. The use of the term glacial in his description of the pace of international justice probably hadn't helped. Duncan had been knocked back by the ferocity of the response and determined to keep the lowest of low profiles in advance of the final stages of the trial at The Hague, whenever the hell that would be. The rumour was that the verdicts would be announced in the autumn, but they had been postponed on four occasions, so he wasn't holding his breath.

Nonetheless, the wedding was a long-standing engagement, and he was damned if he was going to renege. Jason had a been a friend since school and both had followed parallel careers in the party. Untainted by Skyseed, he still held the seat next door to Duncan's old constituency of Edinburgh East, and he was tipped by some as a future party leader, even PM, God help him. Duncan gazed out of the window as the car slowly negotiated the cobbled surface made slippery by the snow. The number of homeless people was soul-destroying, almost every doorway sheltering individuals or families bundled up against the bitter cold. They were opening new camps every week, but still it was impossible to keep up with the numbers of refugees abandoning the snowbound highland communities. The car swerved to avoid a young man lying face down in the road – dead, unconscious or plain drunk, it was impossible to tell.

The ceremony was at the castle, the battlements and towers of which Duncan could just make out through the driving snow. It was not far from his old stamping ground, so he had expected to be met both by old friends and long-standing enemies. He was not to be disappointed. As the car slowed amongst the accumulated slush at the top of the Royal Mile, it was brought close to a standstill by the press of muffled-up protestors; going by the piercings and placard slogans, a cocktail of tree huggers, eco-freaks and pissed-off constituents. Before the too-few police could get a grip, the armoured windows of the Range Rover came under attack – to little effect – from pounding fists. The spit flecks and mouthed obscenities never made it through the polycarbonate toughened glass, but the waves of malice and hatred did. Duncan had run the gauntlet of many a protesting mob, but this singular outpouring of venom made him feel suddenly aware of his vulnerability.

His position as head of state had always bolstered a certain chutzpah in the face of animosity, but no longer. As public enemy number one, all he felt now was unease and a deep foreboding. He tried not to look at the tableau of enraged faces, but it seemed to draw his gaze like a moth to a flame. Despite the chill, he felt hot. Tiny drops of sweat stood out on his forehead, and he ran a finger around the inside of his collar to try and cool down. He glanced across at Jeremy, who was staring straight ahead, calm and unruffled as ever – or so it seemed. Duncan knew that the years since Skyseed's unravelling had taken their toll on his husband. The concealer didn't quite hide the bags under the eyes. His already gaunt face appeared even thinner, and there were more streaks of grey in his meticulously styled brown locks. Somehow sensing Duncan's scrutiny, Jeremy turned and gave him a reassuring smile, but it never reached his startlingly green eyes, which only reflected Duncan's feeling of wretchedness.

In the front passenger seat, Harry swore under his breath and muttered into a radio. All former prime ministers were honoured with protection for life, even disgraced ones, Duncan had been relieved to discover. But he seemed to have been furnished grudgingly with the basic model – Harry.

Presumably in response to Harry's urging, half a dozen more constables arrived to add weight to those already involved in a battle of wills and wits with the demonstrators. Despite slipping and sliding on the snow, they managed, momentarily, to open a wide-enough gap for the car, and Jamie, Duncan's young driver, needed no further invitation. With a triumphant, 'All right!', he put on a burst of speed and surged through, splashing police and protestor alike with a spray of slush, before throttling back and heading at a more sedate pace across the icy parade ground.

A small, frozen-looking reception committee was gathered at the castle's entrance. Duncan could see Jason waving. The shock of black hair and the colourful Gillespie tartan of his kilt made him hard to miss. There was no sign of Cara, who, Duncan assumed, was circling in a holding pattern somewhere close by. He smiled as he imagined the language that must be turning the bridal carriage blue. Patience had never been one of Cara's strong points.

Behind Jason, Duncan noticed, with more than a little irritation, that quite a crowd had gathered. Held back by temporary metal barriers and a handful of police officers, there were a few dozen well-wishers and an almost equal number of journalists and photographers.

Wide smile of relief on his face, Jason opened the door and helped Duncan out, pumping his hand vigorously and slapping him on the back. 'Thank Christ. I thought we were going to have to go ahead without you. Cara would have killed me.' Duncan grinned. 'You know me, Jason. Bad penny and all that.'

Jason was still holding Duncan's hand. 'Aye, well, it's good to see you. You're looking braw. You know… considering…' His voice faltered. It was the first time they had talked in person since Duncan's fall from power. Duncan was quick to spare his friend embarrassment. 'That's kind of you, Jason. Now, today's all about you – you and Cara – let's keep it that way.'

Jason greeted Jeremy warmly and nodded to Harry. After a little more small talk, Duncan stretched out his arms and herded the others towards the castle entrance. He studiously ignored the barrage of questions from the media and turned away from the volley of camera flashes. He waved to the small and motley collection of well-wishers, surprised that any of the species still existed. A thin, straggle-haired woman in a red fleece holding something out towards him caught his attention. At first, he thought it was a pen for an autograph, then he looked in her eyes and knew it wasn't a pen. Harry must have spotted the threat at exactly the same moment, because he screamed, 'Down,' and went for his gun, but too late.

The first bullet pierced Duncan's abdomen. The pain was indescribable. But the bullet's work was not yet done. It still had sufficient velocity to exit his back and strike Jeremy, who was standing immediately behind him, passing close to the right atrium of his heart. The organ fibrillated for a few seconds before stopping altogether. The second bullet was deflected upwards by Duncan's left scapula. It escaped his body at the shoulder and entered again just below the jawline, burrowing into the brain and lodging deep in the cerebellum.

A millisecond after Molly fired the second shot, a small hole appeared in the centre of her forehead. She crumpled to the ground like a puppet whose strings had been cut, her expression a mixture of triumph and relief.

IN BETTER WEATHER AND DIFFERENT CIRCUMSTANCES, Karl would have enjoyed his stroll along the sandy beach at Scheveningen. As it was he was utterly despondent. It was just over a week since he and Jane had met up in London, and her words were a constant companion. Full ice-age conditions within fifty years – maybe sooner. Not for the first time, he felt sick at the thought. An icy wind off the North Sea carried with it a soaking mixture of horizontal sleet and spume from the incoming tide, but he barely noticed.

Later that day, the three judges at the International Criminal Court, a few miles up the road, would hand down their verdict on the Skyseed conspirators – or at least those at the top of the tree. But the prospects for Gort and the others was not the reason for his wretchedness. Karl had no doubt that they would be found guilty and, to be honest, he had no interest in what happened after that. They could throw away the key as far as he was concerned.

Whatever retribution the plotters faced, it could never match the crime. No punishment could ever be harsh enough for those guilty of bringing about global mayhem and quite possibly the end of civilisation. Because that's what the fall-out of the Skyseeder's meddling seemed likely to accomplish. Only now were the dire consequences of their fuck-up becoming clear to the world at large, and it was impossible to feel anything other than despair at the way things were going.

When the Skyseed revelations exploded upon an unsuspecting world, the reaction was ambivalent. On the one hand, the conspirators were universally condemned for the clandestine and murderous way they had gone about their business, and their arrests were cheered across the board. On the other, a fair number of voices were raised in support of the idea of engineering our way out of climate breakdown. For these, it was simply a matter of right end, wrong means.

But that was seven years ago, when the general perception was that Skyseed's tinkering would likely make our planet a little cooler rather than a lot hotter. Mildly irritating for the sun-seekers, but no big deal.

It took a while for the reality to leak out, as monitoring and analysis of atmospheric carbon levels, nanobot concentrations and replication rates began to paint a far more alarming picture.

The public remained blissfully unaware of the likely endgame – the relentless march of the ice from its polar fastnesses – but what many were already experiencing was bad enough. As global temperatures plunged, harvests failed, and freeze and famine brought about mass migration, civil unrest and war, it didn't take long for it to dawn on people that Skyseed's legacy was something far worse than a bit of a chill. Seven years on, then, the depth of feeling against Gort and her cronies was such that they would be torn apart if they ever left the sanctuary of their cells. The shooting of Bannerman earlier in the year provided testimony to that.

Karl looked up and saw that he had almost reached the pier, a twentieth-century concoction of steel and wood, far removed from the Victorian delights of his childhood holidays around the English coast. Barring some idiot in a wetsuit splashing about in the freezing waters, and a well-dressed woman taking her yappy hound for its morning constitutional, there was no-one about. He looked at his watch. It was still only eight in the morning. He had been unable to sleep so had left the small guest house close to the seafront before six to get some air and do some thinking. The judgement wasn't due until the late afternoon, so there was plenty of time to kill. Too much time. What he needed was something to take his mind off the world and its troubles. Mentally he shook himself. Breakfast! That would be a start, anyway. He turned on his heel and headed back the way he had come, eventually climbing some steps onto the promenade. Despite the depressing weather, all the cafés were open, although few were optimistic enough to have tables and chairs outside. Too big a choice made picking somewhere difficult, but, true to character, Karl avoided the more tourist-oriented emporia and plumped for a small, seedy-looking establishment on the corner of a side street. His mood cried out for comfort food, a craving that was satisfied by a plate of waffles topped with fruit, maple syrup and whipped cream. He could feel his waistband protesting at every forkful, but what the hell.

Suitably sated, he sat back, sipped his coffee and checked his phone for messages. There was nothing from Jane or Ralph. Jane's plane was due to land at Schiphol mid-morning, so she was probably still fighting her way through Heathrow security. Ralph had arrived in the Netherlands from the US a couple of days earlier but had been tied up non-stop with the world's media, who were swarming all over The Hague in readiness for the verdict. Every hotel bed had been booked up for months, which was why he was stuck out in the back of beyond. Ralph – the lucky bastard – was shacked up in the five-star Hotel des Indes, everything paid for by CNN. He had no idea where Jane was staying, neither did she, probably. Forward-planning wasn't really her thing.

He ordered another coffee and let his mind wander, something it had been doing a great deal of since the Skyseed revelations. He would be the first to admit that he had been treading water for close on seven years. For much of the time, the limelight had fallen on Ralph, as hero, and Jane – as victim and key member of the scientific advisory group of the new Recarbonation Commission, so he had been able to lie low and get on with his day job, except that his heart and soul weren't really in it.

Increasingly, there didn't seem much point. Drawers of samples were closed and untouched, the papers and articles had dried up, and he trolled out the same old lectures year on year, no updates, no enthusiasm, the line of least resistance. What had once been a joy was now a chore. The fact that he had been going through the motions had not gone unnoticed either, and in this day of academic metrics – papers published, citations accumulated, research grants won – that meant his career was on the line. He'd already had a number of increasingly acrimonious run-ins with the head of department, and the dean had called him in and muttered into his beard something about dead weight and the upcoming Research Excellence Framework evaluation. It was as close as the self-conscious old gimmer would ever get to warning that if he didn't pull his socks up they might have to 'let him go' – as if he were desperate to escape the place. If he thought about it, that might not be a bad idea. Maybe a change of scenery might give him the kick up the arse he needed, although, the way he felt about things at the moment, it would need to be one hell of a kick.

If he was honest, he'd had enough of lying low, calming as it had been initially. Now he was happy to admit that he was feeling out of the loop. Ralph, in the US, and Jane, in the UK, were heavily involved in monitoring and fighting the Skyseeder's awful legacy. He, meanwhile, was pissing around in some northern backwater, half-heartedly tinkering with research that no-one gave a shit about any longer , and that had little relevance in a world that had far more urgent priorities.

Karl's musings were ended abruptly by the loud arrival of a large group of teenagers, who took up most of rest of the small café. He sighed. Time to go. After paying for breakfast he headed back to the guest house to grab his daysack. He had imbibed sufficient ozone for the time being, and suddenly felt the need to be where the action was. The International Criminal Court was just down the road in Scheveningen itself, but it was far too early to turn up. Instead, he would head into The Hague and potter for a few hours, have lunch and try to meet up with the others. He couldn't be arsed with the buses so asked Maria, the young Polish girl in reception, to book him a cab. He hadn't been entirely convinced that her mix of pigeon English and double Dutch was sufficiently coherent to get the message across to the cab company, and was mildly surprised when a car chugged around the corner ten minutes later.

October 2035
The Hague
The Netherlands

THE SHORT JOURNEY TO THE CITY CENTRE WAS
pleasantly relaxing, if malodorous. Like many big cities,
The Hague had adapted much of its public transport stock
and cabs to burn coal. It had last been widely adopted in
Europe and Japan during the Second World War, when
petrol was scarce. Now, though, it was simply a means to
ramping up carbon levels and ensuring the country met its
emissions obligations. It did nothing for air quality, but this
was no longer a priority. Neither was it pretty, with vehicles
having large stoves strapped to their rears, together with all
paraphernalia that converted the gases formed by burning
to liquid that could be fed into the carburettor. Leaving the
sea behind, the route followed small roads lined with rows
of compact modern houses, neat and well-kept, but veneered
now in coal dust and diesel residues. There was still plenty of
greenery – much of it looking the worse for wear in the filthy
air and, inevitably, canals. Karl had been to the Netherlands on
a number of occasions, so the swarms of cyclists, faces masked

against the pollution and the sleet, were expected. He was always impressed by the happy coexistence of motorists and cyclists on Dutch roads. In the UK, the prevailing relationship between the two tribes was best described as an uneasy truce.

The cab coughed to a halt and dropped Karl at the Hofvijfer, a rectangular lake with a fountain and a small, tree-covered island. Most of the lake carried a meniscus of ice, too thin to skate on but perfect for watching the comical antics of ducks as they touched down. Dominating one side of the lake was the Binnenhof, the turreted and cloistered gothic pile that now housed the Dutch Parliament and Prime Minister's office. The sun had made a welcome appearance, taking the edge off the freezing air and bringing out the dog walkers and duck feeders.

He spent an agreeable couple of hours admiring the fairy-tale architecture from without and – where possible – within, before visiting the nearby Mauritshuis art gallery. An overload of Holbein and Vermeer saw him seated at a small café overlooking the lake, where he ordered a coffee and settled down to savour the sights and sounds. The place was busy now, tourists and parties of school kids mixing with civil servants beetling with intent from one government building to another, office workers on their breaks soaking up the weak rays of a bot-veiled sun. All seemed right with the world, but of course it wasn't.

Try as he might, he couldn't scorn the shadow that fell across everything now. How could there be any fun, any enjoyment, knowing that things were starting to fall apart? He couldn't help but view everything through the lens of a world on a path to anarchy and societal breakdown. *This*, he thought, *must be what it is like to have a terminal illness.* He watched a young dad lift up his giggling toddler son and perch him on his shoulders, and tried to put to the back of his mind uninvited images of the bloated stomachs of starving children.

Swearing under his breath, he checked his phone and was buoyed to see a text from Jane. Her flight had landed early and she was about to get on a train. If he was free, she suggested, maybe he could meet her at the station. Then they could grab some lunch and head across to the court together. He looked at his watch. He had half an hour to get to the station, and it wasn't far. Plenty of time to walk. He downed the dregs of his espresso, donned his face mask against the filthy exhaust of the traffic and headed east.

At Den Haag Central station, he sat on a bench close to the platform exit and watched the hustle and bustle, eager to see Jane's familiar figure. He had always been a bit of a railway buff, and it was a treat to watch the blue and yellow double-decker trains that worked the line from Schiphol airport to the capital. The Dutch used to trumpet the fact that their trains were powered entirely by wind-generated electricity, but that was in another world. They hadn't the UK's legacy of steam, so the engines had been adapted to run on the dirtiest diesel, the stench of which permeated the concourse. The double-deckers were absent from British railways due to the fact that the network's ancient tunnels were too small. That was the problem with being a trailblazer. In time, others learnt from your mistakes and moved on. *A pity*, he thought, *that there would be no opportunity to learn from the Skyseeder's failure to think ahead.* Sometimes, you only got one bite of the cherry. Sometimes, failure to anticipate left everyone well and truly in the shit.

Another train came in, disgorging a flood of passengers. Some were loaded down with baggage and looked lost, escapees from already snowbound Scandinavia, Karl speculated. He had heard they were heading south in growing numbers. The furled banners, hand-written placards and grim faces showed that others had turned up for a very different reason. For more than a week now, the news sites had been spotlighting the growing encampment of demonstrators that had sprouted amongst the grass-covered dunes surrounding the court complex. According to some reports, the camp now numbered in the tens of thousands. These latest arrivals, it seemed, were just the last-minute recruits.

As the crowds dispersed and the station concourse emptied, he began to wonder if Jane had missed her train. Then, he saw her diminutive figure, smiled and shook his head. She looked more like she was heading into the field than attending an international court hearing: red cagoule, chunky footwear and big backpack. One hand held an airport carrier bag, no doubt holding a bottle or two of her beloved malt whisky.

He stood and raised an arm, eliciting a big smile and an answering wave. Jane headed his way, still favouring her left leg, even though it was a couple of years since she'd had the latest prosthetic fitted. They hugged briefly and Jane kissed him on the cheek. In gentlemanly fashion, Karl relieved her of her backpack, and then wished he hadn't.

'Jesus! What the hell have you got in here?'

Jane smiled. 'Oh, you know. This and that – girl stuff.'

Karl lifted it onto his back. 'This is going to cripple me.'

'Come on. You're a big strong man.' Jane grinned and gestured at herself. 'I can't wear this stuff at the court, now, can I? I can see you've made an effort, though,' she said, taking in his open-neck shirt, denim waistcoat and battered sports jacket.

He looked down at brown moleskin trousers that had seen far better days and scuffed, black Chelsea boots. He hadn't thought about dressing up. It just wasn't something he did.

It was Karl's turn to grin. 'This is what I wear. You know that.'

'Hmm,' said Jane, closing the subject. 'Anyway. Can we eat? I'm starving.'

'Some things never change,' said Karl. How she could eat so much and still remain petite had always been a mystery to him.

Pretending to struggle under the weight of Jane's backpack, he picked up his own daysack by the handle and trudged slowly towards the station exit. Jane followed behind, bottles clinking tantalisingly in her carrier bag. 'Come on, man... mush, mush.'

They made short work of a croque monsieur and a beer each at a small café just round the corner from the station. Time was getting on, and they knew it would take a while to get through court security and into the building. Karl hailed another coal-burning cab and the driver chuntered back in the direction of the coast. After ten minutes or so, they turned right down a long, straight road that took them to the northern edge of the city, a place of semi-vegetated dunes and woodland, not far from the sea. A few minutes later, the driver signalled and pulled over. Karl and Jane had been to the court on several occasions, giving evidence and providing support for the prosecution case. They knew they were nowhere near.

'Sorry, madam,' said the driver, in response to Jane's query. 'This is as far as I'm going. They've closed the road about half a kilometre ahead. This is the last place I can turn.'

Jane did everything bar batting her eyelids, but to no avail, so she paid the man, and they decanted and stood around as he unloaded their bags. The sun was disappearing behind a veil of thin cloud and the temperature falling fast, so Karl shrugged on his cagoule.

After a bit of a struggle, they managed to cram Jane's duty-frees – a couple of bottles of Lagavulin – into Karl's daysack, which Jane insisted on taking charge of. The short straw drawn once again, Karl braced himself for a long slog with what seemed like the whole world on his shoulders.

There was a complete absence of traffic – something that had passed them by during the last moments of their cab journey – so they strolled up the middle of the road. With all the fuss on the news sites about the massive demonstration, Karl was a bit surprised by the silence, then he saw why. Ahead, the road intersected another at a major junction close to the curious chequerboard cubes and central lattice-clad block – like a giant crystal – that made up the court complex.

Demonstrators were packed together like sardines here, thousands of them, stretching along both roads and onto the scrubby dunes surrounding the complex's outer security fence. It was a motley gathering: men and women, young and old, well-dressed and down-at-heel, even a few toddlers – noses dribbling down pinched faces, fidgeting and whinging, desperate to be home and out of the cold. There were no shouted slogans, no expletives, no rushing the fences. The protesters stood in absolute silence. Many wore black and they carried identical placards, which Karl and Jane could only make out once they drew closer. Each of them carried an image of one of the leading conspirators: Gort, Bannerman, Adams, Aitken, Petrie. Overlain on each image was a closed inverted fist giving the thumbs-down sign. Underneath was a single word in languages from across the planet. All had the same meaning – 'Death'.

As they reached the rear of the multitude, it parted without the need for encouragement, allowing them passage. They picked their way slowly through the host, the eerie silence broken only once when someone – it sounded like a young girl – yelled in English, 'Join us!'

Eventually, they found themselves facing a line of metal barriers arranged so that they were shepherded back and forth towards a checkpoint. Perhaps two hundred Dutch troops formed a cordon in front, which stood firm until an officer came forward, checked their ID and sent them on their way. Behind the barriers, the road and the adjoining car park were packed with television vans, winnebagos, camera gantries and the like, through which they meandered to the main entrance. Here, their papers were checked again, their bags sniffed and searched, and they were directed through an impressive glass and steel foyer to a waiting area.

The place was swarming with media, some working on their laptops, others doing dry-runs to camera, many just standing around chatting. The atmosphere was subdued. They looked around for Ralph but couldn't see him, so Jane took the opportunity to find somewhere to change.

She returned as a different person: white blouse, dark-blue trouser suit, a touch of make-up and grey-streaked brown hair tied up in a bun. *Very business-like*, thought Karl. She certainly did scrub up well. Before he could tell her so, Jane gave a cry of delight and rushed past him. Karl turned just in time to see her throw her arms around a tall black man in military garb. He followed and stood smiling, waiting for Jane to let Ralph go, which took some time.

Arms free, Ralph stretched out a hand, beaming and resplendent in a USAF colonel's dress uniform.

Karl took it and pumped it vigorously. He hadn't seen Ralph in the flesh for more than a year, and never in uniform. He was impressed. 'Promotion,' he observed.

Ralph shrugged. 'Kicked upstairs. I'm seconded to NOAA at present, back in DC. You know – keeps me out of trouble.'

'A bit late for that,' said Jane, still hanging on to Ralph's arm.

Ralph made to reply but was interrupted by a photographer's flash. Jane was amused, but Ralph's face was like thunder. He shepherded Karl and Jane towards the nearby café, and scowled over his shoulder at the man. 'I've had three days of this and its really beginning to piss me off,' he said through clenched teeth.

'Ah, well,' said Karl, 'the price of fame, old chap, the price of fame.'

'Is that what it is?' said Ralph. 'Well, you know where you can stick it… Anyway, it's great to see you guys. Sorry I couldn't meet up earlier, but you know I've got this deal with CNN. Not my idea, but apparently I'm a great advert for USAF, so the higher ups…' Ralph pointed to the ceiling, 'made me an offer I couldn't refuse.'

The three found a table, and Jane volunteered to get the coffees. Ralph followed her with his gaze.

'She's chirpy enough, but she looks exhausted.'

Karl nodded. 'I think the government work's taking its toll.'

'What about, you know…'

Karl was non-committal. 'On the surface she seems the same old bubbly Jane, but she can't be, can she? The things she's seen, been through – even seven years on? Sometimes, I get the impression that her mind is on other things. She stops in the middle of sentences, stares into space, that sort of thing.'

Ralph sighed. 'Having your kid die before you – in both senses. What could be more harrowing? You would never be the same. Never.' ·

Jane returned with a tray bearing three coffees and a large blueberry muffin. 'Talking about me again?' she said, only half jokingly.

Ralph frowned in mock seriousness. 'Jane, when you're around, we talk of little else. You know that.'

She sat down. 'Just as it should be.' She picked up the muffin. 'I know you guys like to watch your figures, so I just got the one. Want a bit?'

Ralph and Karl laughed and shook their heads, happy just to watch Jane devour the cake with such obvious pleasure.

The three shuffled along to the end of one of the rows of seats crammed into the glass-fronted viewing gallery. The room they looked down on was spare in the extreme. A double-tiered dais of blond wood at one end, the top level for the three judges, the lower one for court officials. On either side, three rows of matching desks topped with microphones were arranged for the use of legal teams and their advisors and more officials. Above these were windowed galleries, two on either side, a much bigger gallery – the one they were in – taking up most of the rear wall. All were packed and the floor of the court was teeming. Few people were in their seats. Most milled about, often migrating from group to group. Some stood in quiet conversation, others talked excitedly, some gesticulated expansively.

After a few minutes, the courtroom hubbub, filling the gallery via the wall-mounted speakers, began to die down. Those below started to take their places, conversation slowed and the atmosphere became one of quiet anticipation. Then, as one, everyone turned and looked towards the rear of the court.

Karl leant forwards to see a couple of blue-clad prison officers entering through a small door. Following behind came ex-President Abeline Gort, Jacob Adams, Norbert Aitken and Augustus Petrie. More than a hundred others had been implicated in the plot but had been dealt with far more speedily in the appropriate national courts, nearly all in the US. No Malachi brothers, of course. They had provided the financial clout but had made damn sure that nothing concrete led to them. It said everything about the state of the world, that it was easier to impeach and convict a US President than lay a finger on a pair of billionaire businessmen. Then again, Karl had punched the air when he'd heard, the previous year, that Palatine Industries had gone bust and that Enoch Malachi had taken the coward's way out. It was the least he could do.

Two more guards brought up the rear. No Duncan Bannerman. He was still in a coma, had been since the assassination attempt in the spring. The likelihood of any recovery was close to zero, but the prosecution had insisted he be kept alive until the judges' verdict and sentence were handed down.

Jane said nothing, but grabbed Karl's hand and held it tight, nails digging uncomfortably into his flesh. Her face never left Abeline Gort, and he could feel she was trembling. On his other side, Ralph seemed unmoved and stared straight ahead.

None of the defendants were shackled and they all wore their own clothes. Like his boss, Aitken had been bailed, but the Americans had been locked up for close on six years, and it had taken its toll, mentally and physically. Gort looked frail and walked with a slight stoop. Jacob Adams' hair had gone completely white, while Augustus Petrie's bloated frame had wasted away to almost nothing. Only Nobby Aitken looked unaffected by the passage of time. The four shuffled along the dock and took their places. None looked up except Gort, whose imperious gaze, as it swept the courtroom, said it all: *I did what I had to do – and I would do it all again given half the chance.*

'Arrogant bitch,' muttered Karl under his breath. Jane looked at him for a moment, and he noticed that her eyes were moist. Then she returned her gaze to Gort.

Moments after the accused had sat down, the court usher announced, 'All rise.'

Everyone, including those in the galleries, stood as the three judges – two women and a man – entered and took their places. They were clad in the blue gowns of the ICC, embellished with white bibs. Their faces were expressionless. Karl understood that the judges would hand down their verdicts and sentences at the same time. It was an unusual step, designed to preclude any further gerrymandering by the defence, which had already drawn the proceedings out for more than six years despite the prosecution's cast-iron case.

Considering the calamitous ramifications of the Skyseeder's crimes, holding the perpetrators to account on the international stage had proved to be a tortuous process. Even after Gort and Bannerman had been impeached and stripped of office, there was work to do. The US didn't even recognise the ICC and only public protest on a massive scale forced the new President's hand, releasing Gort and her confederates into ICC jurisdiction. As a signatory, it required less jiggery-pokery to realise the extradition of Norbert Aitken. Duncan Bannerman was also handed over to ICC jurisdiction, despite remaining oblivious in an Edinburgh hospital bed.

Once everyone had taken their seats, the senior judge, a tall, middle-aged woman of East Asian origin, began to speak. Her voice was subdued and disconcertingly expressionless, and Karl struggled to make out the words. He shouldn't have needed to, as she was speaking English, but he donned the translating headphones just so he could hear more clearly. There was a good ten minutes of legal preamble, during which his attention began to wander. Then, without warning or change of tone, he realised that the verdicts were being pronounced. It was a wordy proclamation, but the gist of it was that the defendants had been found guilty on all counts, including murder and conspiracy to illegally and unilaterally modify the climate, and thereby threaten the well-being and existence of human civilisation.

The defendants were silent. They had expected nothing else. How could they not? Gort's shoulders slumped almost imperceptibly, but she held her head high. The others looked down at their hands.

The senior judge paused for a time to consult with her two colleagues before scribbling something on a piece of paper in front of her. She looked up and her eyes roved around the courtroom, as if to make sure everyone was paying attention. You could have heard a pin drop. Then she cleared her throat, turned towards the Skyseeders and began to read, a little louder this time, no doubt acutely aware that the eyes of the world were upon her. There was again an excess of verbiage, and the attention of the court and the defendants began to wander as the judge's castigation of their actions went on – and on. Karl saw Norbert Aitken sneak a look at his watch and had to admire his coolness.

After maybe fifteen minutes, the judge paused to take a sip of water. When she went on, it was in a voice tight with emotion. 'You have been found guilty of unprecedented crimes against humanity. For your own ends, you participated willingly in an illicit conspiracy, without regard for risks or consequences. You gambled with the future of human society. You gambled, and you lost, so that now billions of innocent humans will pay the price.' She paused and took another sip of water. 'Extraordinary crimes require extraordinary punishment.'

At this, a stir went around the courtroom and the gallery. The defendant's heads came up as one and turned to look at the judge.

'You will return now to your cells. You will have one week to compose yourselves and settle your affairs. Then you will be taken to a place of public execution, where you will suffer death by hanging. That is all.'

For a split second there was utter silence. As the death sentences were announced, Jane's nails dug deeper into Karl's flesh, so that he winced, and she uttered a barely audible, 'Yes!'

Ralph turned to look at Karl, eyes wide.

'Serves the bastards right,' said Karl. Around them in the gallery, and below in the courtroom, there was pandemonium. The usher's call for the court to rise was drowned out in the uproar, and the judges almost tripped over themselves in their hurry to flee the scene.

In the gallery and on the floor of the court, everyone was standing, shouting, gesturing. Some smiling widely, others grim-faced. Karl looked down at the guilty. Norbert Aitken was shaking his head and smiling, as if at the absurdity of it all. Jacob Adams was standing and pointing a finger in the direction of the departing judges, eyes wide, mouth working in a full-blown rant that no-one could hear. Petrie was screaming, pleading for his life. He made a desperate attempt to climb out of the dock but was dragged back by a guard and cuffed. Abeline Gort sat unmoved, head tilted back, eyes shut, lips moving as if in prayer. *Too late for that now*, thought Karl. *May you rot in hell.*

The bar was small, dingy and quiet, so it suited their mood and their needs perfectly. Ralph had stopped off at his hotel and swapped his uniform for a pair of jeans and a checked shirt, topped off by a chunky green sweater. Jane had made the most of a toilet stop to change, bundling up her trouser suit and stuffing it into her backpack. Like Karl's, her hotel was a way out of town, and she reckoned she needed a drink more than she needed to check in.

Ralph went to the bar and returned with three large beers. They clinked glasses in silence and in unison supped the strong, pale liquid. Karl smacked his lips with pleasure. 'Good stuff.'

The others nodded their agreement and took further gulps. They sat in amicable silence for some moments, bound up in their own thoughts. It had taken forever to battle their way out of the ICC. They had come under a barrage of requests for quotes and interviews as they struggled through the media scrum in the direction of a cab that had been ordered for them, Ralph in particular. But he'd had his fill in the run-up to the proceedings, and he blanked the lot. Giving interviews wasn't Karl's thing at all and Jane just wanted to get the hell out of the place, and as far away as possible from Gort and her cronies.

In the cab, they had talked non-stop – gabbling, almost – as they struggled to get their thoughts and feelings out fast enough. They were stunned, but hardly saddened, by the sentences; the first time since the Nuremburg and Tokyo war trials that an international court had imposed the death penalty. They hadn't even thought it was within the court's gift – if that was the right word. But it was the fact that the executions would be public that really shocked them. Then again, as the judge had said, extraordinary crimes…

Karl broke the peace, blowing out his cheeks and exhaling noisily. 'Well, that was one hell of a day. Thank God it's all over.'

Jane was about to take another drink but put her glass down and looked at Karl.

Karl's face reddened. 'Jane. I'm sorry. I didn't mean… I know it'll never be over for you.'

Jane put a hand on his arm and gave him a gentle smile. 'I know you didn't. I was just thinking. It will be a long while yet before this thing is over. And when it is, I'm not sure there will be anyone around to celebrate.'

Jane paused and took the postponed drink. 'Nothing's changed since we talked in London last week. We have to face the fact that things are going to get bad – really bad.' She nodded across the table. 'Ralph knows the score.'

Ralph had been looking down at his drink during the exchange but looked up at his name. His face was grim.

'We've been running a new model at NOAA for the past week and I had a look at the output just before I left. It doesn't make for easy reading. Seems there's just over an eighty per cent probability – give or take a few points either way – that we're into runaway cooling. Summer ice and snow cover across North America and Eurasia is expanding rapidly, and the model suggests it's already self-sustaining. Every year, more and more solar radiation will be reflected back into space. A tipping point has been passed and it looks like whatever happens with bot numbers or the recarbonation programme, we're well and truly stuffed.'

For a few moments, no-one said a word.

Karl fiddled with a beermat. 'How long?'

Jane looked him in the eye. 'As I said, nothing's changed since last week. The model output confirms it. Twenty years, thirty. Fifty, tops.'

There was really nothing more to say. As one, they picked up their glasses and supped long and deep, each preoccupied with thoughts that followed parallel lines. Barely seven years earlier, a couple of centuries of humans spewing out carbon had conspired to thicken the insulating blanket of greenhouse gases encircling the planet to a degree that runaway heating was a real possibility. Now the blanket was in tatters, torn apart by a multitude of self-replicating, carbon-gorging nanobots, their numbers supercharged by the volcanic raw material blasted out by the unforeseen Uturuncu eruption. Global heating was fixed, all right, quite possibly forever. In its place, the world of the deep freeze beckoned. At least they knew what to expect. Hardly twenty millennia earlier, when ice and snow last ruled the Earth, there were barely a few million humans, living in caves and struggling to survive.

It was Ralph who interrupted the brooding, pointing at Karl's empty glass. Jane drained hers – she never did have a problem keeping up with the lads – and Ralph headed to the bar for refills. Round followed round. As the drink took hold, the conversation became increasingly maudlin, and the mood more and more fatalistic. By midnight they'd plumbed the depths. Jane could hardly keep her eyes open, and Ralph and Karl had supped their fill of booze and bad vibes. In the end, they ran out of things to say and decided to call it a day.

They were staying in different hotels and heading in different directions the following day.

All were subdued as they stood outside the bar in the gently falling snow and said their goodbyes, promising to keep in touch but unsure if they would ever all be together again.

JANE'S FINGERS WERE FROZEN AND SHE STRUGGLED with the key to open her front door. She wondered if the lock was iced up, but then there was a small click and she was in. As she had expected, the power was off and it felt almost as cold inside as out. The freezing rain that had followed the recent blizzard had taken out a fair chunk of the grid in the south-east, encasing transmission lines in thick cocoons of glassy ice that brought them crashing down.

It was just getting dark and she took one of the torches from the hall table and used it to light her way up the steep staircase to her bedroom. She dumped her backpack in the corner, rested the torch on the bedside table and sat on the edge of the bed. Her stomach rumbled, but she was too tired to fuss with food, especially with the power out. Standing again, she stripped off as quickly as she could, leaving her clothes where they fell, and struggled with icy fingers to remove her prosthetic. Steeling herself against the inevitable shock, she dived beneath the frigid duvet and curled herself into a goose-pimpled ball, teeth chattering.

It took a good ten minutes to warm up, after which she stretched out, lay on her back with the duvet over her head, and relived the events of the last few days. It had been good to see Ralph again – and Karl, of course. The intimacy between them the previous week had been unlooked for, but welcome nonetheless, and it didn't seem to have affected the tenor of their friendship. She smiled as she recalled Karl's reticence in bed. After all she had been through, he seemed to think she ought to be treated like some sort of fragile flower. She had soon put him right.

It had been a couple of years since she had last met up with Ralph – at one of the endless preliminary hearings of the International Criminal Court. But they talked on the phone often and Jane had gained the impression during recent chats that the latest dire projections for the climate were beginning to get to him. In person he had seemed the same old Ralph, breezy and positive, but by the end of their bar session, on the evening of the verdict, he had been pretty down. She knew it was guilt. He couldn't seem to shake off the idea that, if he'd been able to act sooner, he could have bought more time, so that maybe the world wouldn't be quite so deep in the shit now. It was frankly ridiculous, and she – and Karl – had told him so, on more than one occasion. The stage had been set for catastrophe as soon as Uturuncu spewed its ash high into the bot-infested atmosphere. There was nothing more he – or any of them – could have done differently.

Ralph had mentioned, a little sheepishly, that he had met someone since he had been back in DC, and they had ribbed him about it. But Jane hoped that Cassie would be good for him. Right now he needed a distraction, someone to care for, someone who could keep him grounded and provide perspective. Especially once the latest bad news reached him.

Jane had stopped off in London on the way back from The Hague for a UK Recarbonation Commission confab

– or, at least, its scientific advisory group. The Commission had grown out of the early COBRA crisis meetings. Since then it had become a monolith with a finger in every pie throughout government and society. The role of the scientific advisory group, of which Jane was deputy chair, was to inform Commission policy based upon the latest findings on bot activities and climate response.

She knew the meeting was going to be tough; the new research findings made sure of that. A paper in the journal *Nature*, evaluating recarbonation effectiveness, had gone online that morning, and made for grim reading. She had known what it contained for several days but hadn't flagged it to Ralph and Karl in the bar. The mood had been dispirited enough without adding more bad news to the mix. Ralph must have heard by now and she had dropped Karl a note earlier providing the link.

The paper addressed an issue that she had been warning for some time might put a spoke in the recarbonation wheel. Burning coal and other dirty hydrocarbons was a great way to manufacture carbon dioxide and get it into the atmosphere quickly. It also produced huge quantities of soot capable of coating ice and snow fields, accelerating melting by absorbing heat from the sun. But it manufactured something else too – sulphur. According to the paper, the world's crash recarbonation programme was generating an invisible veil of sulphur particles across the planet, which was counteracting the effects of the carbon dioxide and soot. In the atmosphere, sulphur scattered incoming sunlight, sending much of it back into space. The result was cooling.

The effect was seen after major volcanic blasts, which pumped out enormous quantities of sulphur. But because the sulphur particles quickly floated back to Earth, the resulting cooling only lasted for a few years. Trouble was now, according to the paper's authors, the recarbonation drive was continuously replenishing atmospheric sulphur, so cancelling out much of the heating effect of the added carbon dioxide. The bottom line was a bombshell that hardly needed to be put in writing – recarbonation was never going to work. With the latest NOAA model suggesting that runaway cooling looked close to certain anyway, this seemed like the final nail in the coffin.

The minister heading up the Commission had been at the meeting, at Jane's invitation. She hadn't taken the news well, blustering and prevaricating, waving it away on the basis that one piece of research couldn't – on its own – be expected to change policy. Even if it proved to be true, she had announced bullishly, the UK's recarbonation programme would carry on. People needed to see action, needed to believe that there was at least a possibility of success. Jane had to admit that she couldn't disagree. The truth, when it came out – as it eventually must – was going to be a hammer blow. The thing was, most problems, when examined more closely, when really got to grips with, had a habit of seeming not quite so bad after all. Occasionally, zeroing in on the detail made a problem vanish altogether. But this was different. The more of the Skyseed legacy they unearthed, the more its complexity was laid bare, the worse the picture painted. Still, recarbonation would go on. It had to. For now.

She still found it hard to grasp how the world's attitude to carbon had changed. Less than a decade earlier, everything had been geared towards slashing emissions. Now, quite literally, they couldn't get carbon into the atmosphere fast enough. The renewables industry was dead, fossil fuels were mandatory, and electric and hybrid cars banned. Every scrap of coal and oil was being wrung from the crust. But it still wasn't going to be enough to curtail falling temperatures and the onward march of the ice.

The air beyond the duvet was still frigid, but she was toasty now. Still, she shivered at the prospect of how she might fare as UK society fell apart under the onslaught of the cold. There'd been plenty of job offers seeking to entice her to warmer climes, some underpinned by her celebrity but most by the fact that she was just damn good at what she did. But her instinct was to tough it out as long as she could. There were no plans to close the university any time soon, and she had work to do. The situation was desperate, irreparable, terminal even, but while there was life, there was hope. She had to believe that.

Jane's breathing slowed, her eyelids drooped and – as always happened before she dropped off – images of Ali came unbidden. A smile played about her mouth as she sampled once more his short life. Then her eyes closed and – gently and incrementally – sleep overcame her.

K ARL'S HEAD WAS STILL MUZZY AS HE STOOD IN LINE
at Schiphol waiting to check in for the London flight. Like
all airports these days, the place was heaving. Flying was a very
effective way of getting lots of carbon into the atmosphere,
and it almost felt like a public duty to get on a plane at every
opportunity. As an added bonus, jet contrails played a part in
heating the planet by trapping warmth radiating out from the
Earth's surface, so the more the merrier. National governments
were playing their part by subsidising flights, so that tickets
were as cheap as chips. The downside was that the aviation
industry was struggling to keep up, making it difficult to get a
seat, huge queues, and interminable waiting times for security
and customs clearance.

At last he reached the desk and handed over his ticket,
passport and carbon card. The clerk gestured for Karl to
look into the retinal scanner to confirm ID, then checked
the ticket, printed a boarding card and handed it over. Then
he inserted the carbon card, tapped a few keys and smiled.

'Congratulations, Dr Slater. You've already reached your carbon target for the year. And you have eight thousand bonus points, which entitles you to a return flight of 1,200 kilometres or equivalent high-carbon purchases of your choice.'

Karl nodded his thanks, took back the card and documents, and headed for the long, winding line that led to security and the departure lounge. After close to an hour, he still wasn't through, and the plane was due to leave in thirty minutes. It had been sleeting on and off all day and there was a humdinger of a snowstorm on its way. If he didn't make this flight, he could be stuck on the wrong side of the channel for days. In the end, he made it – just. There was barely time to belt up before the plane was pulling back and heading for the runway. As the wheels left the ground, he closed his eyes and tried to get in a few winks, but images of the courtroom drama kept intruding.

The verdict had been a foregone conclusion, but the sentence – execution, and public at that – had been unreal. By way of upbringing and personal choice, he had always held staunch socialist views and had never been a fan of the death penalty. He could see how, in this case, it might be justified, given the scale and consequences of the crimes. Even so, he felt the sentence was more a sop to opinion than driven by legal necessity. But the public nature of the executions was something else entirely. As the sentence had been announced, he'd felt it an appropriate and proportionate end. Now that he'd had time to think about it, he had decided it played to the crowd and the darker side of human nature, and he was dead against it. As one of the conspiracy breakers, he had an invitation, but there was no way he was going to accept. Even Jane had demurred, and she had more reason that anyone to rejoice in seeing Gort and the rest of them strung up.

In what seemed no time at all, the plane started to descend. It was just a short hop from Amsterdam's Schiphol to London's City airport, and Karl was soon shivering outside arrivals. It was dark now and a light snow was falling. No doubt the forerunner of the promised blizzard. He took the DLR into the centre and walked to his hotel through the empty streets of Bloomsbury. It was snowing heavily by the time he arrived, and the restaurant was shut. He would have to make do with the complementary coffee and biscuits in his room. In any case, he was pretty shattered, and he was out like a light moments after his head hit the pillow.

He was dragged back to consciousness by cold feet. The heating in the room had gone off in the night – policy or power cut, he wasn't sure – and the place was freezing. He made a break for the shower in the en-suite and held his breath as he waited for the icy water to warm up. After a minute or so it was tepid, and he guessed that was going to be as good as it got. He showered quickly and was out before the water temperature started to tail off.

Fifteen minutes later he was standing in the small lobby, after paying the bill, and looking through the glass doors at the scene outside. It had snowed heavily all night and it was still coming down. He couldn't remember seeing so much snow in his life – certainly not in a city centre – and he had to keep reminding himself that it was still only October. A strong easterly wind had piled up great drifts that half-buried cars abandoned in the road. Nothing moved – neither vehicle nor pedestrian – and he wondered if it was worth heading for the station at all. Surely the trains wouldn't be running in this? Used to be that even a few flakes brought the country and its transport system to a grinding halt. Infrastructure had learnt to cope better, in the last few years, as extreme weather became an everyday fact of life, but how they would handle this he had no idea. There was nothing on his phone about any travel interruptions, but he had learnt to his cost, on a number of occasions recently, that this counted for nothing.

Well, he needed to get back up north, so there was nothing for it. Opening the door, he headed out into a world of whirling white. He was wearing walking boots in expectation of severe weather, but even so, progress was difficult. The level snow reached almost up to his knees, so it was more a matter of wading than walking. Now he was outside, he could see that there were people around, but they were few and far between. Mostly, they seemed to be those imbued with a determination to reach work at all costs. He watched open-mouthed as a young woman in a short skirt and high heels stepped through a drift, legs blue with cold, arms held high holding her phone and a takeaway hot drink.

There was no tube, the trains marooned in their sheds on the outer reaches of the network, which were open to the elements. He preferred to be outside anyway, and the air quality was almost like the old days, so he faced into the frigid gale and headed for St Pancras station.

Most people had clearly looked out of the window that morning and decided on the spot that work was out. The station was almost deserted and there was just a handful of people waiting hopefully on the upper concourse. The place smelt of sulphur and the damp blanket odour of live steam. Two of the newly built Peppercorn Class monsters steamed away gently, fully coaled and carriaged but unable to leave the station for the snow. The departure board showed no trains, just a prompt to listen for announcements. Karl resigned himself to a very long wait and headed for the only open café.

Two espressos and a leftover Danish – unsurprisingly, there had been no delivery that morning – left him feeling warmer and happier. He took out his laptop and flipped it open. If he was going to be here all day, he might as well make the most of it. There was plenty to catch up on. He had been typing for barely a minute when he had a real stroke of luck.

"Ey up, lad. What's tha' doin' 'ere?'

Karl looked up at the soot-blackened face of a tiny man dressed in an engine driver's grubby togs and sporting an even filthier Casey Jones cap. He had to look twice before he recognised, beneath the grime, the wrinkled features of his neighbour, Frank Outram.

'Frank! Trying to get home, mate.'

Frank's face sprouted more wrinkles as he grinned. 'Well, I can get tha' partway, if tha' can put up wi' a bit of dirt.'

Half an hour later, faintly bemused but grateful, Karl found himself squeezed into the cab of one of the locomotives – Falcon – sharing the footplate with Frank and his equally diminutive fireman, George. The engine had been uncoupled from its carriages and a snowplough fitted to the front. The plan was that they would clear the line as far as Bedford, while another engine would come south from Sheffield, performing the same task.

Karl was as excited as a schoolboy but reined in his enthusiasm and kept well out of the way at the back, up against the coal tender. He almost jumped out of his skin as Frank pulled on a cord and an ear-splitting whistle announced their departure. Then they were off. Karl was mesmerised by the mess of brass tubing, enigmatic dials and valves that spoke of another age. He had been born far too late to remember when steam was king, but it wasn't difficult to appreciate why so many people looked back fondly on the time. The roaring steam, the gritty, sulphurous smoke, the red maw of the firebox, the rumble of the huge wheels on the rails. By any definition – barring a strict biological one – the thing was alive.

He watched Frank and George with undisguised admiration. Both must have been well into their seventies and he marvelled at their enthusiasm and seemingly boundless energy. But doing something you adored was never really work, was it?

The government's plan to recarbonise the rail system had been launched a few years earlier with much ballyhoo. Only afterwards had it become apparent that there was next to no professional experience, either in operating a steam railway or in building new locomotives. In desperation, the new BritRail Board turned to the army of enthusiasts, whose whole lives revolved around steam in all its forms and all its glory.

Working steam locomotives were commandeered from more than a hundred heritage railways, and others – liberated from transport museums – made rail-worthy. Hundreds of new locomotives were churned out, built to original plans, and the necessary track infrastructure – water towers, coaling depots, turntables and the like – put in place to handle the wholly unexpected renaissance of steam.

Old hands like Frank and George thought they had died and gone to heaven. They were quickly co-opted into crewing the first of the steam services, as well as helping to train a new generation of footplatemen. They might be filthy and exhausted most of the time – muscles cramping, bones creaking – but for them, life just didn't get any better.

The cab was roofed over and the driver and fireman enjoyed the protection of glass windows. Karl was not so lucky. Great fountains of snow spurted into the air either side of the snowplough, much of which was forced by a freezing gale through the gap between cab and tender. Accordingly, while the lower part of his body roasted slowly in the heat of the firebox, the top half was numb with cold.

Even with the snowplough on the front, they managed to get up some decent speed as they rattled through the northern suburbs of the capital. The snow was deep, but dry and fine, and it offered little resistance as they thrust onwards into the countryside.

They seemed to be the only moving thing in a dead landscape of white, save for the distant grey plumes from coal-burning power plants along the horizon. Despite the stiff easterly, fleets of wind turbines stood uninterested and listless, now surplus to requirements and disconnected from the grid.

The rhythmic clatter of the wheels and the monotonous prospect beyond the cab had a hypnotic effect, and the next couple of hours went by as if in a dream. Karl was taken by surprise when they pulled into a snowbound and empty Bedford station, and happy to see another plough-fronted engine steaming gently on the next platform. He enjoyed a cup of tea with Frank and George who, suitably invigorated, were headed straight back to London now the line was clear, apparently as fresh as when they'd started out.

Karl was handed over, in the manner of a package, to another couple of old-timers, who promised to deliver him home safe and sound. Unusually, the snow wasn't as bad further north, and with the line now clear and no carriages to hold them back, the crew of the second train were able to really give their engine its head. Despite the bitter gale that penetrated the cab and froze Karl to the core, the ride was exhilarating. Barely an hour and a half later, he climbed down from the footplate, stiff but thrilled, waved goodbye to his deliverers and headed for Sheffield station concourse.

The local trains, at least, were running again, and the place was bustling. Karl stopped off at a kiosk to buy lunch and a warming espresso. He stuffed the tuna sandwich in his pocket for later, knocked back the coffee and headed out into the city. There was far less snow than down south and while the pavements were icy, the roads were clear. He flagged down a bus heading past the university, settled down in its relative warmth and checked his phone. There was just the one message, from Jane, providing a link to a new paper in *Nature Climate Cooling*. He wasn't even going to attempt to download and read it on a phone screen on a juddering bus. He would print it out later and take a look when he had a spare moment.

The department, when he got there, was as quiet as the grave. Quite a few staff lived in villages up in the hills of the neighbouring Peak District and, with the weather worsening fast, were beginning to wish they didn't. It wasn't unusual, these days, for the more remote communities to be cut off for weeks during the winter months. If things carried on like this, it would be happening in summer too. He wondered if he should start thinking seriously about selling up while he still could. The diet of optimism fed to the public meant that few yet grasped how bad things were going to get. When reality broke through, neither love nor money would persuade someone to take his house off his hands.

Karl felt a twinge of regret as he passed Steve's room. His nameplate had gone and the room was empty. Karl hadn't been able to find the funding to keep him on, and after almost ten years together, Steve – now Dr. Carob – had been compelled to move on. At least Karl had been able to put in a good word with his colleagues over at ETH in Zurich, and Steve had been over there now for a couple of months. They kept in touch, but Karl missed him. And he still hadn't found another drinking partner.

He picked up the mail from his pigeonhole, unlocked the door to his study and dumped his bag. Leaving his door open, he popped along the corridor to the toilets. He had to laugh when he looked in the mirror. His face was covered in dark, sooty patches and his greying thatch – uncontrollable at the best of times – had been rearranged by the wind into a wild mix of peaks and troughs. That, at least, explained the coy smile of the girl in the station kiosk. And he had thought his luck might be in.

He had a seminar at the tail end of the afternoon, but that still left him with an hour or so to kill. Clearing a space on his desk, he opened his laptop, checking over the news while he forced down the sandwich. The tuna was slimy with mayo;

the bread slices of flat, white foam rubber. Swallowing the last mouthful, he grimaced and wiped his hands on his trousers, an unsavoury habit that had dogged him since he was a small child, but one he had given up trying to rid himself of.

He barely recognised the world as presented, these days, in the news websites. Presumably designed to counteract the appalling weather, the new Information Ministry – created a few months earlier – was having a field day, reflected in the headlines. Humans were winning the 'battle with the bots', bot concentrations were at record lows, recarbonation was a triumph, things could only get better.

The day's big story was the international agreement to further tighten domestic carbon targets across the world. A smiling Met Office chief scientist explained that everyone was doing well, but they just needed to do that little bit more. She went on to describe, jauntily, how the amount of carbon each household was required by law to emit every year was being hiked up another three tonnes. It would, she announced triumphantly, be the final nail in the coffin of global cooling. 'Yeah, right,' muttered Karl.

Closing the news pages, he went onto the *Nature* website and downloaded the paper that Jane had flagged in her message. He keyed in 'print' and went next door to pick up the hard copy from one of the communal printers. Returning to his study, he slumped in the easy chair in the corner and began to read.

It didn't take long, *Nature* papers being limited to just three or four pages. Getting the message across in such a small space, complete with all the supporting evidence, made writing a paper for the journal a skill that many academics never quite managed to acquire. Less than five per cent of submitted papers were accepted for publication, the true pick of the crop.

Karl looked up and breathed deeply when he had finished reading. He was stunned, felt as if he had been slapped. This was the real picture; the chilling picture, not the contrived optimism concocted by a bunch of Ministry wonks and complicit news editors.

For some reason, the new Ministry was yet to turn its attention to the scientific journals and their content. Partly, Karl was confident, because an attempt to introduce any form of censorship would cause uproar. But mainly, he guessed, because they thought that only those breathing the rarefied air of academe's ivory towers ever read the things. In any event, the Ministry always had the option of stymieing attempts by the media to pick up new findings whose publication was judged not to be in the public interest or – in other words – true. This new research qualified with knobs on, and he was certain he wouldn't be reading about it any time soon in the newspapers or on the news feeds. He guessed that the Ministry would already be flexing its powers to get the paper pulled.

He would have liked to have shared his thoughts, his rage, despair, but there was no-one about. He would have liked to have drowned his sorrows with a friend, but Steve was five hundred miles away. In the end, he had to make do with sending a single-word text to Jane: 'Fuck!'

She replied almost instantly, 'Ditto!'

RALPH HAD BEEN LUCKY TO MAKE IT OUT OF Schiphol. He had stayed on another day after Jane and Karl had shipped out. More media commitments he could easily have done without, but orders were orders. Another major snowstorm had moved in from the east, the afternoon of his flight, and created a big logjam on the tarmac. After boarding two hours late, they had sat for an hour waiting for a take-off slot, the airframe being constantly hosed down with de-icer. Eventually the plane half jetted, half skidded along the runway and then they were up, according to the captain, last plane out before the snow shut up shop.

DC couldn't have been more of a contrast. The heat and humidity struck like a hammer when Ralph exited arrivals, the experience made more unpleasant by the throat-catching stench from the new coal-burning power plants on the city's periphery. He dug out his mask and covered his mouth and nose. He doubted it kept out much of the filth, but at least it took the edge off the stink. A couple of weeks earlier, he had seen the latest pollution stats – an estimated three quarters of a million excess deaths in the last year. He couldn't say he'd been surprised.

He navigated his way around the enormous piles of cleared snow heaped up either side of the taxi rank, which said everything about the state of the climate. The polar vortex – the girdle of powerful winds that kept the Arctic's bitter air in and warm air from the tropics out – had just about fallen apart. Extraordinarily wild swings in the weather was the result. As frigid northern air battled heat from the Gulf, episodes of snow and freezing conditions swapped, almost from one day to the next, with baking temperatures and strength-sapping humidity. In the longer term, there was only going to be one winner.

There should have been a car waiting, but he had seen no sign of a driver on the concourse so had no choice but to join the back of the long queue for a cab. For close on three quarters of an hour he shuffled forwards, seemingly getting no closer to the stand. Sweat trickled down the inside of his heavy flannel shirt. He'd swapped his uniform for mufti but was dressed for the Arctic weather he'd left behind in the Netherlands, not tropical DC. He mentally kicked himself for not checking on the weather before he'd left. At the same time fuming at the massive hike in air travel since individual carbon cards had been introduced.

He was almost at the head of the queue, when he noticed out of the corner of his eye, a tall man of South Asian descent, who seemed nervously to be trying to attract his attention. In his hand, he held a piece of card, across which Ralph's scrawled name could just be deciphered. He rolled his eyes, sighed and gesticulated to the man. Waving away the driver's apologies, he followed him to a black Chrysler SUV, which – to Ralph's relief – was both nearby and air-conditioned, and gave directions to his rented house in Del Ray, just south of the capital in Maryland. He had intended to drop in first at the downtown HQ of NOAA – the US National Oceanic and Atmospheric Administration – but the heat had taken its toll, and he wanted nothing more than a cold drink and a nap. He had dinner with Cassie to look forward to that evening and until then, all he wanted to do was chill.

He woke early evening, feeling a great deal better. Lying on top of the bed, still fully clothed, hands behind head, he contemplated the future. He was excited by the night ahead and a little nervous. It was quite a while since he had been seriously involved with a woman. He had only known Cassie for a few weeks, so there was still a frisson of excitement, but it was tempered by the worry that he'd screw up – again. He would be the first to admit that he'd never quite got the hang of long-term relationships, and by that he meant anything more than a month. Maybe this time it would be different. Problem was, the Skyseed business and now the desperate race for a solution had just about taken over his life, and he wasn't certain there was room left over for anything – or anyone – else. The timing of the whole Cassie thing felt a bit like a starving man presented with a banquet in a runaway train careering towards a cliff edge. *Well, what the hell*, he thought. The cliff was a way off yet, and it was still possible – just – that the train might never get there.

He stood, undressed and headed for the shower. A few minutes later, towelling his hair dry, he pointed the remote at the small wall-mounted television permanently tuned to CNN. But there was no CNN. In its place was an image of the White House, with a breaking news bar below. He felt the hairs on the back of his neck stand up as the scrolling words hit home: national state of emergency declared; martial law in force; all national guardsmen to report to places of duty; news media outlets closed until further notice; social media shut down; the right to habeas corpus suspended.

Ralph remained standing, remote dangling in one hand, the other still holding the towel to his head. Then he sat on the edge of the bed and gave the edict further thought. It had been shocking, but only because he hadn't been expecting it at that moment. In fact, it was something he had known must happen eventually. As society started to fray at the edges, there was no way that normal service could be maintained. It wouldn't be long before millions were on the move, food was in increasingly short supply, and civil order started to unravel. Doing nothing – in the longer term – wasn't an option. It would have meant certain anarchy. Thinking about the timing of the proclamation, he knew it must have been triggered by the revelation that recarbonation wasn't going to work and that runaway cooling was almost certain. When that became public knowledge, the shit would really hit the fan. There was nothing worse than the absence of hope to bring out the darker side of humanity.

He shivered, partly it was the air-con, which was still going full blast, but mainly the chilling prospect of what the future held for them all. Shrugging on a bathrobe, he headed over to the window. 'Jesus!' he muttered to himself. A cold front from the north must have crossed over while he was sleeping. Gone was the stifling heat that had greeted his arrival just hours earlier. Now, snowflakes drifted gently from a leaden sky.

'HANGING'S TOO GOOD FOR THEM.' AAZIM AL-HALLAQ had read in the morning paper's editorial. He had always hated the phrase. In a roundabout way, it somehow implied that hanging was not an agreeable end. This was simply not true. Carried out with meticulous preparation, by an expert, it was neat, quick and painless. Well, he wasn't exactly sure about the last bit, but – as he liked to joke – none of his 'clients' had ever complained.

But it was a dying art now, no question. And it was an art. His father Abbas, the greatest hangman of all time – known as the Wizard of the Scaffold – had taught him that. There was technical skill, of course, but there was also fine judgement, a certain finesse and an element of showbiz. A perfectly conducted hanging always elicited in him a feeling of contentment and the satisfaction that comes from knowing you have done your job as well as it can be done. He was certain Beethoven must have felt the same on completion of his fifth, and Michelangelo, as he put the finishing touches to the Sistine Chapel ceiling.

But it was on its way out. Barely twenty countries still disposed of their worst offenders by hanging. Wherever else capital punishment was still permitted, it was all shooting, injections or electrocution, but where was the skill in that? Where was the showmanship ?

Aazim sighed to himself. Well, his time was done in any case. He had been promising his wife that he would retire for years now but had kept putting it off. Lucky he had too. This – the first public execution in western Europe in nearly a century – was going to be the pinnacle of his career. An opportunity to go out with a bang, his swansong. Maybe, then, *inshallah*, his wife might stop the nagging.

There. Done. He rinsed his razor under the tap and splashed cold water over his face to remove any last traces of soap and close the pores. Drying his face on a hand towel, he peered more closely at his reflection in the mirror. *Not bad for a sixty-four-year-old*, he thought. *Not bad at all*. His cropped hair was a grizzled grey now, but his small – almost black – eyes were clear, his skin a dark mahogany, barely touched by wrinkles. The whole was dominated by the great hooked nose, which, in combination with his eyes, had given him his sobriquet – the Vulture. The tall, angular frame and hunched shoulders probably contributed too.

He stepped back so he could see more of himself and stood sideways on, pulling his growing paunch in. Maybe he had let himself go a little in recent years, but what the hell, he deserved it. What was it now? More than eight hundred hangings in thirty years? If he remembered rightly, 846, all in his home country, barring a few 'guest appearances' in other states that lacked the 'resources'. This latest show would take it to 850. He smiled at himself in the mirror at the thought. A nice round number to go out on.

He shrugged on a white bathrobe and opened the door to the living room. The ICC certainly knew how to look after its star turn. The suite was the largest in the finest hotel in Amsterdam. He could get used to this.

His clothes were laid out on the sofa: white shirt, charcoal-grey suit, black tie. He had never liked anything showy. Sober and smart was his style. He dressed quickly, gave his black brogues a last-minute shine, and stuffed his notebook and sheaf of documents into a brown, suede briefcase. Mustn't forget the paperwork. Using both hands, he grabbed the heavy, patterned drapes and swept them aside. Brilliant sunshine filled the room. He opened the window as far as it would go and sucked in the icy autumnal air. What a marvellous day for an execution.

The driver provided for his use by the court eased the big BMW to a stop outside the main entrance to the Amsterdam Arena. The executions weren't for another six hours, but a large crowd had already started to build outside, jostling for prime positions in front of one of the dozen giant screens installed outside to cater to the overspill. There was a small tent city too. Nearly all the tickets had been allocated by ballot, but a very limited number were available on the day. Some people had been queuing ever since the sentence was announced. Aazim thought it odd. He delighted in hanging people, but he didn't think he could be bothered to camp out for weeks just to watch.

Telling his driver he wouldn't need him until after it was all over, he started to thread his way through the crowds. His face had hardly been off the TV screens for the last few days, and it was not one it was easy to miss. There were shouts of encouragement, good wishes and pats on the back as he passed by. *This is new*, he thought, raising his hand in acknowledgement and beaming his most winning smile. As he neared security, scattered applause broke out and spread through the crowd. The guards joined in as he approached and waved him through without examining the proffered

ID. Aazim puffed out his chest and entered the arena on a tsunami of acclaim.

As he came out of the tunnel into the brilliantly lit stadium interior, his mouth fell open. The place was colossal. He had dispatched most of his clients in small, dingy rooms, with maybe half a dozen people present. A few of his executions had been public but conducted out in the open, in front of modest crowds; they had been nothing like this. With the roof closed to keep out the worst of the cold, the atmosphere felt almost intimate, but he could imagine that with seventy thousand people inside, the noise would be overwhelming. He had always been immune to nerves, but a small shiver ran down his spine as the immensity of his task – undertaken in full sight of the eyes of the world – hit home.

He made his way towards the centre of the arena along a narrow passageway between rows of temporary seating that filled the whole of the central area. Ahead, a massive stage held the scaffold, theatrically lit to cater to the broadcast media. Around the stage a collection of small prefabs clustered. One provided temporary housing for the condemned and another a refuge for officials and hangers-on. A third was his 'dressing room'. A strange idea, he thought, as he was already dressed to kill – as he liked to think of it. But it would be nice to have somewhere to compose himself, out of sight of the multitude.

He climbed the metal steps to the stage and nodded to a couple of technicians checking out the sound system, then continued up a further set of steps to the long scaffold. The four ropes hung down from a single wooden beam, a few metres apart. Beneath each was a square trapdoor in the wooden floor, the opening of which he would control, at the appropriate time, with a single lever. He had weighed and measured the condemned at the prison a few days earlier, and had adjusted the rope lengths accordingly. His father had drilled into him the importance of this during the very earliest days of his apprenticeship. Too long a rope for a heavy physique could result in decapitation, too short a rope for a slightly built client and the result was slow strangulation instead of a broken neck and instant death. Neither made for pleasant viewing. But more than that, such cock-ups – and he was proud to say there'd only been a couple over the years – deeply offended a sense of pride in his work.

He had fixed the ropes in place the previous day and gone through a couple of dry runs to check that the trap doors functioned as they should. Still, he couldn't resist giving everything another once-over. Anyone could have meddled with the set-up in between, either from mischief or curiosity. Everything still worked perfectly. Finally, he consulted his notebook to make certain that the name plates mounted above each rope on the wooden beam hadn't been swapped around by some wag or miscreant. It had happened before. He took up his position by the lever and turned full circle, trying to imagine the place later that afternoon – the immense sea of expectant faces, the ferment, the febrile atmosphere. Then he walked back down the two flights of steps, entered his dressing room and closed the door.

Augustus Petrie had never been a brave man and he wasn't brave now. But he was resigned. Over the course of the past week he had lost count of the number of times he had pounded on the door of his cell until his hands bled, screamed over and over again for mercy, cried like a baby or cowered in the corner, his whole body shaking with abject terror. But now, as the red figures on the giant digital clock at one end of the arena counted down the final seconds of his time on Earth, he felt almost calm. He wasn't a religious man, so he had no expectation other than oblivion, but he had managed to convince himself that there were worse things. In any case, maybe he'd be proved wrong. He almost laughed out loud. He'd been wrong about so much else.

Thirty seconds. The clock's countdown was clear, but the brilliance of the stage floodlights meant he could see nothing of the watching masses. There was virtually no sound either, just the low-level rustle arising from a legion of whispers melded together.

A stream of imaginative and shocking invective grabbed his attention, and he turned to his right, the coarse rope chafing his neck as he did so. The hessian hood that etiquette required was thinly woven and barely affected his vision at all. Gort's facade of dignified disdain had cracked at the last, and she shrieked and swore as if demented, struggling like a berserker to free her strapped legs and her hands, which – like his and the others – were shackled behind her.

Twenty seconds. Petrie turned to his left and took in Jacob Adams, his emaciated frame accentuated in an orange jumpsuit that was far too small. Adams' face was devoid of any expression other than a vacant smile. The light was still on, but the house had long been abandoned. His lips moved silently and a long string of snot joined and mixed with the saliva dribbling down his chin.

Ten seconds. Turning to the right again, Petrie looked beyond the still-struggling Gort. Norbert Aitken stood quietly, looking straight ahead, apparently oblivious to everything going on around him. It was Aitken he felt sorry for. A loyal man who had simply been in the wrong place at the wrong time. Without the moral fibre or strength of character to say no, his fate had been sealed the moment Bannerman took him into his confidence.

Five seconds. Petrie faced forward. He felt sick, swallowed hard.

Four. He closed his eyes. His body began to shake uncontrollably.

Three. Beads of cold sweat sprouted on his forehead and his bowels felt watery.

Two. Blind terror. A damp patch spread across his groin.

One. 'Please. No.'

The silence was absolute. Seventy thousand people inside, and billions beyond, held a collective breath. Aazim tugged on a lever. Four trap doors opened and four lives ended. Adams was closest, and Aazim heard a satisfying crack as his neck snapped. He could see on his monitor, that the others – who now dangled out of direct sight – had suffered a similar fate. He smiled to himself, contented at another job well done. Quick and painless. As he never tired of saying, what better way was there to go?

Jeremy sat in the chair by Duncan Bannerman's bed, as he had done every day since his own release from hospital three months earlier. Even now, Duncan's husband found it hard to believe that he still lived. The cardiologist had told him that a couple of millimetres to the right and the bullet would have sliced through the aorta and that would have been that. As it was, the paramedics had managed to get his heart restarted and keep it going long enough for the surgeon's knife to do its miraculous work. He would always have a weakness and would need to take care, but that was – he felt – a small price to pay.

He reached forward to take Duncan's hand. It was limp and cool, as always, dry to the touch and completely unresponsive. His chest rose and fell with the conformity of a metronome, synchronised with the Vader-like wheeze-click, wheeze-click of the ventilator. Duncan had never regained consciousness after the shooting, and the machine had been keeping him alive ever since. In reality, alive was something of an exaggeration, at least as far as most people understood the term. The bullet had caused severe damage to the brain during its passage, and matters had been made even worse by a massive bleed. The surgeons had managed to drain this, but only after further damage to brain tissue had resulted. The official prognosis was worse than dire, and, as far as Duncan's medical team were concerned, the probability of any sort of recovery was zero.

If it hadn't been for the court order, he would have long ago sanctioned turning off the ventilator. But, against increasing public disquiet, the ICC prosecutors had insisted that Duncan be kept alive. While there was any chance of recovery, they said – however slim – he must be at the court's disposal and available to answer the charges. With the trial ended and Duncan's co-conspirators dispatched, he thought he would be free, at last, to flick the switch that would let his beloved go. But no. Duncan's name had been on the charge sheet alongside Gort and the others, and – severely brain damaged or not – he was required to pay his dues. So, that afternoon, executioner Aazim Al-Hallaq, would arrive, to formally carry out the sentence handed down by the ICC judges. It would be a stranger, not Duncan's husband and lover, who would switch off his life support.

In despair, he brought his fists crashing down on the tubular metal bed rail, then buried his head in his hands. Almost immediately, the door opened and the guard's head appeared, eyebrows raised in query.

'Everything all right, sir?'

Jeremy took his head from his hands, nodded silently. The guard gave a tight smile in return and closed the door.

Why the fuck, he thought, *did they bother with a guard? They said the round-the-clock security was to protect Duncan from further attacks, but really, who would feel the need now?* Not for the first time, he shook his head at the absurdity of it all.

Once he had calmed himself, he looked down at Duncan's face. Even partly covered by the breathing mask, it was beautiful. Gone were the lines that had blossomed so rapidly after he became PM. Jeremy had shaved him that morning, and his skin was smooth and almost unmarked. Apart from the ghostly hospital pallor, he looked ten years younger, almost as he had when he'd caught Jeremy's eye in Davos a decade and a half earlier.

They had both been in the Swiss ski resort for that annual jamboree of the great and the good – or the haves and the want-mores, as Duncan liked to call them – the World Economic Forum. Jeremy was there as a celebrity ambassador, crusading for access to clean water in the developing world. Duncan was on hand to build relationships and press the flesh, the young and charismatic shadow chancellor, tipped for great things. They had clicked at once but had taken things slowly. It wasn't until Duncan was elected leader of the opposition a couple of years later that they came out. He remembered the time with a smile. How could he forget? The right-wing tabloids had a collective fit. It was funny, though, how quickly everyone adjusted. When they took up residence in Number 10, after Duncan's landslide election victory, few batted an eyelid. By then, of course, they were married.

He reached out a hand and smoothed the thinning grey hair back from Duncan's forehead. They had always been completely open with one another, but Duncan had never taken him into his confidence over Skyseed. Afterwards, he said it was to protect him. Given the way things had turned out, he was probably right. But he hadn't opened up after his fall from grace either, except to say that he did what he thought was best for the country. That, Jeremy could well appreciate. The UK was already in the shit when Duncan had come to power and he recalled commentators shaking their heads and wondering why anyone would voluntarily accept such a poisoned chalice. The economy had struggled ever since Brexit. The widely touted trade deals had failed to materialise and the coronavirus and a second financial crash had made things far worse. Beleaguered at home and on the international stage, Jeremy could well believe that Gort's seductive offer must have seemed too good to turn down; a last throw of the dice that Duncan decided he had no choice but to bet on. He guessed that Duncan must have felt the risks were small, or at least acceptable, and worth taking if it meant helping the country get back on its feet. Jeremy gently stroked Duncan's cheek. *If only he had really thought it through. If only…*

His retrospective was interrupted by the door opening again. The guard's head popped through the gap.

'I'm sorry, sir.' He sounded apologetic. 'The ICC delegation is here. Shall I tell them to come in?'

Fury swelled again in Jeremy's chest, but he managed to hold himself together. His face was stony as he nodded wordlessly and turned back to Duncan.

He was aware of the door opening wider and a number of people entering before it was pushed to softly. For perhaps a minute, no-one said anything, then one of the newcomers cleared his throat.

'Mr Bannerman, sir?'

Jeremy did not respond.

'Mr Bannerman,' the voice repeated, this time with a mixture of urgency and irritation. Jeremy guessed from the slight accent that the speaker was German. He waited a few moments, then turned reluctantly and faced the execution party, for that was what it was. The speaker was a short man of slight build, straight blond hair cut short, grey eyes behind rimless glasses. He wore a pale brown suit of expensive cut and carried a small leather briefcase. Everything about his appearance and demeanour cried out technocrat.

The man looked slightly nervous. Nonetheless, he crossed the room to Jeremy and held out a hand. 'Juergen Pfalz. Pleased to meet you.'

Jeremy remained seated and ignored the outstretched hand, which the man let drop to his side after a few moments.

Pfalz gestured at his two companions, who remained just inside the door. 'May I introduce my colleagues?'

'Dr Paco Delgado.' In other circumstances, the name would have brought a smile. Jeremy's Spanish was not brilliant but good enough to know that, in English, the man would be 'Frank the thin'. Yet he was as round as a football, swarthy, with black hair, black-rimmed glasses and a five o'clock shadow that Jeremy guessed even the closest shave couldn't touch. The man nodded but said nothing.

The other needed no introduction and elicited no amusement. The hawk-like face of Aazim Al-Hallaq had been everywhere in recent weeks. The man bent his tall, thin frame in a deep bow. 'Salam alaykum.'

Jeremy looked at the three men but remained silent. He didn't see why he should make it easy for them. After a few moments, Pfalz sought to break the impasse with what he clearly regarded as a show of business-like efficiency. He took a sheaf of papers from his briefcase and flicked through them until he came to the one he required.

'Mr Bannerman. I know this must be extremely difficult for you. If there was any other way...'

Jeremy's hostile glare stopped him in his tracks.

Pfalz put a fist to his mouth and cleared his throat. 'Well then.' He proffered the document, which Jeremy ignored, his eyes never leaving the German's face.

Discomfited, he lost some of his equanimity. 'Uhm, this is a court document... It provides the legal authority for the death sentence to be enacted upon Duncan Fraser Bannerman, as handed down...'

Pfalz continued in this vein for some time, but Jeremy had turned away and wasn't listening.

Finally: 'A nurse will arrive shortly to unlock the ventilator and allow justice to take its course.' The life support machine had been fitted with a locking mechanism to ensure that it could not be turned off by anyone keen to finish the work of Molly Patterson, or to present Jeremy with an opportunity he might find hard to resist.

All the time Pfalz had been going through the paperwork, Delgado and Al-Hallaq had remained standing near the door, looking uncomfortable. There was only the one chair in the room and Jeremy was damned if he was going to give it up.

There was a gentle tap on the door, which opened slowly to reveal a nervous-looking young nurse of South East Asian ethnicity. She nodded to the room in general and bustled purposefully over to the bed. Taking a small key from a pocket, she inserted it in the ventilator, turned it through ninety degrees and withdrew it. Recrossing the room, she left without a word.

Al-Hallaq chose the moment to make his presence felt. *He's an impressive and somewhat scary man*, thought Jeremy, *even if you didn't know what he did for a living.*

'Gentlemen,' he said. His English was near-perfect, with just a trace of an accent. 'I think, perhaps, it is time.' He looked hard at Pfalz. 'I think also, as a courtesy to Mr Bannerman, that it might be best if you and Dr Delgado waited outside while the sentence is carried out. It is only right that he should be here, but you don't need to be.'

Delgado just shrugged and turned to the door, but Pfalz blustered. 'I'm sorry, Mr Al-Hallaq, but I must be present to witness the realisation of the sentence.'

Al-Hallaq spread his arms. 'If you want me to do my job, then those are my terms. Take them or leave them.'

Pfalz opened his mouth to argue, then thought better of it. What difference would it make, in any case? The man would still be dead. He gave a curt nod and headed for the door, holding it open for Delgado and closing it noisily behind them. For a few moments, his voice could be heard, talking loudly and irritably, but this diminished as they moved away down the corridor.

Jeremy turned to Al-Hallaq. 'Thank you.'

The executioner smiled. 'It is the least I can do. I should tell you that I didn't want this. It's not what I do – flicking a switch to hasten oblivion. Where's the finesse; the theatre? You know all about theatre, Mr Bannerman.'

Jeremy nodded. He'd been up on stage since the age of six. Not so much since his film career had taken off, but still now and again. He understood where Al-Hallaq was coming from.

'But the show must go on, eh?'

Al-Hallaq smiled again. 'This' – he spread his hands to take in the bed, Duncan and the ventilator – 'was all part of the package, I am afraid. Five executions I was contracted for, so…' He made a face.

'But,' he went on, 'there is something I can do.'

He came over and put one hand on Jeremy's shoulder. 'If it will help, I can place your hand under mine when I turn the machine off.'

Jeremy looked up at Al-Hallaq and his eyes were moist. 'I would appreciate that. I would appreciate that very much.'

Al-Hallaq nodded. 'Are you ready, then, or do you wish a little longer to compose yourself?'

Jeremy shook his head. 'I've had far more time than I needed for that. Let's just do it, please.'

Al-Hallaq helped him out of the chair. He took Jeremy's soft, manicured hand and placed it on the small metal switch that toggled between life and death, between this world and the next. Covering it with his own, mahogany-brown and calloused, he applied gentle pressure until they both heard a small click.

For a moment, there was silence. Then, the small, breathy sound of Duncan's shocked lungs struggling to work on their own after months of redundancy. Duncan's chest rose and fell once, and then again, and momentarily Jeremy felt a surge of hope. But then there was a long pause. The next breath was shallower and the chest barely lifted. Another long hiatus, then a final exhalation – more a sigh than a breath. Jeremy took his hand away, leant forwards and touched his forehead to Duncan's. A single tear traced a serpentine path down his cheek and dripped onto his husband's lips. Jeremy kissed it away tenderly and sat down. He grasped one of Duncan's hands and fixed his gaze on his face, drinking in every feature, every aspect, burning it forever onto the retina of his mind's eye. He registered nothing as Aazim put a comforting arm on his shoulder and gave it a parting squeeze.

KARL LOOKED AROUND THE EMPTY STUDY ONE LAST time. It hadn't taken long to pack up the essentials – books and papers, mainly – and these had already been shipped out. Now all that remained was a desk, a couple of chairs, a disconnected phone and memories, lots of memories – mostly good ones. Karl had been happy here, might even have stayed for his whole career. He had been up for a Readership and would probably have been awarded a Chair in due course and in normal circumstances. And it was home. He'd been born just twenty miles down the road. He loved the countryside and the people. But now he was leaving it all behind. Moving just about as far as it were possible to move.

A post had come up at the University of Canterbury on New Zealand's South Island, and he'd been cajoled by friends Down Under to apply. Even when he was offered the job, he wasn't sure it was for him. But then his hand had been forced by the announcement that the university was to close, gradually shutting up shop over the course of a couple of years. It wasn't really a surprise. It had been an appalling winter, and much of the heavy snow cover across the nearby hills of the Peak District and the south Pennines was forecast to persist throughout the summer. It was the thin end of the wedge. Successive snowfalls would build on the icy base, and it was only a matter of time before glaciers began to form and launched their unstoppable march on the city. The cold and the snow were far worse than down south, so it was increasingly difficult to keep transport links open and sustainable. The upshot was that few wanted to head north for an education any more, so the university just couldn't recruit. Without students, there was simply no point to it.

Karl had defaulted on his mortgage, abandoned his home to the autumn blizzards and moved into a city centre apartment. The bank was welcome to the place – if it could find it. In fact, millions of other homeowners in Scotland and the north had been forced to do the same, so that most lenders were teetering on the edge of bankruptcy, if they hadn't gone over already. The apartment had been furnished, so he'd had little in the way of fixtures and fittings to weigh him down. What there was had already gone on ahead. The way things were, he reckoned travelling light and living unencumbered was the safest bet. He had no plans to put down roots in New Zealand, and who knew what he'd be doing, or even where he'd be, ten years down the line, even five. New Zealand wasn't immune to the freeze, that was certain. The ice on the Southern Alps was already thickening up and spawning glaciers that threatened nearby communities. He viewed the move as less an escape from the ice, more a respite.

Closing the door quietly, he shouldered his backpack and headed down the corridor, boots echoing on the hard floor. The place already seemed deserted. Several staff had moved on, and he and a couple of others were the last in the building to cut and run. There had been a leaving party the night before, but it had been more a wake than a celebration. There wasn't much to make merry about, after all. Barely a dozen people turned up. Most out of a feeling of duty than anything else, he thought, and the majority left after a quick drink and a few muttered words from the dean. Word had it that he was heading off too, retiring. Taking the opportunity to head for the sun before the stampede got going in earnest. Well, good luck to him.

He switched the lights off in the corridor, walked up a flight of stairs and out of the main door. It was dark outside and a light snow was falling on a lethal crust of steel-hard ice formed by freezing rain. Without a backward glance, he pulled up the hood of his parka and headed downhill in the direction of the railway station and the next chapter of his life.

PART THREE

REQUIUM

THE SUN REFLECTING BACK FROM THE MONUMENTAL ice wall was blinding. It was just after dawn on an early autumn day and the air was frigid, so the face of the ice cliff was stable. Soon, as the sun's rays did their work, it would come to life, bits and pieces of ice tumbling down as the glaciers resumed their inexorable advance across the landscape.

Jane Haliwell peered through a thick cloud of exhaled breath at the small screen on the drone controller. The snout of the nearest finger of ice was noticeably closer than a week earlier. At this rate, she speculated, another few months and Oxford's dreaming, and now largely abandoned, spires, would be ground and smeared into boulder clay beneath the rapidly expanding Cotswold ice cap.

She guided the drone lower and along a flight path that followed the edge of the ice. She would use the imagery later to build a picture of how the ice front had evolved over the past week. Monitoring ice movement really wasn't her thing, but with so many of her colleagues having already followed the warmth, it was all hands on deck.

Fingers blue with cold, she fiddled clumsily with the joystick, cajoling the drone back to a bumpy landing on the frost-crusted snow of the small field where she had parked the Land Rover. She stowed the flyer in the back, along with the suite of dust samples she had collected, and turned for a last look around.

The belching chimneys of coal-fired power stations lined the horizon to the east and south. It was a war of black versus white, coal versus ice, filth versus pristine, but the by-blow was grey. A dingy landscape of soot-covered snow and ice, and a sky festooned with drifting wisps of slate-coloured smoke, the sulphurous stench of burning fossil fuel ever-present. *This must have been what it was like*, Jane thought, *in the great Victorian cities at the height of the Industrial Revolution.* Even the surface of the ice sheet was blackened as helicopters flying round the clock dropped black carbon on the surface to encourage melting and slow progress.

But it was all a facade. Had been now for nearly a decade and a half, since it became clear that recarbonation wasn't going to make a blind bit of difference. But she could see why those in power persisted. For one thing, it slowed the advance of the ice and bought a little more time within which to find a solution – not that there was anything in the pipeline. For another, people needed a straw to clutch at, a hope – however faint – that the future wasn't dead and buried just yet. Because when it came down to it, without hope, there was nothing to live for; without hope, there was anarchy.

Now, though, there was a new problem. Available reserves were almost gone. There was only so much fossil fuel to be had, and as time went on more and more coal mines and oil and gas fields were either sucked dry or overwhelmed by the expanding ice cover. Soon, the power stations would stand idle, the steam engines left to decay in their sheds, the coal-burning cars abandoned. Then, the war would be over, white victorious. The world crushed, unhindered, within a fist of eternal ice.

She climbed into the cab, started up the engine and turned the heating to maximum. She hoped the battery would cope. It had been acting up a bit recently and several times she had been forced to choose between keeping warm and getting to her destination. The appalling inefficiency of the big, dirty engine didn't help either and the mileage it achieved was dire. Still, bad was good these days.

It took a long time for the heat to start to work its way into her bones.

'I'm getting too fucking old for this caper,' she muttered to herself. Even after twenty years, the cold made the stump just below her left knee ache and she worried at her prosthetic, trying to reduce the pain.

She reached behind for her backpack, rummaged for the flask of coffee and poured a steaming cup. She grimaced at the bitter taste but appreciated it nonetheless. Coffee was almost impossible to get hold of these days, as killing frosts had near enough wiped out the harvest. Soon it would be just a memory.

Already, there were so many things you couldn't buy for love nor money: tea, sugar, bananas, oranges. God, what she wouldn't give for a big, juicy orange. For a few moments she let herself relive memories of the luscious Jaffas they used to take on family picnics, before the clatter of ice granules on the windscreen brought her back to the present. She turned on the wipers to clear away the icy grains brought by a gusting east wind, gulped the remainder of the brown liquid and disengaged the handbrake. Heavy snow was forecast for later and she had been marooned overnight once before. It was an ordeal she wasn't keen to repeat.

She revved the engine and the gas-guzzler pumped clouds of filthy exhaust into the bitter air. *Doing our bit to fight the ice*, she mused, as she carefully eased away, the Land Rover's considerable weight giving it excellent traction in the snow.

She edged south towards the city centre along streets piled high with filthy snow, through which snowploughs had sliced a path just about wide enough to squeeze through. She saw no people and no other vehicles until she hung a left into Beaumont Street. At the far end was a jumble of army trucks, scattered at random amongst the drifts outside the Ashmolean and completely blocking the thoroughfare. The colleges had been closed for a couple of years now and anything worth removing had been decanted – either that or looted. The Ashmolean Museum had left it late, but now it looked as if the time had come for its treasures to be shipped out too. Under an onslaught of advice and abuse from a grizzled sergeant, dozens of squaddies slipped and slithered as they hauled crates of priceless antiquities and works of art across the ice. With more or less care, they loaded them into the backs of the trucks, which would carry them first to Southampton Docks and then by ship to a storage facility in Gibraltar. What would happen to them next was anyone's guess. The troops' cheery banter echoed back and forth across the otherwise deserted street, out of keeping with the bleakness of the surroundings and wholly at odds with the absolute silence that reigned across the rest of the city.

A roadblock manned by more soldiers toting machine pistols prevented Jane from proceeding further, and a young officer waved her down a cleared side street, which took her through a small square and eventually onto High Street and out towards the M40.

September 2048
Surrey
England

THE TRIP BACK TO THE UNIVERSITY CAMPUS ON THE western edge of London was largely uneventful, and only once was she held up – by a jack-knifed lorry. No-one travelled unless they had to these days and as the grip of the ice grew ever tighter, so many people had headed to London and the major cities that the countryside seemed deserted.

Jane guided the vehicle through bulldozed piles of grubby snow and into the university's main entrance. The barrier was long gone, as was the little cabin that had provided shelter for Dennis and the other security guys. Last she'd heard, Dennis had flown south and was somewhere in North Africa, trying to eke out some sort of existence, along with millions of other northern European migrants, in the straggling favela that stretched for more than a hundred kilometres along the Moroccan coast.

Finding a parking space was easy. There were no undergraduates any longer, just a few postgrads completing their research. She couldn't understand how they were always so cheerful. Most would get their doctorates, but what then? There was no future in academia these days, or in much else, for that matter. Still, it was nice to have a few youngsters about the place. They kept her spirits up and reminded her of Ali, even if that was painful at times.

Dusk was drawing in and there was fine snow in the air as she climbed out of the vehicle. It was excruciatingly cold and the shock, after the muggy warmth of the vehicle, struck like a knife. The great gothic revivalist pile that formed the main university building was three quarters in darkness. It couldn't be long now before the university council gave in to reason and shut up shop for good. Why they struggled on was a mystery. More through habit than anything else, she suspected.

She unloaded the drone and the dust sampling kit, picked up a shallow wooden crate containing the samples, and headed for the lab. An innocuous, single-storey structure of grey brick, it couldn't have been more of a contrast to the glitz of the main building. It was a truth acknowledged by academics at all UK universities, that management always garnered the best accommodation. She paused as she passed the dead stump of the cherry tree. So many memories.

She dumped her backpack in the corridor and considered discarding her thermal suit. But she thought better of it when she noticed she could still see her breath. Looked like the sodding heating was out again.

Pushing open her office door, she turned on the light and stopped dead. Slumped in the chair across from her desk, snuggled down in a bright red parka, was a man, dark-skinned, cropped hair, long legs stretched out in front. His face sported the biggest grin she had seen in a long while. A deep voice rumbled the flat vowels of Boston.

'Dr Haliwell... Long time no see.'

'Fuck me! Colonel Ralph Martinez. What brings you to the frozen frontier?'

Ralph's grin got even wider. 'Just plain mister now, Jane.'

He stood and stepped forwards to give her a hug, head towering far above hers, arms enclosing her spare frame like a bear.

She freed herself reluctantly but held his hands in hers as she looked up at him. They had kept in touch by phone and email over the years, but she couldn't remember when they had last met face to face. He had barely changed at all. Perhaps a little more salt in his salt 'n' pepper crop, but that was it. Suddenly, irrationally, she was acutely aware of her grey unkempt hair and a face that time and grief had been dreadfully unkind to. A combination of sun and ice had done their work too, leaving her skin the colour and texture of wrinkled leather.

'So why are you here?' she repeated.

Ralph shrugged. 'NOAA – Met Office liaison. Waste of time – I knew it would be. But it got me here, which is the main thing.'

Again the raised eyebrows. 'So, you came over specially to see me?' She motioned for Ralph to sit and perched on the edge of a battered desk.

Ralph paused for a moment, framing his words carefully. 'Did you know your government is giving up on the UK?'

Jane looked nonplussed. 'What do you mean?'

Ralph shrugged. 'They don't feel the country has a future. They're planning to abandon everything north of Oxford in the next couple of years and close down all government apparatus within ten – tops.'

'But... they can't!' She was visibly shocked. 'There are still millions of people living in the midlands and the north. There're thousands on the move south every day, right enough, but they can't just leave the rest of them in the shit.'

'Apparently, they can,' said Ralph. 'They're hoping that when the announcement is made, most people will self-evacuate and save them the bother.'

'Bastards!' She kicked at an overflowing waste bin. 'And then what? Where will they go?'

'As I understand it, the government will provide a small resettlement allowance. Other than that, it's goodbye and thanks for all the fish! Ten years to get out and find somewhere warmer or stay and tough it out in a frozen and lawless wilderness. So much for your government of national unity.' Ralph grimaced. 'Which brings me to my offer.'

Jane rolled her eyes. Ralph had been trying to persuade her for years to pack up and move out, and had forwarded details of yet another job opportunity just a month or so earlier.'

'Ralph! How many times have I told you? I'm not moving—'

He raised his arms again. 'Just hear me out, Jane – please. This is a great opportunity.'

She made a face, but let Ralph continue.

'I've just taken up a post at the University of South Florida, down the road from the New White House in Tampa. They're setting up an institute focused on geoengineering solutions—'

Jane snorted. 'As if we haven't had enough of fucking around with the climate?'

'Maybe, but it's our only chance now of ever getting out of this mess, albeit a very small one, I admit.'

She shook her head in exasperation.

'Anyway,' Ralph continued, 'they're looking for staff and they want you on board. You'll have your own team and a good budget. The institute is government-funded, so money's not a problem. Karl's there now. Didn't need much convincing. It's getting a bit too chilly Down Under. And there was really nothing to keep him there.

Jane nodded but said nothing. It was a tempting offer, the three of them working together. She looked around at her tired lab, the cobbled together kit, the intermittent WiFi, the struggling radiators that were more off than on. Yes, it was tempting – especially the thought of hands and feet that weren't frozen half the time. But this was her home, her life. She still had work to do – someone needed to monitor the ice front and check bot concentrations in the dust samples. Above all, Ali was buried just down the road, and she was not yet ready to abandon him to the ice.

Jane gave a tight smile. 'Thanks, but no thanks.'

Outside, it began to snow, a torrent of tiny flakes blasted horizontally by a bitter north wind straight off the ice cap.

Ralph was deflated rather than angry. He had come a long way to make Jane the offer but, truth be told, he never really thought she would take it up. Two decades after Ali's murder, she still wouldn't, or couldn't, drag herself away. It was as if – even in death – the two were bound by a cord, the strength of which time did not seem to diminish. Ralph sighed. He really felt for her, but he knew and she knew – he was certain – that it couldn't go on. He had heard that the university was thinking of shutting up shop completely. It had been unsustainable for years, and the final few research students were writing up and would be done soon. Add to this the increasingly appalling weather and the ever more frequent brownouts, and it was clear that the writing was on the wall. So sometime soon, she would have to cut the cord. He couldn't see any other option.

He was deflected from his ruminations by a sudden worsening of the weather. What had started as little more than spindrift had morphed rapidly into a full-on blizzard. He peered through the misted-up windscreen and slowed to a crawl as red brake lights glowed ahead and were soon replaced by winking hazard indicators as the vehicle in front came to a standstill. He couldn't see what the hold-up was. Surely not weight of traffic; there was barely anything on the roads these days. The M25 orbital motorway, built to accommodate many thousands of vehicles an hour, now probably carried just a few dozen over the same period. For most people the conditions were just too bad to risk. Despite a service only slightly better than appalling, the trains were seen as a safer bet.

After ten minutes or so of growing frustration, he pulled on his gloves and balaclava, and pocketed a handgun from the glove compartment. It was an old US forces Beretta M92 – not the greatest, but better than nothing in a tight spot. You could never be too careful these days.

He knew he'd never get the driver's door open against the full force of the wind, so shifted across and opened the passenger door into the lee of the snowstorm. Even so, he struggled to stop the wind catching it and tearing it out of his grip. The air was staggeringly cold and it felt as if his eyeballs were frosting over as he exited the big Mercedes SUV and squinted into the storm. He couldn't see beyond the car ahead – an old-style Land Rover – so walked around it through the ever-deepening snow. The vehicle's interior light was on, and the sole occupant – a well-dressed man in late middle age – ignored him as he shuffled past, gripping the steering wheel and staring straight ahead. He didn't take offence. Minding one's own business was the safest bet in a society that was rapidly falling apart.

He walked a little further, until a shadowy shape resolved itself into an army jeep stopped across the two outer lanes of the motorway. Another smaller shape detached itself and came towards him. It was a young officer in a grey and white camouflaged jumpsuit, machine pistol held at the ready. The suit was padded and heated, but he looked frozen and scared. He held out a gloved hand.

'Papers.'

Ralph reached inside his parka and pulled out his ID and permit to travel. After much debate, compulsory identity cards had been introduced when it became apparent that climate catastrophe could not be avoided. Travel permits had followed just three years back, a last-gasp attempt by a struggling government to control southward migration. How this would fit with the new plan of abandoning the increasingly snowbound cities of the midlands and the north he couldn't fathom. The whole thing was a shambles. But it was no better elsewhere. Germany was pretty much a lawless state these days and the civil war in China had taken the lives of millions. The low-level conflict between the US and Mexico rumbled on, while unrest simmered along the Mediterranean's south coast as European and North African forces clashed. All-out war seemed only a matter of time as the French, Spanish and Italians sought to expand the enclaves they had established along the African coast for millions of their citizens displaced southwards by the advancing cold.

Satisfied with the papers, the officer handed them back. Ralph nodded his thanks and then indicated with his chin beyond the parked jeep. 'What's the hold up?'

The officer turned to follow his gaze, then back again. 'Overturned petrol tanker. The fuel's pouring out and the place is swarming with punters making the most of it. I haven't got the men to stop them, but I've radioed for support.'

With the oil and gas fields of Russia, Alaska, Canada and the North Atlantic icebound, petrol was like gold dust. Rationing was strictly enforced and reserved mainly for essential services and public transport.

Ralph sniffed the air. The stink of petrol was strong and getting stronger by the second. 'Hope there aren't any smokers out there?' he said, only half-jokingly. 'How long until the mess is cleared up?'

'In this weather?' the officer grunted. 'It could be days.'

'Shit. Can I get around?'

The officer just shrugged. 'Don't know the area, I'm afraid. We were escorting the tanker up from Southampton, heading for Oxford. If they aren't already, any minor roads are going to be impassable soon – even to that.' He nodded in the direction of Ralph's SUV.

'Fuck!' Ralph swore under his breath, thanked the officer and headed back to the Mercedes. It probably saved his life.

The few hundred scavengers swarming around the overturned tanker were mainly householders from a nearby estate – men, women and kids. They were bundled up against the blizzard with anything that came to hand, and weighed down with a variety of receptacles, anything – in fact – that they could use to carry petrol. There wasn't a kitchen sink, but there were a fair few washing-up bowls. Half a dozen or so soldiers looked on but did not intervene. The tanker's double skin had split in half a dozen places and fuel was cascading out. A slushy concoction of petrol and melted snow extended across three lanes and the air was heavy with fumes. No-one was smoking. Virtually nobody did these days, and people weren't stupid enough to smoke around petrol. But this wasn't enough to prevent disaster.

The tanker was on its side, resting partly on a number of metal struts that were taking the full weight of the overturned vehicle. One of the struts was under particular stress and had been slowly deforming since the accident. As the internal strain exceeded a critical threshold, it snapped. The tanker shifted slightly, bringing one of the broken ends of the strut up against the metal exterior of the tank. The result was a spark – tiny, but big enough.

The detonation was colossal, ripping the tanker apart. The shockwave blasted a wall of snow ahead of it and sent the army jeep tumbling. The volley of shrapnel that followed shredded those scavengers closest and tore the limbs from those further away. The ballooning fireball turned the rest into living, screaming torches. The driver of the Land Rover still sat staring ahead, hands gripping the wheel. But now his eyes saw nothing. A single shrapnel fragment had penetrated the windscreen, destroying his left eye before slicing through the brain. Death had been instantaneous.

Ralph had just reached the Mercedes when the blast lifted him bodily and sent him sprawling across the bonnet. His head bounced off the icy metal and for a moment he saw stars. A wave of searing heat followed, hot enough to hurt, but not to burn. He slumped off the side of the bonnet and lay on his back in the snow. It wasn't difficult to guess what had happened. He turned over and crouched on all fours for a few seconds, shaking his head to clear it. He felt weak when he stood and looked around him. How the fuck had he avoided injury? The snow all around was pockmarked with melt holes surrounding fragments of hot shrapnel, and a large chunk of twisted metal had shattered one of the headlights and was lodged deep in the housing. Turning, he squinted into the blizzard and surveyed what looked like a battlefield.

An orange glow suffused the scene and rivulets of melted snow dribbled across the carriageway. The stench of burning petrol and roasting meat was overwhelming. Roaring flames obscured the rump of the tanker, and blazing or blackened remains were scattered across the motorway. He noticed that some still moved and suddenly felt sick. But there was nothing he could do. Off to the left the young officer's legs stuck out from under the overturned jeep. Slowly, he became aware of another sound above the crackle of the flames and susurration of snowflakes sublimating as they met hot metal, the rumble and grind of tracked vehicles. Looking up, he could just make out headlights through the snow, coming down from the north. Army half-trucks, he guessed, called up by the officer to help out.

He turned back to the Mercedes. He had a flight to catch early the next morning and the last thing he needed was to get drawn into some interminable military debrief.

It had cost him an arm and a leg to hire and fuel it, so Ralph was pleased to see that apart from the headlight, the SUV was miraculously intact. He climbed aboard, started the engine and turned the heater up to full blast. The heat of the fires had cleared the windscreen, and it looked as if the blizzard was abating a little. He reversed away from the wreck of the Land Rover, the snow tyres doing their job, turned and headed slowly back down the motorway.

It took three aborted attempts and more than four hours to find his way back onto the M25 beyond the carnage. The tanker incident to the south meant that there was virtually no traffic, and he quickly joined the M4 and headed east into London. Finally, he reached the A4 and the outskirts of the capital. The road was lined with commercial buildings, but all were unlit, by government edict. With oil and gas supplies desperately low, energy was just too precious to waste on illuminating the night. It had always been inevitable that over time the focus would switch from maximising carbon output to managing dwindling fossil fuel supplies.

Still a long way out from the city centre and his hotel, he saw ahead the glow of red brake lights. There wasn't much traffic, but what there was of it was stationary. To add to Ralph's growing irritation, it started to snow again. Not the fine, wind-blown flecks of a few hours earlier, but good and proper, huge flakes that drifted down and stuck. The sort of snow that could block a road in half an hour.

It was just after three in the morning. His flight was at eight and he still had to drop off the car, check out and get to Gatwick airport, a way south of London. *No chance*, he thought. *No fucking chance at all.*

Seeing Ralph again had been a tonic, but it had also unsettled Jane. When he had gone, she closed up the lab and drove the few miles home though a minor blizzard, easing the Land

Rover along almost empty roads. She could still see her breath in the hallway, and flicking the light switch brought no illumination. Another sodding power outage. They were becoming increasingly common as the growing ice cover isolated and shut down the power plants and short-circuited the grid. With the north depopulating fast, there was far less demand, but the much-reduced grid still struggled to cope as ice and snow constantly brought down pylons and transmission lines, leading to power cutbacks and blackouts.

She had plenty of candles about the place and lit a few of them now to light her way to the living room, where she busied herself removing some of the ash build-up in the wood-burning stove. She still had some wood out the back, although even this was more and more difficult to get hold of these days. She had got rid of the walnut in the back garden years earlier. It was the tree that Ali used to climb when he was little and it broke her heart to see it go. But the cold was killing it, in any case, and she needed to commandeer the wood before someone else did. A neighbour had felled and chain-sawn it for her in return for a share of the timber. The avenue she lived on used to be lined with majestic limes, but they had long vanished too, chopped down unceremoniously by residents driven by circumstances to value warmth more than a pretty view. Fortuitously, a farmer friend had a small copse, and dropped over a few logs from time to time. But even this couldn't continue, as tree 'rustlers' were fast depleting the resource. Last she'd heard, he and a group of friends were having to ride shotgun at night to scare them off.

By necessity, she was frugal with the kindling, so it took a while to get the small stove going. Even then, she fed the growing blaze just a single log. The living room was small, so it soon warmed up enough for her to shed her outdoor gear. She slumped onto the sofa, almost on top of the stove, and stretched out her freezing hands to the meagre blaze. As she slowly warmed up, her focus of attention switched to her stomach, which was making grumbling noises loud enough to drown out the hiss of the flames. She had eaten little since breakfast and was famished. Problem was, it was difficult to get enthusiastic about food these days. Almost everything was processed, and so bland as to be instantly forgettable. She had coped by spicing everything up, but now herbs and other taste enhancers – even salt – were nowhere to be found amongst the spartan selection of produce on the shelves of the government stores. Gone were the private supermarkets, off to warmer climes where a profit could still be made and shareholders kept contented, at least for a time.

She went into the still freezing kitchen to see what there was. The fridge she ignored. It had been unplugged for a couple of years at least. If she ever did get hold of fresh produce – and it did still happen, once in a blue moon – she hardly needed somewhere to keep it cool.

The cupboards weren't exactly bare, but they were getting that way. Her own fault, really. She let herself be submerged in her work so that shopping hardly made it to her to-do list at all. Only when there was nothing but scraps left would she think of picking up her ration card and making her way to the nearest state store a few miles down the road.

Soup, she decided, chunky vegetable – again. Root veg, mainly, of course, not much else grew in the UK these days. But it was comforting and warming. She had a single ring on the worktop, fed from a small bottled gas container, and she fired this up now. Mains gas was no more, as most of the UK and European gas fields had succumbed to the ice or extreme weather, and even bottled gas was strictly rationed.

She rummaged in the cupboards again. Bread – she was sure she still had some somewhere. It too was becoming scarce, and nothing but the sliced white pap could be found anywhere. Ah, there it was, right at the back, a few dried-up slices. She scraped off the flecks of mould and was thinking how lovely it would have been to make toast, when the hall light came on and she heard the gurgle of water in the radiators. Power! She switched on the kitchen lights, popped a couple of slices in the toaster, and began another hunt – this time for butter substitute.

She took her supper through to the living room on a tray. The fire in the stove was on the wane. It made the room so much cheerier, but she couldn't really justify using up another precious log. Anyway, now the power was on, the electric storage heaters were slowly warming up the house and she was already looking forward to a hot shower before bed.

She turned on the television. There were just the two BBC channels now, run directly by the Ministry of Information, both providing a constant diet of repeats cut with news bulletins. Making television programmes was hardly a priority any more. Every time she watched the news, she told herself, *Never again*. Even with the worst censored out, it always made her utterly despondent, and that really was the last thing she needed. But she could never stick to her resolution. She was the sort of person who had to know what was going on, so at nine every evening – when there was power, at least – she was there, waiting to hear the latest, hoping, but not really believing, that there would be some nuggets of good news amongst the bad. Tonight, once again, she watched in vain. Wars, starvation, assassination, civil strife and not a cute kitten in sight.

The ends of the Skyseed conspirators had been swift and clean. But for many of the billions left behind, death was proving to be slow and brutal. Tens of millions had already perished in biblical famines or met violent ends in one of the many nasty little wars spawned by wholesale southward migration spurred on by the rapid advance of the ice. The guilty had paid the price, and now, so too were the innocent.

Wishing, not for the first time, that she had held firm, she grabbed the remote and flicked the television off in irritation. The bulletin was over and there was only so much *Fawlty Towers* she could take.

She prodded with a poker at the embers in the stove, to squeeze out the last of the heat, and leant back in the sofa. The food and the warmth were making her feel sleepy, but she needed to do some thinking before a shower and then bed.

She found it hard to believe that Ralph had come all this way to try to get her to join him in Florida. Perhaps she had been too quick to reject his offer? There was no future here, and she knew it couldn't be long before the last students left and the place shut its doors for good. And the warmth of the sunshine state was a real pull. Even when the sun shone, these days, its rays provided illumination, but no heat. And sometimes weeks went by without seeing it at all.

Then again, Florida was far from immune to the effects of the freeze. The state was inundated with migrants from the northern states and Canada, and refugee camps and shanties surrounded the major cities. The steeper temperature gradient between temperate latitudes and the tropics was also spawning super hurricanes that often ended their lives on the Florida coastline. Miami had taken a colossal battering ten years earlier and had never really recovered. Fort Lauderdale too.

She never made a decision without asking herself what Ali would have advised. And she nearly always followed what she thought he would say. Once or twice she went the other way. There was the fling with Tom a few years back. He and Ali would have got on like a house on fire. She knew Ali would have wanted her to be happy, and she was certain he would have told her to go for it. But she kept Tom hanging on for so long that the relationship just faded away to nothing. Bottom line was, she already had a man in her life and she didn't need – didn't want – another. She knew what Ali would have said about Ralph's offer too. 'Take it! For God's sake, take it. I'll always be with you, wherever in the world you are. Live again.' It was good advice, she recognised that, but nonetheless, it was advice she wouldn't take.

Ralph had said she could call any time, or at least when the networks weren't playing up, and he would make the arrangements to get her and her stuff over to the States. But she knew that, however appealing his pitch, it was a call she would never make.

All at once, she felt dog tired. Her eyes were drooping and it took a supreme effort to pull herself upright and stand. As she did so, the lights went out. 'Shit!' She could look forward to another morning waking up to the water in her tooth mug frozen solid. Still, there would be enough hot water for a shower. Simple pleasures as the world fell apart; simple pleasures.

In the end, it took Ralph close to six hours to edge his way back to his central London hotel and drop the car off. But he didn't miss his flight. Gatwick – now the only functioning major airport in the UK – was completely snowbound, and nothing took off or landed at all that day. He made the most of the respite to catch up on much-needed sleep and cater to an empty stomach.

The morning after dawned as bright as a pin and eye-wateringly cold. He was up and about early, refreshed and champing at the bit to start a journey that he had no doubt would be – at the very least – trying. The tube system was all but down and out so, after he had paid his bill, he bundled himself up against the numbing cold and shouldered his backpack, ready to head south on foot.

As he was about to leave the hotel lobby, he caught the eye of a stooped, world-weary-looking man in a grubby raincoat carrying a battered suitcase, who was also checking out. He had assumed that, apart from himself, the place was deserted, but looking around he saw now there were other guests: an old couple shuffling out of the lift, a family group – mum, dad and three kids of various ages – struggling down the stairs with their bags. Looked like the hotel managed to attract just enough itinerants to keep it ticking over. It couldn't last, he thought. He looked over at the man at the check-out desk again. He was bent over, talking quietly to the young receptionist, querying an item on his bill. As she turned away to print something out, the man stood upright. His hair was lank and his chin had accumulated several days of beard growth, but Ralph thought there was something familiar about him. Then it hit home.

'Mr Bannerman. Jeremy Bannerman?' Ralph called out and headed across the lobby to the desk. The man looked up in surprise, then smiled gently as he saw Ralph approaching.

'You have me bang to rights, sir.' The man held out his wrists, as if for cuffing, then offered a hand, which Ralph looked at for a moment, then shook. 'But I go by my maiden name now – Carnforth. Makes things simpler – you understand.'

Ralph nodded.

Jeremy tapped Ralph lightly on the chest with a forefinger. 'I never forget a face, and I certainly couldn't forget yours. Ralph Martinez, is it not? Scourge of the Skyseeders. Macbeth to my very own King Duncan.'

The literary analogy went over Ralph's head, but he sensed trouble and made to say something. Before he could, Jeremy put both hands up in a placatory gesture.

'Please. There's nothing more to be said. You were doing your job. Duncan was doing what he felt he had to do – in the circumstances. It was stupid, dangerous. He would admit it himself if he were here. But that was then. Water under the bridge and all that.' For a moment he was quiet – distracted, maybe, by some treasured memory.

'So, what brings you to snowy London town?' Jeremy went on.

Ralph really didn't want to talk about his failed attempt to hook Jane out of her lab, so muttered something vague about work. 'What about you? I guess there's not much of a demand for actors these days?'

Jeremy grunted his disgust. 'Indeed not. We always used to say that the show must go on, but no longer. Film and theatre are dead and buried, and television – at least here in the UK – is on its last legs.' He grimaced at the thought. 'I'm subsisting on a diet of radio voice overs and government propaganda. Not my thing, of course, but needs must.'

Ralph nodded at the suitcase. 'So where are you headed?'

Jeremy's demeanour brightened. 'Gibraltar, old man. The BBC's shipped out there lock, stock and barrel now – on the coat-tails of the government and the King – and I'm following on a tight leash. Continuity presenter, you know. They said they were sending a car to get me to Gatwick.' He glanced hopefully out of the window at the car-less, snowbound street.

Ralph raised his eyebrows and thought, *Good luck with that*, but said nothing.

Jeremy turned at the receptionist's voice, took a sheet of paper from her and stuffed it in his pocket. 'Expenses,' he explained. 'The Beeb are still real sticklers.'

The conversation ebbed as each thought, unsuccessfully, of how to continue it. In the end, Jeremy stuck out his hand. 'Well, good to meet you, Ralph. Safe journey.'

'You too,' said Ralph, 'and good luck. I'll listen out for you.'

What he thought was, *Poor fucking sod!*

Jeremy was good. He gave him that, but he was an actor after all. He had gone along with Jeremy's narrative but hadn't believed a word of it. There was barely a button left on the man's coat, his Hollywood smile was long gone – stained brown with nicotine and coffee substitute. This wasn't a man heading for a new life in Gibraltar. This was a man at his wit's end. Just one more wretched UK citizen heading for the exit, driven by the likely futile hope of finding something better. Ralph felt a pang of sympathy. He gave Jeremy an encouraging pat on the shoulder, evoking a weak smile, negotiated the lobby's revolving doors and turned south.

The journey from his Bloomsbury hotel to Waterloo Station was only a couple of miles, but the snow and ice made for slow going. The bus services were no more and private cars were a rarity, so he kept to the centre of the road, where the going was a little easier.

Most of the shops and cafés to either side were empty and boarded up, their occupiers driven out by the weather and the losing battle to find anything worth selling, but some still struggled on. Despite the bitter cold, there were plenty of people about, all headed south. Refugees, many hardly dressed for the bitter conditions.

Waterloo Station was on the far side of the Thames and crossing points were now few and far between. As sea levels had plunged, the river had been forced to find a new level, gouging deeply into the soft clays and sands beneath, excavating and widening a gorge that sliced through the capital and as far west as Maidenhead. But now, the advancing ice sheet to the west had cut off the water supply, so the river had run its last.

The growing chasm had played havoc with the transport system, slicing the tube network and north–south rail routes in two. It had also made short work of the existing bridges, some of which had been standing for centuries. In their place, the government had caused half a dozen temporary crossing points to be thrown across the gorge. Two – one each way – carried vehicles only, the rest delivered southward – on foot – the growing spate of refugees from the north and west that converged on the capital on their way to the channel ports or the only working airport of any size. One of the pedestrian crossings occupied the position of the old Waterloo Bridge, and it was towards this that Ralph was headed.

The sun was well above the horizon and its light blinding, even if there was little in the way of accompanying warmth. As he drew closer to the bridgehead, the trickle of refugees became a stream and then a flood, as they were funnelled onto Kingsway from neighbouring streets. There were all sorts, some smartly dressed, struggling to haul pull-alongs across the lumpy ice-packed surface, others in tattered coats, stuffed with newspapers and belted with rope, apparently with no possessions at all. Groups of bored squaddies, in white thermal jumpsuits looked on, assault rifles cocked ready for trouble, but there was no heart for it. Many of the refugees were family groups, adults and children alike loaded down with everything they could carry, only desperation for something better, warmer, keeping them going. Ralph saw in people's faces a weariness that went beyond mere exhaustion. An amalgam of shock, despair and confusion that sapped the soul.

The crowd was so closely packed now that progress was reduced to a shuffle around the curve of the Aldwych. But its passage was almost silent, people speaking in whispers, if they spoke at all. As they approached the end of the bend, Ralph saw the northern end of the new bridge. Here, the Thames gorge had eaten its way back to the Strand, swallowing up all the buildings that had lined its southern side. The new crossing stretched from here nearly all the way to Waterloo Station. Almost twice the length of the original.

The bridge was filled with a multitude, inching forwards beneath a miasma of exhaled breath that hovered in the still, bitter air, like a low-hanging cloud. A nation on the move, even before the coming government proclamation declaring the abandonment of its people. As Ralph approached the bridge, the ground beneath his feet became increasingly irregular. Cracks broke through the thick layer of ice, which widened as the bridge entrance drew closer. With the river now dry, the gorge had stopped expanding. Nonetheless, the cracks suggested to him that the bridge anchors – suspended from a portal high overhead – were beginning to pull away, the immense load imposed by the unending stream of people warping the walkway and straining the fastenings. He hoped to God they held out a little longer.

Enclosing ramparts of filthy snow guided the shambling mass of humanity across what was left of the Strand and towards the bridgehead. A little way in front, a man in a dirty raincoat detached himself from the host and crossed to the snowbank. In his arms he carried a small bundle wrapped in a grubby blue blanket – unmoving. Ralph watched in horror as the man kicked out a small hollow in the snow, within which he gently laid the bundle, before using his bare hands to pull some of the blackened snow down on top. Contented with his efforts, he stood for a few moments, looking down at the pitiful heap, before turning and rejoining the throng. A woman and a teenaged boy on either side each put an arm around him and they shuffled onwards as one.

Bodies were forced together so closely now that Ralph couldn't even see his feet. He was only certain he was on the bridge when he began to feel the surface tremble beneath. The walkway gave under the weight of the crowd, and bounced up and down like a trampoline.

After an hour or so, he reckoned he must be about halfway across. Some distance off to the right, pointing skywards out of the gorge, he could see the ornamented neo-gothic pinnacle of the Elizabeth Tower – home for more than two centuries to the great bell known as Big Ben. Emblematic of the collapse of the old world, it rested now – battered and broken – against the northern edge of the chasm. Teetering on the rim beyond the remains of the tower was the shell of the Palace of Westminster, the interior of its hallowed halls open to the elements. Until recently, the much-diminished Houses had met in circumstances of reduced grandeur in a former concert hall in Croydon. Now, they had decanted to the relative warmth and normality of Gibralter. From the crumbling walls of the gorge, the shattered remains of tube tunnels, sewerage mains and smaller utility pipes, dangled like severed arteries, the capital's deeply buried infrastructure now derelict and on show. A further reminder, if one was needed, of a once-great city in its death throes.

Another hour of shuffling brought Ralph, much to his relief, to the solid ground of the south bank. Once he had negotiated the steps up to the station concourse, progress was marginally faster as the crowd spread out. Even so, the place was heaving and it took another thirty minutes for him to find the right queue for the next Gatwick train. Yet another hour passed before he was able to shoehorn himself onto one of the long trains that shuttled continuously back and forth between the capital and the airport and south coast ports, ferrying the hopeless and the hopeful alike. All the seats had been taken out to accommodate as many passengers as possible, so that each train held thousands. As it clattered through the snowy suburbs, Ralph tried not to imagine the carnage if they derailed.

He had a welcome break when the train pulled into the platform at Gatwick and his carriage stopped adjacent to an exit. Making the most of his good luck, he mounted the steps at speed and got a decent head start on the pursuing horde. The airport concourse was a sea of displaced humanity in all its despondency. Even though there was no heating, the mass of living, breathing flesh had pushed up the temperature of the place almost to comfort level. Though welcome, the warmth had also released the odours – long-imprisoned by the cold – of several thousand people, who had been marinating in their own juices for days, some for weeks. The result was gag-making.

He spotted an official from his airline and waded through the crowd to intercept her. The Met Office had flown him over first class, and he made the most of his status now to angle for special treatment. It helped too that the woman recognised his face, and forty minutes later he found himself in the calm of the first-class lounge, all checked in, boarding pass in hand. He was the only one there. It appeared that anyone who could afford a first-class ticket had already headed south. The hubbub on the concourse penetrated into the quiet of the lounge, and he felt a twinge of guilt at the continuing ordeal of those beyond its walls. But this dissipated rapidly as a rumbling stomach reminded him he hadn't eaten for several hours. Barring further blizzards, the Tampa flight left in two hours, so he had a bit of time to refuel and relax.

The spread was far from that of first-class lounges of yore. Gone were the caviar, champagne and pastries, replaced by stale sausage rolls, processed cheese sandwiches and bottled beer. This was far more to his liking, in any case, and he spent a good three quarters of an hour satisfying his needs. The networks were down again, and he hadn't seen or heard the news for forty-eight hours. There was a television on the wall, which he watched as he munched, and then wished he hadn't. The tanker explosion on the M25 was still the lead story on the news bulletin, 140 people dead, including twenty children. The government was making the most of the incident to warn of the dangers of opportunistic looting. The rest of the news wasn't any better.

He hadn't realised how exhausted he was until he lay down on one of the sofas and closed his eyes. Seconds later – or so it seemed – he felt a hand on his shoulder, gently shaking him. It was the same woman who had attended him earlier. Her smile was bright, but her eyes gave away her weariness. 'Last call, sir. Wouldn't want you to miss your flight.'

Thirty minutes later he was fast asleep in his seat in the otherwise empty first-class cabin of a Florida-bound A380. Seven hours on, he was awake and looking down on a new world. A major Atlantic storm had shifted the plane's flightpath, taking it much closer to the eastern seaboard. He peered out of the window. There was some ragged cloud, but otherwise the sky was clear and the view pin-sharp. Westwards, beyond the Prussian blue of the sea, everything was white, blinding white so that the eyes squinted and watered as they struggled to decipher detail. Ralph was awestruck. He had seen satellite images, of course, multitudes of them, but this was different. It had been ten-tenths cloud on the way out, so this was the first time he had seen the extent of the snow and ice cover with his own eyes. They must have been somewhere a little south of DC, he calculated, but the altitude and the intense glare meant he couldn't make out any landmarks. He knew that the capital had been abandoned to the ice nearly two years earlier, so the White House was down there somewhere, and the Pentagon and the rest of it.

His thoughts turned to his parents' retirement place, way out west in Wyoming. They were long gone now, had died within a week of one another. Probably as well, really. They would have been too old to move again when the climate started to deteriorate in earnest. Now, the state was empty, a wilderness of white where the wolf and the bison reigned once more.

The first patches of green began to show when they were over southern Virginia, and the landscape was snow-free by the time they reached the Carolinas. The plane lost height as it crossed the Florida peninsula south of Jacksonville and Ralph looked out on a world that was hardly recognisable. Barely thirty years earlier, all the talk was of how rapidly rising sea levels would see downtown Miami fifty miles offshore. Now, as the ice sheets had sprouted across the continents, so the oceans had shrunk. Miami, along with all of Florida's coastal cities, was now marooned far inland, the shoreline having shifted more than fifty kilometres towards the edge of the continental shelf. The Everglades were long gone, left high and dry by the rapid retreat of the sea. Tampa's great bay was an immense hollow floored with compacted mud and the flotsam and jetsam of human excess.

The vast expanse of newly exposed terrain that bordered the state's original coastline was barren, the salt-infused sediment toxic to plants. The plane was low enough now for Ralph to make out groups of people meandering across the scabby, pockmarked surface of the former seabed. He guessed they were scavenging, although what they hoped to find he couldn't fathom. To Ralph's jaded eye, the great swathe of blasted landscape recalled images he remembered seeing of the no-man's land that separated opposing trenches during the Great War. And like it, a testament to bleak and hopeless times.

It was just after six in the morning when he picked up his car at Tampa airport. No ice or snow here, but the air was chill and the skies grey. No-one called Florida the sunshine state any longer. Autumn and winter were cool and wet, with snow flurries making their appearance in the north of the state during the darkest months. The summers, at least in the south, were still warmish, but the sun made far fewer appearances than of old. Hurricanes continued to pound the coast, less frequently, but devastatingly more powerful. The only saving grace was that they had usually lost much of their destructive power by the time they had traversed the newly exposed sea floor and reached the major population centres.

Despite the increased land area, the population of the state had dived. Wealthy retirees had decanted to South America, where the sun still shone brightly, leaving behind the poor and the vulnerable. The Floridian economy had all but collapsed as killing frosts wiped out fruit growing. Mass unemployment and food shortages kindled desperate poverty and a culture of intimidation and violence within which life was cheap. The police and national guard tried to keep the lid on, but they knew in their hearts it was a battle they couldn't win. The sound of gunshots formed an ever-present backdrop and fresh bodies littered the streets every morning.

Ralph felt refreshed, having slept for much of the flight, so instead of going home he made for the university. The route took him through the vast shanty town that encircled the city, housing refugees from the north; a sprawling landscape of tin shacks from which streamed countless plumes of smoke from coal-burning fires. His journey was a slow one, progress interrupted twice by military roadblocks and further impeded as he navigated, on half a dozen occasions, through large groups of itinerants straggling across the highway. He knew better than to slow if he wanted to arrive in one piece and felt fortunate that only a couple of shots were aimed in his direction as he swung the vehicle at speed from one side of the highway to the other to present less of a target. Replacing the windows with armoured glass, he mused, had been well worth the arm and a leg it had cost.

It was mid-morning when he arrived at the new institute. Its doors had only opened a few months earlier and it still wasn't fully staffed or equipped. He eased his car around the concrete blocks installed to make life difficult for the suicide bombers of the Earth Brigade and pulled up at the front gates. The armed guards at the entrance checkpoint examined his ID carefully before opening the double barrier and waving him through.

The campus had been expanded enormously since the climate further north had made life there near impossible, and many agencies and research bodies had moved south. Slowed by speed humps and groups of chatting students, it took another five minutes to reach the Geoengineering Institute. There were few cars in the lot and he parked easily. At the main door, another armed guard checked his ID, and he took the lift to the sixth floor, swiping a card reader to gain access to his corridor.

The way to his study was stacked with boxes belonging to a new researcher moving in a few doors down. He didn't recognise her but nodded a greeting that the other – a middle-aged blonde – returned with a wide smile that said, *I know who you are.* He wasted a few moments regretting that it wasn't Jane moving in, then pulled himself together and smiled back. He had phoned ahead on the plane to let Karl know he was on the way, and when he reached his room there was a note from him pinned to the door. It didn't say much, just that Karl needed to see him as soon as he got in. He unlocked his door, dropped his backpack on a chair and binned the note. He guessed it wasn't going to be good news.

The door to Karl's study was open, but he was nowhere to be seen. Ralph eventually tracked him down to the communal area on the floor below, brewing himself an ersatz coffee. He watched as his friend added milk, took a sip and made a face. Karl's mane and beard were as wild as ever, and both now mostly grey. Ralph hadn't noticed before, but he'd developed a slight stoop too. *Well,* he thought, suddenly aware of the arthritic twinge in his right knee, *we're none of us getting any younger.*

'I don't know why we keep drinking that stuff.' He grinned as Karl turned.

'Ralph! Good to have you back.' They shook hands. 'Any luck?'

'With Jane? No. You were right. She's not ready. Not yet, anyway.'

Karl made a face. 'Maybe never.'

'True,' said Ralph. 'Anyhow, your note?'

'Yeah. Something new's come up.'

'Nothing good, I presume?'

'How did you guess?' Karl gave an ironic smile. 'Bring your coffee and I'll fill you in.'

Ralph picked up his cup and followed Karl up the stairs to a seminar room two floors up. There were a dozen or so chairs in the room and the built-in data projector was still switched on, connected to a laptop on a small table in front of a wall screen. Karl gestured to Ralph to take a seat and woke the laptop from sleep mode. A presentation was already open, and a map of the world filled the screen. Picking up a remote, Karl stood at the front.

'I've just finished a presentation to the high-ups,' he explained. 'Thought I'd let you in on the gist. I don't suppose you've been paying much attention to what's been happening in the world of volcanoes recently?' he continued.

Ralph shook his head. 'Not really. I know there have been a couple of big ones in the last few months. The one in PNG and Askja, is it – in Iceland?'

Karl nodded. 'That's just the tip of the iceberg. Take a look at this.' He moved the cursor and clicked on the world map, and Ralph realised it was an animation.

A small triangular symbol appeared halfway down the east coast of Sicily, glowed red and faded. Another appeared in the southern Andes and did the same. Then one in Mexico, followed by another in Papua New Guinea. A short interval preceded two more glowing triangles in the Philippines and the Caribbean. Karl paused the animation.

'In case it isn't obvious, this shows the occurrence of volcanic eruptions over time – the last thirty years – sped up, of course. Now watch.'

Karl restarted the show. More glowing triangles appeared. Initially, pauses were common, but as time went on, the time between eruptions clearly began to reduce. Eventually, triangles began to appear almost simultaneously, with only rare pauses. It was hard to miss the point – volcanic eruptions were becoming more frequent. When the animation ended, Ralph nodded that he understood.

'They've been popping off right, left and centre,' explained Karl. 'Not always biggies, but hefty enough to push up and maintain ash levels in the atmosphere.'

'Shit! That's not good,' said Ralph.

'Shit indeed!' said Karl.

'Is this just coincidence?' said Ralph. 'I mean, so many events in a short space of time.'

''Fraid not,' said Karl. 'There's a clear, increasing trend. Looks like we're starting to see a feedback effect that was described a while back.'

Ralph raised his eyebrows in expectation of elucidation.

Karl continued, 'If you look back at past episodes of rapid climate change, there's plenty of evidence that the solid Earth gets involved too. Well, it's not surprising, really, and it looks to be happening again.'

Ralph wasn't any the wiser. 'What mechanism are we talking here?'

'Mass redistribution. Unimaginable volumes of water are being sucked from the oceans and incorporated into the growing ice sheets. Hell, sea levels are falling so fast you can almost see it happening.'

'So?' wondered Ralph.

'So,' said Karl. 'This has scooped a serious chunk of the ocean's weight off the crust around the continental margins, and any available magma is making the most of the chance to escape. That's why, if you noticed, most of the new activity is pretty much confined to volcanic islands and volcanoes that are close to the coast.'

'Ah,' said Ralph, the light dawning. 'That really isn't good.'

A snort from Karl. 'Ever the master of the understatement. The bot population was way down,' he continued, 'but this is giving them a new lease of life. Bot numbers are already up and climbing fast. And there's more. It isn't just ash that's the problem here; there's a shed load of sulphur dioxide too. That, on its own, would be enough to accelerate cooling.'

Karl closed the animation and powered down the data projector, leaving Ralph to consider the implications.

'Put it this way,' he went on. 'I know we were already fucked, but now we're doubly so, taking it both ways, as it were. Unless the techies can pull something out of the hat, that is – and quickly. I've heard of nothing in the pipeline. You?'

Ralph shook his head. 'But,' he said, frowning, 'surely this is only a temporary response? There's only so much magma can come out.'

'Well, yes, but so what?' Karl said bluntly. 'We're already into a runaway situation. Even another few years of this level of volcanic activity will accelerate cooling beyond our ability to engineer our way out of it. Even if we could work out how.' Karl spread his arms wide and looked around the room. 'And that is, after all, why we're here.'

J ANE SCRAPED AWAY THE PATINA OF ICE AND LOOKED
out of the lab window at the morning snow, big flakes
that fell steadily and vertically in the absence of any wind.
The calendar showed the nineteenth of May. Traditionally,
the month of hawthorn blossom, spring lambs and far-
travelled swallows, but not any longer. The seasons were
no more, melded into just the one: winter, all-conquering,
everlasting. She pulled her battered overcoat tighter and
huddled closer to the tiny, bottle-fed gas stove. The fuel
was near impossible to get hold of now, and she had just
two bottles left.

It was more than four years since the university had
shut up shop for good. The last of the research students had
completed, sent out into a failing world that had nothing to
offer them. The few remaining academics and the dregs of the
admin staff had shipped out. The lucky ones to new positions
in warmer climes, the long-in-the-tooth or less-sought-after
to uncertain futures that were unlikely to end well.

The department had closed, along with the rest of the college, but Jane had battled hard to keep her small lab open. The analytical kit was long gone, the power supply too unreliable to run it, but she made herself useful monitoring and reporting on the advancing ice front. She joked with Major Bellers, who kept a watchful eye on her, that she really wasn't sure why she stayed on, but in her heart she knew well enough. Ali. It was more than a quarter of a century now, but the hurt was still as strong. She just couldn't leave him. Hardly a day went by without her wondering what he would have done with his life. He would have been in his early forties by now, probably with a wife and kids. Then again, why the hell would anyone want to bring children into this shithole of a world, a dead-end place where the best they could ever hope for was survival?

But if he had, she couldn't help speculating, she might have been a grandma by now. *I certainly feel like one*, she thought, rubbing at the knee above the prosthetic. The arthritis had been bad in recent weeks. Well, she was well into her seventh decade, so she couldn't really complain.

When the university refused to listen to her increasingly desperate pleadings to stay on, the government had taken the lab under its wing. For the past few years it had supplied bottled gas for heating and official blue diesel for the four-by-four. Her home was just a few miles down the road, but over time she had found herself spending more and more time in the lab. The house was still connected to the grid, but there was no longer any power supply, so the place was perishing and too big to heat by other means.

A few weeks earlier, she had moved a camp bed, duvet and a pile of blankets into the lab. The place was draughty, and she had needed to stuff a broken window with newspaper, but with the gas stove lit it was quite cosy. Sometimes, on a good day, the temperature even got above freezing.

It had been hard taking the plunge. She had been in the house ever since the break-up with Simon. Not long afterwards – by accident rather than design – Ali had been born there. And that's what made it so gut-wrenching to leave. The house had been her only meaningful connection to him. She had kept his room just as it was the day his life – and, to all intents and purposes, hers   had ended. Every Saturday morning she had dusted, wiped and given the duvet a shake, almost as if she were expecting him back any minute. Sometimes she caught herself talking to Ali as if he were in the room, which was not a little disturbing. Now she just had the photos on her screensaver and – of course – Blue Ted. She looked over at the battered old soft toy, which lay on the pillow of her unmade bed in the corner, and smiled fondly. He still had the one eye, but now, she noticed, he'd somehow lost the other arm too.

Having no mains power, she had to rely for light on a couple of spirit lamps and a good supply of candles. She had a battery pack that charged from the solar panels when the sun was out, and if she'd remembered to sweep them clear of snow. At least, then, she could charge the drone, the radio and the rest of the kit. Food was the real issue. The government shops in the area had shut and the snow was making it increasingly difficult to get to the nearest army supply unit five miles to the east.

But now the government was pulling the plug. They said her position was unsustainable. And, in any case, they had pointed out, there wasn't much point in her monitoring the ice front any longer when it could be seen from the top of the Shard. It was the end, and she knew it. She reckoned she had supplies to carry on for another month or so. For now, that was her horizon. After that… well, she would see.

The snow had stopped and thin, watery sunlight tinged the alabaster landscape a pale urine yellow. It was still early, so she decided to pay the ice front a visit. The weather had been so bad that she hadn't managed to get out for almost a week, but Bellers had said the road out of the university was clear now, and the army snowploughs and bulldozers still worked hard to keep the main public routes open. An advance tongue of the western ice was marching along the empty bed of the Thames, its next victim the large town of Reading. Every major population centre further west was now abandoned – at least as far as officialdom was concerned – so the place had been a frontier town for a while now. Much of the population had gone, but there were still plenty who were unwilling or unable to leave. Very soon, they would have no choice, and it was for them that the army kept an escape route to the east open.

She stood up with difficulty. Sitting still for any length of time was never a good idea these days. Her knees clicked, her stump ached and her back groaned in protest. She grimaced in pain and wished Bellers would get a move on with the painkillers he'd promised her. She pulled an ancient red down jacket over her coat and zipped it up with difficulty. Layering up was the best way to keep warm, even if it did make her feel like the Michelin Man.

She turned the gas down as much as she dared. It never did to skimp, as the lab quickly became so cold that sleep was impossible. Finally, she pulled a pair of thick mitts over the top of the thin silk gloves and woollen fingerless mitts that she wore indoors, more or less permanently. As she was leaving, she caught a glimpse of herself in the wall mirror she had brought from home. For a few seconds she studied her image, then turned and took in the state of the room. *Jesus Christ!* she said to herself. *I've turned into a fucking cat lady. All I need now are the cats.*

The army had supplied her with a Land Rover to replace the one she'd written off in a losing encounter with black ice the previous year. It had huge, chunky tyres and a powerful diesel engine that could handle most conditions. It was already loaded, so she started up, got the heating going and eased out of the snowbound parking area. The road to the main Reading route was surfaced with hard packed snow that had developed a thick glaze of ice, and she struggled to stop the vehicle meandering all over the place. At least there was no other traffic to get in the way.

By the time she reached the Reading road, her hands ached from gripping the steering wheel hard, and she was relieved to see that one of the lanes of the dual carriageway had been scraped bare of snow. She relaxed a little, put her foot down judiciously and picked up speed. It was only about twenty miles or so to Reading; a forty-minute journey back in the day. But her recent accident had made her wary, and she would much rather get there slowly than not get there at all.

After a time, she saw dark shapes ahead and slowed down. As she drew closer, they resolved themselves into long lines of people trudging slowly towards her on either side of the road. At the last, Reading was emptying itself of the stubborn, the stupid and the eternally sanguine. She slowed to a crawl, her heart going out to this latest ragbag of destitute humanity, at the same time cursing inwardly at the time they were costing her. Most plodded onwards without giving the vehicle a glance, weighed down with belongings and wearing, it appeared, as much as they could. A tiny girl peered up at her as she stumbled past. Her hooded face was pinched with cold and her feet muffled in bespoke snow boots cobbled together from what looked like an old duvet. Jane gave an encouraging smile, but the girl's face registered no response as she turned away and carried on walking.

The numbers started to dwindle as she approached the centre of the town. The army were in evidence, watching out for looters – exactly why, she couldn't fathom. It wasn't as if anyone was going to be coming back to reoccupy their homes

– ever. The sky was thick with snow clouds once more and although it was early afternoon, it was as gloomy as a late evening. Most of the buildings were clearly empty, their doors torn open by scavengers and opportunists. Still, in one or two windows, the light of candles flickered. Some, it seemed, would never leave.

She wound her way through snowbound streets scattered with belongings discarded by those too optimistic about how much they could carry: a guitar, a giant fluffy toy rabbit, even a small armchair. An impressive, gold-framed portrait in oils had been left against the wall of a house, its subject – a dour Victorian gentlemen in black – surveying the scene with apparent distaste.

She reached an army checkpoint but was waved through, the squaddies recognising her from previous encounters. One gave a friendly wave, which she acknowledged with a raised finger, while still holding fast to the wheel. She was headed towards the river, or at least where the river used to be, on the northern edge of the town. The snow was deeper here and pristine, many of the residential roads abandoned and untouched by the few clearance crews still operating. She had to backtrack a couple of times before she found the road she wanted. Eventually, she emerged into the open, the flat countryside of the Thames Valley stretching away northwards into the mist. Of the river, there was no sign. It's source to the west had long been cut off by the ice, and the location of its dried up and snow-covered course was given away only by the blackened stumps of the chopped down willows that once lined its banks.

She parked the Land Rover on the corridor of flat ground that marked the long-abandoned route of the Great Western railway line and grabbed her backpack, a handful of marker poles and the mini-drone from the back. The snow was deep, so she donned snowshoes before heading west along the trackbed. Somewhere to the right was the hidden river course, on the left, rows of abandoned industrial prefabs. It had become increasingly foggy, so she failed to make out the ice front at first. What drew her attention to it also made her jump out of her skin. The enormous, grey warehouse she was passing suddenly gave a tortured groan and crashed to the ground in a mess of twisted metal girders and torn corrugated iron sheets.

She stood stock-still, shaken and confused. 'What... the... fuck...?' she whispered.

She peered ahead into the murk and then she saw it, the ice wall. It was perhaps fifteen metres high and vanished, to left and right, into the mists. One of her yellow and black marker rods – number six – was sticking at a jaunty angle out of a snowdrift off to the right. Now she had her bearings. 'My God!' she muttered. The ice front had advanced much further than she had expected. The first five markers – set twenty metres apart – had been overwhelmed, which meant it had moved more than a hundred metres in six days. That was one hell of a speed – for ice. She was lucky that the sixth marker had survived, otherwise she would have had no accurate measure of the rate of movement.

Now she knew what had happened to the warehouse. The ice had exerted more and more force until the building's frame could no longer handle the load and the whole thing had crumpled as one. She had seen the same thing happen to homes on the flanks of Vesuvius, during the big eruption a couple of decades earlier, only there it was lava doing the pushing. Ice or lava, the end result was the same. When nature was this single-minded, there was just no holding it back.

A fine, gritty snow had started to fall and the light was too poor to fly the drone, so she planted another set of markers – ten this time, just to be on the safe side – and headed back towards the vehicle.

She was still a good half mile away when the silence was splintered by a chilling howl that echoed back and forth off the abandoned buildings.

'Jesus!' A shiver ran down Jane's spine.

She had always been terrified of dogs ever since an over-friendly spaniel had nipped her nose when she was a toddler. Whatever made that noise, she guessed, was no spaniel. Bellers had warned her about the feral dog packs, which was the main reason he had insisted she carried a loaded handgun. In her experience, feral people were a far bigger menace. More than once she had used the gun to ward off individuals and small groups intent on mischief.

Guns were few and far between, so she'd had the upper hand in encounters – so far, at least. God only knew what it was like in the US, where assault rifles and machine pistols were just like condoms; everyone carried one – just in case. It must be carnage. According to Ralph's last email – only partly tongue in cheek – it was back to the Wild West, but with grenade launchers. As far as feral dogs were concerned, she had seen neither hide nor hair during her many visits to the ice and had thought Beller's warnings a load of old tosh. Now, though, her hands shook as she put down the drone, took off her backpack and rummaged about for the gun.

When she found it, she stood and immediately felt her knees go weak and her heart start to pound. Barely thirty yards away, between her and safety, was what she assumed was the source of the howl. She wasn't well up on her dogs and, to be fair, she didn't really give a shit what this was. She just knew it was big, mean and – quite obviously – starving. She waved her pistol in the general direction of the animal, at the same time calling out, 'Good dog, good dog.'

'What the fuck am I doing?' she muttered to herself. She gave up on the plaudits and edged forwards slowly. Not wishing to kill the animal, she was hoping it was as scared as she was and would just run away as she got closer. But then, from the left it was joined by another, this one taller and even more emaciated, with jaundice-yellow eyes. Then three more.

'Fuck!' She could maybe have shot the one, even though she had never fired a gun before, but five – no way. She looked around for somewhere to hide, but there was nothing close enough. Anyway, she still had her snowshoes on so couldn't run. When she turned back, the dogs were a couple of yards closer. It was a bit like playing 'What's the Time Mr Wolf' but with the prospect of a much nastier ending.

She couldn't stand there forever. The snow was starting to fall more thickly and a biting wind was making her face numb. The pack was clearly impatient too. Yellow eyes – who seemed to be the leader – made some yapping noises and, as if at his command, two of the dogs moved out wide to either side and started to outflank her. *Shit!* she thought. Half turning, she fired off a shot in the direction of one of them. It missed, but the noise stopped the dog in its tracks, belly to the snow, ears flattened against its head.

She turned back just in time to see the leader hurtling in her direction. Jaws gaping, it hurled itself at her when it was a good few yards away. She fired instinctively, moments before the animal crashed into her chest, sending her sprawling backwards in the snow. For a few moments, she lay stunned; then she realised she must have got lucky, because the beast was stone dead. Big as it was, it was skin and bone and weighed next to nothing. She shoved it aside and stood as quickly as she could. The remaining dogs had regrouped some distance away and were barking and yapping nineteen to the dozen. One down – four to go. The odds were still overwhelmingly stacked against her and she felt her resolve start to weaken. Then she noticed the drone on the ground and had a burst of inspiration.

Never taking her eyes off the dogs, she pocketed the gun, rummaged for the controller in her backpack and switched it on. The dogs' ears immediately pricked up at the thin, whining sound of the rotors and then went quiet. When the drone lifted off, they shifted about nervously and moved back a little way. She fiddled with the controls and sent the drone whirling towards the pack, buzzing low over the dogs' heads. As one, they turned tail and retreated some distance away, growling and yammering.

'Yes!' she shouted in triumph, shouldering her backpack, and walked slowly towards the dogs. Two of them broke away from the pack and, giving her a wide birth, headed in the opposite direction, no doubt to feast on the still-warm carcass of their leader. The remaining pair she drove onwards with the drone. 'Just like herding sheep,' she said to herself.

Fifteen minutes later, the Land Rover came into view, and soon after she was safely inside. No longer intimidated by the drone, the two dogs circled outside, howling at prey lost. One stood at her window and looked at her, its eyes pleading. She felt sorry for the abandoned animals, which ultimately had no hope of survival, but neither did she wish to contribute to keeping them alive. Starting up the engine, she turned the vehicle around and headed back into the centre of town.

By the time she reached the lab, it was almost dark. The snow had stopped and the sky was clear. The cold was literally breath-taking. When she got inside, the lab felt almost hot in comparison, but she knew from experience and from the icy rime on the insides of the windows, that this was purely an acclimatisation effect. She pumped up the gas as high as it would go and took off her duvet jacket and mitts. Already the room was beginning to feel chillier, and she kept on her overcoat and inner gloves.

She wandered down the corridor, past the row of empty studies, to the small kitchen and filled the kettle. Returning to the lab – which she thought of now as her living room – she stuck it on the heat and switched on the radio. It was more than fifteen years since a state of emergency had been declared, which required independent broadcasters to shut down. The BBC was still going, but radio – like television – had long been a government mouthpiece that presented the official line. There were just the two radio channels to choose from. One played nothing but upbeat hits from the late twentieth century, presumably with the intention of keeping people's spirits up. She surmised that for many – and she included herself – all it did was remind them of the good times, the unavoidable comparison making the current situation seem even more desperate – if that were possible. There was only so much forced musical joviality she could stand, so the radio was permanently tuned to the second channel, which broadcast a mix of news – inevitably dismal – and classical music. The BBC had decanted to Gibraltar some years earlier and continued to broadcast back to the ever-shrinking and increasingly beleaguered UK populace from there.

She returned to the kitchen and rummaged about for something to eat. A couple of Beller's squaddies had brought over some fresh supplies a week or so earlier, before the latest blizzards socked the place in. Nothing fresh, of course. Tinned, dried and long-life made for the height of culinary excellence these days. Despite the cold and her exertions, she wasn't particularly hungry, never seemed to be now. The remorseless advance of old age, she guessed, a sign of the body winding down. She chose a can of sausage and beans and a pack of crisp-breads and headed back to see how the kettle was doing. Hot tea – or what passed for tea – was what she really needed. She had no idea what it was made of, but it was just about drinkable and seemed to provide a lift. It would have been quite acceptable with sugar – if there were any sugar.

She made her tea, added some long-life milk, and put the sausage and beans in a saucepan on the heat. The place was warming up a little now, and rivulets of melted frost ran down the windowpanes and collected in puddles on the damp, rotting sills. She could still see her breath in the steamy air but took off her gloves anyway. The osteoarthritis in her fingers made using a knife and fork difficult at the best of times, and near impossible with gloves on.

She had a sip of tea, smacking her lips and enjoying the warmth as it spread down and into her chest. The food was bubbling now, and she took the pan off the heat and dived in with a fork. She couldn't be arsed to heat water for washing up, so she ate out of pans and scoured them with snow. She needed the food to keep her energy levels up, but she would hardly say she enjoyed it. What she wouldn't give for a great slab of cheddar, a chunk of crusty bread and a heap of the rhubarb chutney she used to make.

She sighed, skewered the last sausage and downed the dregs of the tea. She needed to radio in her report, but the news was due, so it could wait. The final notes of Elgar's 'Sospiri' – depending on your mood, calming or achingly sad – faded, to be replaced by the familiar bongs of long-gone Big Ben announcing the seven o'clock news. She steeled herself for whatever bad stories were to come, because they were – always – bad.

The headlines, inevitably, focused on the aftermath of the nuclear exchange between India and China. Even before the flowering of the first mushroom clouds, these two nations, which together once hosted more than half of everyone on Earth, were in deep trouble. The great Asian rivers – the Indus, Ganges, Yellow, Yangtze – were little more than trickles, the growing Himalayan ice cap sucking up all the available water. Severe drought was widespread, at the same time as the cold had sent crop yields through the floor. Neither country could sustain its population, and hundreds of millions had already died in the greatest famine the world had ever seen. Some estimates suggested that India's population had been slashed by two thirds.

It was scrapping over the dregs of the Brahmaputra River that led first to conventional war and then the use of nuclear weapons. It was the very last thing that the world needed. The newsreader played it down – no need to pile despair upon despair – but Jane knew the score. The colossal quantities of dust ploughed into the atmosphere by the nuclear blasts were certain to accelerate cooling, blocking the sun's warmth just when it was needed more than ever. Far worse, the bots would love it. Their numbers had been climbing remorselessly on the back of the ash erupted by volcanoes invigorated by the unprecedented environmental changes. Now they could share in the added bounty of a cloud of radioactive dust spreading itself far and wide. She shook her head in resignation and despair.

There were a few other pieces of doom and gloom, before the presenter turned to the sport. 'Dear God! Does nothing get in the way of football? Not even a fucking ice age?'

She turned the radio off in irritation; then her head snapped up as the glare from a pair of headlights flashed through the steamed-up lab window. She heard the rumble of a powerful diesel, which stopped abruptly. Then the lights went out. Now, who the hell was this? Jane wasn't taking any chances. She fished the gun out of her backpack and stood pointing it at the door. For a while there was silence, then the sound of someone stamping snow off their boots. The knock when it came was quiet, almost polite. She recognised it and relaxed, lowering the gun. 'Come in, Hugo. I'll put the kettle on.'

The door opened to reveal Major Hugo Bellers. In a well-cut, civvy-street suit, Bellers' slim frame would have looked dapper. Shrouded in the cold-weather garb of the army, he just looked overwhelmed by his clothes. He pulled back his hood to reveal a thin face and a big smile. 'Trifle chilly out there,' he said cheerily. His accent was straight RP, a product of Harrow school, Oxford and Sandhurst.

He accepted the chair Jane offered, took off his gloves, unzipped his white, padded one-piece down to the waist and shrugged out his arms.

'Nice and cosy in here, though, Jane,' he said, rubbing his hands together and placing them as close as he safely could to the stove. He noticed the gun, which she still held at her side in one hand. 'That's the girl. Better safe than sorry.'

Jane ignored the indelicate sexism. 'Tea?'

'Yes, please.' He reached in a pocket, pulled out a carton and put it on the small table next to him. Painkillers. She nodded her thanks. 'Oh. And something else.' He rummaged in another pocket and held out a small packet.

Jane put down the kettle and took it. 'Sugar!' She could almost have kissed him. She hadn't tasted sugar in months. She made two mugs of tea and added a spoonful of sugar to each. Then she sat down on the opposite side of the stove and sipped gratefully. Her eyes closed as she savoured the taste. When she opened them, the Major was looking at her, his expression worried, but he quickly turned away. Her delight that sugar was back in her life again faded, as she guessed she was about to hear something she wasn't going to like.

'So, what brings you out on this lovely evening?' she said breezily, hoping she was wrong.

He took a slurp of tea and frowned. 'Look, Jane, I'll come straight to the point. I wanted to tell you face to face.'

She was getting more concerned by the second. 'Tell me what?'

'We're being pulled back. Tomorrow.'

'Lucky you,' said Jane. 'Civilisation calls.'

'Well… it's not that simple. There'll be no-one to keep an eye on you. No-one to call on if you're in trouble. The bottom line is… I'm under orders to take you with us.'

'No!' Jane was distraught. 'I've got supplies for a month – at least.'

'Jane. Did you not hear what I said? This is non-negotiable. When we go – you go. It's going to take the best part of twenty-four hours to get ourselves sorted. I'll come for you tomorrow evening. Before dark if all goes well. Make sure you're ready.'

Jane's eyes were wet now. She hadn't expected this. She thought she had a month to psych herself up for what she would do next, but now…'I can't. I just can't.' She put her head in her hands and sobbed.

Bellers was discomfited, didn't know where to look. Blubbing women had always left him feeling inadequate. The best he could come up with was a gentle hand on her shoulder, which she immediately shrugged off.

'Jane. You've done your bit. There's nothing here for you now. Don't make it difficult for me.'

She looked up, wiped her eyes with a sleeve and tried to smile. She seemed to have come to a decision. 'OK, Hugo. You're right, of course.'

Bellers patted her on the arm, self-consciously. 'You know it makes sense.'

'I'll be ready and waiting,' she said, but her eyes said differently.

St James's churchyard was a study in black and white. Arsonists had left the church a roofless shell of charred stone. The flowering cherries that had long guarded the tarmac drive that split the cemetery in two, were reduced to blackened stumps of dead wood. Only the tallest of the headstones, most from the eighteenth century or earlier, peered above the drifted snow. The sun lurked just below the horizon, its early light sifting weakly through a thick mist that hugged the ground. In a far corner, a young apple tree, that had somehow slipped beneath the radar of the wood foragers, waited in vain for the interminable winter to end. Beneath the tree, a simple headstone of pale granite emerged from a patch of cleared snow, in front of it what looked like a pile of abandoned clothing. The clothing stirred.

It had been a struggle to get to the churchyard. The lab was a good mile away and the drifts were deep. The whisky Jane had been saving for a snowy day had numbed her to the fearsome cold of night but had played havoc with her ability to put one foot in front of the other. She had lost count of the number of times she had fallen. Once or twice, she had just felt like staying down, but she gritted her teeth and kept going.

It was beginning to get light when she reached the place. She lay in the snow for a couple of minutes to get her breath back, then stumbled around, clearing the foot or so of snow that had fallen since she last visited Ali's grave a few days earlier. It was dry and powdery and didn't take much shifting, despite the fact she was three sheets to the wind.

Feeling light-headed, she slumped down in front of the headstone, and pulled her overcoat closer. In her drunken state, she'd forgotten to pull on her duvet jacket. Now the piercing cold was beginning to make itself known through the alcoholic haze, and she could feel it working its way into her bones.

The headstone was frosted with ice, which she gently scraped away with a mittened hand to reveal the simple inscription. The lettering announcing Ali's full name, and the years that bookended his too-short life, had initially been picked out in gold. Over the years, the elements had conspired to remove the bling, and they were now less easy to discern. Below was a faded black-and-white picture, beneath which were the words 'My beautiful boy'. Jane caressed the photo, as she had done countless times across the years. She remembered when it was taken as if it were yesterday. The breakfast table on Ali's first day at big school. She had the camera out to mark the occasion and he turned towards her as she called out, his expression a mixture of excitement and apprehension.

She leant forwards unsteadily and touched her lips to the picture. The headstone was dangerously cold, and when she withdrew, she pursed her lips at the unpleasant tingling.

'I love you, Ali. Mummy's coming.'

She reached in her pocket and took out two foil blister packs. They were the strong painkillers that Bellers had dropped off for her earlier. He was so thoughtful. She needed them now more than ever, had taken as much pain as she could bear. She popped out all the pills – a dozen all told. Three at a time, she put them in her mouth, washing them down with icy water from the plastic bottle she carried in her coat pocket. Then she lay back in the snow and let the whisky, the pills and the cold do their job.

For what seemed like hours she felt nothing. Maybe it wasn't going to work. She began to panic and tried to stand, but her legs wouldn't move. After a while longer, she began to feel warm, but not unpleasantly so. The cosy warmth of a winter lie-in beneath the duvet; the comforting radiance broadcast by an open fire. Her agitation subsided and she closed her eyes, surrendering herself to the cuddly bliss of the moment. Images came to her then. They say, when you are close to death, that your life passes before your eyes, but these were scenes of another life. Jane's lips made a smile as she watched Ali take his first tottering steps, as he sat grinning in his highchair, face a mask of chocolate. There he was, waiting for her in the kitchen on his first day at school, uniform far too big for his tiny frame, desperate to get out of the door; winning the sports day eight hundred metres at the age of thirteen; and again – older – coming out of the sea, hair dripping, surfboard under one arm, elated. And dangling a set of car keys in front of her on a sunny summer morning... *No!*

Had she shouted out? Her eyes were open now, or so she thought. She must have fallen asleep or lost consciousness, because the sun was up. It was astonishingly bright this morning, tearing apart the freezing dawn mist that shrouded the churchyard. She couldn't turn her head so squinted against the brilliant yellow glow that filled her field of vision. Now, there was a patch of darkness at its centre, a shadow that moved and came closer. She gasped and her eyes widened. An arm reached towards her out of the light: bare, well-muscled, youthful.

'Come on Mum. Take my hand.'

And she did.

THE HELICOPTER'S ROTORS SUCKED UP SNOW AND spun it into a maelstrom that half blinded the pilot. Feeling for the ground with the extendable wires on the landing skis, he eased the craft onto the frozen lake with a crunch and cut the power. As the blades slowed to a standstill, the enshrouding blizzard of snowflakes dissipated, revealing a crystalline landscape of white bathed in the orange light of a setting sun. It was Mid-Summer's Day and the silhouettes of the buildings bordering Battersea Park looked as if they had been cut out of the eggshell blue sky.

The pilot tapped Ralph on the shoulder and pointed out of the window to where a pair of figures on cross-country skis, machine pistols slung over their shoulders, struggled through the drifts. He murmured his thanks, opened his door and flinched visibly as the blast of frigid air struck his face. His knees not being what they were, he lowered himself carefully onto the ice and winced at the sudden pain as one of them clicked. Retrieving his skis from the small external hold, he strapped them on, donned his face mask and headed towards the reception committee.

The introductions were cursory: handshakes and a quick name check. Then they were off. His chaperones were considerably younger and set off at a pace he simply couldn't sustain. After a while, one of them turned, saw that he was struggling and signalled to his companion. The two waited until Ralph reached them and, after he had caught his breath, moved off again at a slower pace that he could just about keep up with. The snow was a real bastard, deep drifts that had crusted over so that sometimes the skis slid easily over the top but at others plunged through and stuck there. Every time this happened, he had to release the bindings, pull out the ski, find a relatively shallow patch of snow and put it back on. His chaperones waited patiently and without comment. Somehow, it never seemed to happen to them.

Even once they'd left the open ground of the park, the going didn't get any easier. The wind, funnelled between the buildings that lined the streets, had piled the snow from countless blizzards into prodigious drifts that often formed barriers from one side to the other. Some were far too steep to negotiate on skis, so they had to remove them, struggle up and over, and then put them back on. It was a slow business and all the time the sun was sinking further.

They had been at it for more than an hour, and Ralph's stamina was becoming tested to the limit, when a gunshot shattered the silence. In the absence of any competing noise, the sound echoed back and forth for several seconds before being drowned out by the crack of a second shot. Ralph's basic training kicked in and without a thought he hit the ground. His chaperones had been even quicker off the mark. He could see them now, running at a crouch behind a long ridge of drifted snow, towards where candlelight could be seen flickering in an open window above an abandoned convenience store. He kept his head down while he watched them unsling their machine pistols and train them on the window. For a minute or two, nothing happened, then a head appeared for a moment before vanishing. Another minute passed, then the head appeared again and this time lingered. There was a short burst of fire from one of his companions and the head was knocked sideways, hitting the window frame before falling forwards. The rest of the body followed, tumbling out of the window, almost in slow motion, and plunging into the drifts beneath.

His chaperones raked the window again, just in case anyone else was lurking with intent, then stood tentatively, gazes still locked on the window. After a minute or so, they seemed satisfied that the shooter was a lone wolf and signalled to Ralph. Together, the three of them skied over to the building.

Ralph looked down on the body of a boy who couldn't have been more than fourteen. His pimply face bore a faint smile and he could easily have been asleep if it weren't for the fact that the left side of his head was missing and oozing grey matter. He shut his eyes and shook his head in a mixture of sorrow and anger. What a world! What a fucking world!

It seemed astonishing to him that – amongst this largely forsaken wilderness of ice and snow – there were still people about, derelicts begging, a pair of hooded youths sheltering in a doorway, a group of scavengers feeding the remnants of liberated furniture into a brazier made of an old oil drum. As the three passed, they just stared, faces gaunt, eyes bright with hunger. Ralph had the uneasy feeling that they were sizing them up for the evening meal. Dancing candlelight punctuated the grim darkness of just one or two of the now-abandoned buildings. These they approached with vigilance, but no more disgruntled youths made their presence known.

It took another full hour to battle their way through the drifts to the US embassy in Nine Elms, by which time it was pitch dark. The security gates were open and a couple of marines were on duty at the door, more for show than of necessity. Once Ralph and his companions had removed their skis and shrugged off thick coatings of rime, they were waved through without challenge or comment.

He thanked his chaperones and headed across the cavernous lobby to the reception desk, which was unattended. He called a greeting, but it went unanswered. He called again and started pacing impatiently back and forth, stopping at each turn to rub his painful thighs and stretch his back. *God!* he thought. *I'm getting too old for these sorts of shenanigans. Far too old.* He was about to call out a third time when a marine sergeant appeared from a back office and directed him, without any prompting, to the third floor.

The place was dimly lit and almost as cold as outside. Ralph's footsteps echoed as he meandered his way around the packing crates stacked high on the pale marble tiles of the lobby floor. Power supply was far too intermittent these days for the lifts to be operating, so he took the stairs. He found the waiting lounge the marine had directed him to easily enough. Karl stood with his back to him, looking out of a panoramic window. His mane of hair was quite white now and he was hunched over and leaning on a stick. The perspective was dominated by the Thames gorge, edged with the heaped remains of collapsed buildings. It had started snowing again and the ice pellets clattered against the bullet-proof glass like frozen peas.

Karl turned at the sound of Ralph's booted feet. 'She wasn't there.' More a confirmatory statement than a question. Karl hadn't really expected anything else.

Ralph shook his head. After nearly two months of silence, it would have been a real turn-up if she had been. When Jane had suddenly stopped responding to his daily emails, he felt in his gut that something was badly wrong. He'd hoped that the UK networks had finally given up the ghost, that she'd eventually find a way to get in touch. Sometimes, he even imagined her surprising them and turning up – unannounced – at the Institute. But, as time dragged on with no word, the feeling of unease grew. Karl had felt the same, so finally Ralph decided to do something about it. He had called in every favour, traded on his celebrity, done everything short of selling his soul to grab places for the two of them on one of the last USAF transports into the UK. One final desperate quest to get Jane across the pond. They badly needed her expertise, sure, but their mission was far more about refusing to abandon a friend, one last effort to get her to let go of Ali and leave behind her grief once and for all.

It had taken more than a week to track down a Major Bellers, who seemed to have been the last person to see Jane. According to Bellers, she was due to be pulled back into the capital alongside his troops, in mid-May, but when they went to pick her up she wasn't there. Jane had supplies for a month or so longer, and Bellers had assumed that she had stayed on until they had run out and then followed on. He didn't seem too concerned. He'd always imagined, he said, that she was living it up now – as he put it – somewhere a mite warmer. Ralph thought that was bollocks and told the major so. Neither he, nor Karl, nor anyone else he knew, had heard from her in nearly two months. He held out little hope that he would turn up anything that might shed light on Jane's whereabouts, but he had to try. He knew he could never live with himself otherwise.

It turned out that Bellers did, after all, feel something for Jane, and now that his interest was piqued, he seemed almost as keen as Ralph to pin down her fate. The major pulled a few strings and came up with a chopper, plus a pilot willing to ferry Ralph on the twenty-minute flight out to the lab. There was room for just one on board, so Karl would have to stay behind and twiddle his thumbs. In any case, his arthritic hips made it difficult for him to get around and he would just have slowed Ralph down.

The pilot put the helicopter down on a conveniently snow-free area close to the lab. Gale-force winds had scoured the snow from the surface, exposing dead, brown grass, and piled it up in monumental drifts that almost buried Jane's workplace.

'The lab was abandoned. Door open, snow and ice over everything. Looked like Jane had been living there. There was a bed, blankets, you know – personal stuff.'

'She must have shipped out, then,' said Karl optimistically.

Ralph said nothing and looked at the floor.

'There's more?' queried Karl.

Ralph slumped onto one of the sofas and massaged his temples. He looked exhausted. 'Her laptop was there, still open. And her toothbrush. There was a photo of her son on the desk... along with an empty bottle of whisky and a box of strong painkillers – also empty.'

They looked at each other for a few moments without speaking.

'Shit!' said Karl, turning away again and looking out at what was now a full-blown blizzard. 'Shit, shit, shit!'

Ralph rearranged his long frame yet again and struggled to get comfortable on the narrow sofa. Even in his hooded thermal suit, he was cold, and – unusually for him – sleep wouldn't come. His mind was buzzing and Karl's stentorian snoring didn't help. It hadn't been a good few days. First, just before he left the US, he'd heard that Jojo had bought it in another flare-up of the Mexico conflict – friendly fire, just to make it worse. Then Jane. He couldn't get her face out of his mind.

The thought that she had died alone somewhere in the ice and snow on the edge of London made him feel sick to his stomach. The bomb hadn't done the job, but the bastards had got her anyway, in the end.

He stood, wandered into a small, dimly lit, anteroom and picked up a paper cup. At least the coffee machine was still working. He pressed a button and waited for the cup to fill. There was no milk. He grimaced at the taste – whatever the brown liquid was, it certainly wasn't coffee – and headed back into the darkened waiting room. He stood before the window. It was still snowing heavily and there was no sign of the Thames gorge through the onslaught of whirling flakes.

He peered into the grey murk and – in his mind's eye – beyond it to the ice and snow that stretched now all the way to the pole. A little over a quarter of a century, that's all it had been since he had blown Skyseed wide open. Just a few decades, during the course of which much of the temperate world had been transmuted into a frozen wasteland. In the end, it had all been for nothing. He had always been a glass half full kind of guy, but not any more. The way he felt at the moment, he could sympathise with Jane. Her way out of the shit was more than tempting just now. But for Jane it wasn't so much a way out as a way back, a way back to her son. That boy was her life. She was tied to him, even in death, and there had never been a chance that she would leave him. He saw that now.

He sighed, shook his head, turned and looked at Karl's supine form. He was deeply asleep and if anything the snoring was louder than ever. He looked old, tired. Ralph had often wondered why Karl had never married, guessed the idea had never entered his head. His hair might be white now, but he knew that deep down Karl was still about eighteen. Even now looking to play the field. He smiled at the thought.

Ralph had tried marriage himself. It would have been nice to have had someone to face the future with, an anchor in desperate times. But it just hadn't worked out. He wondered where Cassie was now, if she were still alive. A particularly loud snort from Karl jolted Ralph back to the present. Dropping the empty coffee cup in the bin, he lay back down on the sofa. This time, sleep came at once.

There were no drapes on the windows and Ralph was woken by the light of the dawning sun twinkling through windows frosted on the inside with a thick rime of ice. It might have felt like deepest winter, but the calendar said high summer, so the sun was up before five. Though his body was warm enough, the room was frigid, and he exhaled thick clouds of vapour as he struggled to sit. Never had he felt so old, every muscle and sinew aching after the previous day's exertions. He stood and rubbed his arms and legs vigorously, seeking to bring back some semblance of life.

He looked over at Karl who was still spark out and snoring for England. Partly out of irritation at his friend's knack of sleeping through anything, but mainly because they needed to be up and about, he picked up the cushion he had used for a pillow and hurled it at Karl's head. Apart from cutting short the snoring, it seemed to have no effect. But then Karl raised his head tentatively to look around and smacked his lips a few times.

'Rise and shine, buddy. We're out of here.'

Karl groaned, pulled the hood of his thermal suit closer and snuggled back down.

Right on cue, there was a tap on the door frame and the cropped head of a marine corporal appeared.

'One hour, gentlemen. There are some refreshments down in the lobby if you would like to partake.'

It was the mention of refreshments that did the trick. Karl slowly tilted upwards to a sitting position, like Dracula rising from his coffin, hair a wild, snowy mane of which Einstein would have been proud. He swung his legs over the side of the sofa, made a grab for his stick and groaned with pain as he leant heavily on it to ease himself upright. For a moment or two he stood swaying gently, before rubbing his face a few times and running his fingers through his white locks. Suddenly, he raised his head, nostrils quivering, and sniffed. 'That's not...?' He sniffed again. 'It is... It's bacon!'

Ralph could smell it too now and it set the juices flowing. Within a couple of minutes, they were packed up and heading down the stairs in search of the source of the aroma. The power was still out, and the generator fuel-less, so the lobby was as frigid as the rest of the building. The stacks of packing crates were gone, in their place a small table. On it were a couple of trays of bacon and eggs that some saint had managed to get hold of – God only knew where from – and cook up on a couple of bottle-fed gas rings. Eager soldiers in grey and white camouflaged thermals and bundled-up embassy staff buzzed about the table like flies around a pile of poo. The bacon was on the flabby side and the eggs watery, but Ralph swore he had never tasted anything so good. He wolfed it down straight, but Karl took his sandwiched between a couple of slices of dry and dodgy-looking bread. He looked to the heavens, eyes closed in ecstasy as he munched. 'Bacon and egg sarnie. Utter bliss.' Then he pulled the slices of bread apart and looked inside. 'Shame no brown sauce, though.'

When they were done, the dirty plates were left on the table. No-one collected them up for washing. What would be the point? In thirty minutes or so, they would all be gone, the place abandoned to the ice.

Appetites satisfied, the atmosphere became subdued, conversation limited to the occasional murmur. Some of the old hands at the embassy seemed on the verge of tears. A young soldier laughed loudly and nervously, and everyone turned sharply to look, some frowning at the insensitivity. The soldier looked abashed and stared at his feet.

The roar of powerful diesel engines starting up outside broke the silence and a stir went through the small congregation – maybe thirty in all. A marine sergeant, hood of his thermals already up, waved his arms to attract attention. When he had it, he bawled a ten-minute warning, and everyone began making final preparations. Tinted facemasks were donned against the cold and the sun, hoods pulled up and drawn tight, boots firmly buckled. The revving of engines outside sounded more urgent, and a klaxon echoed throughout the lobby. The sergeant began herding everyone towards the doors, and Ralph and Karl joined the back of the line.

When it's well below freezing indoors, the temperature outside shouldn't come as a shock. Still, as they crossed the threshold into the gelid morning, Ralph and Karl felt as if they had been plunged into a vat of liquid nitrogen. Within seconds, eyebrows and nose hair were crisped with rime, exposed skin marbled to a blotchy white. The sun was somewhere above the horizon, but there was no sign of it behind the ground-hugging fog of icy motes that limited the world to a hundred metres or so in all directions. Lined up in front of the embassy, were three huge, yellow, snow-cats, black exhaust fumes corrupting the virgin perfection of the scene.

The group dispersed, forming three short lines, waiting to negotiate the icy metal steps that led into the snow-cats' brightly lit interiors. As they shuffled forwards, the spine-tingling howl of a feral dog went up close by. Ralph shivered at the sound and others looked around nervously. The lines moved forwards with more urgency as the howl was taken up by others in the pack. To Ralph, the sound of the canine chorale exactly matched the mood of the moment. It was a dirge, a lament for a dying city, a requiem for a doomed world.

Hustled along by the sergeant, the tail-enders climbed onboard, Ralph helping Karl up the lethally slippery steps, and the doors were pulled to and locked behind them. They were wedged, along with half a dozen others, into the lead vehicle. The interior lights were turned off for the benefit of the driver and, Ralph guessed, to make them less of a target for anyone out there still set on taking pot-shots. The driver switched on the powerful headlights, opened up the throttle and they were off. The snow-cats weren't built for speed, but they could grind their way through just about anything in the way of ice and snow.

The headlight beams sliced through the icy vapour, which was beginning to disperse, revealing a low-hanging, watery sun. Karl was asleep within minutes, head clattering periodically against the frosted window.

Ralph scraped away a circle of ice and peered out, trying to get his bearings. It looked as if the small convoy was retracing his route of the previous night. The brazier around which the small crowd had gathered contained nothing now but cold ashes. He looked for the body of the boy, but more than a foot of snow had fallen overnight, and it was now just another shapeless mass amongst an undulating landscape of drifts. No lights showed in any of the abandoned buildings and there was no-one to be seen. He wondered if the derelicts and unfortunates they had encountered the night before had all frozen to death. Surely, if they hadn't, they would do soon. That, or starve.

Just seven years earlier, London had been teeming, the crossroads of a nation on the move. Now it seemed shorn of life, a place of silence and stillness, an ancient city haunted by a glorious past but without a future. After thirty minutes or so, Ralph thought he recognised the open space of Battersea Park. At the same time – above the roar of the snow-cat's engine – he felt, rather than heard, the deep, rhythmic throb of turning rotor blades.

AS THE BIG MILITARY HELICOPTER CLIMBED HIGHER into a sky of cloudless blue, the enclosing vortex of snow provoked by the rotors slowly evaporated. Karl squinted through the window as they banked southwards and headed for Gatwick and the last USAF flight out of the UK.

The blinding rays of the morning sun reflecting back from the great cliffs that marked the ice sheet front, formed a ribbon of red encircling London some way to the north and west, a fiery ligature slowly tightening its grip on the capital. It was the same right across the northern hemisphere. Scandinavia was long gone, its cities ground into rock flour by the relentless march of ice already hundreds of metres thick. The southern margin of the ice bridged the North Sea to straddle northern France and Germany, merging with the mushrooming Alpine glaciers to form a frozen carapace over what was once Switzerland and Austria. Kiev, Moscow and Beijing were long abandoned, Canada was a distant memory, and Boston, New York and Washington had all been relinquished to the ice.

Karl turned to look at Ralph across the aisle. His grizzled head was turned away, gaze fixed on a blazing spectacle of ice and sun barely diminished in its terrible beauty by the darkened window glass. As he watched, Ralph flicked a salute towards the west, to where a friend and colleague lay, stiff and cold, beneath the whiteness, reunited at last with her son. Ralph turned and caught his eye. Karl said nothing but nodded in recognition and understanding of the act.

He leant back in his seat and closed his eyes, thoughts turning to a future he had no doubt would be bleak – barbarous, even. He sighed. Sometimes he felt like chucking it all in. Then some small success, some inkling that all might not be lost, would open a chink in his despair that let in a ray of hope. It was on the cards that there would be no future worth the term. Not for most of the human race, perhaps even all of it. The hunt to find a solution had been morphing fast into all-out panic. Then, at last, the small successes had become promising avenues. Problem was, there just didn't seem enough time, and even the last straw looked beyond reach.

Atmospheric carbon levels were still on the way down, the bots feasting on the clouds of volcanic ash and radioactive dust that veiled much of the planet, their numbers flourishing. If they couldn't find a way of sticking a spanner in the works, the ice would never stop, trundling remorselessly from both poles to meet at the equator, completing the transformation of a once-temperate planet into a lifeless, frigid, hell-hole. It had happened before, far back in deep-time, when natural variations had eventually goaded the ice into returning to its polar lair. But this time, there would be no way back, the final outcome a real-life Narnia with no prospect of redemption. Still, as long as there was the tiniest prospect that they might still come out on top, that the human race might yet – against all the odds – prevail, he would give it his best shot.

He sat up to accept a beer that Ralph had rustled up from somewhere and pulled out his smartphone. There were no longer any functioning networks in the UK, but they had a signal on the chopper. He checked the news. Snow in Tampa. Airport closed. He shook his head in exasperation. That was all they needed. Well, there was nothing he could do. He returned his attention to the scene outside. The sun was higher in the sky now and far below, its warmth was working its magic on the ice front. Slowly, steadily, pitilessly, it began its move on London.